COLD
HEARTED
Casanova

OTHER TITLES BY L.J. SHEN

Cruel Castaways Series

Ruthless Rival
Fallen Foe

Sinners of Saint Series

Vicious
Defy
Ruckus
Scandalous
Bane

All Saints High Series

Pretty Reckless
Broken Knight
Angry God

Boston Belles Series

The Hunter
The Villain
The Monster
The Rake

Stand-alones by order of publication:

COLD HEARTED
Casanova

L.J. SHEN

Text copyright © 2024 by L.J. Shen

Published by Montlake, Seattle

www.apub.com

Amazon, the Amazon logo, and Montlake are trademarks of Amazon.com, Inc., or its affiliates.

ISBN-13: 9781662512476 (paperback)
ISBN-13: 9781662512469 (digital)

Cover design by Caroline Teagle Johnson
Cover images: © MirageC / Getty; © Oat_Phawat / Getty;
© Stefano Valota / EyeEm / Getty; © Bernadett Becska / EyeEm / Getty

Printed in the United States of America

To Mom.
Yes, I wrote all of this myself.
And yes, I am wearing a sweater.

Love is like a tree: it grows by itself, roots itself deeply in our being and continues to flourish over a heart in ruin. The inexplicable fact is that the blinder it is, the more tenacious it is. It is never stronger than when it is completely unreasonable.
—Victor Hugo, *The Hunchback of Notre Dame*

Girls just wanna have funds.
—Unknown

CHAPTER ONE

DUFFY

As I sat in front of *Love Is Blind*, crying into a sleeve of overpriced digestive biscuits, mourning my breakup with the man I thought was the love of my life, it was clear to me that my night couldn't possibly get any worse. Maybe if I died. Even then, I'd get a much-welcome relief from my pain and anguish.

Was love blind? Quite possibly. There was no other way to excuse how I'd failed to read the writing on the wall. To be honest, it wasn't even on a wall. It was on a bloody flashing neon billboard in Times Square, accompanied by a jingle: *Duffy, you're a fool / you are dating a tool / He'll never ask for your hand / how daft are you not to understand?*

All rights reserved, et cetera.

And, it wasn't even a proper breakup. More like a quasi breakup. A half breakup. A don't-expect-me-to-wait-for-you-even-though-we-both-know-that-I-will breakup. A Rachel Green, we-were-not-on-a-break breakup. You get the drill.

"Silver lining? That's as bad as my life is going to get," I mumbled aloud to my biscuit, which in answer crumbled onto my pajama-clad chest.

Don't tempt me, you cow, the universe replied in the form of my mobile buzzing next to me on the couch.

"Sod off," I muttered, before my gaze landed on the phone screen, on which Gretchen's name flashed.

Gretchen Beatty, my boss, was the anchorwoman of *The World Today*, WNT's flagship show. As her executive assistant, I was in charge of her entire life. Until six months ago, when Gretchen announced that she was taking a position as the White House press secretary and would be leaving New York for DC. Which also meant WNT was not going to renew my work visa. The worst part was, I couldn't afford to tell my tyrannical boss just what I thought about her, even though I had only a few days left of work. She was the type of woman who would refuse to give me a reference if I so much as dared to order her grande iced americano with half-and-half instead of a dash of oat milk.

More on my woes later.

Clearing my throat, I swiped the screen. "Hello?"

"Good God, Daphne. Slacker much? It took you ten minutes to answer."

I checked my new watch. It was eleven o'clock at night. "Is there anything I can do for you?"

I was certain there was. If making me work odd times was an Olympic sport, Gretchen would have been its Serena Williams.

"It just dawned on me that it's Lyric's sixth birthday tomorrow, and I was so busy with the handover to Claire, I forgot to buy my baby a gift."

Busy with the handover, my foot. I was the one liaising with the woman who'd inherited Gretchen's throne—investigative journalist Claire Scott—and her flock of assistants.

Since I could see where this was going from two planets away, I gave her my assurance. "I'll buy Lyric presents first thing tomorrow morning. Do you have a budget in mind?"

Gretchen had given me her credit card two days into my employment. Ever since, I'd been in charge of running her entire life. This included getting groceries for her Manhattan flat and paying her bills. I also attended parent-teacher conferences, filled out her ballots, and wrote her op-eds for prestigious newspapers. Truly, to keep my job—and visa—I had done everything short of birthing her children myself. And *only* because, fortunately for me, they were already in existence.

"*Tomorrow?*" Gretchen slurped her drink noisily. "Time is of the essence. It has to be tonight. I'm driving up to Greenwich first thing tomorrow morning. Jason is making me attend the birthday, even though we *literally* have a show to shoot that same evening." She groaned, as she did every time she spoke about her husband. "I told him I'm heading back to the city before she opens her presents. I have a business to run. Why can't he understand that?"

Because you're the mother of his children?

I'd only met Jason a handful of times, but I suspected he was a lot kinder than his wife. Which was something I could also say about a handful of stale nuts.

"You'd like me to go shopping for presents for a six-year-old in the middle of the night?" I asked tonelessly.

Wow, Karma. Wow. What did I do in my previous life? Skin babies for a living?

"*What?*" Gretchen yelled into her speaker over the loud music. "I can't hear you, I'm at this god-awful pub. Full of peons. No one even recognized me here. Uncultured swine."

"About the presents . . . ," I said, raising my voice. "I don't think I can find anything open at this hour."

"Of course you can!" Gretchen sounded appalled. "This kind of attitude is why you Brits lost an empire, Daphne. Step up to the challenge. You can, because you *must*. I believe in you. Now I ask you—do you believe in yourself?"

I believe I should've accompanied these biscuits with some wine. And maybe an Adderall.

"I'll see what I can do," I said.

"And make sure the gifts are with me before I leave for Greenwich at six tomorrow."

"Six in the evening?"

"Six in the morning, silly."

"What?" I shrieked. "I can't—"

But it was too late. The line had gone dead.

I stared at my mobile, calculating my next move. Not that I had many options to choose from. Gretchen was still my boss for the next two weeks. Knowing her, she'd tarnish my name in every news agency in New York if I crossed her now.

Reluctantly, I picked up my mobile and called BJ.

My ex-boyfriend, BJ. The same BJ I broke up with tonight. Yup, that prat.

"Duffy!" He sounded both delighted and smug. Why wouldn't he be? My parting words were that I never wanted to speak to him again. And that was forty-five minutes ago. "Changed your mind, huh? Why don't I call you an Uber, and you can come to my place and discuss everything?"

"Actually, I need your help." *Bold assumption, though.* "It's an emergency. Do you know anyone with a toy store, or someone who could pull strings to open one this time of night?"

The only reason I felt comfortable asking him for a favor was because I'd bailed BJ out of loads of trouble over the years. I'd written his entire dissertation when we both attended Cambridge, made last-minute birthday cakes for his family members, and once physically expressed his mum's elderly Yorkshire terrier's glands.

"Adult toys or toy-toys?" he asked.

"The latter." I reared my head back and scowled at the phone. "Purchasing a vibrator is not usually an emergency."

He let out a grunt. "Gretchen again?" Were we really having a normal conversation, like he hadn't told me earlier that he was leaving for Kathmandu, Nepal, within the next few days, as if we hadn't spent the last half decade together?

"Lyric has a birthday tomorrow," I confirmed.

"Give me a few minutes. I'll hook you up."

"Cheers."

Brendan Ronald Jr. was an Abbott, which meant privilege simmered out of his ears, he was so fortunate. The Abbotts were a well-known family in New York. Their last name opened doors . . . and wallets. BJ being connected gave him a shine I'd only ever seen on telly shows. Me, I grew up in a council flat in Tooting Broadway, with my parents only recently graduating to a semidetached a block away from the flat we grew up in. When I first met him in Cambridge all those years ago—me on a full ride, him with a library section under his family's name—all I could think about was how to keep him. To make his good fortune my own. Literally *and* figuratively.

My stepdad owned a chippy, and Mum was a homemaker. We were the opposite of influential. What would that be called? *Outfluential.* Mum would buy discounted potatoes at the Portuguese shop downstairs and constantly try to find Lidl coupons to buy milk and bread.

My mobile vibrated three minutes later.

I swiped the screen. "Yes?"

"Midnight. FAO Schwarz. A woman named Kayleigh is going to open the store for you. But you only have ten minutes, and the lights are gonna stay off," BJ said reluctantly. He must've been pissed about my not falling at his feet.

"Oh, come on, Duffy. You know I've been working my ass off for the past few years. I deserve this vacation. And it's only for six months. I'm

gonna hang out with monks. Learn how to meditate." Fractions of our breakup conversation, which had taken place at our favorite restaurant, assaulted my memory.

"That's more than I'll need. Thank you."

". . . *you* promised, *BJ. You said you'd pop the question. I counted on you. That's why I stayed put. My visa expires in two weeks. You can't do this to me.*"

"So . . ." BJ seemed reluctant to hang up. "I feel like you're still mad at me. Are you ever gonna hear me out?"

"Jesus, Duff, talk about putting me under pressure. No wonder I'm second-guessing our engagement. I feel like a walking, talking meal ticket. Besides, you can always come with me to Nepal."

"No, I cannot. I can't leave the US if I want to stay, you wanker."

"I heard you out at the restaurant," I clipped out. "Honestly, I'd bleach my own ears if it meant unhearing some of the things you've said."

"If all you care about is the freaking visa, just find some other sucker to marry, Duff. Just because you and my mom are pressuring me to do it doesn't mean I'm ready for marriage. I know I said I would be, but people change their minds. It's called growth."

"I wasn't being snarky. I know how much you love this city. That should show you how much I care!" he protested. "I gave you permission to do something that'd hurt me badly so you can reach your full potential. This is the ultimate sacrifice. You marrying someone else."

Permission. Someone needed to buy the man a calendar. And a clue. We weren't in the nineteenth century anymore.

"Cheers for the help again, BJ. Have a grand night."

"So we're not even gonna hook up before I leave? One last time for the ride?"

I hung up the phone, shaking my fist at the ceiling of my five-hundred-square-foot Madison Avenue flat.

God had failed me. He could well forget about me ever going on Lent again.

◆ ◆ ◆

It was half past midnight when I cabbed it from FAO Schwarz to Gretchen's ritzy flat on the Upper East Side. If I were lucky—which, as you could suspect by the way this evening was unfolding, wasn't a characteristic of mine—she'd be fast asleep, and I could quietly dispose of the wrapped gifts.

"Must be a special birthday girl to get so many presents." The cab-driver eyed me in the rearview mirror. I was buried in pastel-colored gifts—anatomically correct baby dolls, Barbie fanny packs, a ride-on unicorn, and a life-size kangaroo. (Was civilization ever going to address the fact that kangaroos were aggressive arseholes and *not* cute? I needed their PR person.)

"Wouldn't you think," I muttered, peering out the window as sky-scrapers zinged by. Manhattan was especially lovely at night. Elegant, gritty, and dewed with promise and opportunity. "Throwing money at children isn't love. It's an admission of guilt."

The cab pulled up at the curb. I saluted Terrence, the doorman, as I zipped past him. He was used to my coming and going at all hours of the night. After practicing mindful breathing and telling myself that the worst of the night was *definitely* behind me, I stuffed myself and Lyric's gazillion presents into Gretchen's elevator.

When the elevator slid open, I was greeted by four overrun gar-bage bags my boss had decided to position outside her door. Gretchen once explained to me she didn't *believe* in taking out her own trash. As though keeping her flat tidy was aliens or cryptids.

Sidestepping the leaky things, I balanced Lyric's gifts as I punched in the code that unlocked Gretchen's door.

I swung the door open. The bloody kangaroo slipped from between my arms to the floor. I tumbled over it, diving headfirst on a gasp. Luckily—and I use the term loosely—I landed on the fluffy thing. My dress rode up, giving my bum some airtime. To make matters worse, I was still wearing the sexy knickers I'd bought last week in hopes BJ would propose tonight. Black and lacy, with a red bow just above the crack.

With my face buried in a kangaroo's knob (*of course* I didn't fall atop it missionary-style; that wouldn't have been quite as humiliating), I thought tonight really, truly, *undoubtedly* couldn't get any more disastrous.

Yet again, the universe rose to the challenge.

Because as soon as I lifted my face from the kangaroo's crotch, I realized what I had walked into.

My married boss having sex with a man who *definitely* wasn't Jason.

CHAPTER TWO

DUFFY

The image was imprinted on my mental hard drive before I could hit the delete button.

Of my ballbusting boss—the woman who'd moderated the last presidential debate—with a scarf balled and shoved inside her mouth, as a tall, bizarrely well-built demigod slammed into her, his arse muscles contracting each time he did. Her pencil skirt was bunched around her waist, her knickers haphazardly tugged to one side. Her tits bounced happily through her torn shirt. *Lovely.*

Assuming Jason hadn't become a six-foot-four deity with buns of steel, Thor's build, and shaggy, nineties-heartthrob blond hair in the three weeks since I'd last seen him, this was definitely a paramour of some sort.

"Nice panties," he greeted me midthrust, not bothering to stop shagging my employer. "Please tell me you're wearing a matching bra."

"I am," I announced, refusing to appear embarrassed. "They were on sale."

"Great investment." He groaned, obviously on the edge of a climax.

Were we actually exchanging pleasantries while he was defiling my boss? And people said the Brits were overly polite.

"WHAT THE FUCK, DUFFY!" Gretchen shoved the man away, her bare feet slamming against the marble floor. She dashed toward me like a bullet, trying to cover her tits with her torn blouse. I scrambled to my feet, tugging my dress down as I peered at the man behind her, because obviously, ogling hot men was of great importance in that moment.

Bloody hell.

Where did she find this bloke? Not anywhere I'd been frequenting, that was for sure. To say the man was hot was like saying hell was pleasantly sunny. *Sizzling* was more like it. His cheekbones and jawline were comically sharp, his lips pomegranate red, pouty yet well proportioned. And that body . . . *hello*, Michelangelo's *David*. But with *much* better equipment.

Was he an aging model? An actor? Brad Pitt and Chris Hemsworth's love child? They must've had him when they were quite young. He looked to be in his mid-to-late thirties.

Gretchen gripped my shoulders and yelled in my face. "What're you doing here? Answer me!"

"You told me to bring Lyric's gifts to your flat before six o'clock in the morning," I reminded her, in a rather bland tone. Even though this was a colossal clusterfuck, it wasn't *my* colossal clusterfuck.

"I meant in the early morning, you idiot!" Gretchen kicked away the wrapped gifts between us, showing me exactly how much she cared about her child's birthday presents. "Not in the middle of the night. What the hell were you thinking?"

"I was thinking I wanted to get this assignment done so I could be available to tend to all of my other Gretchen Beatty–related duties tomorrow morning." I took a step back, not in the mood to be showered with her spit. "You know, like finalizing your farewell speech, finding that sound bite from that interview with POTUS, working on Lyric's school diorama, and booking you that interview with *Vogue*."

In my periphery, Demigod leisurely buttoned his black Dickies with one hand, then flung the balcony doors open and lit himself a joint. His blue eyes met mine, and he smirked quietly as if we had some sort of alliance. *The things that leave her mouth when my cock's not stuffed in it, amiright?*

"You ladies need a moment?" His voice was rich and smooth and—I couldn't help but notice—quite mocking.

"A moment, a drink, for you to build me a time machine to get me out of this mess." Gretchen picked up one of the presents and hurled it at him.

He seized it midair, then calmly placed it on the credenza. "I can get you a drink and a moment. As for the time machine, I only build shit if it comes with an IKEA manual. Though if you're serious about it, my friend Arsène could probably—"

"I really don't care what your friend Arsène can do. Can *you* strangle and bury her somewhere?" Gretchen seized me by the wrist, obviously worried I'd escape. "No one's gonna miss her."

He examined me through half-lidded eyes, the ghost of a smile hovering over his gorgeous lips. *Bollocks.* Was he going to kill me? Was I going to *like* it? He *was* nauseatingly attractive. And I *was* in the market for a rebound. In other news, I really did have the tendency to surround myself with the worst of people. Between BJ breaking the news to me tonight that instead of proposing to me before my visa expired—*in two weeks*—and my boss plotting to kill me, one had to wonder if the FBI could use me as bait to attract domestic terrorists.

"Nah. I think I'll keep her as a pet." Demigod winked.

"You just try." I narrowed my eyes at him, my feistiness trickling back into my system. "I'll chew on all your furniture, piss in your shoes, and bite your arse."

Chuckling and shaking his head, he glided out of the double-glazed doors, leaving us alone.

Gretchen swiveled to me, a demonic sneer stamped on her face. "You had no right to barge in here."

"I've been coming here three times a week since we started working together," I pointed out. "I reckon you simply forgot you invited me this time around."

"Oh, fuck. I got so drunk. He always makes me lose control. What do I do?" Gretchen let go of me, raking her shaky fingers over her face. She began pacing, shaking her head frantically. "No one can know. This could end my White House career before it even started."

To make matters worse, because WNT had been in the midst of a humongous sexual harassment scandal when I'd joined their forces, the network had decided to waive all NDAs for people who worked with the stars of their flagship shows in an effort to exhibit full transparency. Which meant I had never signed a nondisclosure agreement. Nothing stood in the way of me shopping myself a nice, six-figure interview about how I caught Gretchen Beatty shagging a man who later on toyed with the idea of keeping me as a *pet*. Then plotted my murder in my presence.

Wait, wasn't that a *Coronation Street* plot?

I stood there silently, processing the power shift while Gretchen tipped her face skyward, presumably to demand of one of God's angels that she speak with the manager.

"This isn't happening to me. I've worked too hard, I've given up too much . . . there must be a way to make this go away. To think of something . . ." She paused, seemingly remembering Demigod was here too.

"Bring your ass back here, mister! Don't try to leave me with this mess. Your dick's not even dry yet, and you're already planning your escape."

I forgot to mention—Gretchen wasn't known for her manners.

Demigod took two idle drags, flicked his joint off the balcony, and strolled toward us. Up close, he was positively gigantic—six foot three, minimum—and ruthlessly sculpted.

I didn't even fancy attractive men. Blokes like him were so inaccessible, so out of reach, that I regarded them like aliens. With a *Huh, so you do exist* approach. As opposed to *Why yes, I'd love to be kidnapped, then anally probed by you.*

Besides, well-bred men with receding hairlines and trust funds were more my speed, and this bloke had very few clothes, all of which seemed in poor condition.

"Relax." Demigod wrapped her hair around his fist and tugged teasingly, his biceps flexing. Even his body language could trigger a spontaneous orgasm. "Little Mary Poppins won't breathe a word."

Gretchen swatted him away on a bark. "Easy for you to say. You have nothing to lose if she walks out of here and starts singing to the press. You're single."

"That I am. The best state to be in, and I've visited all of them." He winked as he ambled to her fridge and plucked out one of her ginger juices. Leaning a narrow hip against the counter, he took a long sip before pointing at me with the bottle. "Does Mary Poppins have a name?"

"Daphne Markham." Gretchen twisted her mouth in repulsion, as though the very thought of me depressed her. "She's my assistant."

Now I was standing there in my flowery Ellie Nap jigsaw dress—I couldn't leave my flat in the same jammies I'd collected biscuit crumbs on—being roasted by these two cheaters. The amount of rock bottoms I'd hit today had me sinking to a whole different galaxy.

"Assuming your temper out of bed is as ferocious as it is inside it, I'm guessing there's not a whole lot of motivation on her part to keep her mouth shut," Demigod said to Gretchen.

"*Please*. As though if she liked me, it'd have made a difference." My boss began buttoning her torn blouse. "Money is money, and she's very fond of it."

What gave it away? My weakness for designer clothes or the fact I dated BJ Abbott, the heir to a real estate mogul?

Formerly dated, I reminded myself.

"Then how 'bout we grease her palm a little?" Demigod suggested. "Make it worth her while to keep her pretty little mouth shut."

My eyes ping-ponged between them. For once, I held back my snarky remarks. I wanted to see where this was going.

Gretchen huffed. "Take it seriously, Riggs!"

Riggs. What a peculiar name for a peculiar person.

And a single one too.

"I *am* serious." Riggs flashed a perfect set of teeth. "As you said, money is money, and you've got a fuck ton of it, babe."

Riggs had a tattoo of a mountain on his inner bicep, and beneath it, a list of famous mountains: Mount Everest, K2, Kangchenjunga, Lhotse, and so on. The entire list had been crossed off, other than Denali.

He was a mountain climber. How odd that the only major mountain he hadn't climbed was in Alaska.

How odd that you'd be thinking about his mountain-climbing career while contemplating blackmailing him. Which, by the way, was the direction I was currently leaning toward.

"Fine!" Gretchen swiveled, training her venom-filled gaze on my face. "What's your price?"

"Take me with you to DC," I blurted out.

It was the only way I could stay here and wait for BJ, which, for a reason beyond my grasp, was something I was still entertaining, even after he'd screwed me over tonight.

She stared at me for a long moment before tossing her arms in the air and bursting into a tearless sob.

"They won't let me bring my own staff. Let alone consider a foreigner for a White House job."

"I need someone to sponsor my visa." I laced my arms over my chest.

"I can do that!" Gretchen's eyes lit up. "I can get you interviews with all the networks in Manhattan."

I shook my head. "I'm not talking interviews. I'm talking about a *visa*. One I could use to gain employment anywhere. No strings attached." I was done being metaphorically squeezed by the bollocks by a network that knew I depended on it to stay in the country. Plus, I wanted to make my own hours and negotiate a better salary. And though my inclination was to remain in the news industry—it was fast paced, glamorous, and full of opportunities—I couldn't help but internally admit to myself that I found the news . . . well, quite *boring*.

I turned to look Riggs in the eye. "Mary Poppins here isn't thick."

"But *I* am." Riggs winked mischievously. He was in the process of rolling himself another joint, licking the edge of the paper with expertise. "And no offense, but smart people don't usually work for tyrants."

"At least I'm not sleeping with one," I said pointedly.

He offered me the spliff. I shook my head. He shrugged. "Assholes make great lovers and shitty employers. Source: science."

"I don't think you know what science means." I glared at him.

"Of course I do. It's that thing with the test tubes and smoke bubbling out of them. Oh, don't forget the funny goggles."

He treated the entire thing like it was a joke.

"So you're okay with this behavior?" I motioned to Gretchen, who was busy crying into her palms theatrically, producing zero tears and loads of drama.

"She's my fuck buddy, not my mother."

"Back to the topic!" Gretchen interjected, not seeming to be bothered by how she'd been openly labeled as an abuser by both of us. "How am I supposed to secure you a visa? The last thing I need is to meddle with the immigration office while I work for POTUS."

"There are other ways to secure a visa." I examined my fingernails, which were squarely trimmed and cream colored. I idly wondered if I'd lost my mind, with what I was about to propose. It was possible. *Probable*, even. But desperate times called for desperate measures.

"There are?" Gretchen eyed me warily.

"I could marry him." I pointed at Riggs.

The man was so surprised he actually whipped his head around to see if there was another person behind him. He turned back to me, stubbing his bare chest. "You weren't talking about me, were you?"

"Indeed I was. You're American, aren't you?"

He lit up his spliff, taking a long drag. "I'd like to think of myself as a citizen of the world."

"Do you travel said world with a blue passport issued in the United States of America?" I arched an eyebrow.

His flat-lined expression said it all. "If you want to get all technical."

"Good enough for me. So. When's a good time for us to get married?" I asked, businesslike. I produced my phone from my purse and checked my calendar. "I have a mani-pedi tomorrow after work, and a facial on Saturday, but otherwise I'm free."

Though I could probably cancel the facial if he needed me to be flexible. Teamwork was one of my fortes.

"Sorry, it might be the accent." He fished his black tee from between the pillows of the couch, then slid it on. "But it sounded like you just dropped the m-bomb."

"Marriage is not profanity."

"No. It's not." Riggs slam-dunked his empty bottle into a bin across the room as he sucked on his rollie. "Marriage is worse than profanity. Profanity is fun, creative, humorous; take *cum dumpster*, for example. Great word, right?"

"You mean *two* words." I wrinkled my nose. "Let's hope you don't pass your dazzling math skills to our children." Now I was just being cheeky. Since sperm was mentioned, and all.

Riggs shuddered. "The c-word. You really are a sadistic creature, Poppins."

Gretchen looked between us, growing desperate. "Riggs, *please*."

He sneered. "You're nuts if you think I'd ever entertain this, sweet cheeks."

"It's just a piece of paper. She could destroy my career!" Gretchen threw herself at him suddenly, like a damsel in distress. I stood there, having the distinct feeling tonight was stretching over approximately five months. Was Mercury in retrograde?

But Riggs gave no indication he was about to cave in, instead shaking her off his arm. "Find another career then. I'm sure there's a small repressed country in need of a new authoritarian. I'm not marrying anyone, for any reason, at any time."

"You owe me!" Her palms collided with his chest, and she seemed more mental than ever. "Please. This can't be the end of my career. You *know* there's no going back from a sex scandal for a woman in politics."

She slid down his body, begging him on her knees now.

He stared her down, his jaw square, his eyes dead. What was it that revolted him more, I wondered—the fact that she'd begged him to sacrifice his freedom for her, or the prospect of marrying me?

I knew I wasn't the sort of woman men like Riggs went for. While I was perfectly decent looking, I wasn't as in-your-face sexy as Gretchen, who, at forty, looked like a Hollywood bombshell, with curves for miles, luscious blonde hair, and a pout that had seen more syringes than a drug addict. I'd taken the Kate Middleton route. With fresh brunette locks, conservative dresses, and a willowy frame without much to grab. Le sigh. If only anxiety and insecurities were grab-able.

Riggs clasped her chin, tilting her face up.

"This is not the kind of begging I'm into, and my mind won't change." His voice was soft but final. "Now get up and dust off."

"Bloody hell!" It was my turn to lose my temper. "I was just joking about the children part. I'd rather remove my own teeth with a pair of tweezers than have you contaminating my DNA pool. Give it up, mate."

"Sorry, Poppins, I don't do monogamy." He finished the last of his spliff.

"I don't do *delusional*," I responded with an eye roll. "It's going to be completely fake. On paper only."

"*It* is not going to happen."

"I'll pay you," I blurted out in a fit of desperation.

His jaw dropped mockingly. "You mean I'll have access to the unfathomable wealth and splendor accumulated by a lowly cable news assistant?"

"*National*," I corrected. "And judging by your clothes, you could use all the help you can get."

His shirt was faded, his belt halfway torn off. My comment left a sour taste in my mouth—commenting on people's clothes was bad form, but the adrenaline coursing through me made me say and do unlikely things.

Riggs's eyes widened, and I had a feeling that his funds, or lack thereof, were a very serious business for him. "You're the shallowest, bitchiest, meanest woman I've ever met—and I've met plenty."

My belly slithered with venomous snakes. I was usually thick skinned, but Riggs's impression of me hit home, because . . . well, because I rather agreed with him.

"Just go, Riggs." Gretchen's voice cracked. Her head lolled between her shoulders, like she was boneless. "You're not going to help me, and you're not making things better."

"Don't have to ask me twice." He shoved his feet into dirty army boots and slung an old backpack over his shoulder. "Good luck."

He stormed away, leaving both of us to stand there, like we were in a duel.

Maybe it *was* a duel. Maybe it had always been a duel between Gretchen Beatty and me.

Only now, one thing was for certain.

She knew my gun was cocked, loaded, and ready to fire.

CHAPTER THREE

Riggs

Emmett Stauce was a schmuck.

This wasn't only my opinion but a fact. Another not-so-fun fact: that schmuck was my boss.

The big irony was, I didn't need to have a boss. Or a job, for that matter.

Before my grandfather took his final dirt nap, he'd left me a $1.3 billion fashion empire, about $800 million of it liquidated. I wasn't only rich; I was fuck-you rich. The kind of rich people hated on principle. But because I grew up with people who were loaded, and I'd witnessed how deeply money corrupted the soul, I'd refused to submit to its allure. See, what people didn't know was that being a billionaire was the most boring thing one could be. You spent your life hopping from one vanity venture to the other. The stakes were never high. The outcome of failure and success remained the same. And don't get me started on people who hung on to billionaires like remoras on a shark. Feeding off scraps of prey.

Which was why I'd always lived like I didn't have money.

Money was a great substitute for happiness, but you could always tell the difference—because unlike money, happiness wasn't something you were constantly afraid of losing.

Usually, living like everyday folk was a decision I prided myself in.

Today, I wanted to punch my own balls for the decision.

"Riggs, I'm gonna need you to stay after this meeting." Emmett tapped his pen over his notepad from across the boardroom. "I have something important to discuss with you. A once-in-a-lifetime opportunity. Thank me later."

Yeah, hold your breath, ass-face.

I rarely attended the monthly editorial meetings for *Discovery* magazine, choosing instead to travel the world and actually do photography work. Sometimes, when I was between assignments, I showed my face at the headquarters, but not often. Confined spaces made my skin crawl.

I nodded, glancing at my phone again. Gretchen had been blowing up my DMs since last night, begging me for help with her PA situation. I felt bad for her, but not bad enough to wed an entire fucking stranger. And one who spoke and acted like a Harry Potter villainess, no less.

On top of being a terrible negotiator, Poppins was also rude, overbearing, and snobbish. She was hot, though. I would give her that. Then again, so was the Carolina Reaper, and I didn't want to stick my dick into one of those either.

Gretchen: We need to talk ASAP.

Gretchen: Just the way she looks at me while we're at work, Riggs. You should see her. I know she's in talks to sell our story.

Gretchen: I couldn't even concentrate on Lyric's birthday today.

Gretchen: Please reconsider. You wouldn't even have to see her. It'd just be paperwork. She spends most of her time trying to move her way up the social circles of NY and buying seventh-hand designer bags. Like that fake heiress from that documentary. Only less sophisticated.

I hoped for our nation's sake Gretchen would do a better job being the White House's press secretary than selling this woman to me. My desire to ever meet Poppins again just plummeted to below zero.

Putting my phone away, I refocused my attention on the pile of oxygen-wasters who were employed by *Discovery* magazine.

Everyone sat around the table and discussed what should be the theme for next year's first issue.

"Yemen's the place to be right now," Harmony, the art director, suggested. "Send Riggs and Steven out in the field." Steven was a world-famous journalist, and not one to get high on his own supply.

"That's a good idea." Emmett jerked forward, scribbling something in his notepad. He looked like Edward Cullen's accountant. Sickly pale, with reddish eyes and a hairline that receded all the way to Uruguay. "But I have something else for Riggs, so let's see if Fred's available for photography. Anyone else?"

As long as I didn't stay in New York for a period exceeding two weeks, I was a happy camper. My repulsion with monogamy ran beyond human interaction. It also applied to cities, states, food, music, and TV. I loved switching things up.

"Meeting adjourned." Emmett, who thought himself personable, used a squeaky toddler hammer to bang on the table.

Everyone trickled out of the room.

Emmett turned to me, cutting straight to the chase.

"Alaska," he said.

"Gold mining. Sourdough. Sarah Palin."

"Huh?" He frowned.

"Thought we were playing an association game."

"Why would I do that?" He blinked, evidently confused. Did I mention the man wasn't in possession of a sense of humor?

"What about Alaska?" I sighed.

"I want you to go there." He reclined in his seat, channeling his inner Italian mobster from an eighties film.

"No," I answered flatly.

"Be a sport, Bates." Emmett went from tough to whining in a nanosecond, sitting up straight. "You haven't even heard my pitch."

"Don't need to. There's only one place on my short list of won't-travel-to—Alaska."

"Before you make up your mind . . ." Emmett slammed his notepad shut. "It's a great opportunity, both for the magazine and for you. We're collaborating with a new streamer, Planet-E, on a documentary about deep Alaska. This thing could win us Emmys, Riggs. The producer did *Whale Tale*, that film about whales in captivity?" He ignored my rejection, giving me his pitch anyway.

"The one that got slammed in reviews as a mouthpiece for oil companies?" I elevated an eyebrow. He and Gretchen were a match made in PR hell. Collectively, they wouldn't be able to sell ice to the residents of hell.

"This one's different." Emmett waved me off, huffing. "No one's funding it."

"Shit, Em, you're really selling it to me. A low-budget documentary produced by a washed-up sellout has always been my dream."

Right after becoming a space cowboy, of course.

"You'll be getting into the thick of it. I'm talking eight months of nonstop filming—"

"Here, buy yourself some Q-tips." I threw a five-dollar bill on the desk between us, then stood up and tucked my wallet in my back pocket. "Your hearing's impaired. As I said, I'm not going there. Not for eight months, not for eight minutes."

Emmett jerked his head back, as if I'd punched him.

"The production company told me it's you they want. They put it as a contingent—"

"Should've checked with me first."

He closed his mouth. Opened it again. "Is there any specific reason why you're so revolted by the idea of Alaska?"

"There is," I answered matter-of-factly. "And it's none of your damn business."

Every time Emmett and I spoke with one another, it ended up with a verbal sparring match in which he got knocked out. To be honest, he had good reasons to hate me. For one thing, I'd slept my way through most of his staff, which, while unethical, wasn't prohibited, since I wasn't their superior. For another, I'd made it clear I thought he was a tool bag. Short of tattooing the statement on my forehead, I did everything I could to convey I disliked him.

"See, I had a feeling you might try to dodge the assignment." Emmett sighed, powering up his laptop. "So I took the liberty of peeking at your contract with Discovery Magazine Inc." He turned the screen in my direction.

"This is our standard contract that you signed. I highlighted the important part. Says here plainly that on-location employees are only exempt from travel assignments due to medical emergencies, religious beliefs, and/or family obligations. All of your colleagues are married with children and cannot take the time off. So unless you're planning a funeral or a wedding sometime in the near future, you're legally bound to us."

"In that case, I quit."

I could always go to *National Geographic*. The only reason I worked with *Discovery* magazine was that the workload was bigger, which meant more traveling.

"Aha." He scrolled down my contract, grinning extra smugly. "I anticipated that might be your reaction. I refer you to clause 41c. Because our projects span over several months, and sometimes even years, we have a thirty-day notice period. You can hand in your resignation today, but we're starting to film in Alaska in two weeks, so your dream of never visiting there sadly won't be fulfilled."

"I'm not traveling to Alaska," I repeated, point blank.

"You have no choice." His ears reddened, and his nose started twitching.

I let out a wry chuckle. "Sue me."

"Happily!" Emmett snapped his laptop shut. "You being a billionaire is a great incentive. As you well know, print is dead. Much like your career, if you decide to break the contract."

My spine went rigid. How the hell . . . ?

The question must've been written on my face because the answer followed promptly.

"Don't look so shocked—you've garnered a lot of interest from the company. Especially our female employees." He rested his elbows on the table between us, peering at my face with open satisfaction. "A few months ago, I asked myself—how come Riggs has never asked for a pay raise? You're by far our most acclaimed photographer, with the most experience—and street cred. Yet, you don't even rent out a place in the city. We send your checks and tax forms to a PO box. I was curious about your financial situation. I figured only someone who didn't need it would be so careless about their salary. So I started digging a little. It wasn't hard. *Discovery* mag has most of your information available."

I sat back down. A muscle in my jaw jumped. "You stalked me."

He sulked haughtily. "Don't flatter yourself. Most of the information was available on the internet."

"Liar. They kept my name out of the press," I said through gritted teeth. My grandfather made sure of it in a bid to protect me. Fame was a terrible thing. He didn't wish it on his only grandchild.

"Mostly, yes. But one publication didn't. And that was enough. As it stands, I could use a few extra bucks when I win the lawsuit. I'm sure I don't have to tell you we're doing awful financially. Each year our budget decreases," he said sullenly, tossing a hand in the air. "And I already have an entire legal team at my disposal. Might as well use them."

"There's only one problem." I stroked my jaw.

He picked up his coffee cup, taking a sip. The guy even *drank* smugly. "What, pray tell, might that be?"

"I *am* getting married." I kicked back in my seat, flashing him my most conceited shit-eating grin. "I have a fiancée. Upping and leaving for almost a year?" I tsked. "Not gonna fly with her. She's a feisty one." If *feisty* meant *deranged*, I was on point.

"You?" Emmett spluttered his coffee, leaning forward in a panic. "A fiancée? Since when?"

"Around one in the morning last night." I stroked my chin, basking in his misery, even though I was going to pay for it handsomely. "Call it kismet, Emmett, but I've found the one."

"That's so—"

"Romantic?" I offered.

"Convenient." He pouted like a teenybopper who'd just been told she couldn't get a boob job for her sweet sixteen. "I don't believe you."

"You wound me, Emmett. I thought we trusted each other." I crinkled my face, feigning devastation.

"If that's the truth, then that means you can't go on lengthy assignments *at all* anymore. No Yemen, no Bolivia, no Seychelles. Right?" he challenged me.

Okay. Maybe I didn't think *Operation: Stick It to Emmett* through. But it was too late to back out now. Even at the cost of doing the inconceivable.

"Two weeks max." I smirked good naturedly, knowing it drove him crazy. "Can't stay away from her longer than that."

I wasn't sure what *her* name was, but that was purely semantics.

"So you're just going to give up the variety?" He eyeballed me. "That's unlike you."

"She's worth it." Whoever that fictional lady was.

He squinted, trying to see through my bullshit.

"Tell me about this mysterious lover of yours."

I had to think on my feet, so my mind naturally went straight to the one (and only) woman who had asked for my hand in marriage.

"She's in the news industry," I mused, trying to remember what Mary Poppins was like. "Smart. Quirky. Sex on legs." *If the sex was missionary-style, in the dark. While both participants pondered the weather.* "English."

"*English?*" Emmett repeated, staring at me with unadulterated surprise. "This is too elaborate to make up. You don't normally remember people's hair color, let alone their nationality. You wanna tell me you're really engaged?"

A-fucking-pparently, thanks to your sorry ass.

I nodded.

"To a *woman?*"

"Yup."

I made a note to check her pronouns if I ever met her again. Not that she'd ever find out I'd married us for my own convenience.

"And we'll all get to see and meet her, this imaginary Englishwoman of yours?" Emmett circled the air with his pen.

"In the flesh." I stood up and stuffed my phone into my pocket. Better bail before he started asking me tough questions about her. Or questions at all.

"What's this girl's name?" Emmett's eyes still darted daggers at me as I made my way to the door. "I'd like to look her up. You know, do my due diligence, since there's so much money on the line."

I stopped dead in my tracks.

Was it Deidre or Darlene? It definitely had a *D* in it.

"Desiree." *Fuck.* It was definitely not that.

"Nice name," Emmett said skeptically, rolling it off his tongue. "*Desiree.*"

Okay—second mental note: tell whatsherface to change her name if she wants that visa.

Also—was I really entertaining the idea of *marrying* this wacko for real now? Apparently I was, because she was the kind of woman to *definitely* tell Emmett we weren't married if he ever found her.

"Desiree *what?*" he pressed.

"Are you going to ask for her social security and Wikipedia page next?" In lieu of answers, I decided offense was the best defense. "I'm not going to violate her privacy so you can get your rocks off."

"Don't worry, I intend to do a thorough check to ensure Desiree has a nice, proper, *real* last name. And very soon."

Knowing you, you'll put a PI on my ass the minute I walk out of here.

"She exists," I ground out, pissed now. "So that won't be a problem."

"Well. Let me know when you have a date in mind. For the wedding, I mean. We need to talk through your vacation days."

"Hmm. Vacation days. Sure, yeah." I closed the door behind me before making a beeline to the elevator. "See you later. *Unfortunately,*" I muttered.

The suing-me part wasn't what I was worried about—he could have the money. It was the fact I'd be outed as a billionaire in front of the whole world that bothered me. My life would never be the same again. Every interaction, every hookup, every transaction would be laced with the unknown of what people's motivations were with me. No. I'd gone this far without revealing my filthy rich identity. I wasn't going to lose my tranquil reality because of Emmett's power trip.

Which meant I had an engagement to propose to a complete stranger.

It was either that or going to Alaska.

And I sure as hell wasn't going to Alaska.

CHAPTER FOUR

Riggs

I spent the subway ride to the WNT headquarters *not* hyperventilating into some guy's McDonald's bag, a big win in my book.

I wasn't like my friends Christian and Arsène, who had a perpetual boner for messy conflicts. Those two could pick up a fight in an empty room. Antipathy was their passion.

I got off at Thirty-Fourth Street and entered the main reception of WNT. A bubbly receptionist greeted me. "Welcome to WNT News Corp.! How can I help you?"

You can kill me now. I'll pay you extra if you make it quick.

"I'm here for . . ." *Delia? Davina? Delaney?* "Gretchen Beatty's assistant."

"Which one? She has six."

Six? G was more high maintenance than Disney World. But that didn't surprise me.

"The British one who looks like a sexy nun." I leaned a hip against the counter, jerking my foot impatiently.

"A sexy nun?" The woman tilted her head, clearly confused. I sometimes forgot how most people didn't draw their analogies and cultural references from Pornhub.

"You know, dresses conservatively, with heels and all that jazz. She's got nice . . ." I cupped my hands to my chest in a weighing-watermelons gesture. Oops. I was doing it again. Being overtly me. "Uh, *hair*."

It wasn't a lie. I remembered she had shiny hair. Because I wondered what it'd look like wrapped around my fist.

"What color is it?" The receptionist narrowed her eyes.

"Huh?" Flashbacks of the Brit's impressive rack shot through my mind. She really was a bombshell, and she worked the whole chic European look like nobody's business. Shame about that personality.

"Her hair, sir."

"Oh. Brown. An interesting shade of brown. Like . . ." *Don't say crap.* "Mud."

Though I was in no danger of snagging Pablo Neruda's spot as the king of quixotic poetry, Enola Holmes here put the pieces together.

"That'd be Daphne." *Daphne! I knew it was a D name.* "I'll buzz you up. Who should I say is looking for her?"

The guy who fucked her boss in front of her, then proceeded to offend her. Twice. Then rejected her marriage proposal. Here's a photo of my dick, in case she needs a refresher.

"Riggs." I cleared my throat. "Riggs Bates."

I waited for the receptionist to connect with Daphne on the switchboard. After a quick call, I was sent to the thirtieth floor. A woman who waited at the elevator and introduced herself as Gretchen's fourth assistant led me to Daphne's office. That was where I found the woman I was about to make my fiancée painting a traffic cone with red finger paint while standing inside a Crocs shoebox. She was screaming into a phone pinned between her shoulder and ear. "I'm well bloody aware, Charlie! No need for the weekly fatherly pep talks. I *wish* I could tell Gretchen to shove her attitude up her ars—"

Who was Charlie? Didn't matter. It gave me inexplicable pleasure to see her like this. I knew her kind. She was obsessed with her precious hair, her expensive shoes, and her designer dresses. Her idea of art was probably contouring her face.

I stepped into her office, then leaned against the door and grinned. She didn't look up, too caught up in what she was doing.

". . . can't make it to our drinks tonight, I'm afraid. Raise a pint for me . . ."

Not even slightly surprised the people in her life needed alcohol to see the next day, I decided to make myself known and get it over with.

"This looks . . ." *Almost as bizarre as your behavior last night.* "Therapeutic."

She looked up, her mouth comically ajar. "Oh. It's you." She screwed her mouth in distaste and tossed her phone to her desk. "Gretchen's office is down the hall."

She thought I was here for Gretchen. I'd almost forgotten about the latter's existence.

"Working on a Guinness record for most eccentric piece of garbage?" I asked to initiate some pleasant chitchat.

She didn't look up from the small cone she held, wrapped in brown papier-mâché. The tip of her tongue poked from the side of her mouth. "I'm making a diorama for Lyric's science project. She wanted an active volcano."

"Who's Lyric?"

"Your lover's child, you scoundrel." She squatted down to retrieve more red paint.

"G's kid?" I pushed off the door and ambled into the room. "Shouldn't she be doing it?"

By the death glare Daphne pinned me with, I gathered the Beatty family did very little by themselves. Considering she had six assistants, I'd be surprised if Gretchen wiped her own ass. Mary Poppins should be grateful Gretchen couldn't physically transfer her period cramps to her.

I plopped down on her office chair. She had flow charts with Post-it Notes arranged by pastel color on her desk, freakishly neat handwriting, and an inspiration board pinned with Hamptons mansions and Birkin bags. Gretchen wasn't kidding. She *was* a social climber. I'd grown up around moneyed women my entire life, and the only ones who were gaga for overpriced designer crap were the newly rich ones.

"I came here to continue our negotiations." I popped open a plastic container's lid on her desk to see what was inside. Berries. Figured. She seemed like the kind of woman who viewed carbs as a mortal sin.

"Make yourself useful while you're at it and fill this empty bottle with baking soda and red food coloring." She jerked her chin to my right, where a cardboard box sat with the ingredients. "Don't add the vinegar. She'll have to bring it separately to school."

I picked up the empty water bottle and started working.

"So. Told anyone you caught Gretchen Beatty fucking a punk yet?" I inquired conversationally.

Daphne was still painting the bloodied stool she referred to as a volcano. "First of all, I reckon you're too old to be called a *punk*. A *loser* might be more age appropriate."

And this is why you have to blackmail people into marriage, sweetheart.

"To answer your question, I'm currently shopping around for an interview deal." She let loose a smile that could freeze the sun and its neighboring planets.

"And how's that going for you?" I tilted an eyebrow.

She glared at the shoebox she was standing in, then back at me in a *Take a wild guess* look.

"Well, I come bearing good news." I used the funnel on her desk to slide the baking soda into the bottle.

"Oh?" She picked up a wet towel from the floor and wiped her hands. "Last time you came, the only good thing that happened was I narrowly avoided getting strangled to death by my boss. No thanks to you, of course."

"Shit, Poppins, was that a sexual innuendo?" I laughed.

"Hardly." She scowled and then blushed. "*That* wasn't a sexual innuendo, either, so do behave."

My God, her mouth was more entertaining than her boss's. And it wasn't even wrapped around my cock.

"Actually, I have a confession to make. I didn't come." I put a hand to my heart. "You killed the mood for me."

"The condolences basket is on its way." She untied the apron around her waist. Underneath it was a pleated ankle-length dress that made her look like a stern governess who was a few minutes away from thrashing an orphan for asking for more porridge. Having sex with the woman was probably as thrilling as filing your annual tax return.

"Water under the bridge." I screwed the cap back on the bottle with the baking soda and put it in the box. "Listen, I'm willing to rethink the whole getting hitched thing."

She stepped out of the diorama and carried it to an open window, each of her movements designed to curb her surprise and joy. "Why?"

"Don't worry about the why."

"What is it? Are you in trouble? Have you done something illegal?" She propped herself against her filing cabinet, her tone measured and crisp.

"You mean in general, or recently, in a way that can implicate you?" She scowled. "All three."

"I haven't done anything that could get either of us into trouble."
Not recently, anyway.

"You do know I can't pay you." Her eyes darkened further. They were the closest thing to purple I'd seen on a human, and I fought the urge to drag her to the window, to natural sunlight, and take a picture of them to see what they'd look like behind my lens.

"I don't need your money."

She curved an eyebrow, giving me a slow once-over. Daphne was unapologetically money oriented, which was a huge turnoff. At least there was no risk for us to truly get along. "I do beg to differ."

"Look, Poppins, you wanna get hitched or not?"

"*Not*," she answered decisively and then, after a beat, rolled her eyes. "But I'm afraid I must. First, I want you to tell me what made you change your mind."

She wasn't going to let it go, and I wasn't in the mood to do this song and dance for the next couple of hours. Plus, I needed to get out of her office. It smelled like a candle shop.

"If you must know, I need a fiancée as an excuse to keep me in New York for a while. Work stuff."

"Oh, you have a job. Marvelous." She seemed surprised. "What do you do?"

"I'm a photographer for *Discovery* magazine."

She popped one eyebrow. Clearly, the answer she'd expected was trafficking small children and deadly drugs across the border. "And having a wife would help you, how?"

"My boss won't be able to spring an eight-month stint in deep Alaska on me. Apparently, it's an assignment fit for a single person without responsibilities. I need a responsibility. Some baggage. That's where you come into the picture."

She stared at me with the enthusiasm of an inmate on death row. "I've always wanted to be someone's burden."

"If it makes you feel any better, I'm sure you already are."

Shaking her head, she groaned. "So how do you see this working?"

Her hostility was low-key turning me on. I'd never met someone so immune to my charms, to my looks; this woman honestly only cared about high fashion and men with deep wallets. If only she knew she was standing in front of a man who was worth more than this entire block and its retailers combined.

"By setting expectations and some ground rules." I opened my arms wide.

"Rules." She tapped her chin, frowning. "I do enjoy rules."

"Shocking."

"You're quite rude, you know."

"You called me a loser," I reminded her.

"How else would you describe a man who conducts an affair with a married woman?"

"Horny," I replied flatly, raising my palms in the air. "Guilty as charged, by the way."

"Unbelievable." She tipped her head back, closing her eyes. "Your rules. Start listing them, please."

"First—no catching feelings. I'm terrible husband material. I'm not a bad guy. But I'm not a faithful one either. I can barely stay in a committed relationship with my inner organs, let alone another human. And there's definitely no reliable bones in my body. If we get married, I need you to remember it's all for show. I'll be free to engage in extracurricular activities with other people and travel as I please."

She stared at me with an odd look on her face before letting out a raspy, sexy laugh.

"Dear God, you're serious." She cupped her mouth. "Rest assured, Mr. Bates, I'm in no danger of ever becoming infatuated with you."

This woman was not great for my ego. The amount of humble pie she shoved into my mouth was making me nauseous.

"Remind me why I gross you out so badly?" I was a glutton for punishment. Maybe it was time to try BDSM. I bet this woman would love to smack me around if I asked her.

"Well, for one thing, I'm rather involved with someone else. Before you ask—marrying him is not an option. Secondly, even if he wasn't in the picture . . ." She trailed off, squaring her shoulders. "No offense, but you're not my type. I like ambitious, driven, smartly dressed men with impeccable manners and noble pedigrees."

"You mean you want to marry a rich asshole," I translated, stroking my chin. "You know, Daphne, I think you might be my favorite feminist."

She crossed her arms, her glare deepening. "I'm not going to defend my morals to *you*."

"Thank fuck." I stacked my ankles over her desk and sit back. "I find morals too boring and constrictive to preserve."

Another long-suffering sigh escaped her. "Anything else?"

"Yeah." There wasn't, but I needed to pretend I'd given this more thought than a subway ride. "Don't ask me for a penny. I have none."

"Terms and conditions accepted," she said. "Now my turn."

"Hit me with it."

"You must cosign my petition for a visa and attend our appointments and interviews with the US Department of State. Make sure we're in compliance with everything they need. I know quite a few people who've done that."

Easy-peasy. Worst that could happen if we got caught would be to pay a penalty and get some community service, with her being deported. The world was too full of actual criminals to lock the two of us up.

"Accepted. Now let's get to the good part. When are we getting a divorce, Daphne?"

"It's Duffy."

"Bless you."

"No, my name. All my friends call me Duffy. I suppose you should too."

"Fine. When are we getting a divorce, *Duffy*?"

"So, here's the thing." She licked her lips. "It could take up to thirty-six months for me to get a green card—"

"Three fucking years?" I spluttered. "Aren't you supposed to get a temporary passport stamp or whatever in the meantime?"

"Well, yes, you do. But then if we stick it out for two years—shouldn't take more than twenty-four months, really—and prove our marriage is legit—"

I held my hand up. "Our marriage will *not* be legit."

"Come on. It isn't like they have a way of knowing this." She waved a dismissive hand my way. "Think about it. I can help you with whatever you need at work." She pushed off the cabinet, pacing back and forth in an attempt to come up with more pros.

"Oh!" She stopped, snapping her fingers. "Gretchen mentioned earlier that you don't have accommodations? You could absolutely stay with me temporarily. My fridge is full and my settee is quite comfy."

"Full of this?" I raised the container with the berries. "No, thank you."

"You must need a place to sleep." She frowned at me.

"Finding a place to crash has never been an issue." I could buy a whole damned hotel if I wanted to.

"But why ask for favors? You're what? Thirty-eight? Forty?" She scanned me head to toe.

"Thirty-seven." My ego was dust and a distant memory at this point.

"Right." She smiled politely, revealing a stunning white smile and zero warmth behind it. "Soz."

I couldn't figure her out. Why couldn't she marry her main piece?

Maybe he wasn't American. Whatever he was, I didn't need a jealous boyfriend in the picture. Then again, if Duffy and I were having this conversation, there was no chance the guy truly gave a crap. I'd never been in love, but both my best friends were disgustingly and happily married, so I knew what love looked like. If Arya or Winnie had spontaneously decided to marry someone else, both grooms would be scattered in cube-size pieces all over New York in a *CSI*-style scavenger hunt.

I popped some berries into my mouth as I spun in her chair like a child. "Tell you what. Let's wait for your temporary visa first. That buys you time to find a job that will sponsor you. And if the arrangement works out—and no offense, but I wouldn't bet my chips on it—we can stay married until your green card is secured. If not, you'll grant me a divorce. A nice and quick one, or I tell the authorities you blackmailed me into doing so. Final offer."

She looked like she was about to argue, first opening her mouth, then pursing her lips reluctantly. Finally, she nodded. "Fair."

I stood up and thrust my hand in her direction. She looked down at it like I was offering her chlamydia. Her stuffiness was starting to get on my last nerve. I almost withdrew when she apparently decided to bite the bullet and place her hand in mine. Her shake was cold and dry. Her beauty was sadly wasted on one of the most horrible women I'd had the displeasure to meet.

Duffy despising me was great news to both of us. The last thing I needed was for my fiancée to tolerate me.

"How does it feel?" I peered down at her purple eyes.

"How does what feel?" She glowered.

"To catch genital herpes through a handshake."

If she enjoyed my joke, she chose to show it by visibly gagging. She stepped back and wiped her hand on her dress.

"Don't be so stuck up. I promise to keep my STDs to myself."

"I appreciate it."

"Oh, and Dina?"

"*Duffy.*"

"One more thing."

"Yes?" She looked like she was bracing herself for a blow.

"How open would you be to changing your name to Desiree?"

CHAPTER FIVE

RIGGS

Later that night, I stopped at the Brewtherhood, a bar favored by aging hipsters. There was nothing overtly special about it, other than the fact that it was too run-down to attract tourists, and the playlist swung heavily toward '90s and early 2000s music.

Arsène, Christian, and I sat at the bar. I was crashing at Christian's while in town. Since I had just become betrothed, I was racking my brain for a creative way to tell him his bedroom would be needed for a few more weeks while Duffy and I tied the knot and filled out paperwork. No fucking way was I sharing a confined space with Cruella de Vil. Cohabitating a city seemed too much at this point.

Both my friends' wives were great catches, albeit in different ways. Christian's Arya was a bossy, sassy, red-heeled ballbuster with world-domination aspirations, and Arsène's Winnie was a doe-eyed actress with a southern drawl and the best peach pies on the East Coast. They both seemed chill about my using their places as hostels. It was Arsène and Christian who wanted me out of their hair so they could continue humping their partners' legs uninterrupted.

"What can I get you, gentlemen?" A new bartender, with spiky green hair and a collection of piercings, winked my way as she slid coasters across the bar.

I ordered a local brew, Arsène a Japanese beer, and Christian a whiskey, neat.

"Coming right up." She beamed at me behind her shoulder, peppering the gesture with a wink.

"This new one seems extra jolly." I patted my jeans. "Did she just steal my wallet or something?"

"For what purpose? You look like the kind of guy who only holds used gum and a Costco membership in it. No, you porked her," Arsène articulated graciously, an astronomy book propped under his elbow.

"*Fuck.*"

"Aptly put." Christian was typing an email on his phone.

"When?" I may or may not have promised my friends to stop hooking up with the staff here. Quality, quiet dive bars were becoming hard to come by downtown.

"Between Chile and Mozambique," Christian supplied, reluctantly ripping his gaze off his phone. "She asked about you a dozen times after you went away. Apparently, you told her you had one year to live and were on a mission to travel the world, so no relationships for you."

That sounded like something I'd say while zipping up my pants on my way out.

"We figured you wouldn't remember her, so we told her you were suffering from amnesia."

"Thanks, pal." I clapped his shoulder.

He shook me off. "Instead of thanking me, stop feeding women bullshit stories. We're tired of cleaning up your mess, Bates."

What else was I supposed to tell them? The truth?

"You're great, sweetheart, you really are, but due to a fucked-up childhood and deep-rooted abandonment issues, I would rather feast on my own leg for the next week or so than get attached to another human."

After our drinks were served, and the bartender gave me a *poor thing* pout and told me she was always here if I needed to talk, Christian swiveled on his stool in my direction. "So when's your new assignment starting?"

"You mean, when am I getting out of your place?" I tipped my beer in my mouth.

He swirled the amber liquid in his tumbler. "You speak Christian Miller fluently."

This was my in to break the news to them.

"Actually, now that you mention it, it might take a minute or two before my next project."

"Let me guess, you're banned from most civilized places for impregnating the locals and causing overpopulation." Arsène flipped his phone to check if his wife had texted him. He was so thoroughly whipped I was surprised she didn't use his balls as a door knocker.

"That too. But mostly . . ." I flopped back on my stool, opening my arms wide with a victorious grin. "I'm getting married."

Christian sprayed his whiskey all over the bar.

Arsène's quiet, skeptical glare dug its way under my skin as he watched me from behind his beer bottle.

"You do understand that part of telling a joke is making it funny," Arsène drawled.

"It's not a joke." I shook my head. "I'm getting hitched."

"Sorry, I'm not buying what you're selling." Christian had recovered, wiping his chin with napkins he'd retrieved from behind the bar. "You. Marriage. The fact that you put the two in the same sentence. You jumped the shark."

"You not only jumped it, you're not even in the same body of water as said shark." Arsène raised his beer in agreement. "You lack the capacity to recognize a woman you hooked up with last month. *Twice.* You taking a stab at monogamy is probably going to kill the concept completely."

41

"Sorry to disappoint, ladies, but I'm about to become a taken man."
Taken hostage, more like.

"Are we gonna do this for a while?" Christian flagged the bartender for another round of drinks. "Because, as previously established, this joke isn't funny. Be serious."

"I *am* serious." I knocked back my entire drink. "What's so hard about envisioning me getting married?"

"I find it easier envisioning you shitting in your own hand and clapping." Arsène squinted at nothing in particular, as if watching a film of the situation in his head. "Frankly, you seem happier clapping on your own crap too."

"Domesticating you is akin to herding a six-pack of Bud Light," Christian explained, using an unfortunate analogy. "No woman in her right mind would marry you. Wait." His face clouded. "She *is* in her right mind, yeah? Is she of age, fully mature, and doesn't live in a closed psychiatric ward? New York State's laws are pretty strict about that."

Smiling cheerfully, I dug through my front pockets and produced two middle fingers, erecting them Christian's way.

"Notice you haven't answered my question." Through his squint I could see him already calculating the bail they'd put on my ass if I got arrested.

"While it's true I don't have a lot of experience with relationships, my settling down isn't more outrageous than you two getting hitched." I peeled a sticker off the bar, quietly but thoroughly pissed. "If anything, I've never been mean or abusive to my partners." I pinned Christian with a glare. "Nor have I ever *bullied* anyone." My gaze shifted to Arsène. "I always try and say my goodbyes while inflicting minimum damage. Compared to both of you, I'm a gentle soul."

"A gentle soul who keeps mason jars with his farts in a Brooklyn storage space from when we were in ninth grade." Christian raised his new whiskey glass in a dropped-mic gesture.

"They'll be worth a fortune one day." I gave him a chiding scowl. "When future scientists will need to know shit about the twenty-first-century diet, who do you think they'll turn to?"

"Good question." Arsène pretended to mull this over. "Our generation is grossly undocumented. I wish they'd invent the internet already."

I made a mental note to return these friends to the store and get new, less contentious ones.

"Keep laughing at my business ventures. I just might release one of these jars' contents in your house one day."

They both shifted in their stools, probably remembering the sheer amount of chili con carne I consumed during the days I'd filled those jars. I wasn't really keeping them for anthropology experiments. I was keeping them because the knowledge amused my friends, and even though we often gave each other shit—zero pun intended—I enjoyed seeing people I cared about happy.

"Back to the subject—so you're really getting married?" Arsène eyeballed me.

"Yeah." I polished off my drink and reached for the second bottle immediately. "But you're right, there is a stipulation involved. She needs a green card."

Christian frowned. "How is her needing a green card your problem? You didn't knock her up, did you?"

I shuddered. The idea of touching Daphne made my skin turn inside out. She'd probably ask me to bathe in Purell and deep-peel my cock beforehand.

"We're not involved like that. I'm doing her a solid."

"What's in it for you?" Arsène insisted.

"She caught me nailing her boss and blackmailed me into it. The boss is married and high profile," I explained. "Turns out, her timing was perfect. I need a placeholder. A responsibility. An excuse not to do a shitty task *Discovery* is asking me to do."

"You need responsibility? Get a fucking hamster," Arsène suggested.

"You do realize this is a federal offense. You could get fined out of your ass." It was Christian's turn to shit all over my parade.

"Since when does Riggs care about money?" Arsène wondered aloud. "He's been beefing with the concept ever since we met him."

"We both need this cover story," I said mildly. "It's a done deal."

"You're digging yourself a pool-size hole." Christian scowled.

"More room for me." I tipped my beer up in a *cheers* gesture.

Christian pointed at me with his drink. "You can't just marry someone for a green card. There are rules, regulations; you'll have to meet specific requirements to make her eligible for a visa."

"Break it down to him," Arsène goaded, a cruel smirk on his lips. "Use simple words. Maybe some illustrations on a napkin."

My grin widened. They were giving me shit because I was good looking, rich, and worked a job I loved. Christian, meanwhile, worked his ass off to support his lifestyle, and Arsène did what he did because of deep-seated daddy issues.

"For one thing, you'll need to live together," Christian explained. "And have utility bills with both your names on them."

"That's not a problem." I shrugged off this piece of news.

Actually, it was a MAJOR FUCKING PROBLEM, but I'd already gotten so much shit from them about this stupid marriage, I wasn't backing down on principle. "She's already offered that I move in with her. What else?"

"You'll need to establish some kind of history together. You'll have to take mutual pictures, introduce each other to people in your lives, book vacations together, the whole shebang," Christian proceeded. "There's a list somewhere online, and it's extensive. Immigration law officers are no dum-dums. They'd want receipts to back up your story. I can refer you to a colleague of mine. She is a star immigration lawyer, but she ain't cheap."

This whole thing sounded intense. Much more intense than Duffy led me to believe.

The green-haired girl glided her elbows across the bar, getting in my face just as I was shoving my arms into my leather jacket.

"Hey. So, you probably don't remember me, after everything you've been through . . . with your emergency surgery . . . and the amnesia . . ."

Staring at her, I pretended to be confused. In my periphery, Christian and Arsène tittered like two teenage girls sharing a secret. I couldn't believe these asshats had saddled me with a side plot of a soap opera.

"But I just want you to know that if you ever want to, uh, talk to anyone, I'm here. My aunt was in a coma for three days, so I know how it is."

Jesus Christ, I needed to stop lying to avoid me having to call her the next day. Or at least keep a notepad on my phone to keep all my lies straight.

"Thank you." I reached to squeeze her hand. "You'll never know how much I appreciate it."

I got up, fished out my wallet, and threw a wad of cash onto the counter. "I'll see you fuckers around."

"Aren't you crashing with us today?" Christian looked confused. He sounded like the mother I never had. "Arya said she'll make your favorite refried rice, but this time you have to remember to take your laundry from the washing machine. You're stinking up the whole place."

Suddenly, I realized Duffy wasn't completely off when she said having a place of my own wasn't the worst idea. Throughout the years, I thought renting a place in New York—or worse, *buying* one—was useless with all the traveling I did. I didn't want to be tempted by comfort and banality. I lived a shark's life. Always on the move. But there was a flip side to being on the go. I was at my friends' mercy. Always ping-ponging between them, abiding by their house rules. It almost felt like an extension of my years at the Andrew Dexter Academy.

"Nah." I shoved my fists into my jacket's pockets. "I'll stay at hers." She *did* offer.

"Sure you're not mixing business with pleasure?" Arsène arched an eyebrow.

If only they knew Duffy's company was about as pleasurable as shoving your dick into a KitchenAid mixer set to the fastest speed.

"Positive."

CHAPTER SIX

RIGGS

My next stop was Duffy's apartment. I got her address from Gretchen's assistant number five, Trudy. I got *Trudy's* number earlier today, when she gave me a grand tour of WNT and offered to let me fuck her mouth in the break room. I wasn't going to take Trudy up on her offer—she couldn't have been older than twenty-two—but after being treated like a walking, talking used condom by my future bride, it was a nice balm on my wounded ego.

Like a lot of young professionals, Duffy opted to live in a trendy neighborhood, in conditions you could find in a sewer. In New York, unless you were very wealthy, you had to choose between location and comfort. Judging by Duffy's graffitied, smoke-stained building, she'd chosen the former. The place wouldn't have been palatable to a Ninja Turtle, let alone a prissy Brit.

I showed myself up to her apartment on the second floor, slipping through the building's entrance door when an older, dashing neighbor of hers walked in. His apartment was on the same floor, and when I stopped by her door, he frowned at me curiously. I knocked. It was already pretty late. I hoped she wasn't entertaining Prince Charming.

I didn't mind stepping into some action, but it was probably going to suck for him to hear the news while he was inside that human ice cube.

Her door swung open, and in front of me stood my future wife, dressed like a medieval prostitute.

I'm talking burgundy bodice dress paired with golden, elbow-length gloves and an elaborate, crown-like braid. And she had a belt with a sword. An honest-to-God *belted sword*.

What in the *Game of Thrones* shit did I get myself into?

"Riggs?" Her mouth fell open. She looked like she'd seen a ghost. Specifically, of someone she'd murdered with that sword who then came back to haunt her.

"Is this a bad time? Are you on your way to slay a Lannister?"

"What . . . *how* did you find my address?" Her delicate brows furrowed. I could tell I was an unwelcome surprise. Too damn bad. We had a lot to unpack, including my backpack and, with it, all my worldly belongings.

I strolled past her, inviting myself in. Her place was the size of a porta-potty. This was going to be an issue. For her, not for me. I was used to sleeping in inhumane conditions.

"Before I answer anything, please confirm the sword attached to your belt is fake." I pointed at her waist.

"What, this?" She yielded the plastic weapon, waving it between us. "Faker than Hilaria Baldwin's accent."

"I don't know who that person is." But I was sure she hadn't invented any important medicine or made a breakthrough with the battle against global warming.

"Of course you don't." She held the sword like you would a baby, not a weapon. Very good news to my limbs, as I seemed to have a knack for getting on her nerves. "I wouldn't be so lucky that you'd be well versed in pop culture. Now tell me how you found my address?"

"Trudy gave it to me."

"How presumptuous of her. Why didn't you ask me?"

"Because the thought never occurred to me while we were at the WNT offices. I asked her an hour ago."

"You exchanged numbers with your future wife's *colleague*?" She blinked rapidly. "Are you barking mad?"

I opened my arms wide. "Every second marriage in the Western world ends with divorce, Poppins. We're definitely going to fall into the wrong side of that statistic. Never put all your eggs in one basket. Going anywhere fun?"

I threw her fridge open. She had salads organized in containers with dated Post-it Notes on them on one side, and homemade dressings in small sealed cups on the other. Bottled water. Fresh fruit. And were these . . . *pickled eggs*? Or her enemies' eyeballs?

"Just got back." She crossed her arms, watching me hawkishly. "From a Renaissance fair."

"Fan of the time period?" I took a bottled water, closed the fridge with my boot, and plopped on her couch.

"Oh, I couldn't give a toss about the period." She stomped around the tiny space, then stopped in front of me, tugged at a shawl I was sitting on, and wrapped it around her shoulders to hide her cleavage. "I went with my boyf . . . *ex*-boyfriend. He's rather fond of lager."

Can't blame him, considering who he dates.

"Ex-boyfriend, huh?" I arched an eyebrow. "That's one hell of a thing to tell your *fiancé*."

"My fiancé hit on my colleague," she said in a deadpan.

"Technically, she hit on me. What made you go then?" I sat back. "I'm sure even you aren't so masochistic as to willingly hang out with your former boyfriend."

She stopped tramping about and shot me an unsure glance. "If I tell you, you'd laugh."

Putting a hand on my chest, I said, "Sorry to break it to you, but I'll be making fun of you no matter what. It's carved into my genetic alphabet. Better start getting used to it."

She sighed. "Well, a big part of it was to show him I was unbothered by the sudden breakup. We'd discussed going weeks ago."

"And the small part?" I tilted my chin down, scanning her face.

"I'm always on the lookout for the perfect American waffle, and the Renaissance fair seemed like a good destination."

"'Perfect American waffle'?" Was that a euphemism? A *dirty* one? Maybe we could get along after all.

She made her way to a recliner and sat down, spine stiff, hands perched in her lap. "Growing up, I'd heard so much about Americans having the best waffles in the world. I hadn't actually tasted a waffle until I was about thirteen. I grew up watching others eat them on TV. They always looked fluffy and airy and just . . ." She trailed off, staring at the ceiling dreamily. "*Perfect*. Something about the symmetry of a waffle just called out to me. So when I moved here, I decided to find it. The perfect American waffle. The best this country has to offer. I take every chance I get to taste new waffles. I always order them whenever I'm at a new diner. I've tried maybe a hundred waffles since I moved to the States."

This was both impressive and peculiar. I liked people with a mission. Even if that mission was to get type 2 diabetes.

"Please tell me you keep a list of places on your hard drive and rank them." I knocked back the rest of the water. "That's such a Daphne Bates thing to do."

"Daphne *Markham*," she corrected sternly. "And don't be ridiculous."

"I'll take that as a yes."

Her cheeks pinked, and she tossed her hair snootily. "Actually, the list is in a journal."

I pressed my knuckles to my lips, stifling a laugh. "The pages are laminated, aren't they?"

"And if they are? Accidents happen all the time. Better be safe than sorry."

Now I was full blown laughing. I couldn't believe this person was real. I thought women like her only existed in Colin Firth movies, where it takes him two agonizing hours to win her over, even though she has no redeeming qualities other than quirkiness.

"So how were the Renaissance fair waffles?" I leaned forward, oddly invested.

"Dreadful!" She tossed her hands in the air. "I reckon they were frozen."

"Sacrilege." I pretended to gag.

She grinned before seemingly remembering I was the enemy and pinching her eyebrows together. "So what brought *you* here?"

"Business." I plucked my phone out of my front pocket and popped the USCIS website on. "Just had drinks with a lawyer friend, and he pointed out we need to jump through several hoops to make sure we're eligible for your visa thingy. Did you know it was a pain in the ass?"

By the way her cheeks ripened into a bright-red blush, I figured the answer was both *Yes* and *Bugger, he found out.* I was 110 percent sure she loved the word *bugger*.

"I'm sorry." She winced. "I was at a point of disadvantage. I thought you wouldn't want to do it—"

"I didn't want to do it," I confirmed.

"Well, yes. Precisely."

There was a pause, in which I briefly contemplated drinking my own weight in bleach in order to remove myself from the situation.

"We'll have to move in together for real. They could come here and check," I said, repeating what Christian had said to me at the bar.

"That's not an issue. You may live here rent-free. Provided you do your chores, of course."

My gaze traveled around the tiny, run-down place. "I can hardly contain my joy."

"Oi." She wagged a finger at me. "A roof is a roof. Neither of us is a millionaire."

Right. I was a *billionaire*.

"But one of us is dressed like one." I eyeballed her Louboutins by the door.

She ducked her head, clearly embarrassed to be called out. "Secondhand stores and hand-me-downs are my best mates," she explained.

"I'll need to have my name on the utility bills," I continued.

"I'll add you. I'll still pay for everything. Hey! This could help you build your credit score. I reckon yours must be quite underwhelming, what with your lack of possessions."

I was almost tempted to tell her all billionaires had embarrassing credit scores. We paid for everything in cash.

I put a hand on my chest. "Your generosity knows no bounds."

We went onto the government site on her laptop and scrolled through the entire supermarket list applicants had to check, printed it out, then proceeded to book an appointment at City Hall to get married. It was the nearest appointment they had available, and it was still a few weeks away.

"Overwhelming, isn't it?" Duffy tucked her feet under her ass next to me on the couch, her laptop balancing on her knees after we were done.

"You're not gonna get cold feet on me, are you?" I shot her a glare. "That would be really bad form, considering you extorted me into this mess."

"Don't be thick." She gave me an aghast look, and damn, she had a knack for looking at me with disapproval. "Of course not. I'm just a bit . . . I don't know, shocked, I suppose."

There was a beat of silence. I wasn't going to console her for strong-arming me into this plan. Besides, I was now fully devoted to the task of screwing up my life and marrying this stranger. First, because of Emmett, for daring to question the authenticity of my fake engagement, and second, because of Christian and Arsène.

"Oh, one more thing," I said casually. "We're hiring an immigration lawyer. Felicity Zimmerman. She's the best in the business and apparently knows some of the people at the local USCIS. It's gonna cost ya, though."

"You mean us." She tilted her head.

"Sure, if you use the royal *we*."

Her shoulder slacked, her mouth flattening into a thin line.

"Better start going through that list." I jerked my chin toward the paper between us.

She picked it up but froze midway, frowning. "You wouldn't mind if I opened a bottle of wine, would you?"

"Mind? I would volunteer my teeth as a bottle opener." I could kiss her at that moment. I didn't even mind the frostbite. "Do you have anything stronger? Whiskey? Tequila? Cyanide?"

She stood up, swaggering to her kitchenette cabinets. "The cyanide I keep for election week. That's when I pull eighteen-hour shifts. I do have tequila, though. Forty-three percent alcohol, I believe?"

Maybe she wasn't such a bad idea.

A printed (and laminated) sheet of our to-do list and six shots later, Duffy and I opened a joint bank account online.

"It asks for your annual salary here," Duffy said apologetically, turning her laptop toward me. "I understand if you don't want me to see. Just put the number in and click the 'next' button. I won't look."

I took the laptop from her, then downed another shot of tequila and put in my *Discovery* salary, which was laughable by New York standards.

"Er, I almost forgot . . ." Duffy pretzeled like she was made out of Play-Doh. "If you're making less than twenty-three K a year, it could pose some issues with your sponsorship. Something about the government wanting you to pay your fair share in taxes to be eligible. You'll have to load your last few tax returns."

Considering I paid more taxes last year than the state of North Dakota, I didn't think we had a problem. As a matter of principle, I didn't tell anyone about my wealth. Least of all someone who'd soon be entitled to half my fortune.

"Twenty-three, you say? I'll make it work. Might take me a second or two to find my tax returns, though, so let's leave it blank for now." I returned the laptop to her. She nodded, tucking flyaways from her braid behind her ear. She had nice, small ears. And she smelled good. Not fruity and seductive like the women I stumbled into bed with. More like . . . *drywall*. I could understand how some men found her attractive. Or maybe it was the tequila that could understand it. I *did* drink on an empty stomach. And by *empty stomach*, I mean we shared one of her salads and a tofu steak earlier.

The woman ate like a rabbit.

She was still talking as I reared my head back, squinting to try to get her face back into focus.

"Well, that's the bank account sorted! Next, we should go to a restaurant or something, somewhere with friends, and take pictures together. We should aim for casual yet affectionate. Perhaps I'll wear my hair differently so they'd think it was taken a long time ago? There must be a tutorial online on how to fake a fringe—"

"I'm crashing here tonight." The words tumbled out of my mouth with a slur.

"Oh." She opened her mouth, then closed it, then opened it again. "Jolly good. I have clean sheets in my room. I'll sort you out a spot on the settee. It's quite comfy, or so Kieran says."

"You let your boyfriend sleep on the couch?" Sadly, I could believe that.

"What? No! Kieran is my twin brother."

"There are *two* of you?"

54

"Bugger off." She pouted, but I could tell she was amused more than annoyed. "Or I'll make you sleep on the floor."

"Is this a degradation kink? Because I might be into that."

"Oh, dear." She ignored my quip. "You're going to stink up my sofa with your weed smell, aren't you?"

"We could share a bed, you know." Now I was just riling her up, watching as her eyes flared and her skin tone turned into that of a Solo cup.

"A *bed*?" Her purple eyes widened comically. "I don't think so." She stood up, hurrying toward her kitchenette. "Clearly we've both had a bit too much to drink. I reckon a strong black tea is just what the doctor ordered. I'll put the kettle on."

"Worried you'd be tempted?" I spread my limbs, intentionally dwarfing the couch. She knew damn well I couldn't fit horizontally on that thing. I could barely squeeze into her entire *apartment*. "There'll be no hanky-panky. I'll keep my hands to myself. All the other important organs too. Even though you smell like drywall."

"Like drywa . . ." She was about to finish the sentence, then thought better of it, instead producing two beige mugs from a drawer and dropping teabags inside them. "Never mind. The answer is no. As I mentioned before, I am still involved with my ex-boyfriend."

"Does your ex-boyfriend know you're getting married to a stranger?" I asked, watching as she spun around the place listlessly.

"Uhm, not quite."

"It's a yes-or-no question. No gray area here, I'm afraid."

She twisted around like she was trying to worm her way out of her skin. "In that case, no, he doesn't know. It's complicated, though. We're going through . . . something."

"Some-*what*?"

"His faculties taking a leave of absence. He is sort of searching for himself. We aren't together currently, I suppose."

"You suppose?" I slanted my head. "I've never been in a serious relationship, but I've always *known* I wasn't in one."

"I'm sure we'll get back together!" she said defensively. "He's just going through some things right now. He is . . ."

"A wishy-washy asshole?" I offered charitably.

"A *complicated* man." She shot me a scolding glare. "Anyway, it's just for six months. He's going away to clear his head for a bit."

"Where to?" Not that it mattered. There was only one kind of man who was happy to leave everything behind him for six months and travel—a man who didn't have any pressing issues back home. He wasn't serious about her.

"Kathmandu."

"Aha."

"What do you mean, *aha*?" She prickled.

"Nothing." I raised my palms in mock innocence.

She squinted at me with suspicion. "You've clearly got something to say. Go ahead, you won't offend my delicate senses."

"I bet he watched *Everest* and decided it'd be cool to see the mountain up close."

Mount Everest was by far the most gorgeous sight I'd ever laid eyes on. I planned on climbing it again before I hit fifty.

"I'll have you know he'll be teaching English to monks," she said protectively.

I threw my head back and laughed, while Duffy stood there and stared at me, lava-tipped arrows shooting from her eyes straight to my face.

"What's so bloody hilarious?" she demanded.

"Those programs are semiscams. They're for patronizing Westerners who want to feel good about themselves. You know he needs to actually *pay* to stay there, right? Like, a couple hundred bucks a week. About twenty-five thousand Nepali rupees. I survived on that kind of money for an entire *month*, in semiluxurious conditions last time I was there." I slapped my thigh, cackling. "Only white rich dudes from New England go around thinking *they* can teach monks shit and not vice versa."

Duffy's lips were now pressed into a disapproving line. "He's not from New England. He's from Westchester."

That only made me laugh harder. "You're killing me, kid."

"I'm not a kid."

"Yes, you are, and a very sweet one, under those ridiculous high-end clothes and fake posh accent."

That last comment made her flinch, which confirmed my suspicion she was putting on a show. She poured water and milk into our teas and brought them over to the coffee table, shaking with anger. "You wouldn't understand. It's about self-growth. He doesn't care about the money."

"You mean he's rich, unlike me?" I grinned, pleased. "Well, that explains why you're only semibroken up and not completely finished."

"He's doing well for himself, yes. There's no shame in that."

"You still think he'll have a change of heart and you'll get to be Mrs. Moneybags."

She gave me a blank stare. "Believe it or not, I love him."

The only thing that helped me calm down from my fit of laughter was the knowledge she was extremely tempted to toss hot tea in my face. To my surprise, she handed me two Tylenols.

"For your head tomorrow," she mumbled.

"I'm not that drunk," I pointed out.

"God, I was hoping you were. The things that come out of your mouth are outrageous."

I accepted the tea and acetaminophen gratefully.

"At any rate, I should let you know up front." Duffy tipped her chin up. "Once he comes back and realizes the error of his ways, this arrangement is over."

I covered my mouth with my fist to stifle another laugh. This woman was marrying a whole-ass stranger, and she was talking to me about being in love with her ex-boyfriend. I wondered at what point in recent history logic had filed a restraining order against her.

"I understand." I nodded solemnly. "Thanks for clarifying."

"Look, I gathered you're quite the lothario." She took a sip of her tea. "Props to you, I'm not one to judge. But BJ and I—"

"Hold the press." I held up a hand. "His name is *BJ*?"

"Brendan Jr."

"Please tell me everyone calls him Cocksucker."

"Riggs!" She stood up, wanting to be horrified by my words, but—I noticed—biting down on a smile. She *liked* that I was making fun of him. Why shouldn't she? Asshole probably fucked up her plans of marriage, babies, and all the other boring stuff and made a run for it.

"So, I guess you met in college? How long ago was that?" It would be nice to know my future wife's age. "Three, four years?"

"Almost eight years," she corrected. "I'm twenty-six; he is twenty-seven."

Riggs Jr. sighed in relief in my Dickies. She was young, but not so young that it was terrible for me to beat one off to her mental image. Touching her, however, was firmly out of the question.

"Wait, you were with Cocksucker for seven years and you didn't even live together?" I spluttered my milk tea. More because it was terrible than because of shock.

"First of all, stop calling him that. Second, his family is quite conservative."

"Were you two having sex?"

"How is that any of your business?" She was tiny and furious, like Tinker Bell. Just like with Tinker Bell, I'd have loved to smack her ass and watch her fairy dust fall.

"So you did. Nice setup, Cocksucker. Guess he's happy to please his family by delegitimizing your relationship and keeping you out of his apartment, just as long as he doesn't need to keep his dick in his pants."

"This conversation is over," she declared. "I'm going to fetch your linen and a towel in case you'd like to shower. Which, by the way, is advisable. You smell like a subway urinal."

I laughed so hard I thought I was going to explode, then tripped over the couch while sitting down.

This was going to be fun.

CHAPTER SEVEN

DUFFY

The day after Riggs and I had booked our wedding was remarkably dreadful, even by my poor standards. The only ray of sunshine was that my neighbor Charlie was kind enough to leave me my favorite Starbucks order and a pastry at my door in the morning, accompanied by a scribbled-on napkin.

Saw a strange man entering your apartment yesterday. Just making sure you're good, Angel.

I wasn't good. I was the opposite of good. I couldn't wait for the next time he and I went down the pub so I could unload. Charlie was a fab listener.

At work, Gretchen was an absolute nightmare, moaning and whining about everything under the sun (including, ironically, the sun itself; apparently, she'd been worried about dark spots ever since she'd started her retinol treatment).

I wondered if she was privy to my arrangement with Riggs. Not that breaking the news to her was high on my to-do list. I had bigger fish to fry. Like telling Mum, Tim, and Kieran I was tying the knot. And possibly slipping my neck into a noose in the process.

Don't forget about BJ. Though, bitterly, there was no denying he'd forgotten about me.

Speaking of my traitorous ex-boyfriend, he called earlier today to ask if I could give him a lift to the airport. For a reason he refused to share, he had deplorable ratings on both Uber and Lyft.

"*I refuse to be defined by cold ratings on a stupid app,*" he had once told me when we discussed his aversion for the app. "*I know my worth.*" That worth, apparently, was less than a hundred bucks, which was the fare most cab companies asked for a trip to JFK, and BJ refused to pay.

The very idea of driving him anywhere was audacious. Especially as he'd used our time together at the Renaissance fair last night complaining about his mum wanting to sell his Range Rover while he was abroad. She'd promised to buy him a newer model once he was back, but BJ argued there was a backlog due to supply issues, and that public transportation gave him a rash.

Yes, I knew he was a rich prat. Frankly, that was his entire appeal. His ability to promise me a life full of security, lavish vacations, and beautiful houses.

Though stabbing him in the eye with my plastic sword had been my preferred response to his whinging, I'd chosen to remind myself that Kate and Wills had also split before the prince realized she was his one true love. Was Kate bitter about it? No. Did she throw a fit? Also no. That's right. She kept it classy. And look at her now. A princess.

Which was how I found myself reassuring him that giving him a ride was no problem at all.

"When shall I pick you up?" I asked as I maneuvered my way among sweaty tourists and Instagram influencers who thought it was appropriate to walk the street in a bikini.

"Seven's fine. I'm going for drinks with Dan beforehand," I heard BJ say on the other side of the line.

I took a tiny bit of pleasure in how Riggs had referred to him as an indulgent Western idiot yesterday. My future husband seemed well traveled enough to recognize an eejit when he saw one.

"Give Dan my regards," I said airily, wondering at what point, exactly, it was appropriate to tell your runaway boyfriend you were betrothed to another.

"Thanks, babe."

"Oh, and BJ . . ." I stopped at a red pedestrian light. "There's something we should talk about before—"

"*Fuuuuuck!*" he screamed, cutting into my words. "I just remembered! That asshole Quinton still has my good luggage. The Prada Mom gave me last Christmas? I gotta call him."

Deep breaths. Kate and Wills. All the roads to happiness are bumpy.

"Right. Yes. The Prada luggage. Of course."

"Gotta go, babe. I'll see you at seven. Bye."

The light turned green. I charged ahead, ready to rugby-tackle anyone in my way. My mobile rang again. Probably BJ wanting to know if I could pick up his dry cleaning on my way to him. Thankfully, it was Kieran.

I slid my AirPods into my ears, then swiped the screen and took the video call.

Kieran was leaning against the white-and-blue Formica of his fish-and-chips stand, a fag tucked behind his ear. He looked like an untended-to male version of me. With floppy overgrown hair and droopy violet eyes and a Joy Division tee that had seen better days. In the eighties.

"Lil sis!" he cooed.

"Stop calling me that, I'm literally five minutes younger than you." I continued my march toward my flat, cutting through the stream of human bodies.

"You could've been two minutes younger than me, but no, you *had* to be breech. Always so special, Duffy." He grinned at me. I smiled back. Mum still held a grudge against me for sending her for an emergency

C-section after she'd had Kieran the way God intended. Apparently, I'd refused to cooperate with her doctor and flip to a head-down position, which earned me the nickname "Arsehole" in the family. Since I was butt down when the doctor cut Mum's belly open and fished me out. What could I say? I'd been strong willed since day one.

"I have something to tell you." I stopped in front of my building's front door. Riggs was probably inside, and I didn't want to have this conversation with him around. Unfortunately, every minute I was outside was a minute I spent sodden with sweat. Today really was unbearably hot.

Kieran pushed off the wall, greeted a client, and served them fish-and-chips while sighing, "BJ finally popped the question, huh? Took him long enough. Mum was getting worried he wasn't serious about you."

Kieran wasn't insensitive per se. He was just . . . *Kieran*. Chronologically twenty-six, but mentally a decade younger. Other than co-owning the chippy with Mum's husband, he didn't have one responsible bone in his body. Still, his words hurt.

"BJ didn't propose to me." I cleared my throat. "But I *am* getting married."

"Bit confused here. You may want to elaborate." He popped open a bottle of Irn-Bru.

"I'm marrying someone else." I licked my lips, averting my gaze to the redbrick building in front of me. "To stay in the States."

"Christ, Duffy." Kieran coughed out his drink. "To who?"

"A man."

"Well, that narrows it down!" he thundered. "Who? When? How? Do we know him? Is he a friend of BJ's?"

"What does it matter? It's not real, is it?" I tried to sound pragmatic. "He seems like a reliable chap. Very . . ." *Old. Chaotic.* "Mature. Adventurous. And honestly, I don't think he's going to be around very much. He's a photographer for a nature magazine."

"What does BJ think about all this?" Kieran seemed somewhere between entertained and puzzled. If I was a go-getter, he was a stay-sitter. My antics always amused him.

"BJ and I are on a break," I informed my brother, proud that my voice didn't crack. "He's going to Kathmandu to volunteer at a monastery."

Kieran's eyes were so wide and so big they looked like the mouth of a laundry machine. "Someone had an interesting forty-eight hours."

That, I did. Saturday couldn't roll soon enough. I needed to bury my face in my pillow and cry into Monday morning without interruption.

"Do you think Mum and Tim are going to kill me?" Tim was Mum's husband. Actually, he was much more than that. He was like a father to me.

"Kill?" Kieran brushed his knuckles over his stubble, giving it some thought. "Seems a bit drastic. But maybe, you know, take you out of their will or something."

"Well, don't tell them!"

"My lips are sealed." He pretended to zip his mouth, then threw away the imaginary key behind his shoulder. "When *are* you going to tell them?"

"I'm thinking . . . never?" I winced. "It's not like the marriage is real. I could bide my time until I get my green card and pretend this never happened."

"Dunno. Marriage is noticeable, innit?" Kieran poked his lower lip out. "Sort of like plastic surgery. Or death."

"Not this one." I pushed the entrance door open, starting for my flat. "This marriage will be like a tampon."

"Bloody and uncomfortable?"

I screwed my nose. "No one will ever know."

"Bad example. I always knew when you had your period," Kieran mused gamely. "You went mental and became the Antichrist, and no Cadbury chocolate bar was safe under our roof."

"You'll see." I ignored him. "It's going to be a piece of cake."

It was not, in fact, a piece of cake. Though there might have been a cake involved.

There was an actual party in my flat.

A *smelly* one. All sorts of odors hit me when I pushed the door open. None of them the signature Jo Malone London candle I'd shelled out a hundred bucks on.

There were also two women queueing for my loo (just *who* was occupying it?), two suited men on my settee, a *dog* on my recliner (not even a tiny one from an expensive breed; I'm talking a proper, seventy-pound beast that also looked quite old and blind), and a half-eaten pizza spread across my coffee table and counter.

I dumped my Chanel bag onto the floor, the chain clinking softly at my feet.

A toddler burst out of my loo, naked from the waist down and holding a toy dragon.

"I did it, Daddy! I did a big poo in the real potty all by myself!"

"Actually, some of the floor and wall got hit too," confirmed one of the women, who hastily slipped into my bathroom with wet wipes. "I'll go clean it up."

Her golden-haired friend ran after the toddler, calling out, "Hey, Louie, come here. No, no. You definitely can't sit on the couch before I clean you up."

I was going to have three consecutive heart attacks followed by a mental breakdown.

"Louie!" Riggs scooped the child midrun like he was a puppy, tossing him in the air. He barely missed the ceiling. "The potty, the wall, *and* the floor? That's talent, my friend. Let's celebrate with a treat. Ice cream?"

"Digno wants cookies!" Louie erected his little fisted toy in the air, almost taking one of Riggs's eyes out with his dragon.

"How about that? I'll stock this fridge up with all of your favorite junk food from now on."

"Hey, Riggs, can you make some popcorn?" one of the men asked. "I want something to munch on when your future wife sees all this. And this time try not to set the whole kitchen on fire. Doubt she has insurance on this place."

I didn't have *any* insurance. And this wasn't a dumpster. Panic and rage simmered in my veins, making my blood boil.

Since no one acknowledged my existence—or noticed it, for that matter—I took a step deeper into the living room and crossed my arms. The stench intensified from unpleasant to dumpster fire. Were they boiling skunks in here? What was that smell?

"Oops!" The blonde woman snatched little Louie from Riggs's arms. "Honey, can you take Brisket out for a walk and see if she needs to go? I think she farted again. Poor thing." She stopped to pet the dog on my vintage recliner on her way to the bathroom. "It's not easy being seventeen, now, is it, girl?"

"It's also not easy to be married to a woman who always adopts the oldest, sickest dog in the shelter." A dark-haired man stood up and expertly secured a harness over the canine. He was the sort of man who dripped wealth just by existing. Something about his unrelenting confidence and ruthless poise. He kissed the blonde's forehead gently on his way out.

Tall, Dark, and Probably a Billionaire passed by me with the dog, shooting me a cynical smile. His eyes were flatlined, devoid of any warmth or emotion. "Guess you're the unlucky girl. My condolences." He tipped an imaginary hat and left.

Which was when everybody collectively realized I was there and the commotion started.

I tried not to let the fact I looked like a soggy sock bother me. After all, I couldn't give a toss what they all thought, could I?

"You must be Duffy." The man next to Riggs stood up, sticking out his hand. "I'm Christian. Congratulations."

"What for?" I inquired politely, shaking his hand.

He let out a delighted laugh, jerking his thumb in my direction. "I like her."

"Oh my God, is she here?" The dark-haired woman traipsed out of my bathroom, the wipe bag in her hand now empty. She looked glamorous and wore this season's Valentino, and I wondered just where Riggs had found these fancy mates of his.

"Hello, I'm Arya, Christian's wife. I've heard so much about you. Thanks for taking him off our hands."

She reached to shake my hand. I complied on autopilot.

Why on *earth* did these people talk like we were a real couple? And how could she possibly hear about me? Riggs and I didn't know each other.

"I'd say my pleasure, but I'm not sure that it is." I glanced around me, shell shocked.

The blonde woman returned with a much-cleaner Louie in her arms. "Howdy, I'm Winnie. Arsène's wife."

Who is Arsène? *Am I even in the right flat?*

She put the (now clothed) toddler down and hugged me. I froze in her embrace, overwhelmed with good intentions and compliments. These people needed to be gone. I still had to shower, doll up, cry hysterically, redo my makeup, and drive BJ to the airport.

"Riggs?" I asked through a tight smile. "May I speak to you privately?"

"Sure, if we can find somewhere private in this shoebox." He raised his eyebrows à la *I'm in trouble* (which won him some laughs) and swaggered my way. I proceeded into my bedroom. He closed the door behind him, then leaned against it. When I turned around to face him, the force of his beauty hit me like a freight train.

I reminded myself he was a corrupted man of questionable scruples. If anything, he was *distastefully* good looking. It was appalling, really. I was certain you couldn't look like that and not be a professional knobhead. And he was. He'd had an affair with a married woman.

Confident I'd got myself sufficiently riled up against him, I proceeded to pick a fight.

"How dare you?" I exploded.

He stared at me, puzzled. "How dare I . . . ?"

"Throw a party in my flat!"

"It's not a party. Just a gathering of a few old friends. 'Sides, you were the one who said 'Mi casa es tu casa,' kid." He ruffled my hair with a laugh, like I was an adorable pup.

"I've never said that!" I waved my balled fists in his face, frantic with rage. "Mi casa will never be tu casa. Tu has *no* casa. This was what landed both of us in this unfortunate situation. All I said was you could crash on my sofa, rent-free. This place is not designed to entertain."

A skeptical smile tickled the corners of his lips. His crate-size dimples made a guest appearance. My goodness, he was a treat to look at. Maybe not a treat. A full-blown dessert. Perhaps . . . a five-tier cake? Yeah, that sounded about right.

I couldn't recognize myself in my attraction to him. I wasn't the same obsessively ambitious girl who studied her way to a full scholarship at Cambridge so she could buy herself a one-way ticket from poverty through career opportunities and the chance to bag herself a rich husband.

With Riggs, I was different. Impulsive. Emotional . . . quite frankly, a *mess*.

"Why not? Don't worry, I made sure the body bags were tucked all the way behind the frozen meats in the freezer."

"It's too small!" I stomped. I'd *never* let myself stomp with BJ. It was so unbecoming.

"Welcome to New York." He spread his arms. "Where dreams are big and the real estate is minuscule."

"I'm too tidy for company," I whined. Another first I wasn't used to doing.

"Tidy is a trait, not a quality. I'm ridding you of bad habits. Thank me later."

"Well, it's *mine*!" I cried out, ready to throttle him. "Tell them to bugger off. I've got to jump in the shower."

"What for? You already seem pretty wet to me."

"Oh, you arse!" I shoved at his chest. Well, this was a mistake. His pecs were magnificent. I actually felt the individual ridges between them. *And* I couldn't make him budge an inch. "I have to drive BJ to the airport."

"Shame. My friends really wanted to meet you." He seemed genuine, which was quite disturbing.

"About that . . ." I frowned. "*Why* are they acting like this is all real?"

He tipped his head back, laughing. "To piss me off, probably. I was the last man standing, see."

"Then why aren't you?"

"Pissed off?" He looked at me funny, like the answer was obvious. "Giving someone the emotional reaction they're shooting for means losing, and I'm no loser. Go get showered, Poppins. I'll kick them out. Don't worry about it."

Astonishingly, this made me feel like a complete twat. I expected him to push back, to hurl insults at me, to tell me I was being difficult and prissy.

"Fine, but when I come out, we're making a house rules sheet. A *laminated* one." I wiggled my finger in his face.

"The fun just never ends with you." He dropped his gaze down to my cleavage and gave me a big, wolfish grin. "I love it when you talk dirty to me, *wifey*."

◆ ◆ ◆

Half an hour later I felt marginally better, once I was in clean, dry clothes after a cold, refreshing shower. By the time I exited the bathroom, the flat was sort of tidy, but it still smelled like a sweaty, infested crotch. Riggs, in his perpetual good mood, was whistling to himself while stuffing pizza cartons into a bin bag.

He stopped and watched as I shoved my feet into my Louboutin sandals. I stole a glance at his face. I couldn't help it. It was like running your tongue over the same mouth ulcer, even though you knew it'd hurt. He raised his eyebrows with a friendly smile. "See something you like?"

"Oh, drop dead."

"I'm about to marry you. That seems close enough."

Flushed, I hurried to change the subject. "I think our first rule should be no pets." I stood up and walked over to my laptop.

"Does your landlord forbid it?"

"Haven't asked." I began typing. "But it doesn't matter. The place is too small, and animals are filthy. They do terrible things to fabrics."

"And awesome things to the soul," he countered, but when I shot him a scowl, he raised his palms. "Fine. Souls are overrated. No pets. I'm always on the go, anyway. It wouldn't be fair to them."

"The second rule is no bringing home hookups," I proceeded. I knew I would have absolutely no issue fulfilling this part of the bargain. My sex life was nonexistent before BJ, *during* BJ, and assumingly after BJ. Riggs, on the other hand, was a lovely, outgoing creature. Gorgeous and warm. I bet he slept with loads of women, all the time. I didn't care to meet any of them over morning coffee while I was getting ready for work.

"Is this two sided?" Riggs arched an eyebrow.

"Of course!" I huffed. "I'm fair."

"Are you?" He double tied the trash bag and brought it over to the door.

"Very fair," I confirmed with a nod.

"Then I have a rule too."

"What's your rule?"

"No more than three rules." He threw his slow sexy grin behind his shoulder. The one I suspected compelled women to offer him a kidney. "That's all you get."

"Why?" I asked, flabbergasted.

"Because what you need right now is as few rules as possible, and to have a whole lot of fun. You're about to be single for six months. Live a little."

Putting my fingers to my wrist, I pretended to examine my pulse. "Sorry to disappoint, but my vitals seem quite good." Then, remembering he was committing a federal offense for me, I sighed. "All right. One more rule. But you accept rule number two, right? No bringing bloody women into my apartment?"

He held my gaze. "You have my word they will not be bloody."

"Riggs!"

"Fine. Or that they will exist at all."

Phew. This left me with one more rule. I felt like a poor kid at a candy store. How could I possibly choose?

I peeked at my mobile. I needed to leave in the next ten minutes if I wanted to be on time for BJ.

Think, Duffy, think.

Then, eureka! Creativity struck. My fingers flew over my keyboard.

"You look way too pleased to be typing this one down." Riggs had an indulgent smirk on his face as he leaned a shoulder over the wall, watching me from his vantage point of being seven foot four or whatever. "What is it?"

"No fraternizing with your spouse." I hit the print button, then listened to the printer on the credenza spewing out our house rules sheet. "This means you absolutely cannot try to hit on me, flirt with me, or pursue me sexually. And vice versa, of course," I said after a slight pause, realizing it was silly to assume this real-life Adonis was going to fancy me.

"I'm going to try, but I gotta tell you, everything in this place screams sex." He gestured toward my decorative pillows, scented candles, and fresh flowers on the coffee table.

Rolling my eyes, I stood up and plucked the sheet from the printer. This was getting *double* laminated, just in case. "And another thing."

"Hit me."

Don't tempt me.

I took my time getting the sheet sealed, then plastering it over the fridge, so he couldn't miss it.

"This is not a rule, but a preference. Under this roof, you're going to start eating your greens. You're not so young anymore. You can't eat pizza and cookies for eternity. There's a veggie casserole in the fridge. I expect it to be gone by the time I come back."

"Does that mean I can throw it straight into the trash?"

"If by *trash* you mean *your gut*, then yes."

"Okay, Mom."

We both stood in front of the fridge, examining our list.

House Rules
No pets
No hookups
No fraternizing with your spouse

Now *that* looked like a good marriage to me.

CHAPTER EIGHT

DUFFY

"I can't believe we're saying goodbye." BJ unbuckled himself in my neighbor Charlie's prehistoric Toyota Camry. Charlie let me borrow it, even though I knew what he thought. BJ didn't need a ride. He needed to jerk me around one last time to ensure I was truly and faithfully his. We were parked outside the terminal of JFK. The heat was still unbearable, perhaps even more so, because everything—the concrete, the trees, the streets—was already permanently hot.

"Me either," I said hollowly. I wore my gray-checked Donna Karen dress, minimal makeup, and my hair up, the way BJ liked it. Now if only I could muster the courage to tell him I was marrying someone else in his absence.

"So. We agreed on no emails, no calls, no connection until I'm back, right, babe?" He gave me his puppy face. This was his idea, not mine. Something about making sure we had time to reflect. My pride wouldn't let me tell him I wanted to keep in touch. Not that it mattered. BJ said he wouldn't have access to a phone unless he traveled from the monastery into Kathmandu to an internet café, which he didn't intend to do often.

"Right." I smiled tightly. "I'm starting my love life detox, in which I'm going to lose a hundred and seventy pounds of boyfriend."

"A hundred and sixty-eight. I'm still riding that clean-juice weight-loss high from June." BJ chuckled. "I'm going to miss you so much." He pressed his lips against my cheek. "My heart physically hurts from this."

So don't leave.

Stay.

Propose, so I can at least get a fiancée visa.

Right. Speaking of. "I do need to tell you something."

"What is it, babe?" he cooed, and I was beginning to get quite agitated with how he treated me like Winnie's blind/old/half-dead dog.

I cleared my throat. *Here goes nothing.*

"Since I'm running out of time, and my visa expires at the end of the month, I decided to—"

"*Holy shit!*" BJ interjected. *Again.* This time he flung the passenger seat open. "Look who it is, Duffy! Kane! Kane from Cambridge. I thought he lived in Bristol? I wonder what he's doing in New York."

I clasped my mouth shut. I didn't even remember Kane. Nor did I care to.

"BJ, wait—"

"You think he works in the city now? I gotta catch up with the guy. I'm gonna call after I pass TSA, 'kay? Thanks for the ride." He leaned in to kiss me quickly, palming my cheeks and pressing his forehead to mine. "Love you to the moon and back. We'll get through this. *Mwah.*"

I sat in the car, watching BJ dragging his luggage from the boot and hurrying toward a man I now vaguely recognized as someone from the rowing team. He turned to BJ, looking pleasantly surprised. I clutched the steering wheel in a death grip and told myself that I was being unreasonable. BJ couldn't know what I'd wanted to tell him. And I'd hardly stood my ground, had I? Besides, did it truly matter? If I wanted to marry into money, I needed to appear less desperate.

I pressed my forehead against the wheel, sucking air into my lungs.

It wasn't until a few minutes later that I realized I *fell asleep* on the wheel, thankfully not while the vehicle was in motion. A police officer knocked on my window. I rolled it down with a wince.

"Ma'am." He parked a hand on his waist, staring at me pointedly.

Christ, I couldn't catch a break today. *Ma'am?* I was quite clearly a *miss*.

"Hello!" I smiled politely. "Did I do anything wrong, Officer?"

"You? No. Your forehead, however, was honking that horn for thirty seconds straight."

Bugger.

"You under the influence?" He arranged his belt over his stomach.

"Ha. I wish." The joke did not land as well as I thought it would, as his face remained stoic. "Sorry. It sounded funnier in my head. I just dropped my boyfriend off. He's going away for six months. I'm quite distressed about the whole thing. Sleep's not in the cards for me these days, you see, so—"

He held his palm up. "I asked if you had a drink, not for your life story."

"Right. Yes. No, I'm completely sober." *But I am going to rectify the situation as soon as I return to my flat.*

"Drive safe and straight home."

He didn't have to ask me twice. There was a half-empty bottle of a cheap tequila with my name on it.

◆ ◆ ◆

When I came back to the flat, I found my future husband's head stuck in a sink full of water and ice. I should specify that the head was completely attached to the rest of his body. Which made the scene a lot less gory than it could have been, but still quite odd.

"Please tell me it's not a cult ritual of sorts," I mumbled, trudging inside. He jerked his head back and shook the water off like a dog. *"Fuck."*

His face was the shade of an ice cube. And still, he was infuriatingly handsome.

"Christ, Riggs!" Without thinking, I hurried to the bathroom, grabbed my robe, and returned to wrap it around his head. He may have been morally corrupt, but he was still my ticket to a green card. I needed him alive. "What were you *thinking*?"

"I'm thinking you're cutting off my oxygen supply, wrapping this thing around me. How'd it go?" He shook the robe off, allowing me to lead him to the settee, where I threw a duvet across his massive body.

"Brilliant. A smashing success." I sat next to him, tucking the duvet behind his back on both sides, like he was a human burrito. "Why was your head in ice water? You could've gotten hypothermia."

He leaned back, screwing his fingers into his eye sockets. "Headache."

"And your first reaction wasn't to reach for the Tylenol, but to my *freezer*?"

"It's a trick a Greek physician taught me." He peeled the duvet off him. The imprint of his abs was visible through his henley. "I get them often. Migraines."

"Well, an English newswoman recommends some ibuprofen." I stood up and went to the kitchen to retrieve a bottle of water. "My special recipe is three pills."

I handed everything to him. He raised the pills in the air in a salute motion before knocking them back. "Compliments to the chef."

"Stay hydrated," I urged him.

"Yes, Mom."

He'd been saying that a lot. The Mum thing. This was my cue to go to my bedroom and cry into my pillow, hugging the tequila bottle I'd been fantasizing about the entire journey back, but I decided to stand in my living room instead. I didn't want to be alone with my thoughts right now. And surely, he'd ask me about Brendan.

Riggs didn't disappoint.

"So now that Cocksucker's gone, are you guys over?"

"His name is BJ," I said icily, as if the question itself was invasive and prodding. "And as I said, we're just on a break."

"A very long break."

"Time is relative."

"Relatives are time-suckers," he fired back.

"Suckers can sometimes be relatives," I managed, playing his stupid word game.

"But sucking relatives is a big, fat no-no." Riggs grinned.

"All right, you win, I cannot possibly top that."

We both stared at each other before exploding into hysterical laughter. To be fair, I was quite sure I was laughing from exhaustion, overwhelmed by my impending marriage and runaway boyfriend and complicated employment situation.

"Is Nepal nice?" I asked on a sigh. "Do you think he'll have a good time there?" I wanted the answer to be no. For Riggs to tell me Nepal would be awful and BJ would run back home before his jet lag was over.

"Nepal is stunning." Riggs had the good manners to smile ruefully at me. "Fascinating culture, great food, rich history, and the views are some of the best I've seen."

He must've noticed my crestfallen face, because he added, "And I don't think Cocksucker can appreciate any of those things, so I wouldn't worry too much about it. He is going to hate the lack of Starbucks."

I barked out a laugh. "He *did* say his favorite city is Vegas."

Riggs gagged. "Vegas isn't even a city. It's a never-ending main street full of drunks and people looking to make a buck."

We stayed like this for ten more minutes, talking about Vegas, and cities, and holiday destinations, until I felt better. Like I could handle being alone in my room.

"Good night, then," I said finally.

Riggs smiled. He always smiled. "Night, Poppins."

CHAPTER NINE

Two days after Cocksucker fled the country, my future wife informed me that she'd booked us an appointment with a family lawyer.

"What do we need a family lawyer for?" I asked, cleaning my photography equipment on her coffee table. I used a rocket blower to remove dust from the lens. "We're not even married yet. Even *I* think getting a divorce is a little premature."

She was running like a headless chicken around the apartment, scrubbing every surface five times.

"To sign our prenuptial agreement, of course." Duffy smiled apologetically, her cheeks turning pink. "Please don't take this to heart, and I say that with no prejudice at all, but I assume you and I aren't in the same financial situation."

I put my camera down, turning my full attention to her. "No," I agreed. "I can guarantee that you and I aren't in the same economic group."

She rocked on her heels, her expression awash with relief. "Which is fine. Money's not an incentive for you."

"It isn't," I confirmed. "And you're a gold digger."

"If you want to call it that." She hitched a shoulder up. "I worked quite hard for my savings—"

"How much savings are we talking about, exactly?" I cut through what I imagined was a prepared, ruthlessly boring speech.

She hesitated, then finally swallowed. "I have twenty-five thousand dollars in savings, give or take."

I whistled low. "And you said you couldn't pay me for the visa."

"Oh, but I couldn't!" Her mouth went slack with horror. "Some of it is tied up in bonds, the rest in stock. And this place is horrifyingly expensive. My parents are skint, and even if they weren't, I would never ask them for a penny. I still have to find a new job and—"

I raised my hand to stop her. "Calm down, I don't want your money."

Her shoulders relaxed, and she propped the broom against her counter. "Cheers."

"But I'm not going to sign the prenup either," I deadpanned.

If there was logic behind my decision, I couldn't find it. In fact, I knew that if Christian and Arsène found out that I was marrying this girl without an ironclad prenup, they'd kill me themselves, making her the sole beneficiary of everything I owned.

What they wouldn't understand was that in order to sign a prenup with Duffy, I'd need to declare my funds and possessions, and I didn't want her to know I was rich. She'd try to become my girlfriend for real, maybe even my wife, and there was nothing I wanted less than more Daphne Markham in my life. Especially since she'd actually be my wife.

Yes, Duffy and I had had one amusing conversation the night she'd dropped Cocksucker off at the airport—was his ass too precious to get a taxi like the rest of humanity?—but other than that, all evidence pointed toward the woman trying to marry her way up.

"You won't?" she asked, picking up the broom again and sweeping ardently. "Why?"

"Because"—I angled my camera sideways, using a LensPen to remove residual dust—"a relationship should be built on trust."

"But we *don't* have a relationship."

"We do," I said around the unlit joint in my mouth. "It's just not romantic."

"I don't think I could ever trust you."

"Don't marry me, then."

"Bloody hell, you know I must." She made a face and swept harder while staring at the floor, like Cinderella. "You're not going to ask for half my money, right? I really can't afford . . . I mean, even if BJ did ask me to marry him afterward . . ."

Unbelievable. She was still banging that old drum, even after everything he'd done to her. He'd flown to the other side of the motherfucking world when she needed him the most. How money obsessed was this chick?

"No prenup," I maintained, resolute. "This is our trust fall. You have to trust me, and I have to trust you."

"Trust me with *what*?" she cried out. "You don't even own an iPad!"

"There's more to life than money." Even though I lived by this motto, I also knew it was a provocative thing to tell a working-class go-getter. I sounded like those zen Bitcoin billionaires who thought they were spiritual because they grew a beard and did goat yoga on Pfeiffer Beach.

Duffy tucked the broom into her storage space. "If that's the case, then tell me what you gain from marrying me. Yes, you said you want to stay in New York for your job, but why don't you want to do this task you're dreading?"

"If I tell you, would you drop the prenup discussion?" I sighed.

She hesitated before nodding.

"Alaska," I said.

"Pardon?" She frowned.

"Alaska. My boss wanted me to move there for eight months for this documentary project. I don't like Alaska. Well, I've never been, but I never plan to either. Apparently, the only reason he insisted on my going was because I'm not tied down to New York. No family, no partner. I needed a responsibility."

"Why do you hate Alaska so much?"

"That's another story, for a much drunker time."

She stared at me wordlessly, and for the first time in my life—in my entire years of goddamn living—I felt genuinely seen. It was exhilarating and terrifying and, above all, fucking weird. I filled the silence with more words.

"The drawback is I'm supposed to stick around here for a few months. I've never done that before."

"You've never stayed in the same place for a few months at a time?" she asked from the other side of the room.

"Never."

"Why?"

"Another story, for *another* drunken time."

"Do you drink to tackle uncomfortable situations often?" She frowned in concern.

"I'm not an alcoholic," I clarified.

"An alcoholic usually doesn't admit to being one," she pointed out. "At any rate, I'm the same. I love a good drink. And I also love a not-so-good one, if I'm in a bad mood."

"You might be able to hold a drink in." I rose up to my feet and picked up my jacket and wallet. "But I'm an actual *expert*. It took years of unaddressed emotional instability, daddy and mommy issues, and deep denial to get to where I am today." I patted my torso.

"You're not the sole proprietor of being damaged," Duffy said with a sad smile. "I'll have you know, I drink my problems away too. 'Tis the English way."

Speaking of English, her throaty voice and sexy accent were doing weird things to my libido. I think they reverted it back to my adolescent years, because the only thing I could think of around her was sex.

"Yeah, well. Bet I can outdrink you with one liver tied behind my back." I shouldered into my jacket.

"Rubbish!" she bellowed. "I can drink you under the table."

"I can drink *and* eat you under the table."

I paused, realizing it didn't sound good. Or, more accurately, it sounded *very* good, but by the way her skin turned crimson, Duffy didn't want my mouth anywhere near her Bermuda Triangle.

"Not that, I'd never do that." I cleared my throat. *Shit.* Now I couldn't unsee the mental image of me going down on her, slurping her juices like they were a sundae. "I meant, in terms of food—"

"Food. Yes. I love food!" She grabbed her broom for the millionth time, still sweeping the same spot. "Do you like food too? You must, I suppose. You're quite the big guy . . ." She faltered.

"I'm glad the eyeful at Gretchen's impressed you."

"Not big like that!" She was pale with horror now. "And, of course, I haven't peeked. I mean, I don't doubt that you are. Everything else about you is, well . . ."

I cocked one eyebrow, daring her to continue. She moaned, slapping her hands over her eyes.

This was painful. And awkward. And *hilarious.* Everything we said sounded sexual.

"What I meant was your height . . . and width . . ." She pantomimed with her hands. "Dear God, I feel like I've just taken my mouth on a test drive and I can't find the brakes on the thing."

"Just pull the hand brake," I said with a laugh.

Her eyes dropped to my crotch.

"Not *that* hand brake, Duffy."

"Oh, bugger," she moaned, dragging her hands over her face. "Who even am I?"

I couldn't believe this conversation had started with a prenup. I could also believe she was capable of being fun if she just abandoned her six-ton reservations and prim-and-proper-lady act at the door.

"I'm gonna go now." I pointed at the door, like there was any doubt I would leave through there and not, I don't know, the fucking window.

"Sure. Right. Marvelous idea," she chirped. "Have a good day. I mean"—she glanced at her watch—"afternoon, I guess. It's my last day at WNT tomorrow. I need to prepare, and there's no redemption for me in this conversation."

"Anyway. So. No prenup."

"No prenup." She made a Scout's honor sign with her fingers. "But no taking my money either."

"I'll try to resist temptation."

"Are you coming to see Mrs. Zimmerman with me?" She meant the lawyer Christian recommended to us.

"Yeah. Of course. We're in this together."

"Right. Right."

We stood like this for a few more seconds.

Leave, you idiot. Did you forget how to use your feet? They climbed mountains for you.

Finally, I turned around and padded to the door. Practically *ran* to the stairway. When I got to the first floor, I heard a door open. Duffy burst out, gripping the banisters and peering down at me.

"Riggs! Wait!"

I looked up. Her face was the color of bubble gum. I was feeling funny, too, in a way I couldn't describe.

"You forgot your mobile." She reached down to hand it to me.

Our fingers brushed for a nanosecond. It was brief, but enough for me to feel how velvety and soft her skin was. Was she like that all over? I'd never find out.

"Thanks."

"Sure."

But she didn't leave the stairway, and neither did I. Not until her phone rang from inside the apartment.

What the fuck was going on with me today?

CHAPTER TEN

Riggs

Emmett: How's Desiree doing?

Riggs: Dessert-who?

Emmett: Your fiancée . . .

Riggs: Oh, yeah. Her. Never better.

Emmett: You know I'll sue if you're lying.

Riggs: Can you hear it?

Emmett: Hear what?

Riggs: My balls shaking, I'm so scared.

Emmett: I'll need to see that marriage certificate at some point, Bates.

Riggs: It's okay. I'd be obsessed with me too, if I were you.

Since I didn't have any assignments outside New York for the next few months, I took the train to Jersey. If I thought visiting another state would cure my claustrophobia, I was sorely mistaken. If anything, I felt even worse. Jersey was unapologetically, depressingly . . . well, *Jersey*. They didn't call it the Armpit of America for its buzzing nightlife, cultural significance, and stunning views. It stank. I wandered aimlessly on Atlantic City's boardwalk, taking pictures, knocking back a few beers. The place was about as inspiring as a used panty liner. The entire reason why I got into photography was because I wanted my job to take me to wild, exotic places.

Two things New Jersey definitely wasn't:

1. Wild
2. Exotic

But what were my options? Go back to Duffy's apartment and watch her fuss over work and salad dressings?

Then there were my friends. While I enjoyed their company, they also had their own lives. Said lives were boring, anyway, so sticking around during the daytime felt futile.

Somehow, I managed to stay out of the apartment until nine that night. By the time I went up the flight of stairs, I was sure Duffy was past her organic, healthy dinner, either working on her laptop in her room or hitting one of those late-night SoulCycle classes she was fond of.

I was about to slide the key into the keyhole when the door next to hers opened and a man in his late fifties emerged, a manila folder tucked under his arm. It was the man who'd opened the building's door when I'd ambushed my fiancée the other day. Intense Asshole Guy.

He wore a seventies-style tweed jacket and a baseball cap and was about my height. A hobo *GQ* type. He took one look at me and groaned.

"You again. Tell me Duffy hasn't moved in with her rebound."

"Duffy hasn't moved in with her rebound," I said, deadpan, as I unlocked the door. "She moved in with the love of her life."

Hey, why the fuck not? We needed to make this thing believable in case the government came knocking on this guy's door. Plus, I knew Poppins would be horrified if she found out I'd said those things to her neighbor, and the banter alone was going to be the highlight of my day.

"'Love of her life'?" The man rubbed the back of his ball cap. "She just broke up with her boyfriend. Plus, you're definitely not her type."

Was this guy competing for the Nosy Bastard Award?

"Are you writing her autobiography?" I pushed the door open with my shoulder. "Actually, don't answer that. I'm going to respect her privacy and let her fill you in if she feels like it."

If this man was creeping on my fake fiancée, I was going to for real strangle him.

"She will," he confirmed, frowning at me like my very existence disturbed him. "In a couple days, when we have our weekly drinks. I'm Charlie." He stepped forward to shake my hand.

"Riggs."

"Briggs?"

"Without the B."

His eyebrows shot up. "That's not a common name. What does it mean?"

"No clue. Parents fucked off before I had a chance to ask." I slid my hand from his before things got even weirder.

"Sorry to hear that."

I laughed. "I survived."

"Yeah. I can see."

Was this building full of socially impaired people?

"Hey, wanna grab a pint?" He pointed downstairs. "It's still a little light out, and your upstairs neighbor has a cello lesson until ten."

"Nice selling point, but I'm gonna call it a night." I was one step into the apartment when Charlie tsked behind me.

"Too bad. I'm wrapping up this documentary about Maasai Mara, and I need a professional eye to help me pick the film poster."

I stopped. Glanced behind my shoulder. "And you know I'm a photographer because . . . ?"

"You're holding a professional camera." Charlie gestured to my shoulder. "And I'm not a complete idiot."

That remained to be seen. Most people definitely fell into the *idiot* category.

Actually, going over someone else's photos of one of Kenya's most breathtaking wonders wasn't the worst thing I could do with my evening. Especially when the alternative was bickering with the hot prude from hell.

"Yeah, okay." I closed the door. "One drink."

At the bar, Charlie and I ordered Carlton Draughts and went through the Maasai Mara photos. They weren't terrible, but they weren't groundbreaking either.

I pointed at one of the pictures, of an elephant standing next to a tree, dwarfing it. "This is your cum shot. Background's insane. The desert looks like Mercury, but it could use some work."

It could've been better if the photographer had used a Canon 100–400mm. The filter was all wrong too. Charlie propped an elbow against the sticky bar, tapping the photo.

"See, it was my favorite, too, but for a completely different reason."

"Oh yeah?"

"If you look carefully, the elephant looks like it's crying."

I squinted, paying better attention to the photo. The elephant did look like it was crying.

"You've been making documentaries long?" I eyed him, taking a pull of my beer.

"Long enough to call it a job and not a hobby." He laughed easily. "For a couple decades now. But I started out late, and only because I ran out of money."

"What'd you do before?" I asked.

"Older, affluent women, mainly." His hand shook as he gathered all the photos scattered on the bar. Was he an alcoholic?

I nodded. "It's a hard knocks life out there for an aging fox."

"And you?" Charlie eyed me. "You've been a photographer long?"

"Since I graduated from boarding school." I fidgeted with my coaster, wondering idly if my fake fiancée had more lingerie like I'd seen the night she walked in on Gretchen and me. "I knew academia wasn't for me and wanted to see as much of the world in the least amount of time. We never know when we'll drop dead, right?"

"If we're lucky, we don't." Charlie stroked his chin thoughtfully. "If we're unlucky, we do."

"Okay, Socrates." I was too jaded for his philosophical ass tonight. "You get my point."

"Do you have any reason to think you might die young?" He picked up his beer, his hand still shaking. Something was wrong with this guy, but just because he'd shoved his nose into my business didn't mean I was going to return a favor.

"Nah." I looked around the bar, people watching for potential hookups. "I just needed an excuse to be a nomad."

"So now you live here, in the city?"

I shrugged. "For the next few weeks, I guess. I don't have a base. I take jobs and travel. During my time off, I visit places on my own dime."

"You must have a mini hub," Charlie insisted.

"Nope."

"What about your family?" Charlie ordered us more beer and two cheeseburgers. If nothing else, this was a nice reprieve from Duffy's fridge, which looked like a dispensary with all the greens.

"No family." I sipped my beer. "Free as a bird."

"Or lonely as a tooth in a crackhead's smile." He grinned big.

I barked out a laugh. "It's all about your outlook, I guess."

"Yeah, well, I've got more mileage than you, and let me tell you, family's important." He popped a french fry into his mouth. "So, Duffy. How'd you meet her?"

I contemplated how much to tell him, if anything. On one hand, the man was a complete stranger. On the other, I didn't want to shit all over my plan with Poppins. We'd never smoothed out the kinks about our engagement story.

"It's complicated," I said finally.

"No, it's not." Charlie wiped ketchup from the corner of his mouth. "Duffy doesn't do complicated. And anyway, it is a one-line question. Coffee shop. Club. Work. Tinder."

"Yeah, definitely not Tinder." I gave him a once-over. "You seem to know her well."

He picked up his beer, then put it back down, as if it weighed a ton. "Well enough to know she's better than that suit she's parading around as her boyfriend. That guy is no good." He made a face. "Where is that mouth breather, anyway? Did she really break up with him?"

"Nepal," I answered, oddly interested to hear more tidbits about Cocksucker. So he wore a suit and came from money. That was predictable. But a mouth breather too? Duffy clearly had zero standards other than having a trust fund.

"Nepal, huh?" Charlie sat back and tossed the balled-up paper napkin onto the bar. "Probably volunteering somewhere, thinking he's holier than thou."

I smiled. The old man was growing on me like fungus. Despite my best efforts not to like him. "She seemed to have bought into that whole savior-and-saint act."

"Duffy?" Charlie chuckled. "Nah. She just decided he's going to be her ticket out of poverty. Can't blame her, with her rough start. More power to her."

Shaking my head, I drained the rest of my beer, not sure I agreed with him.

"Maybe we should do this more often." Charlie glanced at me, smiling.

I tipped my bottle against his. "Maybe you're right."

CHAPTER ELEVEN

DUFFY

It was on my last day at WNT when I decided it would be a great time to have a full-fledged mental breakdown.

Mercury must've been in retrograde. Reversing at a trillion miles an hour, more like. Everything that could have gone wrong had done so. And everything that couldn't—still did.

BJ didn't call me from Kathmandu, even though he had promised to give me a sign of life when he landed. It had been three days since I'd dropped him off at the airport, which meant, according to our no-contact rule, the next time I'd hear from him would be when he came back home.

Mum *did* call, but I wished she hadn't. She was panicked because Kieran (a.k.a. the Traitor Who Shall Not Inherit a Penny Should I Ever Become Rich) told her BJ left me, which wasn't even (entirely) true.

Then there was work.

Everybody seemed to fuss over Gretchen like they were losing a limb, not a high-maintenance anchorwoman. No one paid attention to me, even though I was her highest-ranked assistant. I knew exactly why. I was the snotty, neurotic go-getter who frowned upon those who came to work to socialize and who skipped social functions in favor of trying to impress BJ's family. To be honest, I hadn't thought I'd need to be there for much longer. Sure, I'd stay gainfully employed until *after* my wedding to BJ, but as soon as I was pregnant with my first child, I'd quietly quit to raise the next generation of Abbotts.

Only now there was no BJ, no wedding, and definitely no babies.

Gone was the dream to take two years off to focus on building my family and soul-search what I wanted to do for a career.

Meanwhile, Gretchen's office overflowed with flowers, chocolates, and fluffy teddy bears, to the point I had to start carrying them out and giving them away to randoms outside the building.

I marched several times in and out of her office, removing chocolate and fruit baskets. Gretchen explained that she hated the pollen in flowers and loathed having sweets around her because she was doing keto.

She sat at her desk with the air of a saint who'd just been appointed by the pope, receiving visitors. You'd think she herself was going to be the president of the United States, not just his mouthpiece.

Gretchen and I still hadn't broached the subject of Riggs, but she stopped glancing at me anxiously, like I was about to spill her secret during staff meetings. From this, I deducted she knew that Riggs and I had entered into an arrangement of sorts and felt confident I'd keep my mouth shut. Which could explain why she'd gone back to treating me like I was a piece of gum that was stuck onto her Jimmy Choos.

I wondered if Gretchen and Riggs had slept together since I caught them red handed. Not that it mattered.

As it turned out, I got my answer anyway. It was on my fifth run to her office. I opened her door, then stopped abruptly. Riggs was in the room, sprawled on the edge of her desk lazily. My heart dropped to my knickers, which, unfortunately, were already dampening at the sight of him.

He wore cargo pants, an asymmetrical smirk, and an army-hued henley that clung to each of his muscles like a Harry Styles fangirl. It felt weird, seeing him not in the confines of my flat. A wild, wanton thing.

Gretchen had her hand on his arm. They stood close. Too close to not be sleeping together anymore. And I couldn't help but remember how they were fused together as he shagged her raw against her wall. How his arse muscles contracted with each thrust. The hedonistic, sensual look on his face as he tipped his head back, displaying his square jaw . . .

Stop this right now. Think about something else. Something sad. BJ being a terrible boyfriend. Poverty. Climate change. J.Lo taking Ben Affleck's name like it wasn't 2022.

I didn't know why, but Riggs was the straw that broke the camel's back. Come on! The woman was *married*. How many men did she need? Didn't she know that there was a shortage? For every hundred women in the US, there were only 97.95 males! This was pure greed. Attractive men weren't a hot dog eating contest. You didn't have to shove as many as you could fit into your mouth to win a trophy.

Plus, I thought irrationally, he was *my* future husband.

"Ugh, Duffy." Gretchen didn't bother stepping away from Riggs, her tits plastered against his chest. "Barging in without knocking again. Don't you ever learn?"

Do not kill your boss, Daphne Markham. You are not meant for a life in prison.

"Sorry," I mumbled, gathering more chocolate and flowers in my hands. I kept my head down, refusing to make eye contact with Riggs. "Didn't realize you had company."

"Knock, Duffy, knock. It'll do you wonders." Gretchen flipped her blonde hair patronizingly before dragging her manicured fingernails down Riggs's chest. "I'm all packed up and ready to leave. You coming to my place?"

A box of chocolate fell from the mountain in my hands. I picked it up, flustered, letting out a pathetic whimper. I hated that he was seeing me like this.

He clamped her wrist and removed it from his chest. "Rain check. I gotta check out some new photography equipment in Brooklyn."

"I'll come with." She grabbed her purse, rummaging through it to disguise her embarrassment at his blatant rejection. "I don't have to head back home until later tonight."

"No need. I'm meeting Christian afterward."

"You're choosing your boring, married friend over me?" she asked incredulously.

"That he's boring is unfortunate, but I like his wife more than you, so."

Ouch.

Gretchen obviously didn't like his brush-off and decided to direct her wrath at me.

"Oh, you're still here." She scrunched her nose. "Well, don't just stand there. Your last shift isn't over yet. Offer my guest a drink." She motioned to Riggs.

God, I hated her. But not enough to cock up my future job prospects by giving her the golden opportunity not to write me a glowing reference letter.

"Would you like something to drink, Riggs?" I asked as blandly as possible, balancing her farewell gifts in my arms.

"It's Mr. Bates to you." Gretchen rested her chin on her knuckles demurely. "Now's a good time to remember we're just doing you a favor. It's not like he—"

"I've never seen a female pissing contest before, but I have to say, I'm not a huge fan," Riggs interrupted, throwing Gretchen a put-off look. "Anyway, I just came to say goodbye before you fly to DC. Hey, Poppins, need me to pick something up for dinner?" He threw me one of his sultry glances. Or maybe it was just his default sexiness. His existence alone probably encouraged ovulation.

Goodbye was probably code for loads of sex. Well, they could have sex until their genitals fell off and their crotches had carpet burns. I didn't care, as long as it wasn't under my roof.

"I'm fine," I bit out to Riggs. "I'll let you two . . . *goodbye* privately."

I removed myself from the premises as quickly as humanly possible. I was marching to the elevator when I realized I'd forgotten my employee card on Gretchen's desk.

Though seeing those two again was the last thing I wanted, I couldn't walk in and out of the building freely without it. With a groan, I made a U-turn. The door to her office was slightly ajar. Just enough for their conversation to drift to the hallway and into my ears.

". . . no one even gave her a *card*, Riggs. I always knew she was stuck up, but *wow*, the girl is unlikable."

My heart fell to the pit of my stomach like a ten-ton stone. They were talking about me. Agony ripped through my chest, which I couldn't make sense of, because none of this came as a surprise.

I knew what people thought of me. That I was a slow-burn gold digger, an overachieving she wolf; no one had ever bothered to ask *why* I was the way I was. People just wrote me off. Put me in the stereotypical box and shelved me in the Do Not Befriend category.

Riggs answered in a deep, low tone, but I couldn't decipher his words.

Gretchen sighed in response. "All I'm saying is, make sure you don't get too involved with her. She's so *daunting*." I dug my teeth into my lower lip until it bled. "And . . . between you and me?" Gretchen dropped her voice an octave. "Not the most trustworthy employee. There are a few designer items missing from my wardrobe."

An electric shock of rage sizzled through my body. How dare she? I'd never stolen as much as a pencil from her desk. She'd trusted me with her apartment code. With her credit card. With her *children*!

"Did *you* get her anything?" Riggs asked, ignoring the heavily implied theft claim.

"*Me?*" the cow replied. "Well, it's not like I had time, between Lyric's birthday and the move to DC. And besides, she doesn't deserve it."

There was a pregnant pause.

"Don't look at me like that! Might I remind you she is *blackmailing* us?"

I decided then and there to do the first uncalculated thing in my life since I'd been born. I burst straight into her office, not bothering to close the door behind me. I dumped her gifts onto the floor, bowing deeply with a flourish.

"Here, Your Majesty. Want to know why nobody gave me a card?" I shrieked, knowing full well I probably looked as sweaty and deranged as I felt. "Let me tell you why. Because of *you*, Gretchen. You made me the villain in this studio. True, I was never the most approachable human being to begin with, but *you* insisted I fire any assistant that was too tardy, too loud, too slow, too blonde, too much bloody competition!" My voice shook, much like the rest of my body. Behind me, a cluster of WNT employees gathered, peeking curiously. I saw them through the glass walls bracketing Gretchen's office.

"When you needed someone to be told off, you sent me to do it. When the stylist made you look like Big Bird, I was the one who had to write her a scalding review. Whenever you had an oopsie on air, you blamed it on me." I stubbed my chest with my finger. "I was the only executive assistant at WNT who never socialized with anyone else, because *you* forbade it. You were so scared I'd spill one of your trade secrets, you would barely let me grab a coffee with the runners!"

I knew I shared some of the responsibility as to why I was about as popular as Neapolitan ice cream within WNT hallways. I never made a genuine effort, but to pretend the fault fell squarely on my shoulders was ridiculous.

"Don't blame me!" Gretchen tossed her hands up, her roar very nearly throwing me across the room. "Hold yourself accountable for the way people perceive you. You're in charge of your own behavior."

"Oh, I *am* to blame!" I laughed shrilly. "I'm beyond responsible for doing your ugly bidding. You molded me into your perfect little machine." I pointed my index finger at her face. "Knowing I couldn't quit because the channel was sponsoring my visa. You abused your power." I laughed incredulously. "No wonder you ended up in politics."

The silence that followed was so loud I swore I could hear people in Maine asking one another what they should have for supper tonight. I peered behind my shoulder. There were at least fifty WNT employees behind me, their phones directed at Gretchen and me, recording my public showdown.

Time to do something, Duffy. Anything at all. Whenever you're ready. Preferably this year, though.

It was obvious Gretchen was too stunned to produce words. Not that I wanted her to. I couldn't believe I'd behaved so commonly. So crudely. I'd always measured every action of mine carefully, desperate to be a Goody Two-Shoes.

Do something. Right. Now.

I snatched a box of Godiva from her desk and waved it in my boss's face. "You don't deserve this good chocolate. I'm taking it with me. This is my goodbye present. My 'Thank you for your service, Duffy.' Don't forget to check out all of the thirty-five toilets in the White House. We all know how full of shit you are!"

Okay, maybe not that.

Nonetheless, the deed had been done. And so, committed to my public fall from grace, I tornadoed out of her office, after which I anti-climactically waited for the lift for three minutes under excruciatingly dumbfounded gazes before it pinged open.

To make matters worse, Gretchen's assistant number two, Billy, appeared next to me, a pile of flower bouquets in her hands. She, too, was helping my boss with getting rid of all the goodbye presents.

"Hi, Duffy." She pushed her reading glasses up her nose.

"Hey, Billy." I rubbed my forehead tiredly.

"There's something you need to know," she said in a hushed voice when we entered the lift and the doors closed. I angled my face toward her. Had I spoken the mind of the entire office? Were people cheering for me? Had I become her role model? Hope bubbled in my chest.

But Billy looked unnaturally pink and insisted on staring at a spot above my head. "I think you got your period. When you made that speech? There was a red stain showing."

I collapsed on the stairway leading from the WNT building, then proceeded to stuff my face with Swiss chocolate I couldn't even taste and was already regretting.

I was into my seventeenth truffle when someone plopped down beside me. A large someone. A tall and muscular someone who smelled like wild woods and leather and sex.

Someone I *really* didn't want to talk to right now.

"So." Riggs reached to steal a Black Forest truffle before popping it between his lips. "When's the next show? I didn't even have time to make it to the concessions."

"Ugh." I hiccuped into my chocolate box. "I'm mortified. This is the first time this has happened to me."

"That's supposed to be my line."

"That's your pep talk?" My head shot up. "A sexual innuendo?"

"Well, now that I know I'm being *graded* for it . . ." He took another truffle, sucking on the cherry-jam topping. "How about this? 'Tomorrow is another day. The best days of your life are still to come.

There is no such thing as bad publicity. What doesn't kill you makes you stronger. Our biggest breakthroughs often come after the darkest times.' How am I doing so far?"

I glared at him with open annoyance. "You sound like my Pinterest inspiration board."

He chuckled softly. "You okay, Poppins?"

"No. Clearly, I'm never going to be okay." Wasn't he there a second ago, when I'd annihilated my entire reputation and career? "I made a complete eejit out of myself. I should just move back to England and change my identity." I covered my face with my hands.

"Yeah, that's not gonna fly." He ribbed me. "You owe me a marriage."

"You'll have plenty of eligible women to choose from," I said, realizing I was probably right. He was handsome and worldly and oozed big-dick energy. Not everyone wanted to marry a walking, talking wallet.

"But I don't want an eligible woman. I want an unhinged one who yells at her boss and laminates random documents and arranges her salad dressings by date, fat percentage, and list of ingredients."

Well, excuse me for not wanting to eat my greek salad with blue cheese dressing. Not all of us thrived in chaos.

"There's a fine line between insanity and genius," I reminded him primly.

"And you straddle it like a seasoned stripper." His aqua eyes sparkled with mischief.

"Everyone must think I'm mental." I felt my lips wobbling and knew I was close to tears. More than anything, I was gutted to be comforted by my boss's lover. No one promised me he wouldn't go straight to her afterward and tell her about this pathetic scene.

"And you care about what people think because . . . ?" He elevated an eyebrow.

"Social standing equals power."

"Not giving a fuck about what people think equals power," he corrected me, tapping the tip of my nose as if I was an adorable fawn. "And right now you're choosing to be power*less*. Change that, Poppins."

"I still want to run away and change my name."

He stroked his chin. "Would you consider Desiree?"

This was the second time he'd brought up this name.

"Why on earth would I—"

"Got your name wrong accidentally in front of my boss."

"You cad." I gasped. "We've been living together for—"

"Relax, it was before we moved in together." He waved a flippant hand. "It's all different now. I know everything about you."

"You do not."

"Try me."

Normally, I'd pass. But my other option was sobbing into a box of chocolate on the stairway of my previous workplace, and I was eager to cap my embarrassment quota for the decade.

"What's my full name?" I quipped.

"Daphne Helen Marie Markham."

"Okay. That's on my gym membership on the fridge. Favorite biscuits?"

"Digestives."

That was easy, though. They were the only kind I kept in the flat.

"Wardrobe quirk?" I wanted to see if he noticed I color coordinated my dresses with my purses.

"You never wear underwear." He grinned winningly. "Which I approve of, by the way."

"Oi, of course I do!" I slapped his thigh. *Ouch*. Was he made out of iron?

"Then how come they're never in the washing machine?"

"I wash them by hand. They're delicate." I fisted a couple of truffles, then shoved them into my mouth and chewed.

"Just like you," he said sarcastically. "By the way, your teeth are brown from the chocolate."

I opened my mouth, spitting the half-chewed truffle back into the box, horrified.

His jaw pulsed. "You're doing this again."

"Doing what?"

"Caring what people think."

"Would you please just stop?"

"Stop what?"

"Stop being funny and charming."

"So you find me funny and charming?" That sultry zing in his eyes was back.

"You're *trying* to be," I amended, glad I'd run out of chocolate. A wave of queasiness washed through me. "It's not working. I know your game."

Riggs leaned on his elbows, smirking. "I have a game now, do I? Please fill me in as to what it is."

He was grating on my nerves, but at least we weren't talking about my public meltdown upstairs. I hoped I wasn't becoming a viral meme this very minute.

British Karen lashes out at boss with a period stain on her bum.

This made Elvis's dying on his toilet seat look like a graceful departure.

"You love female attention. You don't care how or where you get it, or who you destroy in the process." I crossed my arms.

People sidestepped us on the stairs. It was time to evacuate. I rose up and dusted off my dress, too preoccupied to care that I was sporting a *period* stain. I wasn't even supposed to get my period until next week. BJ must've thrown me out of cycle with his traumatic news. I made my way to the subway, with Riggs tailing me.

"And what evidence do you have to support this claim?" he probed as I slam-dunked the empty Godiva box into a bin.

"You're having an affair with a married woman." I suppressed a burp. "You're ruining a family."

"Don't tell me you grew sympathy for Gretchen Beatty in the last ten minutes." He put a hand to his heart.

"Hardly." I tilted my chin up. "But think about the children."

"I prefer not to. I have a strong aversion to them, generally speaking."

"Color me shocked." I snorted, getting more riled up, although I noticed he stayed close behind me, hiding my period stain. "I've never met a man quite so reckless. You're nearing forty and don't even have a place!"

"I could have a place," he said dryly, in a way that almost made me believe him. "And a car. And all those little insurances you have to pay monthly. I choose not to."

"Why?"

"Freedom. Did you know the word *mortgage* means *dead pledge* in French? When you own something, it is bound to own you back."

"Maybe I'd like to be owned. Living like a wild weed, without a place to call home . . . seems like a miserable existence to me."

Riggs followed me down the stairs to the subway, his movements panther-like—sleek, long, and graceful. He was drawing looks from women and men alike, and the sheer presence of him made me lose my balance.

"I was never in any danger of ruining Gretchen's marriage," he said finally.

"How come?" I challenged, passing through the turnstile. He *hopped* over it after me. My future husband was a delinquent. Lovely.

"Because." He leaned against the wall on the subway platform casually, one leg propped up. "It was already ruined when I entered the picture. Jason has been having an affair with Gretchen's sister for ten years."

"What a bunch of crock." I rolled my eyes, producing a small mirror from my wallet and then checking my lipstick. "Gretchen's daughter Presence is already nine."

"She named her daughters Lyric *and* Presence?" Riggs wore a repulsed smirk. "She's crueler than I thought. Anyway, that's the God-honest truth. Gretchen found Jason and her sister in a compromising position the same day they arrived back from their honeymoon. Their marriage hasn't been legit since."

Shamefully, this piece of sordid information filled me with plea-sure. Gretchen had always been on the winning end. I'd never seen her wronged.

"So why did she stay married to him?" I demanded.

"Didn't you just say Presence is nine, soon to be ten?" He quirked a knowing eyebrow. "Do the math, Poppins."

"Stop calling me Poppins."

"Stop sounding like her."

That made me shut up for a second while I digested the information.

Gretchen was pregnant when she got married to Jason. That made sense. Gretchen was the kind of woman to tick marriage and kids off her to-do list and move on to her next conquest. And by this stage—ten years ago—she was more concerned with not losing her position at the network than working on her marriage.

"And when did you enter the picture?" I crossed my arms over my chest.

"About four years ago." Riggs adjusted the leather strap of his mes-senger bag over his shoulder. "We were both covering the Olympics in Greece."

"Who hit on who?"

"Does it matter?"

"You know bloody well it does."

"The attraction was there from both sides," he said diplomatically.

"Who made the first move?" I insisted, filled with fresh rage toward Gretchen for hitting on my fake fiancé.

"Me," Riggs said carelessly. Unconvincingly. "What can I say? All that cardio made me want to have a workout myself."

I didn't believe him. He was covering for Gretchen. I couldn't figure him out. He had the thoughtless, hedonistic air of a villain and the moral code of a hero.

"Do you love her?" I narrowed my eyes, drowning in those ocean-hued marbles of his.

He threw his head back and laughed heartily. "Love is not an emotion I'm capable of, so don't worry about your future husband pining after another."

The train arrived at the platform, and Riggs and I both slipped inside. Since it was crowded with rush hour folks, we had to squish together against a plastic partition, with Riggs towering over me. His chest was flush against mine. He smelled outdoorsy and fresh.

"Even if Jason and Gretchen aren't 'legit,'" I said, air-quoting the word as I grabbed one of the straps, "what you two are doing is immoral."

"Why?" Riggs spoke to the crown of my head, his warm cinnamon breath fanning my hair. "What kind of double standard is that? Men are expected to be forgiven and excused for cheating on women all the time, while women have to take the moral highway. Is this the deal you want to take?"

My face twisted in revulsion. "Just because Jason is an arsehole—"

"Doesn't mean Gretchen should be one too?" Riggs finished for me, arching an eyebrow. "She responded to his indiscretions in kind. An eye for an eye, an orgasm for an orgasm."

"Quite sure that's not how they phrase it in the Bible."

"Did you read the new edition?" he challenged, a teasing smirk gracing his mouth. "*Much* more explicit. I highly recommend."

I don't care about Jason, you wanker. But I'd love it if you could stop screwing my office bully.

Swallowing hard, I changed the subject. "This is not the way to Brooklyn."

"Huh?" he asked, his attention already drifting to the phone in his hand.

"You said you're heading to Brooklyn. You should get off and take the A or C line."

"Don't worry about it." He reached over to tuck a wisp of hair behind my ear. My breath hitched. It was the first time he'd touched me intentionally. Thankfully, I didn't crumble into rubbles of hormones. "Brooklyn was never in my plans tonight."

"So why did you lie?"

"Because Gretchen wasn't either."

I masked my relief with a headshake. "It is unlike you to pass on an opportunity to have sex."

He frowned. "Who said I'm passing on sex? My friend Ingrid is in town from Denmark."

It felt like he'd stabbed my chest with an icicle. Must've been my longing for BJ. Which reminded me—perhaps I was foolish to sit around and wait for him. It would be a good idea to start exploring other opportunities.

I patted Riggs's chest with a salacious smile. "Good for you, my primal, basic fiancé."

"Uh-huh. She's sarcastic now." He smirked again. At least one of us found our banter pleasurable. "What did I do now to upset your delicate notions?"

"You couldn't upset me if you tried," I lied.

"Spit it out, Poppins."

"You haven't even given me an engagement ring."

Madame, what are you on about, and who gave you the authority to say such a thing? I already knew I wasn't in full control of my motor mouth when he was around, but this was scandalous.

"A fake engagement ring?" He tucked his finger into the loop of his belt.

"Obviously."

I had officially lost my mind. I very much doubted it was on the same continent as me at this point.

"What do you need a ring for?" His tone was nonchalant, but he gave me that look again, like he was worried for my sanity. That made both of us.

"To authenticate our engagement, of course, why else?" I rolled my eyes. "A diamond ring is the blue checkmark of nuptials. It is utterly unskippable."

"Blue checkmarks are a terrible invention. They solidify the false narrative that famous people are more important."

"Thanks for the TED talk, Riggs, but the immigration officer would hardly care what you have to say about modern-day society," I replied tersely. "We need to look convincing, and I can't be the one to buy myself a ring because my taste is too highbrow for someone like you to choose it. It must look authentic."

"You're so lovable. It's beyond me why you haven't won Miss Popularity at the office."

"That was because of your girlfriend," I said.

"Is she also the reason why Cocksucker ran for the hills—sorry, highest mountain on Planet Earth?"

"I can't believe you went there." I reared my head back, staring at him wildly.

"I can't believe *he* went all the way to Kathmandu to avoid asking you to marry him."

I was about to bite out something snarky back when nausea clawed at my throat. Must've been the seven-pound chocolate assortment I'd decided to propel down my gob. *Bugger.* I didn't want to throw up somewhere public. And on a ludicrously attractive man, no less.

"So help a tasteless guy out. What kind of ring would you like?" Riggs ignored a woman who "accidentally" threw herself at him when the train stopped, giggling an apology.

"Just go with your natural instincts," I mumbled. My mouth felt like it was full of wool. "BJ always said he wanted to get me a marquise diamond engagement ring."

"You mean Cocksucker the mouth breather?"

My head snapped up. "How did you . . . he's *not* a mouth breather!"

"I bet his breath smells like a wet dog." He grinned down at me, obviously getting off on my anger.

"I'm not even going to dignify that with an answer."

Though, just for the record, BJ's breath was absolutely fine. Possibly because I always snuck packs of mints into his wallet, but still.

"Hmm, Poppins?"

"What?" Was I actually answering to this nickname now?

"You're green."

I pursed my lips, holding back from puking.

"You're not about to vomit, are you?" His forehead creased.

The desire to shake my head was strong, but I knew any movement would inspire me to throw up. So, I didn't answer. Didn't move. Didn't breathe.

Riggs flipped his bag open, angled it between us, and pulled out a Polaroid camera and a phone. "You're not gonna make it to a public restroom. Throw up into this."

My eyes flared. Was he mental?

He let loose a groan. "You can't keep it in. The next stop is a few minutes away."

I shook my head no. Huge mistake. My nausea intensified.

He pried the jaws of his bag open wider. "Just do it here before you throw up on someone's shoes. I really don't feel like getting into a fistfight because my fiancée can't control herself around truffles."

"Stop it. I had a day," I muttered around the bile assembling in my mouth.

"Yeah." Riggs began gathering my hair from my face expertly. He was surprisingly kind. Fatherly, even. Which was ironic, considering he didn't want kids. "Trust me, half of New York's corporate media was there to witness it."

"I'm not throwing up into your messenger bag," I maintained, even as cold sweat broke through my skin and I became light headed. "It's not ladylike."

"Ladylike left the station when you tramped around the streets of Manhattan with a period stain the shape of West Virginia on your ass."

I pinched his bicep, outraged. "That you'd ever even mention this to me in public—"

He laughed brusquely. "Now that I've pissed you off, could you please do the world a favor and just throw up in my bag already?"

Well, he *did* deserve it.

That was when I keeled over and vomited into Riggs's bag while he held my hair in his fist. I didn't stop until it was completely full. My forehead collapsed on his chest. He stroked my head the entire time, his pecs shaking with laughter.

All in all, it was the most romantic thing anyone had ever done for me.

CHAPTER TWELVE

RIGGS

Emmett: Alaska looks mighty nice this time of year. Perfect temperature.

Riggs: I'll buy you a one-way ticket.

Emmett: Are you ever going to tell me what your problem with the place is?

Riggs: No.

Emmett: Am I getting a wedding invite?

Riggs: Also no.

Emmett: I still don't buy that you decided to settle down and give up the variety.

Riggs: Good, because my relationship is not for sale. Get your utensils out, buddy. You're about to get a big piece of humble pie.

"Talk me through the logic of buying your *fake* fiancée a *real* diamond again." Arsène snapped his fingers when we were at a jewelry store. It had been a week since Poppins and I had the ring conversation. My best friend waltzed around the white marbled space, squinting at diamond bracelets and emerald necklaces.

"She's so uptight she might get a heart attack if someone notices she's wearing a fake." I drummed on the glass counter irritably, waiting for the salesman to return with some samples.

"And you care about her getting a heart attack because . . . ?" Christian cocked his head sideways, wrinkling his forehead.

"She's unemployed and uninsured. Her hospitalization alone would cost more than an entire wedding." I scanned my phone, scrolling through messages.

"Look at you, you hopeless romantic," Christian tutted sardonically. "Is it possible that you like her just a teeny-tiny bit?"

"You've *met* her." I shot him a bewildered look. "Does she seem like my type?"

"Your type is anyone with a pulse—no matter how faint and shallow—so the answer is yes," Arsène deadpanned.

Putting aside the fact that she vomited into my bag, blackmailed me into marriage, and referred to me as the *village idiot* at least twice a day, Duffy also had a quasi boyfriend. I didn't *dis*like her, but I sure wasn't her number one fan. More than anything, she possessed the one trait I despised about people the most—she was money hungry.

"She's gorgeous," I admitted gruffly. "But would also marry a convicted child murderer if he had his own yacht. She's the definition of a gold digger."

"And you play the poor Oliver Twist," Arsène finished, fingering an expensive pair of earrings for consideration for his wife. "Which means there's no risk of her falling for you. Not that there would be if she knew you were a billionaire. You have fewer boyfriend qualities than a bottle of Flonase."

Ever since Arsène fell in love and decided to marry the widow of his girlfriend's side piece, he'd fancied himself the twenty-first century's answer to Romeo.

"Thanks for the unasked-for opinion. I'll be sure to ignore it." I parked my elbows on the counter. The salesman came back with an array of engagement rings arranged on a white satin pillow.

"There you are, sir. Please let me know if you have any questions."

I did have a question—*What the fuck am I doing?*

I still couldn't believe I was getting married.

"Looks like you're a little overwhelmed." Christian eyed me. "You sure you've thought this whole thing through? Marriage is baggage. Real or not."

"I'm not afraid of marriage." I began plucking up the engagement rings one by one and examining them. "But, like hard drugs, I prefer to stay away from the concept."

"Because—also like hard drugs, it gets you addicted." Christian pointed at a silver ring with a cushion diamond.

I needed to find something not excruciatingly expensive. Didn't want to blow my cover as a billionaire to a woman who would marry a no-show mouth breather with an oral sex name just so she could afford to shop on Fifth Avenue.

Arsène pushed his face into the pillow of rings with a scowl. "Which one screams Daphne Markham to you?"

"Dunno." I skimmed through all of them. "Is there anything that looks like it would look good on a thirty-year-old divorcée with two children and a time-share in Aspen Highlands?"

Arsène chuckled. "Aren't you a lucky bastard?"

I knew she wanted something mouthwateringly gauche, with a diamond the size of her head. But I also knew she'd tell immediately if I got her something expensive, and I wasn't in a hurry to please her.

"She'd probably hate an heirloom ring." I scrubbed the stubble on my chin. I pushed the pillow with the rings toward the salesperson. "Which means that's exactly what she's going to get."

"An heirloom?" Christian glowered at me. "You need a family to have heirloom pieces. Your ass is lonelier than a brain cell in Congress."

"Thanks for the reminder."

Arsène clapped my shoulder. "Where there's a will, there's a way."

"Are we going to rob a nice elderly lady?" Christian inquired calmly. "Because that's the only *way* he is getting this woman a family heirloom."

"Granny needn't worry." Arsène turned around, heading for the glass door. "We're going to a place where you sell your soul for a few bucks."

"Wall Street?" Christian and I both followed him reluctantly.

Arsène laughed, already hailing a taxi. "Pawnshop hopping."

Seven Brooklyn pawnshops and one purchase later, I returned to my love nest with Poppins, a.k.a. the woman who vomited into my messenger bag, then had the audacity to tell me I was uncivilized for throwing it into a public trash can because it would leave a terrible smell.

I pushed the door open. Her voice filled the apartment like soap bubbles. She seriously had the poshest accent I'd ever heard, including the royal family.

". . . no, Kieran. Mooning thy neighbor is absolutely *not* a form of courting."

"Why?" I heard a male voice rising from the speakerphone in the kitchenette.

"Because it's harassment, isn't it?" Duffy leaned against the counter, sipping lemon water. She hadn't noticed me yet. "Besides, she won't fancy you for it."

"Why not?" Kieran demanded. "I have a great sense of humor, and an even greater arse."

Wait, wait, wait. That was Kieran, her twin brother? Why did he sound like Michael Caine? She sounded like a gently bred, privately educated princess, and he . . . like the person who cleaned her chimney.

Then the penny dropped. Duffy didn't come from money. Of course she hadn't. That was why she was so obsessed with it.

"Honey, I'm home!" I sauntered in, deciding to mess around with her a little. After all, it had been four hours since I'd last done so.

She raised her head from her gargantuan gallon of water and stared at me like I'd just handed her over to ISIS.

"Who's this?" Kieran probed on the other line.

"No one." She shot me an intimidating *Don't you dare talk* look, sprinkling it with violent hand-waving gestures.

"Her fiancé." I popped open the fridge and grabbed one of her green juices.

"Hey, mate. I'm her older brother, Kieran," the person replied without missing a beat.

"*Twin* brother," she amended. "He was born a few minutes before me."

"That was because she was arse first."

"That explains a lot." I downed her lettuce juice or whatever it was in one go. "Riggs. Nice to meet you."

"Thanks for breaking the law for my sister."

"My pleasure, just needed an excuse." I winked at Poppins, saluting her with her empty green-juice bottle. She grumbled something inaudible to her gallon of water.

"So, why are you doing that, anyway? Marrying her, I mean," Kieran asked. "Insanity? Boredom? Are you a minger?"

I let out a raucous laugh. Hard to believe these two shared a womb. He was a working-class hero, and she—a Kate Middleton wannabe. Oil and water.

"I need a fake wife to get my boss off my back."

That piqued his interest. "She's making a move on you?"

"*He* wants to send me to Alaska for eight months."

All this time, Duffy was standing there like a decorative plant, her phone angled toward me, hating every moment of my conversation with her brother.

"Well, mate. Good news is, you won't have to miss the frigid weather, sharing a roof with my sister."

We both laughed. Duffy jerked her phone back.

"All right, I've actually got some plans this evening, so you'll have to continue this little bonding session later."

"Later when?" Kieran asked. "I bet Briggs could give me apt advice on how to lure the neighbor into my bed."

"It's Riggs," Duffy ground out. "And I wouldn't trust him to take care of a dead cactus, let alone give out love advice."

"Can a cactus really be dead? Or deader than it already is?" Kieran pondered aloud.

"It can," I supplied. "If you overwater it."

"Stop talking. Stop bonding. Just . . . *stop*." Poppins shook her head exasperatedly.

"Your sister can't get enough of me." I slapped the towel Duffy had allotted to me over my shoulder, sauntering to the bathroom. "Anyway, I'll have her text you my number. We'll figure it out. Hot Neighbor will be rolling in your sheets in no time."

"Cheers, mate."

After a quick shower, I strolled back into the living room and noticed Duffy was all dolled up. She wore one of her Duchess of Boredomville dresses, and her hair was plaited. It was unfortunate that the more proper she tried to look, the more sexy-librarian fantasies sprang into my mind.

Poppins didn't only look like a naughty nun; she also looked mighty guilty.

"What's up?"

"Nothing." She avoided eye contact, securing her earrings in front of a small hallway mirror.

I hoped she didn't barf into any more of my stuff. That was one quirk too far for me.

"What's with the face?" I stopped in front of her, shirtless, running the towel over my hair. I was muscular in a sinewy, athletic way, and she was the first woman I'd come across who didn't try climbing me like a tree when I flashed my six-pack.

"Nothing, nothing."

"Did you pee in my shoes or something?"

Her jaw fell open. "Why would I wee in your shoes?"

"Because you seem like a vindictive creature, and pissing you off is an untapped talent of mine."

"I can't believe you're pushing forty." She massaged her temples. "No, I didn't wee in your shoes."

"Why're you looking all guilty then?" I patted my back dry, pondering what I should DoorDash tonight. Nothing in this place was edible. Other than my roommate.

Poppins finally noticed the fact I wore nothing but a towel to my waist and gulped audibly. "I have a favor to ask you."

"I'm touched." I bowed my head. "And you're about to be touched, too, if you're asking me what I think you're asking me."

"Please stop acting like a man whore."

"Then please stop staring at me like I am one."

She ducked her head, twiddling her thumbs.

"You know what?" She let out a nervous laugh. "Forget it."

She grabbed her purse, shot up to her feet, and ran to the door. She made it halfway before swiveling back on her heel.

"Okay, fine! A bunch of former colleagues from WNT invited me over for goodbye drinks. I was wondering if you wanted to be my date. We could take a few pictures. Be seen in public. This could establish our . . . eh . . . relationship."

My mental hard-on dropped to half mast. My crap-o-meter, however, was dinging so hard it was about to shoot out of the atmosphere.

They decided to be nice to her all of a sudden, for no apparent reason? Un-fucking-likely.

"Your date," I repeated dully. I was still hoping there'd be nakedness involved when she asked for a favor.

"*Fake* date," she corrected with a prim nod.

This was a good time to remind her that these people had seen me with Gretchen and may have some questions, the primary one being— *What the fuck?*

No part of me wanted to tag along to this get-together, but an annoying (and unwelcome) sense of protectiveness tackled my conscience to the ground. I wasn't prepared to send her to the lion's den knowing she might get eaten whole. She could use a win. Especially as she seemed to be struggling with some confidence issues. Otherwise, she wouldn't adopt a fake accent to go with her secondhand designer clothes.

"Fine." I sighed. "But don't forget to take pictures and file them. I'm not gonna suffer through these hipster assholes in vain."

"Oh, Riggs, thank you!" She ran to me, but when she actually got *to* me, she stopped, her gaze colliding with my naked chest. Her cheeks reddened. She punched my bicep clumsily. "You're . . . uh . . . the best."

"But it's gonna cost you." I jabbed a finger in her direction.

She took a step back, her mouth pulling into a hard line. "If you think I'm going to hand out sexual favors every time you—"

"I'm not that desperate, and you're not that hot." I made a cross sign with my hands, lying blatantly. She was all seven deadly sins combined, once you fished her out of those Elizabeth Bennet dresses. "I mean you'll literally have to *pay*. I'm broke, remember?"

Her face relaxed. "Right. Yeah. I'll buy you a pint or two, sure."

"Food too."

"Don't push it, boy toy."

Man, she was going to blow a gasket when she realized I was going to order appetizers too.

◆ ◆ ◆

An hour later, we were at a swanky restaurant on the Upper East Side. Duffy introduced me to her former colleagues, Sadie, Warren, Dalton, and Amber. I immediately forgot who was who, refusing to waste any memory space on these professional pretenders. The men wore the uniform of smart pants and rolled-up dress shirts. The women looked like they were auditioning for a Netflix real estate show. A cross between the vulgarly rich and sex workers.

It was obvious from the get-go they just wanted to see where Duffy had landed, postmeltdown. They expected a broken mess a week after her train wreck departure.

Our table ordered appetizers and bottles of wine. Duffy sipped on a glass demurely.

"Thanks for including me," she murmured into her wine. The only reason she came was to establish a history with me. I appreciated a good hustler when I met one.

"The pleasure is ours, girl." One of the women threw her friend a *When is she going to break down in tears?* look. Her cleavage was so generous it made Bill Gates look like a cheapskate. "We were actually super impressed with how you handled Gretchen the other day."

"Yeah. She had it coming." One of the men nodded, nibbling on his antipasto bruschetta. "I mean, the woman had some nerve, accusing you of stealing her garments."

"You're not even the same size. She gained *so* much weight this year." One of the women stabbed at her cocktail's ice cubes with her straw, leaning forward. "Is it true, by the way? Is she a size six now? One of her stylists told me she could barely squeeze her into a size four pencil skirt the other day. Keto, my ass. This woman eats carbs. Probably every day."

Poppins frowned. "Gretchen's problem was never the size of her body. It was always the size of her gob."

No complaints here, but I had a different experience with Gretchen's oral skills.

"So, are you going to sue her or something?" one of the talking heads wondered. This was officially the Mean Girls Olympics.

"No." Duffy reached to smooth out her folded napkin on the table. "I know I overreacted. I shouldn't have . . . you know, gone bonkers. I was under a lot of pressure."

The entire table nodded solemnly. Now that it was clear Duffy wasn't on suicide watch and wasn't going to spend the entire dinner shitting all over her former boss's reputation, everyone quickly lost interest.

I knocked down two more glasses of wine, wondering why people held a liquid that was made by people stomping on fruit *barefoot* to a higher standard than a perfectly hygienic beer made in a brewery. Maybe my new neighbor, Charlie, would have good input on that.

"So, are you guys, like, together?" Clone Woman One motioned between Duffy and me with her finger.

Poppins looked ready to barf again. "Quite."

I draped my arm over Duffy's seat, grinning winningly. "We're very much together. I mean, how could I resist the temptation? Duffy *did* dump her long-term boyfriend for me."

If I was going to lie through my teeth, I was going to have a good time doing it.

Duffy slammed her heeled foot over mine under the table, unimpressed and unafraid to break my bones.

"Why'd you break up with BJ?" Clone Man Two asked.

"Was it because he was a mouth breather?" Clone Woman Two inquired.

"Was it because he wore a trilby in the winter?" Clone Woman One shuddered.

"He didn't breathe from his mouth, and I thought the trilby was sort of adorable." Duffy kept her composure as she answered their questions. "As for your main question, I suppose we grew apart. I do wish him all the best. He is in Nepal now."

"Nepal? I *love* Italian food," Clone Woman One exclaimed.

"That's Napoli," I drawled into my drink.

No wonder Duffy didn't collect any friends at WNT. These people had the combined IQ of a trash can.

"Wow. You're so smart," Clone Woman One purred, batting her lashes at me. "Guess it's true what they say. All the good ones are taken, huh?"

After this inspiring conversation, Duffy insisted we all take pictures together. The scene seemed as organic as synthetic grass, with my fake fiancée insisting we all squeeze into a few photos and smile. Luckily, these people loved taking photos of themselves.

"Hey, weren't you in Gretchen's office the other day?" Clone Man Two snapped his fingers, pointing at me. "Shit, it's you! I'd recognize those forearms anywhere."

And just like that, in a crapalicious turn of events, our cover was blown.

Instinctively, Duffy slipped her hand under the table and squeezed my fingers. Her palm was small, hot, and sweaty.

I felt a smidge of solidarity toward her. Enough to throw Gretchen under the bus. I mean, the woman *did* ask me to sacrifice my life and freedom and marry a complete stranger for her career's sake. That classified as her throwing me under a tank.

"Yeah." I slipped an oyster into my mouth. "Came to give her a piece of my mind. Nobody treats my lady this way."

"You did?" Clone Woman Two fanned herself dreamily.

"Duffy had been hurt and upset over Gretchen's behavior, and I wasn't gonna sit there and watch her take it." I used my arm on Duffy's armrest to stroke her hair. Amazingly, she didn't light my limbs on fire.

"Ohmigod, she was *such* a nightmare to our Duffy. It was terrible to watch." Clone Woman Two pouted. Then, without being prompted, she added, "You know word around town is that she's cheating on her husband?"

Duffy jerked in her seat with a gasp. I had to physically pull her down by the shoulder before she hit the ceiling.

"What? Who told you that?" she asked in a high-pitched voice.

"Heard it in a barre class."

"Doubt anyone would put up with that woman unless he's legally obligated to," I chipped in.

"*So* true." Clone Woman One nodded.

"Ugh, Duffy, you have the best taste in men." Clone Woman Two sighed.

"Okay then." Clone Man One glanced at his watch. "Guess it's time to wrap it up. I have a six a.m. spin class tomorrow."

"With Julio?" Clone Woman Two cooed.

"Yes!" He clapped. "He is doing a new Madonna special."

And this, ladies and gentlemen, was why I didn't stick around in New York City more than absolutely necessary. The amount of brain cells I lost just by sitting here listening to privileged middle-class, over-paid pretenders was too damn high.

"Duffy, it was *so* good to see you." They all stood up, collecting their jackets and purses. "Thanks so much for dinner. And it goes without saying—if you ever need anything, a recommendation letter, a reference, a good word, all you have to do is ask."

Poppins and I were left there with these words of encouragement. *And* the check.

Clone Woman Two also slid her number into my hand. According to my nonbinding arrangement with Duffy, I could call her. But somewhere in the back of my head, I'd already decided not to mess with anyone affiliated with my fake fiancée. She only had, what, three, four people in her life? It wasn't much of a sacrifice, and she didn't deserve to have another crappy partner. Even if it was fake between us.

Plus, somewhere in the back, back, *back* of my head, all the way in the storage room, I still thought there was a minor chance of us bumping uglies at some point, and messing around with an ex-colleague of hers would kill that chance with a blazing fire.

"These are the people who give us the news?" I shot her a sidelong glance. "I wouldn't touch them with a bag of Fritos."

She closed her eyes and groaned. "I can't believe they left me with the check."

"I can. They're assholes."

"You knew it was a bad idea, didn't you?" She sucked in a breath. "Why didn't you tell me?"

"Experience breeds wisdom, Poppins." I shrugged indifferently. "Scars are great reminders to avoid future mistakes."

"Do you think they know about you and Gretchen?" she asked as she flagged the waitress for the bill.

"Nah." I stood up, tapping my front pocket and stretching with a yawn. "They'd have interrogated us to death. Be right back, doodie calls."

"You did not just say that." She speared me with a wrathful glare. "'Doodie calls.'"

"Problem?" I curved an eyebrow.

"Sometimes I think you insist on aggravating me."

"You really think highly of yourself, don't you, my secretly working-class fiancée?"

I slipped away to take care of the check. Then, I returned, calmly tugged my fiancée by the arm, and whispered in her ear, "How fast can you run on these heels?"

"Why?" Her back stiffened.

"We're dining and dashing."

"No, we're n—"

But then I started running, and she had no choice but to follow me.

After all, I *did* take her Kate Spade purse ransom.

CHAPTER THIRTEEN

RIGGS

We took the subway back to her apartment. I sprang over the barriers again.

After she stopped chastising and berating me about the unpaid check, she felt so charitable she stopped at a Duane Reade and treated me to a few pairs of new socks, because mine, as she explained, had "more holes than a plot in a porn."

"Have you ever even watched porn?" I walked shoulder to shoulder with her across the platform now. I couldn't imagine the woman touching a penis. No, scratch that—I definitely could. *Mine*. Kneading, stroking, spitting, kissing. But I wouldn't have been surprised if she was still a virgin.

"I'm not going to answer that question."

The air stood still, hot and humid, as summer soaked the walls of the subway. There were only a few people loitering on the platform.

"Just tell me you know babies don't get delivered by storks."

A look of confusion marred her delicate face. "I beg your pardon? I've just ordered one from the internet. The stork agency offered a great discount."

I chuckled, pushing my fingers into her hair and messing it, just as an excuse to touch her. She wasn't so bad when she was being her true, undiluted self.

"If you ever want to watch porn, I have some recs," I offered.

"Color me surprised."

"We could do a fake-movie date to go with our fake relationship."

"That's a *real* pass from me." She scrunched her nose.

"Is that because I'm poor?"

"It's because I don't do one-night stands, especially with people I have to share a flat with for the unforeseeable future."

Cocksucker must've been a shitty lover if she was so prickly about discussing sex. We were both grown-ups. Me, mostly chronologically, but still.

"The offer still stands," I said easily. "Everyone should watch porn at least once in their lifetime. It's an experience."

"Right. So!" She clapped her hands together, seemingly eager to change the subject. "What are you going to do now that your boss thinks you're staying in New York for a while?"

"Wanting to get rid of me already?"

The train approached the platform with a loud shriek.

"Don't pretend like our arrangement is ideal." She crossed her arms defensively.

It wasn't. And she was right: I needed to find a project to throw myself into. There was no way I was going to sit around in the same place for months.

"I'll just do short trips for a few weeks, then tell Emmett you were a huge mistake, and we're getting a divorce. You won't mind if I spread a little rumor you gave me syphilis, right?"

"And what if . . . *you know.*" She cleared her throat. "This works out, and we wait until I get a green card? The time period between a CR1 visa and a green card is just a couple years."

"What's the point in that?" I frowned. "Don't you wanna marry up?"

"Marrying up would take time if BJ and I don't get back together." She licked her lips, looking down. At least she was honest enough not to deny her life's ambition.

"Is that really the height of your dreams? Marrying for money?"

"I won't be marrying for money. I'd be marrying for security. For peace of mind. For the privilege of not having to worry about where food is going to come from, paying the electricity bills, or having something warm to wear during the winter. Marriage has been a pragmatic arrangement between families and individuals since the dawn of time. Love is a recent, unwelcome development. Indulgent and self-centered. I personally reckon it's all Jane Austen's fault. Couldn't she have written a murder mystery? She would have spared all of us gold diggers the hassle."

Now I was laughing so hard I couldn't fucking breathe. She didn't mean to be funny, but she was. My fiancée was reddening next to me, apparently mistaking my amusement for mockery. I wasn't mocking her. I had a feeling her need for financial security was deeply rooted in some really dark memories, and I couldn't judge her for it. It was her ruthless hardheadedness that I found refreshing. She was like John D. Rockefeller. She had a talent to find opportunity in disaster.

"Hey, don't pretend like what *you're* doing isn't pragmatic." She stubbed my chest with her finger. "You're marrying someone because of your work. Couldn't you look for another job?"

I could. And, frankly, I *should*. But I didn't want to let Emmett win. Quitting would be an admission of defeat.

"Don't give me any ideas, Poppins, or you'll end up groomless."

We hopped onto the train. It was packed. Only one seat was available. I motioned for Duffy to take it. She sat prissily with her back straight and her hands in her lap.

I towered over her, my arm slung over a pole. Speaking of Emmett, I needed to throw my engagement to Duffy into high gear. The fucker had been calling and texting me nonstop, trying to call my bluff. He didn't believe Duffy was real. A little PR to boost this fake relationship was just what the doctor ordered.

The train started moving. I looked around. There was a nice mix of commuters. Students, millennial hipsters, tourists, and blue-collar workers. I was willing to bet my left nut that they all had working phones. It was time to execute my plan.

"Hey, Poppins."

Her head was tilted down. She was engrossed in her phone, scrolling through secondhand designer bags in a fashion app.

"*Duffy*," I said again.

"In a minute, Riggs. I think I found a quilted Chanel for two hundred bucks."

In a minute, we might not have this kind of audience. With each station, the train was emptying out, and so was my patience.

"Duffy. Duff. Daphne. Desiree."

"Jesus, *what?*" She looked up, her eyebrows dancing aggressively on her forehead, indicating her contempt. "Can't you see I'm doing something?"

"And I'm hoping that someone is going to be me. For the rest of our lives, baby." I shot her a tacky, heartthrob smirk I knew made her want to strangle me, then stomp on my lifeless body.

When I slowly lowered myself to one knee, bowing my head humbly, she opened her mouth—no doubt to give me a piece of her mind. The chatter on the train stopped. People unglued their gazes from their phones and tablets. Two girlfriends who sat opposite us gasped audibly, clutching each other's shirts. And my soon-to-be fake fiancée stared at me with horror mixed with resignation.

She wasn't a fan of public gestures.

I wasn't a fan of losing. And Emmett wanted me to lose.

Duffy cupped her hands over her mouth, more to stifle a curse than in shock.

"Daphne, sweetheart, the love of my life, I can't imagine growing old without you."

You're already old, I could hear her sass in my mind.

"You're my reason, my inspiration, my person. Most importantly, you're my *one*. From the moment I met you. It was unorthodox, and weird, and I definitely didn't make the best first impression." I offered her a dimpled smirk as people in our periphery held their phones up in the air and recorded my proposal from every angle possible. "But that just makes our kismet even more special. Our ability to love one another, flaws and all, for eternity and beyond."

For the record, I pulled every word out of my ass on a whim. Of course, I'd googled *Things to say when proposing* while Poppins was buying me discounted socks, but I didn't expect the lies to fall so naturally from between my lips.

"Oh my God!" a woman screeched behind my back.

"Dreamboat alert," someone cooed. "Sign me up, Mr. Hottie."

"Is that Chris Hemsworth?"

"*No.* Chris doesn't have this bone structure and lips."

"I think I just manifested a Greek god."

I dipped my head, pretending to be embarrassed by the attention. Maybe I was laying it on too thick, but it wasn't like I was shooting for an Oscar.

"Daphne, would you do me the immense honor of being my wife? I promise to love and respect you. To give you everything your heart desires. To put your happiness before mine, and to give you the fairy tale you deserve."

Duffy's face was blank and white with shock. She obviously welcomed my gesture just a little more than she would an intrusion of an entire army into her apartment.

And she *still* hadn't said a damn word.

Through a tight, unwavering smile, I ground out, "Take your time, Poppins. It's not like we have an audience."

"Eh . . . of course I'll marry you . . . uhm, *darling*," she mumbled, finally, with all the enthusiasm of a woman who had been offered a trip through a minefield. Barefoot. "It would be my honor."

The lukewarm acceptance didn't stop people from darting up to their feet, clapping and cheering for us. Dozens of people bracketed Duffy's seat as I produced the ring I'd purchased at a pawnshop and slipped it onto her engagement finger. It was a simple, thin golden band with a square emerald at the center. The guy at the pawnshop said it was at least two hundred years old, which happened to fit into the kind of marriage style my fiancée wanted for herself.

"My God," she murmured under her breath, wiggling her delicate fingers, admiring the thing. "It's *stunning*."

This, I knew, wasn't an act. Her purple eyes sparkled like diamonds. I was surprised she found the cheap jewelry so lovely.

"Not half as stunning as you." I lunged forward, grabbing the back of her head and kissing her temple. Her skin was hot and soft and fucking delicious. Too pure to belong to such a cunning, superficial creature. She froze the minute we touched, her breath stilling. I pulled back more reluctantly than I cared to admit.

Our eyes met and locked in a strange trance.

"I've been told there's an engagement going on," the conductor's voice pierced through the silence in our car, making people go wild with cheers and laughter. "Congratulations to the happy couple."

Poppins glanced around, looking self-conscious and disoriented.

"Hey!" a woman dressed in a suit who angled her phone toward us shouted. "That was the best proposal I've ever seen. The least you can do is give your man a real kiss."

"Kiss!" the crowd began chanting. "*Kiss! Kiss! Kiss! Kiss!*"

I peered down to catch Poppin's mien. She looked like she was about to faint. I widened my eyes in what I hoped conveyed *You don't have to do this. We don't owe these people anything.* But the truth was, it was going to look weird as hell if she didn't kiss me.

"Kiss! Kiss! Kiss!"

"Hell, girl, if you don't kiss him, I will, and I'm not gonna stop there!" one commuter threatened with a giggle.

Duffy looked around us in a daze. She was clearly overwhelmed. Sweat began coating her forehead. Suddenly, I felt like a class A shitbag for putting her through this. I *knew* she wasn't a public-declarations kind of girl. Still, I'd done it for my own selfish reasons.

Sorry, I mouthed. I really was. Not enough to do it differently if I could—I'd grown too accustomed to putting myself above everyone else—but seeing her so miserable made my stomach feel like that time I got intense food poisoning in Spain.

With her lips flattened in disgust, Duffy rose on her toes. Everything happened in slo-mo. She put her hand awkwardly on my chest, which flexed instinctively under her touch. That made her jolt back, which made *me* wrap my arms around her waist, making sure she didn't fall. She tilted her head up. Her eyes were full of misery and trepidation.

She was also the loveliest fucking thing I'd ever seen in my entire life, every landscape on Planet Earth included. No mountain, no hill, no lake, no ocean even came in a close second.

"You don't have to," I hissed. "Remember what we discussed? Don't give people power over you."

"I . . . I . . . I . . ."

"Want to kill me?" I offered as the entire population of the car continued chanting for us to kiss. The voices somehow drowned us out in the private capsule we both seemed to share.

Duffy moved her tongue around her mouth like it was numb. "I have stage fright."

"Lucky we have a captive audience."

"Kiss! Kiss! Kiss!"

"No, you don't understand, I . . ." She took a ragged breath. "When I was little, I wasn't very popular at school. I went to a gifted public school on a full scholarship, while Kieran went to a 'normal' school. I was the only poor kid there. And I was . . . well, *very* poor. During recess, other students used to gather around me and shout what they thought about me. About my uniform, my family, my . . . my lunch box. How empty it was. I don't like attention."

So that was where her obsession with money stemmed from. She was ridiculed for it.

"These people are not your asshole bullies," I said quietly.

She blinked, processing it all very slowly. "I'm also a terrible kisser."

"You have no way of knowing that." Unless Cocksucker told her so, in which case I was going to personally make my way to Nepal and shove him off Everest myself.

"No, truly, I'm quite awful."

"Kiss! Kiss! Kiss!"

"You are? All right." I sighed. "The wedding's off, then."

"Really?" She winced, vulnerable all of a sudden.

"No."

"I can't—"

She really couldn't. I'd seen Aunt Bessie's meals less frozen than this woman. Which was why I took charge, dunked my head down, and kissed the living crap out of her without further ado.

. . . Fine, I did no such thing.

But I did lean down to give her a dry, respectable peck. It was brief. No more than a brush. I'd had more action from TSA officers giving me a pat-down at the airport, and still, somehow, my cock saw fit to nod appreciatively.

The car exploded with whistles and cheers. Camera flashes blinded us. People were obviously satisfied with our lackluster display of affection.

Duffy fell back to her seat. Her hand shook as she wiped her lips clean. "I can't believe I told you about my school years. How mortifyi . . ." She trailed off when she realized her future husband's penis was semihard and staring right back at her. Eye level.

Her eyes dragged up to my face. Shock gave way to anger.

"You have some nerve, sir," she whisper-shouted.

"You have some lips," I said by way of explanation. If God did exist, I was going to meet the second pair in her body too.

"Put that thing away. It looks like it's about to stab me in the eye," she complained, and I managed not to laugh. Just barely.

"No one told you to sit down."

"No one told you to sexually *harass* me."

"Excuse me? If anyone should be crying under the showerhead while hugging their knees, it should be me. You mentally licked my chest just a few hours ago," I reminded her. "When we were in your apartment."

"I did *not*," she hissed, her cheeks enflamed.

"Did *too*."

"Again, I can't believe you're pushing forty."

"You think once you hit a certain age you start talking like Morgan Freeman?" I frowned, fed up with this line. "Thirty-seven-year-olds still say 'fuck' and make dick jokes and play Xbox and prefer Cheetos and soda over broccoli and chicken and *still* think *Stranger Things* is better than documentaries about migrating ants."

"But they don't say 'doodie calls.'"

"Yes, they do. And what's more—you're about to legally bind yourself to someone who just might tattoo the phrase on his ass."

"You wouldn't dare." Her jaw ticked, and I knew she actually thought I was capable of it.

I smiled winningly. "Wouldn't I, now? May I remind you, I am marrying a complete stranger because of a pissing contest with my boss."

"Are you guys okay?" Ready to Kiss Me if My Fiancée Wouldn't Lady cut into our argument. "You seem . . . *tense*."

"Brilliant." Duffy offered a fake, icy smile.

Brilliant, my ass.

She couldn't wait to get back home so she could gargle some bleach.

CHAPTER FOURTEEN

RIGGS

Emmett: . . .

Riggs: It's the middle of the night, Emmett. Don't you have women to stalk?

Emmett: Send me a picture of you two together.

Riggs: My dick might be big enough to be its own entity, but the royal "we" is unnecessary.

Emmett: You and Desiree, smart ass.

Riggs: With or without clothes?

Emmett: . . .

Riggs: Pervert.

◆ ◆ ◆

I woke up to the sound of the world ending.

There was screaming, crying, pounding, and doors slamming. If I had to guess, I'd say Duffy had decided to wrestle a bear in the living room. And was losing.

Cracking one eye open from my vantage point on the couch—I'd somehow gotten used to sleeping with my feet on the coffee table—I spotted my fiancée weeping over the sink, FaceTiming someone on her phone.

"*Of course* it's the end of the world, Kieran!"

Shit. The apocalypse. I wondered if I had time for a quick booty call. It seemed wrong to depart without a last hurrah. Especially after the dry spell I'd had since fate chained me into a shoebox apartment with a snotty Brit who possessed the sex drive of a Coke can. My so-called Scandinavian friend I told Poppins about on her last day at work was a figment of my imagination. Designed to poke at her prudish senses.

"No, it's not. If anything, it's a good thing," her brother piped up.

"How's that a good thing?"

"Maybe your tosser ex-boyfriend will see this and finally get his head out of his arse."

Poppins gulped, proceeding to wail even harder. "BJ! I hadn't even thought of that. How could him finding out be a *good* thing?"

"Maybe he'd stop taking you for granted."

Kieran was obviously more street smart than his twin.

"He doesn't take me for granted." Duffy slammed more cabinet doors, bulldozing around the kitchen with a towel and Lysol. She was stress cleaning. Last time she did that, the apartment smelled like someone was trying to cover up a murder. "You know, I'm sick and tired of everyone judging him. Give the man some grace."

"In BJ's case, he'd shag Grace too," Kieran deadpanned.

I barked out a laugh.

She turned toward me, her eyes narrowing on me, like she was ready to shoot me with the Lysol.

"Ah. The arsehole is awake. I'll call you later."

Kieran perked. "Can I speak to him?"

"Absolutely not."

"Don't kill him, darkling. I'm getting rather attached here."

"No promises. Bye." She ended the call, then pinned me with red, bloodshot eyes. "I'm going to kill you."

I sat up straight, digging the bases of my palms into my eye sockets.

"Can we fuck first?" I asked gruffly. "I'd like to go with a bang. All puns intended."

"No."

"Thought I'd try. What did I do this time?" I reached for my pants. I only slept in my briefs, which meant Poppins normally spent her mornings bumping into furniture while trying desperately to stare at the floor and avoid getting an eyeful of my morning wood.

Her thumbs flew across her phone screen now. She turned the device around and thrust it in my face, almost breaking my nose in the process. "*This* happened."

I was looking at a YouTube video of our engagement scene in the subway from the day before. The resolution was crappy, but our faces were recognizable to anyone who knew us. The caption of the video read: *Surprise Proposal on NYC Subway!*

"So?" I shoved my legs into my faded Dickies. I tried to ignore the hangover-like headache that was hammering rusty nails into my brain.

"Look at the number of views, you wanker!"

Squinting, I could now see the reason for her rage.

"Six million." I whistled. "Guess we're a power couple now."

"You know what it means?" She collapsed on the edge of the couch and sat closer to me than she normally would, a sure sign her guard was down. "My parents are going to see this!"

"Not necessarily. Boomers don't do well with technology."

"This was featured on two morning shows. My phone has blown up with TV people wanting us to give an interview." She hit refresh.

The view count turned to six point two. I patted the side of the couch, retrieved my phone, and frowned at it. There were two missed calls from Emmett. *Bingo.*

"Just tell them the truth." I turned to Duffy.

"Mum and Tim are not even my biggest concern." She shot up to her feet, then returned to her towels and Lysol for another round of scrubbing the counter. "What if BJ sees it?"

"Isn't he on an electronic ban while in Nepal?" She'd mentioned something about that the other day, while I was knee deep in trying to tune her out.

She licked her lips, nodding. The thought must have encouraged her. "I suppose he is, but when he comes back—"

"When he comes back, he'll be too busy begging for forgiveness to give a crap. It's not like we shared a passionate kiss. I've gotten more action from my aunt during Thanksgiving dinner."

"Ew, perv."

"Just kidding. I don't have a family."

"Wait, what?" She paused, looking at me with her big purple eyes. "Are you serious?"

Yes.

"Point is, there's nothing overtly incriminating in the video."

"Ugh." She poured bleach into the sink. The scent hit my nostrils, making me want to throw up. My headache was out of control this morning.

I got the idea to go viral when I saw how Duffy's video with Gretchen had made waves on the internet. I thought it was a nice way to redeem her pride, and—let's admit it—the quickest, most efficient way to show Emmett that I had a fiancée. Only I hadn't taken into consideration how bad she was going to take it.

Because you've never considered anyone else in your entire life.

Also, because I wasn't privy to her past scars. To being ridiculed by other students. Getting the wrong type of attention.

"Hey. Good luck with the interviews," I told her retreating back.

She drifted out of the room, taking her Duffy scent and Duffy wit and Duffy everything with her.

◆ ◆ ◆

Four Tylenols and a chain of curses later, I made a call to Christian. The man had a bevy of people at his disposal who knew how to get shit done. He'd hooked me up with a colleague of his, who assured me that for a suitable amount of money, I could get the video taken down from YouTube. Once he'd found the owner of the account, he was able to send them an offer they couldn't refuse. And they didn't.

The video was removed from the site an hour and a half after it was loaded. I had no intention of telling Duffy I was the reason her ass—and imaginary relationship with Cocksucker—had been saved. It would cost a normal person an arm and a leg to do what I'd done.

She sent me a text not even two minutes after the video was taken down.

Unknown: They took the video down.

Me: Who is this?

If I couldn't fuck her, I could at least fuck *with* her.

Unknown: Duffy. Who else do you have a video with? ●●)

Me: See, this is why I asked you if you ever watched porn. I'm kind of a big deal.

Unknown: Hilarious. Program me into your device.

Me: Done.

Duffy: So? How do you think it happened?

Me: I clicked on your number, then info, then create new contact. I thought you youngsters knew all those things.

Duffy: I meant the video. 😊

Me: IDK. Maybe the person realized it was an intimate moment.

Duffy: Or maybe it went against YouTube's policy or something.

Or maybe I paid the YouTuber an entire annual salary to do it.

Duffy: Job hunting is going rubbish in case you were wondering.

Me: How come?

Duffy: I'm either overqualified or too nuclear after my viral showdown with Gretchen.

Me: You'll figure it out.

I put my phone down and tended to the very important task of taking a shower and masturbating to a mental image of my fiancée. When I came back to the phone, there was a message waiting from Duffy.

Duffy: Would you like me to lick something when I get back today?

Me: Don't play with my tender feelings. You were the one who said no hooking up.

Duffy: *pick.

Duffy: I meant food, you uncultured swine.

Me: More of your rainforest greens? Nah, I'm good.

Duffy: We could always eat something else.

Me: YES.

Duffy: I mean strictly food items.

Me: ☹

Me: Pizza?

Duffy: No need to get carried away. Tacos can be nutritious and tasty without destroying my body.

Me: Now you're just begging for another sexual innuendo.

Duffy: Goodbye, Riggs.

◆ ◆ ◆

While Poppins spent her day running around town trying to find gainful employment, I invested my time in scratching my balls on her couch and staring at the clock. The few weeks' sabbatical didn't agree with me.

I'd never stayed in in my entire life and didn't like that my body was getting used to one time zone.

That was how I found myself sitting in front of *Jerry Springer* reruns on cable TV. I was one pack of bonbons away from being Peggy Bundy. How could people do this day in and day out? Stay home and do nothing?

A knock on the door snapped me out of an altercation between a man who'd come to the show to have a paternity test and his stepsister, who was also his baby mama.

After unplastering myself from the couch, I dragged my ass to the door, wondering who it could be. Duffy wasn't exactly a social butterfly. A busy bee, more like.

"Who is it?" I called out.

"It's Charlie."

"Duffy's not here." In the time that had passed since I'd moved in, she and Charlie had met for drinks twice.

"I know."

I swung the door open and leaned against the doorframe, eye-balling him.

"What's up, Charles? Need a cup of sugar?"

"Sugar's poison. You know it's more addictive than crack, right?" He gave me an intense stare. I hadn't seen him in a while. He had a weird pattern. Sometimes he was in the hallway twice a day, but then he'd disappear for days on end.

"Been out of town?" I probed. "It's been a hot minute."

He yawned, looking around disinterestedly. "Not really. Some days I'm just holed up in my cave, doing art shit."

"So what brings you here?" I asked.

"I'm doing a freelance job for an urban magazine. I need to take some pictures of buildings and scenery in Spanish Harlem. Thought you'd wanna tag along."

"And why would you think that?" I rolled myself a joint. His eyes halted on the thing, and he grimaced. That was a plot twist. I didn't peg him for the stuck-up type.

Charlie was nice enough, but he was a little clingy for someone who had known me for exactly two seconds.

"Because I bet you have cabin fever," he said easily. "I used to travel the world too. I still have the bug."

Was he me in twenty years? Fuck, I hoped not. Something dark lurked behind his eyes. Like a washed-up child actor who'd grown out of his glory days.

"Actually, it's nice to chill for a few days," I drawled out.

"No, it's not." He smiled good naturedly.

He was right, but that still didn't mean I wanted to spend time with this stranger. I was about to marry a random. No need to befriend the entire goddamn building.

Evidently seeing the doubt on my face, Charlie rolled his eyes. "I'll buy you a beer."

"And lunch." I really slipped into the poor-man role easily.

"On a budget." Charlie jabbed a finger in my direction. "Or I'm gonna lose money on this assignment."

"Fine, but I'm choosing the place." I grabbed my backpack from the floor.

"You're lucky I like to feed you." Charlie was already taking the stairs down.

I made a note to tell Charlie I was very straight.

A half hour later, we were on Lexington Avenue. It was a mercilessly hot day. Too hot not to wonder if New York wasn't, in fact, a section of hell. Charlie was taking pictures of children at play—faceless, or I'd have informed the authorities—small bodegas, and graffitied buildings with more character than I'd witnessed in all of Duffy's WNT colleagues combined.

I brought my camera along and took some pictures too. When we were done, we walked across the street from a row of food stalls to a small café. We were almost at the door when someone burst open a fire hydrant.

Gallons of water sprayed everywhere, filling the street with gushing puddles. A flock of small children and teenagers ran toward it shirtless, splashing one another. Charlie and I exchanged looks. We were both thinking the same thing. This made for an epic picture. We took out our cameras at the same time and started working silently. Far enough away that they were just flashes of movement in the pictures. About a minute or two into taking the pictures, Charlie handed me his camera, a modest Nikon D5600.

"Hold this for me, will you?"

I tucked his camera into my backpack and watched this oldish, fully crazy man hightailing it toward the kids.

He ran into the thick circle of children, limping a little, like he carried an injury from when he was young, and started jumping over the puddles on the concrete floor, splashing them. They giggled and tugged him in different directions, luring him to play with them. Normally, I would look at this and think this should be illegal in all fifty states. But I couldn't deny the innocence Charlie was oozing just then. At some point, one of the kids jumped on Charlie's back. Charlie gave him a piggyback ride, running around the fire hydrant in circles while making siren noises.

"My turn, my turn!" the kid's friend cried out.

Before I knew it, kids were jumping on his back in turns, using him as a human police car. Charlie didn't skip one kid. Not even the one who looked like he weighed about the same as him. Even when his muscles gave up and I saw the exhaustion on his face.

After we wrapped things up, we went to a Dominican café and ate green bananas, longanizas, and cornbread. We downed two beers each before either of us spoke.

"You're good with kids," I said, finally. I didn't know why, but the silence between us wasn't awkward. Maybe because we were both used to being alone. Silence was my friend more often than not.

He waved a flippant hand. "Just as long as I don't have to take care of them."

"You don't have kids of your own?" I took a lazy pull of my beer.

He leaned across the window, his eyes following a bunch of teenagers smoking cigarettes and laughing. "No."

I frowned. "You sounded thoughtful. Is that your final answer?"

"I had a kid," he said with a sad smile.

That could have meant any number of things, all of them tragic.

"She died when she was eight months old."

"Fuck. Sorry."

"What about you?" He turned to look at me. "Any little Riggses running around in different continents?"

I smiled ruefully. Arsène and Christian always speculated that I'd sired a kid or twelve during my travels, but condoms were my religion and pulling out *while* wearing them was my temple. Better to be safe than (incredibly) sorry.

"None that I'm aware of."

"I think you should try it. You'll make a good dad." Charlie tipped his beer in my direction. The sun dipped behind the buildings over his shoulder, washing the rooftops in orange and yellow hues. New York was beautiful in the summer. I'd almost forgotten.

You forget a lot of things about a place when you never stick around long enough to appreciate it.

"A kid would cramp my style. Besides, I haven't had the best family life, so I wouldn't know the first thing about raising one."

"I think it's precisely the people who don't come from perfect families who create the best ones." Charlie fixed his gaze on my face. "It's like kids of divorced parents always try extra hard to make their marriage work. Experience shapes you, and heartbreak defines you."

"With all due respect, divorce is a walk in the goddamn park in comparison to my childhood. I'd eat divorce for breakfast if I could, with a side of poverty."

"Tell me about it." He shoved cheese bread into his mouth.

I didn't share my life story, not with anyone, and I wasn't going to make an exception with this nice yet oddly clingy stranger.

"Just take my word for it. I'm not father material." I waved a hand. I wouldn't trust me with a fucking houseplant. "What about a wife? Ever had one of those?"

"Almost." He scratched the damp beer label off his bottle.

"Your baby mama?" I asked.

He nodded. "What about you?"

I thought about Duffy. It seemed insane to count her as anything other than a headache. But that was exactly what she was about to become. Though I wasn't going to divulge any more information about our lives without her consent after my little stunt in the subway yesterday.

"Never been married," I said finally.

Charlie balled the damp beer label into a wad. "We should do this again sometime."

"Talk about depressing shit?" I took out my rolling kit, and he gave me a funny look again.

"Do projects together," he explained. "Gotta keep busy."

"Dunno what you're talking about. I had a great time watching Jamie Spinner."

"*Jerry Springer*."

Maybe he did have a point.

CHAPTER FIFTEEN

DUFFY

I forgot the bloody tacos.

That, in itself, wasn't even the fifteenth most terrible thing to happen to me today. But considering everything went wrong from the moment I opened my eyes—other than the proposal video disappearing from YouTube—that was my tipping point. The forgotten tacos.

I'd only noticed when I walked into my empty flat and my stomach made a sound eerily similar to a bear's yawn.

Feed me, you daft cow.

But I had nothing to feed it with, because I'd forgotten. I'd forgotten because I'd gone to three job interviews that day. All of them ended prematurely, with none indicating any interest. Either my meltdown video had done the rounds and landed on my potential employers' desks or nobody wanted to hire someone without a visa. Likely, it was a combination of both.

I dragged my arse to the shower. Riggs wasn't home yet. I could only imagine where he spent his days. Probably hopping between one model's bed to the other. Breaking our marriage vows before he'd even uttered them.

Not that I minded one bit. Not even half a bit. Not even a quarter.

Oh, but he was so lovely. So very handsome and sort of funny in his own juvenile way. And he never made me feel like he had the upper hand in our relationship, the way BJ did. Never used my weaknesses against me.

Speaking of BJ, his sister Brenda (yes, I was aware that Brendan and Brenda were the tackiest names for siblings) called me today to let me know that he was safe and sound. Apparently, he'd called his family to let them know he was okay. Well, I *wasn't* okay. I was put on the back burner while he did his thing. I was starting to see that Riggs had a point. BJ was a total tosser.

The worst part was that I couldn't channel my anger at BJ, because I had no way to contact him. He was undumpable. MIA. Which begged the question—how had I allowed myself to leave the door open for a comeback to someone who'd cut off all contact with me for six months without batting an eyelash?

Because you care about money more than you care about pride. And you care about never allowing your children to go through what you did. Walking with torn shoes to a one-hundred-K-a-year school.

Flashes of my treading through the vast corridors of Saint Anthony's School for the Gifted in my tattered Mary Janes zinged through my mind. Back then, I had my real accent, my authentic, awkward sense of humor, and a dream to become an investigative journalist. I shook my head fiercely until the memories evaporated.

I stepped into the shower and lathered my body soap until bubbles ran down the expanse of my flesh. I turned the water to extra hot and closed my eyes, practicing deep, long breaths.

Everything is okay.

No. That seemed wrong.

Everything will be *okay.*

That sounded slightly more believable.

Everything will be okay.

Everything will be okay.

Everything will be o . . .

A loud noise of glass smashing came from the living room. It was followed by the sound of glass crunching over the floor, like someone had stomped all over it.

Riggs had a key, so it couldn't be him. I lived on the second floor, but my window was directly in front of the fire escape.

Instinctively, I decided the best course of action was to wrap myself in a towel and confront the intruder in my living room. After all, there was no better thing to do than to *greet* one's burglar half-naked.

Why not simply stick a RAPE ME note on your forehead, Poppins? Riggs's wry voice taunted in my head.

Still in the bathroom, I caught myself. I couldn't go out there empty handed. I needed a weapon. Something sharp and discreet. I looked around frantically. The only thing that was remotely practical was my pink shaving razor. I pulled it from the suction holder and dashed out of the bathroom, waving the thing in the air like it was a sword.

"Who is there?" I demanded in a shrill voice before coming to a stop in the middle of the living room.

My window—my *only* window—was smashed. Broken beyond repair. That was the bad news. The good news was that my burglar was also my fiancé. And the man I was about to murder.

Riggs was standing in the middle of the small room, calmly tucking his photography equipment into its cases, shards of glass adorning his gargantuan booted feet.

"Hey." He popped a cinnamon gum, not bothering to look up. "Water must be hot after today, huh?"

The water was actually lovely. It was one of the things I liked the most about summers in the city.

Focus, Duffy, focus.

"Hmm. Did you just . . . ?" I motioned at the broken window.

He raised his head distractedly, then nodded. "Oh, yeah. Sorry. I smashed the tripod against it when I organized my shit. Don't worry about it. I'll call someone to fix it first thing tomorrow morning. Get them to install the triple-glazed stuff. You had a crack in the glass, anyway."

How could he be so calm? This was going to cost a fortune. A fortune neither of us had. He couldn't even pay for a subway ticket.

"Riggs, this is a rented flat!" I bellowed, balling my fists in anger. "You can't just break things."

"I said I'll take care of it." He bypassed me by stalking to the kitchen and filling himself a glass of tap water. He was uncharacteristically taciturn, but I wasn't in the mood to ask how his day had gone.

"So what if you did?" I followed him, perching my fists on either side of my waist. "If something goes wrong, I'm the one who's going to have to deal with it."

"You'll have a brand-new window in less than twelve hours." He leaned against the counter and filled himself another glass. He threw open all the cupboards before rummaging through them relentlessly. "Shit. Where's your Tylenol?"

"Second cupboard to your right," I gritted out. He was making a right mess, and I was in the wrong mood for it.

Riggs had some nerve brushing me off. I was living off my savings, with no job prospects, in one of the most expensive cities in the world. "And do you reckon you'll pay for that wind—"

"Duffy, just shut up for a sec, will you? My head feels like someone is trying to drill oil out of it," he snapped.

For a moment, I was speechless. Did he actually tell me to shut up? He'd never spoken to me this way. I had two options: calmly explain myself or go mental on his arse.

Normally, with BJ, I would choose option number one and try to reason with him. After all, I had loads to lose. With Riggs, I felt confident I could be free to be who I was—whoever that may be.

Which was how I found myself flinging my arms in the air.

"HOW DARE YOU—"

I didn't get to finish the sentence, because something terrible happened. Something so terrible, in fact, it took me a few moments to fully digest it. The first giveaway was the breeze between my legs, followed by my cold nipples. My gaze traveled south, down my body.

Yup. Suspicion confirmed. I was completely, gloriously, *dreadfully* naked.

My towel fell off halfway through my scream. Currently, my nipples were pointing at my future fake husband accusingly.

Oh God, my cellulite was my first thought. *He can see my cellulite. And those horrible stretch marks on my waist.* Followed closely by *I haven't shaved down there in a while, have I?* There was no point now, with BJ gone. This was succeeded by *Duffy, you daft cow, would you cover yourself up? He's staring!*

And he was. Riggs didn't even have the decency to pretend otherwise. He flat out ogled me, his mouth agape, his pupils dilated, his penis . . .

Don't look at his penis!

After a few moments of channeling my inner deer in headlights, I gathered the towel and secured it around me. My teeth were chattering with adrenaline.

"Bugger, bugger, bugger, bugger, BUGGER." I was running like a headless chicken now. First, toward the bathroom, before realizing I didn't have any clothes there, then toward my bedroom. Then sensible Cambridge Duffy left the building, and the one from Tooting Broadway finally reared her head, coming back from a decade-long sabbatical. "BOLLOCKS."

"I didn't even see anything." Riggs was as believable as George Clooney in *Batman & Robin*.

"Yes, you did." I made a beeline to my room, slamming against the wall in the process like a fly trying to penetrate a closed window. "You stared!"

"Okay, I stared." In a few graceful strides, he was right in front of me, blocking my way to my door. "But I don't regret it. It was the best thing I've seen all year."

Really? More than Gretchen? More than all the others?

"Please move." I crossed my arms over my chest, mainly to keep my heart from jumping into his hands.

"No can do." He leaned against my door, hogging all the space with his massive frame. "You're just prudish enough to never leave your room."

I closed my eyes, drawing a shaky breath. "I can't believe you saw me naked."

"Don't be a baby."

"You're the one with the poop jokes!" I cried out.

"Look at me, Poppins."

I was now covering my face with my hands, pretending he couldn't see me, like a dog sitting under a table.

"No."

"This is crazy." I felt his rough, big, *sexy* palms covering mine, trying to peel my fingers off my eyes gently. I jerked back in horror.

"Don't touch me!"

"Okay. But can you just listen?"

While I couldn't listen, I could, apparently, launch into an incoherent tirade.

"What kind of perv stares at someone when they're naked?" I bit out, my nonposh accent sneaking through. "And it's not just you being a creep. Everything has been shite today. I failed all of my job interviews. And BJ hasn't called since, since—you were right, he *is* a twat. And . . . and . . . money's tight. I might have to sell my Equinox membership next month. And then I forgot the tacos!" I let out a pained moan. "*Our* tacos."

There was a lengthy silence. Granted, six seconds seemed like an eternity after my verbal diarrhea.

"Are you done?"

"Not quite." I cringed. "But go on."

"I'm going to touch you now," he said gruffly, around the time my chest stopped rising and falling like I'd just run a marathon.

I felt Riggs's hands prying my fingers from my face gently. He kept my palms in his, rubbing circles with his thumb over a sensitive spot between the base of my thumb and my index finger. He waited patiently until my eyes had fluttered open. I couldn't look at him, even though he stood directly in front of me, only a couple of inches away. His body heat rolled against mine, making my skin prickle everywhere.

I very maturely kept my gaze stuck on the ceiling.

Riggs cupped my cheeks. My body temperature shot to a dangerous degree, and an invisible string under my belly button clenched and tightened. I had to remind myself he was just Riggs, the friendly roommate who joked about having sex with me, without ever actually initiating anything. The same Riggs who didn't have a penny, didn't want children, and didn't even own a bicycle.

"You had a crappy day, Poppins. It happens. Bad days will keep happening. You'll just have to brush them off." He was staring into my face, and I felt more naked than I had a few moments earlier, when I was *actually* naked. "I'm sorry I was snappy. My headache was no excuse. Now, go get dressed, and I'll get us tacos in the meantime. My treat."

My mouth fell open.

"*Your* treat?" He'd never offered to pay for anything before. I'd never even *seen* his wallet.

"Yup."

"But you don't pay for anything. Ever."

"I'm a fan of trying everything at least once."

"Can you afford it?" I demanded. "I don't want you to go hungry tomorrow or something."

Now that I was a little less angry about the window, I begrudgingly admitted to myself I didn't want to put him in an awkward position. What if he was skint because he was paying for huge medical bills or something?

He gave me an exasperated look. "I can pay for a few tacos."

"You sure?"

"Eighty-three percent positive."

"Where are the remaining seventeen percent?"

"On the floor. You shaved them with the razor you intended to use as a vicious weapon."

"All right." I reddened with mortification. "Cheers, I suppose."

He grabbed the key and pocketed it. "This is to ensure you don't lock yourself inside for eternity, just in case." He stepped around me as he strolled to the door. "Oh, and don't expect any guacamole. That stuff costs extra."

Half an hour later, after I'd collected the broken glass and the remainder of my self-esteem from the floor, I was completely and blissfully dressed, eating tacos (*with* guacamole and queso; Riggs was apparently feeling extra generous), and sipping one of his beers. I couldn't remember the last time I'd consumed so many calories, but everything tasted so good that I couldn't even feel properly guilty about it.

"I can't believe you're eating carbs, Poppins." Riggs wolfed down a shrimp taco. Salsa ran down his chiseled chin. If he ate his women out like he ate his tacos, he'd most definitely be the eighth wonder of the world. Although, to be fair, I didn't need to see the way he ate to know he was a good shag. There was something wanton and blithe about Riggs that oozed mind-blowing sex and guaranteed heartbreak.

"I can't believe that either," I murmured around a small piece of fish. I still hadn't looked him in the eye.

"Why's that?" He threw a tortilla chip between his lips, chewing loudly. "Were you attacked by a carb when you were young? Stabbed with a baguette? Roped to a tree with spaghetti?"

I giggled, surprising myself by opening up to him. I suppose it was fair that he knew why I was so horrified by the scene earlier.

"Growing up, I was a bit of a plump kid. I'd struggled with my weight my entire life, trying every diet under the sun—Weight Watchers, Atkins, Jenny Craig, South Beach . . . ," I admitted quietly, swirling guac from a plastic container and sucking on the pad of my thumb. "I never quite managed to drop the weight, which was dreadful news for my social life, since I was already the poor kid in the posh, rich school. But it was hard, with my family only able to afford frozen food from Aldi. I lived off fish-and-chips the first decade and a half of my life." I let loose a tense breath. "The summer before I started uni, something just clicked. I managed to stay on the wagon and lose about a stone, which was enough to push me into the Fit Girl category."

Riggs stared at me intently, waiting for me to continue.

"That summer was a great time to reinvent myself. Different accent. Different wardrobe. Different manners. That first year at uni changed me. I'd become popular for the first time in my life—or at least, not *un*popular. No more sticking gum in my hair, laughing at my torn shoes, pouring piss into the cracks of my locker." I licked my lips, frowning at the coffee table, laden with our leftovers. "I met BJ. After years of swimming against the stream, struggling to get somewhere, I felt like a wave had been carrying me to my destination. I guess I linked my trim waistline and fancy accent to my new fortune. Thus my weight became an obsession." *Right along with having money.* I was beginning to realize I was obsessed with shallow things, because I thought they'd guarantee I could keep the important ones.

"Do you think BJ wouldn't have dated you if you were a few pounds heavier?" Riggs asked seriously.

"*No*," I snorted out. "Nor would I have expected him to. He has a certain type."

"Malnourished and a doormat?" he asked wryly. "Weird taste, but to each their own, I guess." He was quiet for a moment before adding, "You'd look beautiful no matter your weight. Just so you know."

"Thank you."

"It wasn't a compliment." I felt his eyes, ablaze with scorn, heating the side of my face. "It's a stated fact. And if he was too dumb not to notice—"

"We have no way of knowing he wouldn't have dated me." I lifted a hand up, stopping him. "Remember you took the piss out of me for being a bad feminist when I said I wanted to marry BJ? Here's another something you can toss into my Bad Feminist pile. I'm obsessed with my weight and allow the scale to alter my mood."

His eyebrows pulled together, his face clouding further. I stared down at my hands, wringing my fingers together. The engagement ring still felt weird and heavy, but it was so deliciously perfect that I was already wondering if I could buy it off Riggs when this charade was over. He needed the money, and I'd need the memory.

"I don't keep tabs on your shortcomings, Duffy." There was a beat. "And for the record, you shouldn't either. But if it's worth anything at all, seeing as it's coming from me and not from Cocksucker—you will always be beautiful in my eyes. Thin, big, and in between."

"You can't possibly—"

"I can," he said, cutting me off, dead serious. "I just fucking did. And meant every word of it."

"Bugger off. You hate me."

"I don't hate you. Up until recently I didn't like you, either, but I think I'm beginning to understand you."

I wanted very badly to laugh this moment off, but something in the intensity of his voice made me want to fall apart in his arms like a sinner pardoned. To confess to him that this was what I had always wanted to hear. That it killed me that, when I'd told BJ about my weight loss when we'd first started dating, he'd responded with a callous, *"Good work, Duff. Make sure you're on top of it. You know how easy it is to pile on the pounds."*

I pressed my lips, staring at the floor. My feelings were all over the place. A mixture of elation, pain, and hope.

"So." Riggs snapped us out of the moment, standing up and then gathering the rubbish on the coffee table. "What are we gonna do about the fact you can no longer look me in the eye?"

"Don't be ridiculous," I protested, rushing up and helping him clear the table. "That's not true."

"Do it then." He swiveled, crowding me with his body, his gaze drilling into my face. "Let's see."

I shifted my stare to the kitchenette, laughing. "Christ, Riggs. A bit aggressive, don't you reckon?"

"Coward."

"Give me some time. I'll get over it." I dumped our leftovers into the bin.

"No, you won't. There's only one solution." He flicked on the faucet and started doing the dishes.

"Kick you out of my flat?" I asked hopefully, leaning against the counter, facing him but concentrating on a spot behind his head.

"I see we're still doing this thing where you pretend not to like me." He turned off the tap and wiped his hands with a kitchen towel. "Get even."

Our bodies were angled toward one another. My heart felt like it was about to burst through my skin and roll at his feet like a stone. What did he mean by that?

"Even?" I stared at his prominent Adam's apple. Anywhere but his eyes.

"You showed me yours . . ." He took a step in my direction, and just like that, the oxygen had dispersed from my lungs. "It's time I show you mine."

"Your . . . ?" I suspected my eyebrows hit the ceiling in that moment.

"If we both know what the other looks like naked, there's no awkwardness. Tit." He pointed at my breasts. "For tat." He pointed at his knob.

I could really use a rock to crawl under right now.

"So what do you say?" he probed.

"I say no." I marched toward my room again. At least my mouth said no. Every other part of me screamed yes. When was the next time I was going to see a deity naked, up close?

Riggs followed me. "Too bad. It'd solve all of our problems."

"Not the most pressing one," I pointed out, "of you being mentally sixteen, and my not wanting to take advantage of a minor."

"For your information, I'm mentally eighteen, which means I'm game in all fifty states."

I stopped in front of my bedroom, pinning him with a glare. "Cheers for the offer, but I'm good."

"No, you're not. What's more, you should say yes just to get out of your comfort zone. Loosen up a little."

"No, thank you. I like being wound tight," I maintained, but I didn't enter my room either.

Get inside, you silly cow. Before he gets completely naked and you do something weird, like lick his nipple.

"If not for your self-growth, do it so you can shove it in BJ's face when he comes back," Riggs coaxed, his slow, sexy smile on full display now.

"You really want to get naked, don't you?"

He put his hand on his chest. "Nudity is my passion."

"Fine." I rolled my eyes. "Take off your bloody clothes already."

"Thought you'd never ask."

"I literally wasn't askin—*oh*."

He tugged off his shirt and was now standing shirtless in front of me. I'd seen him shirtless before, but not *this* close. He was naturally smooth and cut sharper than cheddar cheese. And lickable. So incredibly lickable.

I swallowed audibly.

"Now off go the pants." He hooked a thumb into the edge of his Dickies. "You may wanna clutch your pearls."

With one go, he took off his trousers, standing in front of me in a pair of briefs only.

This sight is surely more pleasurable than watching your firstborn making their first steps.

"You purchased a new pair." I was openly staring at his willy now. And we both wanted it to be free. I'd never achieved this kind of intimacy with BJ.

Which is a good thing. BJ is a sane, reserved man. Not the lust child of Johnny Knoxville and Tarzan.

"What can I say? I'm a hopeless romantic." Riggs chuckled, and as he did, each individual muscle in his six-pack flexed. "Ready for the money shot?"

I couldn't breathe and speak at the same time, so I simply nodded. He slid his briefs down inch by inch, until his cock bounced out, bobbing up and down. He was hard. *So* hard. And beautiful. *So* beautiful. And I was screwed. *So* . . . well, you know the rest.

It was the first time I'd found a cock to be aesthetically pleasing. Normally, they looked like inside-out socks. Riggs had a long, thick ridge, a prominent vein, and a perfect crown. He had the Rolls-Royce of knobs. Twelve out of ten. Inches, probably.

"You can pet him if you want," Riggs cooed, holding himself by the root.

But again, I couldn't find my voice to offer him a snarky reply. We just stood there, me staring at his member, him staring at my face.

"That thing should not be petted. It should be put on a leash," I finally managed.

"Now you're just threatening me with a good time. Better?" he asked on a smirk, his voice raspy and thick. My eyes traveled up, meeting his. Purple on blue. I'd never had a one-night stand before. Not even a half-night stand. I'd only been with three men, one of them BJ. This was the first time I had genuinely contemplated such a thing.

"Ah . . ." My throat tingled. "I think so."

"You're looking me in the eye," he observed huskily, eyes half-lidded. "Told you it'd work."

Riggs's eyes darkened, becoming stormy and full of intent. So this was what *smoldering* meant. I'd always wondered while bumping into the bloody word. My body tipped forward despite my best efforts, seeking his touch.

Don't do it. Remember the house rules. No pets. No hookups. No fraternizing with your spouse.

He dipped his head, closing the distance between us. He was so close I could see the individual stubble on his jaw. His magnificent, nibble-worthy jaw. His lips nearly brushed mine. His breath—of beer and cinnamon and pine—tickled at the column of my neck. A kiss from him was going to annihilate every past smooch I'd ever experienced. Still, I couldn't stop what was about to happen, even if I wanted to. My body felt boneless as I melted against his broad chest and burrowed into his warmth, his steady heartbeat, his drugging scent.

Show me what I've been missing all this time I've been busy being a presentable, serious, marriage-worthy woman.

"And now . . . ," Riggs announced suddenly, ripping himself back from me at the speed of light. "I'm hopping in the shower to flog the log."

For the first time, he looked flushed and disoriented, not his usual playboy self.

Where was the snog his body had promised me?

I stumbled backward, bumping against my door. I put my hand on my cheek. It was hot enough to fry an egg on. "Is that code for . . . masturbation?"

"Yes, Poppins. Yes, it is. See now?" Riggs tromped around the flat and grabbed his towel from the settee. "That wasn't so har—*fuckkkkk*." His toe smashed into the leg of the settee. I let out a surprised giggle. He was one of the most elegant creatures to grace the earth. Was he actually affected by this? By me?

The thought made me flush with pleasure. I couldn't wipe the foot-long grin off my face.

"Everything all right?" I purred.

"Peachy." He slapped the towel over his shoulder, marching to the bathroom. Nestled between his thighs was the barrel of a tank. "Never been better."

I kept gawking at the spot where he'd been long after he'd closed the bathroom door.

One thing was for sure: I found my fiancé tragically attractive.

There was only one thing to do: avoid him as best I could and hope it'd all go away.

CHAPTER SIXTEEN

DUFFY

Charlie was being weird during our weekly drink. Which wasn't out of the ordinary. Charlie was always a bit of an oddball. It made us kindred spirits. But he never seemed so . . . *pokey* before.

"So you and the photographer. Tell me all about it." He brought his pint of Guinness to his lips. I pouted at my extra-dry martini accusingly. I didn't even *like* martinis. I wanted a bloody cider with a side of chips. I was just so used to being a cardboard copy of every attractive cultural cliché men were attracted to that I sometimes forgot to break character and be my true, authentic self.

"Nothing to tell," I said firmly, shoving away all thoughts about last night's almost-kiss and my almost-meltdown that followed it. Since there *was* plenty to tell, I decided to go with a condensed version of the truth. I trusted Charlie. "We're marrying so I can stay here."

There. Out in the open. That wasn't so bad, was it? Then why was pesky guilt nibbling at my gut, telling me I was a liar?

Charlie gave me the flat, unnerving stare of a headmaster who's just been fed an emotional story about a dog who's eaten one's homework. "Yeah, I figured out that part pretty early on. But you guys are more than just friends, right?"

Were we even friends? It was hard to categorize my relationship with Riggs. Sometimes it felt like we were an actual couple. Other times, I swore the world wasn't big enough for the two of us to coexist.

"I have a boyfriend," I reminded him curtly.

"*Ish*," he corrected, raising his Guinness in the air in a mock-salute. "And let's admit it, he isn't around to fight for your affections, is he?"

"No." I swirled the untouched martini in my hand. "I don't think he's ever . . ." *Given a crap? Properly courted me? Not taken me for granted?* ". . . done any of that."

The more time passed, the less I remembered BJ as a well-rounded, three-dimensional person. I couldn't explain it, really, but he was becoming more of a symbol. A prop in my seriously, and I mean *seriously*, messed-up book. It wasn't a romance; I knew that for sure. Was it a thriller? A horror? One thing was certain—it wasn't self-help.

"Now, I don't know much about relationships, angel, but I do know this—love isn't a privilege. It's a necessity. You're acting like you and Brendan can mend whatever's been broken, but if I'm being honest . . ." Charlie hitched a shoulder up, licking the Guinness's foam off his upper lip. "I think you're hedging your bet on the wrong horse."

"There are no more horses in the race," I reminded him. "The horse is more of a . . . lone wolf?"

"There's another horse," Charlie countered.

Do you reckon?

"Riggs doesn't even like me." I studied Charlie acutely, desperately wanting him to dispute my theory.

"Oh, he likes you. He just doesn't like coming to terms with liking you."

"That is . . . very confusing."

"All matters of the heart are." He swept a finger along the edges of his pint, hunting for foam.

"Charlie, don't be ridiculous. We don't fit."

"That's okay." He finished the remainder of his stout, then plucked his jacket from the back of his stool and slid into it. "You're not a pair of shoes, so that's not a requirement."

"Wait, where are you going?" I was still sitting in front of my lack-luster martini, avoiding my Riggs-infested flat like it was a mosquito colony I had to brave through.

"Doctor's appointment." Charlie tucked his wallet into his back pocket. "Wanna come hold my hand?"

"Do you need me to?" Even if I did want to go home, which I decidedly didn't, I wouldn't mind tagging along. Although Charlie was perfectly handsome, worldly, charming, and sought after, he always seemed like a tragic hero to me. Someone I wanted to shield and protect.

"Nah. I'm good."

I sighed. "Next week, same day, same time?"

"If life grants me another week—I wouldn't miss it for the world." He winked.

Rolling my eyes, I shooed him away. So dramatic, this one.

"You're lying." I pressed my fingers to my eyes, fighting off tears.

"Why would I lie about something like that?" Kieran's voice drifted into my ear while we were on the phone. "It's not like I have an incentive for it."

"I just don't see why he'd do that."

"Because he's a wanker, Duff. Always has been."

I shook my head, even though my brother couldn't see me. This was yet another blow in my already shitty-licious week of job hunting and trying to ignore my roommate slash fiancé slash teeny-tiny-totally-minuscule crush. The same one I was going to marry in less than three days. After which a flurry of paperwork and bureaucracy would ensue, and I'd apply for my marriage visa.

Kieran sounded like he was eating something crispy. "I can forward you the email if you want."

"Go on, then."

"'Kay. Don't shoot the messenger."

I rose up to a sitting position in my bed, grabbed my Mac, and turned it on.

I logged straight in to my email, where the forwarded email from Kieran was waiting.

—————Forwarded message—————

From: Brendan Abbott <brenfjr333@gmail.com>

Date: Fri, July 20

Subject: Things and stuff

To: Kieran Markham <kkktookmybabyaway@gmail.com>

Kieran, my dude. Hope life's treating you well. Things over here are awesome, but I miss your sister a lot (please don't tell her I touched base with you. Poor thing's only gonna miss me more, and between you and me, the more I have time to reflect, the more I feel like I'm ready to propose when I go back home).

Anyway, I got a few questions about opening a restaurant. I know you and your stepdad have a quaint fish and chips thingy. Just general questions about supply chains, contractors, staff hiring, etc.

Lemme know when you have a few minutes to spare.

Your almost-brother-in-law LOL

So he *did* have access to the internet.

"He thought you wouldn't tell me?" For some reason, this was what I chose to focus on. Not the fact that BJ was getting ready to propose. He must've been a complete eejit to think my own twin would keep secrets from me.

Kieran snorted. "You know we get along fine, but BJ tends to be full of himself. He's the kind of guy who thinks I won't snitch on him because we shared an eggnog one Christmas."

"But . . . why would he want to open a restaurant?" I asked.

"Listen, Duffy, something's dodgy about all this . . ." Kieran trailed off. "Makes me wonder if he's telling us the entire story about his getaway."

BJ never showed any interest in opening a restaurant. He was also a horrible cook. If this was him looking for a new career direction, he clearly needed a better map.

"Thanks for telling me." I sniffled.

"Course. It just seemed odd, innit?"

"Odd. Awful. Your pick."

"What else is new?" Kieran's voice brightened, signaling he was uncomfortable with my brazen display of emotions. "How's that fake fiancé of yours?"

"Riggs?" I asked, distracted. "Good, last I checked."

Which was a considerable time ago. I had been avoiding him all week, but I was positive he was alive. His mess was all over my flat, serving as vital signs of life.

"He's been giving me advice about my fit neighbor, Shelby. I think she's thawing."

"Oh, goodie," I mumbled distractedly. "Very nice."

"I googled his name, you know. Found loads of photos he's taken. He's not a professional loser like BJ."

"Hmm. Quite." I was still contemplating the BJ thing. "Sorry, Kieran, I gotta go."

After I hung up with my brother, I paced the living room. It was Saturday morning, and the job sites wouldn't resume posting until Monday, so there was no point in checking.

Thankfully, Riggs didn't sleep the night here. I knew he was hooking up with other women, because how else would you explain his night away? *Not* that I cared. He could shove his behemoth willy inside whoever he liked, as long as it wasn't me. I tried lifting my spirits up by reminding myself that our City Hall appointment was in three bloody days, and with it, our meeting with Felicity Zimmerman, the big-shot lawyer Riggs's friend had hooked us up with.

"Honey, I'm hoooome." The door opened and Riggs swaggered in, looking deliciously rumpled and thoroughly fucked.

Bugger. Normally, I could hear him coming up the stairs and disappear into my room before he was able to chat with me. Today, it was almost like he'd tiptoed his way up here.

Right. Because he's just been dying to talk to you.

"Hello," I greeted coolly. "How was your night?"

"Nine out of ten." He sauntered over to me while I opened the fridge, about to make breakfast. He slammed it closed before I could retrieve the egg white carton.

"I got a better idea." He grinned down at me.

"Better than eating the most important meal of the day?" I raised a skeptical eyebrow. He stank of another woman's perfume, and suddenly, this lie I'd been feeding myself, that I didn't care about his manwhoring ways, wasn't working quite so well.

"Oh, we're having breakfast." He flung his heavy arm across my shoulder, headlocking me and kissing the crown of my head. "And just like me, it's going to be the best you've ever had."

"Oh my *God*, Riggs." I dropped my head back, moaning, à la Meg Ryan in *When Harry Met Sally*. "I think my mouth just orgasmed."

I dropped the fork I'd just sucked clean on my empty plate. This was hands down the best waffle I'd had since I moved to the States.

We were at a small, unassuming diner in Park Slope. It had checked black-and-white floors, bright-red booths, and pink-and-blue neon lights. All the staples of an underwhelming culinary joint.

"You know," he said, elevating a thick eyebrow, "I could give the rest of you an orgasm if you—"

I raised my hand. "Absolutely not."

"Not even as my wedding present?" He wiggled his brows rather adorably.

"How'd you find out about this place, anyway?" I circled the air with my fork.

Riggs picked up his coffee and took a slow sip. "Doesn't matter."

"Yes, it does," I insisted. "I've been waffle hunting for years, and suddenly you just happened to stumble upon the best waffles in the city."

"Walked past it."

"Coming from where?"

He glowered at me, clearly annoyed that I wasn't dropping it. "I stayed over with a friend."

"A *friend*?" I grinned, shimmying my shoulders. Inside, it felt like I was being knifed in the chest by every felon in the zip code. "From school? Work?"

"A fuck buddy."

"Nice that you'd think about me right after having sex with someone else."

His lips twitched. "I always think about you. You're my girl, Poppins."

Despite my best efforts, I couldn't control the butterflies stretching their wings in the pit of my belly.

"And your fuck buddies?" I asked casually, dumping too much creamer into my black coffee as a distraction. "What are they?"

"My outlet," he answered shortly before flagging a waitress.

She came over quickly, shooting him a flirty smile. "Can I help you, handsome?"

"You sure can. Got any Advil?"

She threw him a pout, resting her cheek against her shoulder. "Sorry, but we're not supposed to give away any medication. Liability stuff. We could get sued."

"I won't sue you." He gave her his I'm-about-to-fuck-your-brains-out grin. The one I'd been avoiding all week. As expected, it worked like a charm.

Her gaze ping-ponged between us. "Doesn't your girlfriend have any?"

So subtle. So smooth. Quick, someone give this woman a medal for diplomacy.

Well, as it turned out, I'd had enough of women trying to get a piece of what was about to be *legally* mine.

"Actually, I'm the wife." I wiggled my engagement finger, flashing Riggs's ring.

"But we're getting a divorce," he hurried to say. "As soon as today, seeing as wifey here is dead set on my not getting painkillers."

I could see the waitress's internal struggle before she sighed.

"All right. Be right back."

Once she was gone, I swiveled to him. "Headache again?"

He nodded, rubbing his temples.

"You seem to get them a lot."

"Yeah," he groaned. "For a couple years now. They keep getting worse."

"And you never got it checked?" I eyed his still-full waffle plate.

He shrugged. "One in every fifteen men has chronic migraines."

"If you have to pop fifteen to twenty painkillers a week, they're not *just* headaches. You should see a doctor."

"Don't have one," he hissed out, obviously in pain.

Maybe he didn't have any health insurance. Didn't the magazine he worked for cover anything? They sounded like a bunch of twats.

"Anyway." He nodded in thanks after receiving the painkillers the waitress disposed in his hand, along with a handwritten phone number and some water. "Let's talk about something else."

"Like what?" I asked.

"We're getting married this week."

"May I?" I reached over to his waffles. He nodded. I knew he wouldn't judge me for it. When I looked up at him with a mouthful of hot, fluffy waffles full of whipped cream and syrup, Riggs's eyes gleamed with joy.

"If this was a real wedding, who would you invite?" I asked.

"It *is* a real wedding." He swiped his finger over his whipped cream, sucking on it. "And I invited the usual suspects. Christian, Arsène, Arya, and Winnie. Maybe Alice. She's Christian's faux-mommy."

"Sounds . . . delightful. What about family?" I asked.

"They're my family."

"I mean extended one. Parents, uncles, cousins. You must have someone." I reached for his plate again, but he was quicker, switching between our plates and taking my empty one.

"Nope." His eyes caressed my face. "No relatives whatsoever. Not even a pet hamster."

"How come?" I remembered the offhanded way he'd told me he'd had a miserable childhood, and how I hadn't pressed for more details, and I suddenly felt terrible for being so selfishly focused on myself in that moment.

"Well, I'm always on the road, so no sense in getting a pet. But hamsters specifically freak me out. They eat their young. *Literally.*"

"Riggs!" I chided. "How come you don't have a family?"

"It's a long story," he said.

"I've nowhere to go," I pressed.

"It's depressing too."

On a whim, I reached out, touching his palm across the table. It was the first time I'd initiated anything physical with him. "I absolutely *love* depressing stories. They're my favorite. Remember, I'm the same person who told you I think Jane Austen should've killed off Mr. Darcy and had Elizabeth and her family join Scotland Yard and find his murderer. The same person who told you I went to school with torn clothes and empty lunch packs. Depressing life stories are my comfort zone."

He hesitated, a smile on his face, before dropping his head in resignation.

"I'll give you the condensed, comma-free version: My very gay grandfather ran away from Scotland to San Francisco in his twenties after his Catholic family disowned him because of his sexual orientation. There, he met an older man with a daughter from a previous marriage. That daughter was my mom. Elderly Gentleman and my grandfather fell in love and lived together. Elderly Gentleman kicked the bucket three years later, when my mom was fourteen, and left pretty much everything to my granddad—daughter included. He got full custody and raised her as his.

"When she was eighteen, my mother got knocked up with my ass. The guy who impregnated her was some no-good bum, completely insignificant to this story. As soon as she pushed me out, she ran away with the asshole, and my grandfather raised me. Then, when my mom was nineteen, she died in a car accident. Fast-forward to when I was a preteen, my grandfather died. So, yeah, basically. No family. My grandfather had friends and colleagues, but no one to step up and actually take care of me."

I stared at him, my jaw on the floor. He really didn't have anyone. No wonder he was a commitment-phobe. He had no idea what it felt like to belong.

"And your biological dad?" I managed through a choke I hoped he didn't hear.

Riggs hitched a shoulder up. "Don't even know his name."

"The family in Scotland?"

"Can shove it." He sat back, looking disgusted. "They sounded like assholes. When he died, they'd offered I move to Dundee with them. Thanks, but no fucking thanks. I don't have a taste for homophobia."

"I'm so sorry," I said quietly.

He slipped his hand from underneath mine, tipping his coffee cup in salute. "No need to be. I turned out fine, didn't I?"

"Yes," I said seriously, feeling my cheeks heating up. "You turned out perfect."

"And you?" He jerked his chin in my direction. "Who would you have invited? Other than your parents and Kieran, I mean."

My parents, who somehow hadn't heard or seen my viral proposal video before it was taken down, thank goodness.

I popped a strawberry into my mouth. "Most definitely Cocksucker."

He smiled tightly. I didn't know why. I thought he'd be beaming that I'd used his nickname for him.

"And . . ." I looked up at him, taking a final stab with my fork in his waffle. "Definitely, *definitely*, Gretchen."

The day I'd dreamed about from the moment I was born—my wedding day—ended up costing thirty-five bucks. Forty-six and some change, if you count the iced americanos I'd chugged beforehand as liquid courage.

The bride wore powder-blue trousers from Marks & Spencer and a white Topshop blouse her stepdad got her two Christmases ago. The groom opted for casual black jeans and a V-neck shirt. He looked like a hunky Hollywood star, but one who was going on a vegan acai bowl run, not attending a red-carpet event.

Everyone in attendance was from the groom's side, highlighting just how lonely I was in this city. There were Christian and Arsène, the rich-looking blokes, as well as their wives, Arya and Winnie. No farting dog, though, thank heavens.

We were all standing outside the courthouse, on the stairway, slurping iced coffees, ignoring the blistering heat wave. Arsène was scowling at tourists as if they'd personally attacked him, Winnie offered me homemade wedding-themed red velvet cupcakes, and Christian and Arya periodically checked their phones, obviously disgruntled about having to unplug from their busy day to attend this sham wedding.

"I still can't believe you're getting hitched." Christian side-eyed Riggs through his Ray-Ban Wayfarers.

"I still can't believe we're treating this mess as a real marriage." Arsène scowled, and I gathered he was the bad cop in this group's dynamics. "The man picked up *two* women at the Brewtherhood not even a month ago."

"Jesus, Ars." Arya glowered, flicking his arm. "Duffy has ears, in case you haven't noticed."

"She also has a brain." Christian slid his shades off. "Which means she knows better than to treat this as anything more than an arrangement. Right, Duffy?"

I nodded numbly. My mind was reeling. Riggs had a threesome? I hated that I was letting this piece of information crawl under my skin, but I chalked it up to the fact I was getting over BJ. Emotions were obviously bleeding into one another.

"Just make sure you sanitize that sofa." Arsène shot me a glare that could freeze the Sahara Desert. "Our boy here is a piñata of STDs."

Riggs laughed, enjoying this exchange, and in that moment, on the steps of a courthouse, minutes before what was supposed to be the most important moment of my life, I got cold feet.

It made no sense at all. *I* was the one who had begged Riggs to marry me.

I couldn't help but feel deep sorrow that my marriage was being wasted on a coldhearted Casanova who enjoyed nothing more than picking up randoms on the weekend, wasting away as an eternal bachelor.

The worst part was that I couldn't undo the chain of events that was unfolding.

Even if BJ did come back and propose, I would probably not accept. My life had started to fall apart like an elaborate domino display on the day he'd told me he was leaving, and things had been unraveling ever since.

I was never going to get my perfect wedding. This was as good as it was going to get. A detached exchange of vows with a relative stranger in a courthouse.

Suddenly, I couldn't breathe.

"Excuse me," I piped up, beginning to make my way down the stairs and onto the street. I didn't even have full control of my feet. They'd just left the premises of their own accord. As if they knew something my brain couldn't fully comprehend. That marrying this man was going to be a terrible mistake, punishable by great heartbreak.

Before I knew what was happening, I was charging down the street, zipping past storefronts and commercial buildings and shoppers, my breathing labored, my forehead dewed with sweat.

Why did I want to stay in New York? I had virtually no friends here, no job, and a shoebox of a flat, and my most prized possession was a thermal laminator.

I was about to round a corner when someone jerked my wrist from behind. They tugged me into an alleyway before pressing my back against the sizzling brick wall.

I was crowded by a huge, male body. I sucked in a breath. It was classic Duffy Markham to get robbed on the day I'd decided to ditch my sham wedding.

"Out of all the crap I thought I'd have to deal with in this lifetime, a runaway bride wasn't one of them." Riggs's beautiful face materialized an inch from mine. As close as he was the night we'd almost kissed.

"Christ, Riggs." I pushed at his chest, snarling. "You scared the hell out of me!"

"You ran away on our *wedding* day." He stared at me with what almost looked like raw pain. "A wedding day which, by the way, *you* blackmailed me for."

"I wasn't running," I lied haughtily. "I just . . . needed air."

"There was a sufficient amount of air on the courthouse's stairs." He turned to point at the direction of the courthouse. "Same level of air as anywhere else in this city. What's going on?"

"I f-f-freaked out," I said, stuttering out the truth.

He blinked at me, looking confused. "Care to give me some more information that wasn't evident from you taking the fuck off?"

Whoa. He *was* pissed. I'd never seen Riggs this livid. Annoyed? Yes. Disinterested? Plenty of times. Even when he had his headaches, he was mostly irritated. But never, ever angry.

"It just dawned on me that this is my wedding day. I imagined it very differently growing up. And . . ." I gulped down a sob. "Well, there hasn't been one day in my life when I haven't thought about my wedding day. So it feels really sad that nothing about it is going to be as I planned."

His frown collapsed.

"You wanted this," he said quietly, after a pregnant silence.

"I know." Tears filled my eyes. The first tear escaped before I could wipe it. It ran down my cheek. Riggs brushed it away with his thumb. "The pragmatic part of me—the one who wants to marry rich—thought it was a good idea. *Still* thinks so. But I guess . . . well, I guess there's another part to me. One that loves *Pride and Prejudice* just the way it is."

I wasn't making much sense, was I? And yet, it seemed as though my future husband knew exactly what I was getting at.

With a sigh, he pressed his forehead against mine, closing his eyes. I did the same and found that I soon lost my hold on gravity with him so near. It felt like I was drifting on clouds.

"You'll still have that dream." His thumb brushed across my cheek, back and forth, in a soothing, repetitive motion. "Just not with me."

"I know." My voice cracked.

"And if there is a God, not with Cocksucker either."

I snorted out a laugh, burying my face in his shoulder. Not because I was devastated—even though I was—but because I didn't trust myself not to kiss him when he was so close. That was a whole new problem I wasn't eager to unpack.

It was just that sometimes, when my eyes were closed and my heart was open . . . Riggs Bates felt like he was truly mine.

He stroked my hair, sweeping his hot lips across my temple. "There, Poppins. Everything'll be fine. Take my word for it. I don't throw promises around very often."

I loathed that he called me Poppins. Was that all I was to him? An odd, eccentric character?

We stayed like this for a few minutes, wrapped in one another, breathing each other in, before Riggs's front pocket danced with an incoming call. He pulled his phone out.

"Yeah?"

"You're going to be late to your own wedding, lovebirds," Christian's voice announced on speaker. "And not fashionably so, if I may add."

"We're coming," Riggs said shortly.

"Do you even have a bride anymore?" Arsène asked.

"Just barely," Riggs gritted out, giving me a look. "You did a good job of almost scaring her away."

"Not good enough, if the wedding's still on," Arsène said easily, not a hint of sorrow in his voice.

"Careful, Riggs, or I might suspect you actually want to marry me." I tried to sound casual.

"I do want to marry you." He killed the call and glanced at me. "Emmett's going to have a really shitty time when I text him a copy of that marriage certificate."

An hour later, Riggs and I stood in front of a court clerk and exchanged our vows. Riggs's friends surrounded us in the simple, albeit offensively brown, room. Our backdrop consisted of wooden walls and a judge stand. The clerk was wearing a black robe. A fairy-tale wedding it was not.

The clerk introduced herself as Allison. Allison was extremely nice and seemed enthusiastic about her job marrying people, which deepened my guilt, since in our situation, the bride was in love with another man's wallet and the groom was probably going to spend tonight with a different woman. Or *two*.

"Are you lovebirds ready to get hitched?" Allison shimmied her shoulders.

"Been ready my entire life for this woman," Riggs confirmed with one of his dazzling smirks. Allison purred. His smiles should 100 percent be outlawed. The man could knock a woman up with a smirk alone.

"You're doing amazing," Winnie whispered in my ear, squeezing my hand.

"God," I moaned. "Why did you say that? Do I look that frightened?"

Winnie flashed a warm smile. "Just a tiny bit."

What was she doing with Satan's more sadistic cousin? I wasn't sure, but props to her for taking him off the market.

"You're such a beautiful couple," Allison gushed, oblivious to the farce she was becoming a part of.

"Believable too," Arsène deadpanned before Winnie elbowed him in the ribs.

"You may hold hands if you wish." Allison's eyes ping-ponged between us, likely puzzled by the fact I stood six feet away from my future husband. "No need to be shy. Many couples don't realize a court-house wedding can be romantic too."

Riggs didn't have to be asked twice. He comically flicked away Winnie's hold on me and grabbed both my hands, jolting me close. His touch was warm and dry and full of strength. I couldn't believe I was marrying the same impossibly hunky god I'd caught only a few weeks ago screwing my former boss. Gretchen seemed like a distant memory now.

Allison began the ceremony with the "dearly beloved" speech I knew so well from the dozens of weddings I'd attended in my life back in London before reminding us of our duties and roles in marriage. The entire time, I had an out-of-body experience. I couldn't believe my parents weren't here—that they didn't even *know* about the wedding. Plus, the part I had been trying to push into my unconsciousness finally reared its ugly head. I was going to be a married woman when BJ came back to New York. Our relationship was doomed from the start.

Riggs threaded his fingers through mine, tickling the inside of my palms in a bewitching way that made every hair on my body stand on end. When my eyes met his, he grinned.

"Hey, kid." Riggs winked.

My entire being somersaulted. "Hello, old man."

He laughed. I ducked my head and blushed. In our periphery, Christian slapped his forehead. "This has *farce* written all over it." He grimaced. "In Riggs's cum."

"I believe you just lost a bet," Arsène drawled.

"She seemed more levelheaded last time we met her," Christian explained defensively.

"No woman is immune to the charm of Riggs Bates," Arsène hissed. "He could seduce a nun in between bites on his lunch break."

I was about to turn around and remind them I was *literally* right there, listening, when Allison decided it was time to get real.

"Are you, Riggs Carson Bates, free lawfully to marry Daphne Helen Marie Markham?"

"I am."

"And are you, Daphne Helen Marie Markham, free lawfully to marry Riggs Carson Bates?"

"Yes." My voice came out thick and awkward.

Allison smiled. "I now pronounce you husband and wife. You may kiss the bride."

Riggs tugged me toward him by our linked hands. Then, smoothly—so smooth I didn't realize what was happening at first—his hand wrapped around my waist and his lips locked in on mine. Unlike our subway kiss, this wasn't a peck. It was a *kiss* kiss. With intention, wrath, and enough passion to burn down the entire place. His mouth opened against mine. My eyelids slid shut, and a feeling of drunken, achy euphoria took over as the tip of my husband's tongue reached to touch mine.

A hot wave rocked through my body, and I clutched the lapels of his shirt while his tongue swirled around mine, circling it, rough and full of purpose. My breath hitched before I started chasing his tongue with my own. Soon, we were full blown snogging, really kissing, and I forgot everything non-Riggs related. Like time. And place. And *myself.* Goose bumps danced along my back.

His long fingers laced through my hair and moved across the back of my head until he grabbed the back of my neck. He leaned in, deepening our kiss. I groaned into his mouth. He laughed into mine.

Allison cleared her throat loudly, trying to bring us back to earth.

"Mr. and Mrs. Bates. I believe you'll have your entire lives to polish off your kissing skills."

A lopsided smirk on his face, Riggs disconnected from me. So easily, so casually, that I stumbled all over him. He righted me with the hand he still had on my waist.

"My bad. I got a little excited."

His voice showed no trace of emotion, tightness, or elation. He seemed entirely unaffected.

I blinked up at him, waiting for him to acknowledge me. Somehow, this kiss had felt real. Different and wild, separate from everything I'd ever experienced.

But Riggs didn't look at me at all.

"See you back home, Poppins." He gave me a half-arsed hug with one hand, plastering his hot mouth to my ear as soon as Allison had left the room.

With that, he turned around and walked away with his friends.

Leaving me feeling like I was falling into an abyss so dark and vast I couldn't even see the sky anymore.

CHAPTER

SEVENTEEN

RIGGS

Riggs: <forwarded a document>

Emmett: What am I looking at?

Riggs: My marriage certificate.

Emmett: Says here Daphne, not Desiree.

Riggs: Yeah. Desiree is her nickname.

Emmett: You understand what you're saying makes no sense at all?

Riggs: I'm not here to make sense, Emmett. I'm here to tell you to fuck off and take your precious Alaska with you.

Riggs: What, no congrats? Silence has never been this golden.

Emmett: I'm still not buying it.

◆ ◆ ◆

Fuck.

Fuck, fuck, fuck, fuck.

My wife was a good kisser. I did not expect that. Duffy seemed like the type to be allergic to anything that smelled like fun, not to mention looked like it.

Turned out, she had moves. She knew what she was doing. Or maybe it was the fact she was so young, so different from my usual hookups, that made her exotic enough for my chest to constrict when we exchanged fluids in that courtroom.

Your chest did not constrict, Riggs Bates. You probably just had a minor heart attack or something.

I was so disoriented with that little ping in my otherwise-dormant heart that I had to pull away and stagger out of the courthouse like a drunken fool. And where did a drunken sailor end up whenever he got off a ship? That's right, the bar.

"Did you just abandon your wife at the altar?" Arya barked out, catching up with my step as I shot out of the courthouse. I was counting on those four-inch heels to slow her down.

"I didn't abandon anyone." I blasted through the courthouse's doors, seeking the nearest bar with my eyes. It was five o'clock somewhere. Sure as fuck not in New York, but in Asia, for sure. "She has things to do."

"What things?" It was Winnie's turn to challenge me. I noticed their husbands kept their mouths shut and trailed behind us. Cowards. That was exactly why I never wanted to get marri—*ah, never mind.*

Out on the street now, I detected an Irish pub across the road.

"Immigration-document stuff."

"That could've waited until tomorrow."

I choked on a laugh. "You don't know Duffy. She's not big on postponing things she wants. I wouldn't put it past her to become a naturalized citizen before dinner, and the wife of a *Forbes* list billionaire before midnight."

"You were straight up rude out there, Riggs Bates," Winnie persisted, power walking to keep up with my stride. "Why'd you kiss the poor child if you don't have feelings for her?"

"I do have feelings for her," I protested, slapping the door to the pub open. "I feel strongly that she's a pain in the ass."

My friends wobbled behind me like baby geese. I fell on a stool at the bar and rapped the wood three times. "Redbreast, neat. Make it a double."

A triple might have been a better idea, actually. How much did I have to drink to rid myself of the taste of my wife? Her sweetness lingered on my mouth, and I had to remind myself she was over a decade younger. Not to mention, she'd married me so she wouldn't get deported. Not to mention, she'd thought I couldn't afford her.

The fact she had a price tag at all should've made her undesirable to me.

I'd tried to be good. A week ago, when we'd almost kissed in her apartment, I'd put a stop to it before we did something stupid. But today, when the clerk gave me the green light, and Duffy stood there with her little frown and surly pout and posh outfit and purple eyes, I couldn't help myself. I indulged.

Indulged? You scorched every boundary you've ever agreed to by kissing her.

Confusion and horniness gave way to anger. Did I just sexually harass my own wife? Ten seconds into our marriage?

"Seems that way." Arsène slithered to a seat next to mine on the bar like a dark shadow.

Shit. I said that out loud.

"You did." Christian perched on the other side of me. "And that last sentence too."

I knocked back the whiskey in front of me, then motioned for a refill. Christian chuckled, shaking his head. Arya and Winnie disappeared to the restroom, probably to plot my execution.

"Back to the topic. You didn't sexually harass your wife," Arsène murmured, then ordered a whiskey as well. "The tongue-thrusting was mutual," he reflected. "*And* uncalled for. I was planning to eat today."

The women joined us and ordered fruity schnapps and truffle fries.

"You have to go back to her." Arya put a hand on my shoulder. "What you did today was lame for a thirteen-year-old, and disastrous for a thirty-seven-year-old."

"She'll get over it," I said. Duffy didn't give two shits about me. She was still full-fledged obsessed with the idiot who left her behind.

Just in case, I pulled out my phone to check if I had any missed calls or texts from her. I didn't. She was probably vomiting into a trash can this very moment, brushing her teeth with hot coal and hoping she didn't catch anything deadly.

"Why did you run off, anyway?" Christian tilted his head sideways.

"Because he likes her," Arsène supplied.

"As a friend," I corrected, though I wasn't sure that was true anymore. I did like Duffy, weirdly enough. But I also wanted to fuck her. What would that be called?

Marriage, you moron.

"Sure!" Winnie said brightly. "And I only liked Arsène as a boss."

She *hated* Arsène when he was her boss. In fact, she ran all the way back to Tennessee when she'd worked as an actress at his theater.

"No, I actually do only like her as a friend." I tapered my eyes, shooting Arsène a don't-be-a-dick glare. "You know my thoughts on monogamy."

"What I know is you've never stayed in a place long enough to get attached to anything." Arsène draped an arm over Winnie's shoulder.

"Now that's changing, and so are you. If this is how you kiss your friends . . ." He trailed off, his gaze drifting to the woman tucked under his arm. "Stay the fuck away from my wife."

◆ ◆ ◆

An infinite number of drinks later, I decided to face the music.

I was about to open the door to Duffy's building when my phone rang. It was Emmett, the world-class douchebag. Not normally my conversation partner of choice, but this was the one time I wanted to speak to him. I swiped the screen, taking the stairs two at a time.

"Emmett." I said his name in the same tone I would the word *douchebag*.

"Fine. So the wedding *did* happen," he huffed on the other side of the line. "I'll give you that."

"Hello to you too. And what do we say when we wrongly accuse our employees of faking a wedding . . . ?"

"Sorry," he grumbled, and even though my marriage wasn't real, the pleasure of seeing this fucker backing out of sending me to Alaska was very genuine. "How was it?" Emmett asked dispassionately. I could tell it had cost him a mental arm and a leg to call me.

"Great." I got to our—*Duffy's*—floor and stopped by her door. I didn't want to have my attention on anything or anyone else while I faced her. "How's life at the fishbowl?"

"Stop calling my office a fishbowl."

"It's not just your office." I yawned. "It's *any* office."

"I like my fishbowl," he maintained.

"I like my freedom," I retorted.

He laughed. "Well, you just signed it over when you got hitched."

"Funny," I said dryly. "Is that why you called? To congratulate me?" I found it hard to believe.

"Actually, I called to tell you I'm still not buying your marriage, and I'll be keeping a close eye on you. I hate to be lied to." There was a pause. "Also, you'll be glad to know that now that Alaska is off the table, I have a new, *local* assignment for you."

"Hit me with it."

"Abandoned prisons."

"How many are there in the state of New York?"

"Two," he answered. "One more in New Jersey, and one up in Connecticut."

I tried to ignore the claustrophobia tightening around my neck. I was going to stay in New York for a while.

I cleared my throat. "Sounds good."

"I'll email you the details tonight," Emmett chirped.

"You do that."

"Oh, and Riggs? We still want to meet this wife of yours." Then he added to clarify, "The entire *Discovery* family."

I smiled big, so he could hear it. "She would love to see you too. Just give us a time and a place."

After we finally hung up, I shoved my key into its hole. I was about to turn it when a voice stopped me.

"Hey, Riggs."

Dammit. The one time I wanted to speak to my wife, the entire world and its uncle decided to talk to me.

The one time? Really? What about the time you sneaked in on her after she ignored you after that almost-kiss? You tiptoed your way upstairs so she wouldn't hear you come.

It was the first and only time I'd actually contemplated fucking someone else for the entire duration of our engagement, and pathetically, I couldn't even do that. I ended up falling asleep on that chick's couch, then did the walk of shame back to the train station the next day, only to get giddy about finding Duffy tasty-looking *waffles*.

I turned around, smiling tightly at Charlie, who exited his apartment in a Hawaiian shirt and Bermuda pants. He looked like he hadn't slept since 1995. Wrinkled and worn out.

"Charles, my man."

He advanced my way before stopping a couple feet away from me, shitting all over my personal space.

"Where've you been?"

"Uh." I looked around, ruffling my hair. "Just here and there. Places."

"You look a little drunk."

Who the fuck died and made you a Celebrity Rehab *episode?*

I chuckled. "Nah. It's all under control." Other than his fifteen heads, which were currently swimming in my vision. "You good?"

"Yes. Good," he said distractedly, looking around us. "Wanna grab another one downstairs?"

"Another what?" I blinked.

"Drink."

What was up with this dude? He was a grown-ass man, and not a bad-looking one. I bet he had plenty of lady friends. And buddies he could drink with. Why was he hell bent on humping my leg?

"Rain check." I started swiveling back toward the door, feeling another headache forming behind my eyelids. "If you could *smell* my last few hours on my breath, I better call it a day."

He took another step in my direction, now standing uncomfortably close. I only felt comfortable being so close to people I was interested in putting my dick in. Charlie was in no danger of ever falling into that category.

"I have a proposition for you." He snickered awkwardly.

"Sorry, pal, I'm as straight as a mummy's life line."

"Did you think I . . ." Charlie's eyes flared with horror. "No, no . . . just . . . *no.*"

"Why, I'm offended, Charles." I put a hand to my chest. "I'm sure you've seen worse-looking men."

"You're a handsome devil indeed." He took a step back, just in case. "But I don't swing that way either."

"How can I help you then?" I was beginning to lose my patience.

He gulped, and I could tell my short attitude was making him wary.

"I'm going to the British Virgin Islands next Friday for two weeks to scout some filming locations, maybe hit a few waves while I'm there. I was supposed to take an old friend of mine, but her daughter gave birth four weeks early today. I have a spare ticket. Thought you could use a little vacay."

Was he offering me a two-week holiday with him? Could this guy get any weirder?

"I . . . uh . . ." *Could use ditching New York, but not with you.* "I have a busy few weeks with work."

He nodded, his spine shriveling, making him a few inches shorter. I knew he didn't buy it.

"That makes sense. Just thought I'd put it out there."

"Thanks, though."

"Yeah. Sure."

He ducked toward the stairway, and I didn't know why, but I felt like the biggest pile of shit known to mankind. There was something broken about this man. What was his deal?

Not your circus, not your monkeys, I reminded myself. See, this was exactly why I didn't get an apartment or stay anywhere for too long. Getting attached was inevitable. I had to physically stop myself from jogging down the stairs, having a beer with Charlie, and asking him if he was okay. Fuck, even the thought of taking him up on his offer for that trip had crossed my mind before I mentally torched it with gasoline.

Resolute, I turned back to the door and threw it open.

Duffy wasn't home.

◆ ◆ ◆

Wherever Duffy was, she didn't return all night. I knew, because my pathetic self decided to stay up and wait for her. I told myself it was because I was platonically worried for her. And I was. New York was a dangerous place. And who knew if she'd even made it home from the courthouse?

I could've texted and asked her where she was. But I didn't. I wasn't sure if it was my desire to give her space or my need to prove to myself I didn't have feelings toward this woman.

At four o'clock, I threw in the towel and passed out. I didn't wake up until eleven. When I opened my eyes, I was still alone.

Whatever you do, don't be a dick and check her bedroom.

Naturally, I went ahead and checked her bedroom to see if she was there, ignoring my internal voice of conscience. In my defense, I knocked on the door for five minutes straight beforehand. And that voice was more of a whisper, anyway.

Duffy wasn't in her room, as I suspected. I contemplated calling Kieran, but then realized I might throw her entire family into the arms of hysteria when there could be a perfectly innocent reason for Duffy's absence. Maybe she went on a Tinder date and was currently having wild sex with a stranger. The thought made me want to vomit.

No. It's not the thought. Just yesterday's three gallons of whiskey.

I was beginning to suspect my inner voice was a dumbass.

Proceeding to the coffee machine before calculating my next move, I noticed a handwritten note on the kitchenette counter. Naturally, it was laminated, like everything else in my wife's life.

My pulse picked up as I grabbed it.

Riggs,

I booked you an appointment with a neurologist.

I wasn't sure what your insurance situation was, so

I paid out of pocket, which means you absolutely CANNOT cancel, because I will MURDER you if you do.

You need to find out what's causing your headaches. No one deserves to live with chronic pain.

Get your blood work done before the appointment. Below is the number you should call for places and availability.

P.S.

I really do mean it. If you made me spend all this money for nothing, I will do very violent things to you.

P.P.S.

We're never talking about yesterday. Ever.

—Poppins.

She paid out of pocket to get me to see a neurologist because she thought I lacked the funds? That must've been hundreds of dollars. Maybe thousands, with the blood work.

Two things happened simultaneously: I felt very bad for making her spend all this money when she was unemployed, and very good, because for the first time in my life, someone gave a genuine, God-honest shit about me. I'd never been taken care of. Not since my granddad passed away. And that was so long ago that I could barely remember his face. My only recollection of that period was that I wasn't *as* fucked up. I guess that Maya Angelou quote was true. You do tend to forget what people say or do, but you always remember how they made you feel.

Duffy made me feel seen, and I cruised through my existence being the guy who slides in and out of people's lives unnoticed and unaccounted for.

I staggered to the couch with the note still in my hand. Everything about it, from the fact it was laminated to the way she'd finished it off with her nickname, made me feel. Anger, delight, excitement, fear, courage, and this was just an incomplete list.

I hadn't the greenest clue what it felt like to be loved. To be important to someone. The story of my origin—of *my grandfather's* origin—was my most important possession. Everything I knew about our relationship I'd learned through his estate lawyer. When I turned eighteen and became the beneficiary to all his wealth, I'd met with the man, and he'd filled in the blanks about my childhood.

If it wasn't for this random attorney, whom I'd met at eighteen in San Francisco when I was informed I was officially a billionaire, I wouldn't know about Granddad. About Scotland. About my mother being a runaway teen who cared more about the dick she was riding than her infant son (still bitter about that, in case you were wondering).

I felt my eyes burning. I was dangerously close to shedding a tear. I'd never cried before. I didn't like all these firsts I was beginning to experience under Duffy Markham's roof.

You're not catching feelings. You just have cabin fever, my inner voice maintained, this time much louder. *Get up and get the fuck out of this place. Go to a museum. A movie.*

It was a weekday, and Duffy was probably out all day, running around between job interviews. Her hunger to survive alarmed me. Her entire life was planned around finding a good job, a partner who could provide for her, and opportunities to get ahead. She wasn't ambitious. She was scared. Her past experience had left her scarred. She was hungry, even when her stomach was full. I would never know what that felt like.

I hopped in the shower, put on some clothes afterward, and went downstairs. My phone pinged with an email from Emmett as I made my way to the subway. Details about the prisons assignment. I stopped in front of a diner to shoot him a quick reply. When I looked up, I noticed Charlie through the diner's window. He was sitting in one of the booths alone, frowning into his cup of coffee.

He looked like a stenciled version of himself. Sunken cheeks, skin the color of chipped ice. How hadn't I picked up on that yesterday when I ran into him in the hallway? But the answer was obvious—I was too busy having a meltdown about my nonexistent relationship with my fake wife.

He hadn't seen me. I could atone for the way I blew him off yesterday. Walk inside. Buy him a meal. Ask if everything was all right.

Get attached.

Thing was, I was already feeling all kinds of emotions toward the woman I was living with. Adding another person to worry about was out of the question. Already, I was losing my grip on my most fundamental personality trait—being a loner.

With a heavy sigh and a healthy dose of self-loathing, I turned around and resumed my walk to the subway.

Charlie needed help.

But giving it to him just might cost me my principles.

CHAPTER EIGHTEEN

DUFFY

I managed to avoid my newly wedded husband for two full days after our wedding.

The first night, I'd phoned a friend from Cambridge who was now working at a law firm in Manhattan and suggested we grab a drink. Laura (pronounced *Lou-ra*) had been trying to catch up with me for a couple of years now, ever since she'd moved to the States. I always dodged her attempts. BJ had detested her ever since she was caught doing cocaine on Cambridge's campus halfway through her law degree. After that, she quietly transferred to Durham, but she frequently visited to catch up with mates.

After five vodka and sodas, and a gossip session in which Laura brought me up to speed about all the scandals our year's alumni were up to across the pond, I confessed that I'd married an American man for a visa, that he'd kissed me, and that I was now too mortified to return to our shared flat from fear I might hump his leg.

Laura was quite understanding, and, once she realized I couldn't be persuaded to sleep with him (*"But BJ is all the way in Nepal! And, may I add, a total knobhead who isn't worth your loyalty"*), she let me crash at her place.

Two nights I slept on her couch before Laura decided to put her (heeled) foot down.

"Listen here, missy, I love you to bits, but I also want my personal space back. It's time you leave." She parked a hand on her waist, standing in the middle of her living room, the Manhattan skyline her backdrop through her floor-to-ceiling window.

"Oi!" I bemoaned, burying myself deeper under the throws on her settee. "You're supposed to be my support system."

"*You* dumped me and our friendship for a bloke named *BJ*," she reminded me, thrusting a finger my way. "You deserve no support and no system. Not to mention, I'm doing you a favor. I'm making you face the music."

"Oh, but the music is rubbish." I flung the throw off me and shot up. "The music is . . . is . . . Olivia Rodrigo–bad."

"You did *not* just diss Olivia Rodrigo under my roof." Laura held up her index. "The woman penned my favorite breakup song. I listen to it every time I dump a guy. Which means several times a week." She trekked toward her kitchen, which was stark white and . . . well, in *existence*. It wasn't my measly counter with a microwave and one burner. "Anyway, marriage is not disposable. You're not Kim Kardashian, darling."

"He hasn't even texted me since he ran away from our wedding," I complained, following her to the kitchen island.

"You're both emotionally twelve." She threw her fridge open.

"Maybe, but at least I'm chronologically closer to that age," I said, sulking.

Laura rolled her eyes, producing two fat-free yogurts, one for her and one for me. "Old or not, you'd love to dance the horizontal tango with him."

"What if I do sleep with my husband?" I nibbled on my lip.

"Then I would literally cheer you on. Pom-poms and all."

"*Laura.*" I grabbed the yogurt from her hand and shoved a spoonful of it into my mouth. "Even if he was my type, he is not looking for a relationship."

She sighed. "*Unfortunately*, you will exercise perfect self-restraint. You always do."

"You think?" I perked.

"After he left you in that courtroom?" She scrunched her nose. "I bet as soon as you see him, you'll pick a fight. Now, please get out of my flat. I would like to dance around naked to Olivia Rodrigo on full blast."

◆　◆　◆

It was in my Uber ride home when the final nail in my BJ coffin was driven into the wood.

The minute I slid inside, my phone flashed with an incoming video call. For a second, my heart played Twister in my chest. Was Riggs finally checking in on me?

My shoulders sagged when I saw Kieran's name on the screen. I swiped reluctantly, like it was my brother's fault he wasn't my husband.

"Yes, big brother?" I rolled my eyes, humoring him. But Kieran's face was as white as Mum's signature boiled chicken, and it looked like he was home, even though he was supposed to be at the chippy this time of the day.

"Hey, are you alone?" He peered at me nervously, as if he could see my surroundings.

"Why? Oh, God. Shelby is not suing you for sexual harassment, is she? I told you it was a bad idea to flash h—"

"What?" His eyes flared. "No, no. This has nothing to do with Shelby. She and I are grand."

"What's happening?" I scowled. "Last time you looked unsure and nervous, you shat your trousers, Kier."

"First of all, it was a *shart*. Somewhere in between. And it was a Portuguese buffet, Duffy. I needed to make sure I had a taste of everything." He scrubbed his stubble. "Ah, fuck. I do have bad news, though."

"What happened?" I demanded.

His eyes—purple like mine—were swimming with trepidation.

"So . . . it's about BJ."

I pressed my lips together, waiting for more. Kieran blinked rapidly. He was trying to find the right words, and I knew then and there that there weren't any.

"Duffy, he's an eejit."

"What did he do?" For an unexplained reason, I was feeling much better knowing this wasn't about Kieran running into trouble.

"—literally the dumbest bloke I've ever met in my life."

"Kieran." My voice was tinged with edge.

"—almost think it's a crime to mix our prime DNA with his if you ever get married."

"Kieran!" I snapped.

"Okay, okay." He raised his hands in the air. "So, last night before I logged off for the day, I checked my laptop to see if maybe Shelby answered." He was studying me very carefully, as if I was about to burst into flames. "She didn't, by the way, which is a whole other story. Did I tell you I spoke to Riggs about her? He rang the day after you and I had the conversation. Thought I should ask her out next time I see her at the newsagents'. But how would I know when she—"

"Holy ADHD, Kieran, just finish your story."

"Right, right, right. Where were we?"

"You operating a laptop," I groaned.

"Yes! So, there were eight emails from BJ."

"Eight?" My jaw dropped. BJ was a one-syllable texter.

"Weird, innit?" He nodded. "They were all on the same thread."

"Well . . . what did they say?"

"I'll just forward them to you."

My mobile pinged with an incoming email. I opened it.

—————Forwarded message—————-

From: Brendan Abbott <brenfjr333@gmail.com>

Date: Wed, September 28

Subject: WHERE ART THOU

To: Kieran Markham <kkktookmybabyaway@gmail.com>

Kane, my dude, where u @? I'm so drnk.

◆　◆　◆

Kane, u still here? did u catch a cab bck?

◆　◆　◆

Fuckkkkkkkk. I fucked up. lol. I totally screwed blondie. The girl from Finland? Hahahahaha. U were right. tits nt real.

◆　◆　◆

Duffy can nvr find out.

◆　◆　◆

> Im legit gonna pass out im so drunk. Not sre how I
> even managed to get it up. call me

Bile gathered in my throat, and my heartbeat escalated to a perilous speed. I couldn't believe what I was reading. Couldn't believe this was the person I'd spent so many years of my life with. Planned to live the rest of my years with.

The next email had a different time stamp, six hours later.

Hey, Kieran, it's BJ. I'm really sorry for the chain of emails from yesterday. That was . . . less than a good representation of me. A friend of mine, Kane, hacked my email and started pranking people. Please don't take this seriously. Obviously, I would never do any of those things in the email (drink excessively, cheat on Daphne, etcetera).

I'll try to call you in a bit.

BJ

Hey, Kieran, it's BJ again. Upon reflection, I'd like to come clean about something. I don't want to make this even worse by lying to you, and I know I messed up really bad. I've been vomiting all morning and I can't stop thinking about what I did. I'm hoping we could keep this between us. I know it's a big ask, but please hear me out.

I'm currently in Thailand, not Nepal, with a friend. That's why I asked you about opening a restaurant the other day. My friend, Kane, is wanting to open one in Koh Samui.

As you probably figured out, I got you and Kane mixed up because your name starts with a K and you were the last person I emailed.

We were at a party on the beach last night. Things got a little out of hand. I got really drunk. This was the FIRST and ONLY time I've been unfaithful to Duffy. And technically not even unfaithful because she kinda dumped me before we said goodbye in New York. I know this means little right now, considering all the lies I told her about this trip. The destination, who I was going with, and why. But please don't let this mishap taint your view of me. I've been with your sister for almost a decade and I love her. This is supposed to be my last hurrah before I ask her to marry me. It's ALWAYS been just about that. Getting some fun out of my system before we both settle down.

Look, I'm sure if we hop on the phone and talk, I can explain myself better. Can you please pick up?

BJ.

Kieran? You there? I tried calling a few times . . .

My eyes slammed shut, and I focused on my breathing. Somehow, in a span of a few weeks, my life had completely fallen apart. I lost my job. I lost my boyfriend. I managed to somehow *marry* a manwhore with commitment issues, and BJ cheated and lied to me.

"Duff," Kieran groaned, looking pained. "Please say something."

My insides singed. Not with hurt as much as with anger. At myself, mostly. I had no one else to blame. I'd placed my bet on a spoiled rich man I'd had little in common with, and paid a hefty price. Perhaps Riggs was right and it was time to think about what I wanted to do instead of how I wanted to live.

"I've got to go," I heard myself say.

"Duffy . . ."

I hung up, turning to the Uber driver in a daze. "Can you make an unplanned stop?"

"Hmm . . ." His gaze swung to mine in the rearview mirror. "You'll have to get into the app and—"

"My boyfriend of seven years just told my brother that he slept with someone else at a beach party, even though he told me he was away helping monks in Kathmandu. How about now?"

This was the part in the movie where the driver would say something like, "Girl, I've got you, let's kick some ass!" But this wasn't a movie. This was my life. So the man just suppressed an eye roll and muttered, "Yeah . . . that sucks . . . but I'll still need you to reroute your trip on the app."

"Just pull over right here, please."

I stumbled out of the Uber, feeling raw and disoriented. I was quite a few blocks away from my flat, but if I had to sit in a confined place one more minute, I'd probably hurl myself out the window.

I walked into a bodega, bought myself a bottle of vodka, wrapped it in a paper bag, and started making my way home.

If I drew disapproving glares from people on the street, I didn't notice. I was fully and completely dedicated to the part of the sloshed, cheated-on girlfriend.

My mobile rang in my purse. I dug through it while sipping my vodka, letting the hot, burning sensation coat my throat. When I tugged my phone out and saw BJ's name on the screen—*of course* he'd kept his phone working this whole time—my heart didn't even miss a beat.

How sad that I had spent weeks hoping and praying for him to call me while I thought he was in Nepal, and now all I could feel was reluctance to have an official breakup call. I declined the call. He called again.

Bloody Kieran. He must've told BJ that I knew. I hit the decline button again. The third time, I put my phone on silent and shoved it back into my purse. Let BJ get a taste of what it felt like to be ignored.

I didn't know how long it took before I was in front of my building. I felt sufficiently plastered and dissolute when I tripped up the stairs. Passing by Charlie's door, I made a mental note to check on my neighbor. I'd been so busy avoiding my new husband that I'd neglected my responsibilities. One of which was to give the lonely man some much-needed companionship.

I jabbed my key four times into its hole before I managed to unlock the door. The lights were off. The dim, bluish light of the TV danced in the darkness. I dragged my feet across the floor, hiccuping and kicking Riggs's worn-out leather boots from my path.

So he *was* here. Wonderful. Splendid. Better nip that conversation in the bud.

"Duffy." He stood up from the couch, like a pupil who'd been waiting outside the principal's office. He looked particularly dashing, after not seeing him for a few consecutive hours straight. "Hey. I didn't want to bother you, b—"

"Oh, bollocks!" I moaned, loudly and rather aggressively. "You just *have* to be gorgeous. With your bedhead and dimples and muscles and . . . and . . . lack of shoulder hair. It's like nature didn't get the memo you're middle aged."

Riggs stared at me with confusion. "Uh . . . thanks?"

"You're fit." I took a swig of my vodka. "And I fancy you."

"Why are you yelling?" He frowned. I couldn't tell for sure, but he looked a bit upset. And by a bit, I mean a lot. And by a lot, I mean IMMENSELY. His cheekbones were flushed, and his eyes were so dark they looked like an endless abyss.

"Because I'm wasted." I laughed, feeling incredibly empty on the inside, the echo of my laughter bouncing in my lungs.

"No shit." He gave me a slow once-over. His jaw locked. "Where've you been?"

"My mate's place."

"A boy-friend or a girl-friend?"

"A none-of-your-business friend," I declared cheerfully. "Let's not pretend you're not visiting your lady friends whenever you fancy."

"And you couldn't send a text? Spare a phone call? 'Hey, Riggs, by the way, I'm staying over with a friend, not dead. So don't send a search party.' You know, like a normal person?"

"Why didn't *you* text?" I stumbled toward him, poking my finger in his chest.

His nostrils flared, and his eyes tapered. "I wasn't the one who—"

"Yes, you were," I said, cutting him off. "In the courthouse. You left me."

Incredibly, I didn't think I was taking my BJ rage out on Riggs. I genuinely felt more hurt about my fake husband not spending time with me after our sham wedding than my *real* boyfriend for the last decade running off with some plastic-tit Finnish girl. Or was she Swedish?

Riggs looked ready to toss me out of the Empire State Building. "You can't just run off like that."

I tipped my head back and laughed. "Why? You've made a career out of it. Running off is literally your entire personality."

"We're not talking about me," he said tightly.

"I second that statement." I took another generous gulp of vodka. "We *never* talk about you. I don't know the first thing about you. Why all the mystery, Riggs Bates? What do you have to hide?"

Even though I desperately wanted to know more about him, what I really wanted right now was to unbutton his jeans, drop to my knees, and suck him off until he couldn't stop himself anymore and enjoy a round or two of his wife. Revenge sex was the best kind of sex, or so I'd been told.

But Riggs didn't look sultry and turned on. He looked like he was ready to pump my stomach and send me off to a wellness center. "Look, I owe you an apology, and an explanation for what happened the day we got marri—"

"BJ cheated on me," I said, bursting into his speech again.

"What?"

"Aren't you happy?" I giggled, leaning against his body shamelessly, fingering the long column of his neck. "You were right about Cocksucker all along."

"No, I'm not happy." He captured my shoulders and guided me gently to the settee, where I flopped down bonelessly. "What happened?"

I waved him off with a snort. "Please stop pretending you care about anything or anyone. I happen to know you, Riggs Bates."

"You don't know the first thing about me." He took my shoes off, which was when I first found out I had blisters the size of my nose from wandering aimlessly through the streets of Manhattan for the past few hours. "Now spill it, Poppins."

I squinted at him, tossing my head back to bring him into focus.

"Do you fancy me?" I asked all of a sudden.

"What?" He blinked.

"Do. You. Fancy. Me? I mean, would you sleep with me, given the chance?"

He stared at me like I'd left my faculties at Laura's. To be fair, I might have.

"Why does it matter?" he sneered, finally.

I climbed over his lap, resting my bum directly on his crotch. I laced my arms over his shoulders and puckered my lips, taking a stab at this whole seduction thing. "It matters because I'd very much like to be shagged by you tonight."

He went rigid, pinning his hands to his sides like the settee had been superglued. His breathing was labored, and he didn't move a muscle. Other than one, which kept growing rapidly and thickly under my arse.

"You're drunk." His voice came back gruff and sultry.

"You're *hard*."

"I'm always hard," he grunted, looking torn and miserable and, for once, not so cocky and self-assured.

"Well, I'm not always drunk, so we better go about this quickly before I come to my senses," I bantered, reaching for the hem of his shirt.

He caught me by the wrist, then lifted me up and planted me back on the couch with frightening ease.

"You're not yourself tonight."

"Actually, I don't think I've ever been this authentic in years." I skimmed my fingers along his broad shoulders. I couldn't stop touching him. "Go on, Riggs. You've shagged half this world's population. What's another notch on your belt?" I leaned closer to nibble his ear, but missed the mark and instead grazed his jaw with my teeth.

Riggs let out a low grumble that made his rock-hard chest flex.

"Duffy."

"It's our Christian duty to consummate our marriage," I urged, licking a path from his ear to his neck. He didn't stop me, but he didn't touch me either. "Don't you want to secure a place in heaven?"

"That ship has sailed. I won't be surprised if they'll greet me with confetti in hell," Riggs drawled.

"It's never too late. Jesus forgi—"

"I'm an atheist," he said, cutting through my speech.

"Course you are. My sinful husband."

"You're not making too much sense today, Poppins." He inched backward, away from me. But still, he had that pining look, of a child reluctantly turning their back on a colorful birthday cake.

"But what if God does exist?" I reasoned, internally recognizing that I was probably breaking some Guinness record at being the least attractive seductress on earth. "What if He's watching us right now? What if it's a test and we're failing it?" My mouth fused to his collarbone, where I sucked hard.

"All right." Riggs jumped up to his feet. "That's enough molestation for one day. I'm not going to fuck you while you're skunk drunk. I'm not a fucked-up consolation prize for Cocksucker."

"But Riggs!" I threw my hands up in the air, whining.

He jammed his feet into his boots, looking extremely pissed off. "I'm gonna let you sleep this one off and never mention it again, because apparently, on top of everything else, you've turned me into a gentleman now."

Oh, no. I wasn't going to let him go anywhere. He was just going to sleep with someone else. A fantastic idea sprang into my mind.

"Wait!" I jumped to my feet, immediately regretting it. My head swam.

Riggs turned back to me. "What?"

"I want to take you up on your offer."

"*What* offer?"

"To watch porn together."

He scowled. "When did I offer that?"

"On the subway." I smiled sunnily. "That night when we dined and dashed, remember?"

The night he'd stood up for me. The memory made my spine tingle.

Riggs swiped his tongue along his bottom lip. His throat bobbed. I could tell he was struggling to make a decision.

"I'm not going to regret it," I lamented. "I'm even willing to sign a declaration. *And* laminate it."

Finally, a reluctant smirk tugged at his perfect lips. "You need help."

"Help me, then!" I opened my arms. "Help me discover my sexuality. BJ was terrible in bed, Riggs. Terrible. He humped me like a dog, then flopped over before I was even done. And I swear he couldn't find my clit with a map, a search party, and if there was a huge neon sign attached to it."

It felt lovely saying this aloud. It might have been uncharitable and petty, but it was also something else: the truth.

"What's your plan?" He arched an eyebrow. He had nice, thick eyebrows. I wanted to run my fingers over them.

"To screw BJ out of my system," I announced, then added, "but I get that you don't want to take advantage of me. So that's why I'm willing to watch porn with you, which is technically not touching each other, and therefore not exploiting."

"*No touching*," he warned.

"None whatsoever." I lifted two fingers in the air. "Scout's honor."

"Were you ever in the Scouts?" He eyed me skeptically.

"No," I confessed. "I was too busy studying, honing my fake accent, and filling lottery tickets."

We both laughed.

Even though I was plastered, I did recognize the truth for what it was—I'd been attracted to Riggs from the get-go, and I wasn't going to regret the decision to sleep with him, if he was willing to go there.

I waited with bated breath for his verdict.

Finally, he picked up his phone from the coffee table between us. "Grab your laptop. I'm going to rock your world, Poppins."

Half an hour later, we were sitting on the settee with my laptop on Riggs's lap, balanced on his mammoth erection, watching *Throbbing Hood*.

As far as the plot went, *Throbbing Hood* did not have one. But Throbbing, the hero, was a very prolific thief, in a sense that he'd already stolen four women from their husbands and given them all orgasms.

At the same time, naturally. Which meant he had to get creative with his toes.

Personally, I couldn't really get the fascination. Sure, Throbbing's willy looked like a pool noodle, but everything was so manufactured. All the moans and the groans, the perfect silicone tits, and the orchestrated orgasms. No rare acting talent had been wasted on this body of work. I could tell every single participant only did this for the paycheck.

Which was how I found myself yawning halfway through the thirty-minute movie, checking the time and wondering how many viruses were currently leeching into my laptop from the porno website.

Riggs, who didn't seem too into it, either, and in fact didn't seem to have breathed for the last half hour, turned to look at me.

"Not your thing?"

I shrugged. "You really hyped it up. I thought there would be . . . more."

"More?" He seemed on edge. "What more could you want? There is enough jizz to fill an Olympic pool, and we haven't even made it to the anal-beads part."

"Thanks for the spoiler." I made a face. "Next thing I know, you'll tell me which one of them he ends up marrying."

"Marrying . . . ?" His face fell. "Poppins, he's not going to marry any—"

Realizing I was joking, he let out a gravelly, sexy laugh, shutting down the laptop. Oh, no. Now there really wasn't any chance of us doing the deed. And he was extra gorgeous, now that I was mostly sober and able to fully appreciate him.

"How's your head?" he murmured.

"Full of depressing thoughts, but otherwise fine. How's *yours*?"

His features softened, probably as he remembered the appointment I'd booked him. My cheeks pinked. Did he think I was in love with him or something? Because I truly wasn't. It was just a silly doctor's appointment. Anyone would have done it. It was the right thing to do.

"Mine's good," he said softly. "Thanks."

"You're still going to that appointment, though."

He grinned. "I see you've started bossing me around again. You've clearly sobered up."

"I've only had about half a glass, actually." Both our gazes drifted to the vodka bottle on the coffee table. Riggs nodded.

"Good to have the real you back."

"The real me *still* wants to have sex with you."

His jaw constricted. "To get back at Cocksucker?"

I shrugged. Honestly, I wanted to have sex with Riggs simply because he was the most attractive, fascinating, thrilling man I'd ever come across. But admitting so to him was a terrible idea. He was allergic to monogamy.

"Tell me, Daphne, do you think I'm some kind of a party trick?" His voice was so unbearably cool that I couldn't believe it had come out of him. Icy.

"What? No!" I said breathlessly. "Obviously not."

"You sure about that? I *did* sleep with half the fucking universe." His voice was mocking, but his eyes were two frosty lakes of pain.

"Did I offend you?" My eyebrows creased. "Riggs, even your mates—"

"You're not one of my *mates*. You don't have the flight time and context to form an opinion about me," he said flatly.

Horrified, I sat upright. "Look, I didn't mean that at all. I just . . ." *Wanted to convince you to sleep with me for my own pathetic, selfish reasons.* "I thought I was paying you a compliment. Most men would love to be known as womanizers. This is a no-strings-attached offer."

"We're *married*." I couldn't take my eyes off his. They were so stormy, and for the first time, I realized Riggs did have feelings. Loads of them, quite frankly. And nobody had really paid them any attention thus far.

"Fake married," I said weakly.

"Real living together."

"I'm a big girl," I said, surprised by the avalanche of emotions rippling in my own chest. "And I've been good for a very long time, doing the right thing, playing by the rules." I paused. "I'm done playing the sensible go-getter role. I want to do something because I want to, not because I think it's a means to an end."

"And that something is me," he finished, a sardonic smile tainting his Cupid's lips. "I'm touched, but it's a pass."

There was something so final about the way he said it that I knew better than to ask again. My pride wouldn't let me. Suddenly, I was full to the brim with remorse for putting him in this position. What was I thinking? I treated him like some sort of sex machine.

I nodded solemnly. "I'm sorry."

"No need to be. No hard feelings, yeah?"

I forced myself to look up and smile at him. "No hard feelings."

Then, to break the tension that had built up in the room to a point there was barely any oxygen left to breathe, I announced, "Now excuse me while I go iron my blouses. It always puts me in a grand mood."

This time, he didn't award me with his usual chuckle. I drifted to my room in silence, wondering at what point Riggs Bates's laughter had become my favorite soundtrack.

◆ ◆ ◆

Since I didn't have room for cutlery, let alone an ironing board, whenever I steamed my clothes, I'd do it on my bed, using a piece of tile as a buffer so as not to burn my duvet. It made ironing quite the operation, seeing as I had to bend over in an R shape to ensure my clothes were crisp and wrinkle-free. Strangely enough, I did not derive my usual pleasure from doing something that would make me appear upper class.

I kept running the hot iron over the same crease on my cherry-red blouse distractedly. I managed not to think about what had happened with Riggs out there, instead refocusing on my newly found hatred toward BJ.

I wondered if he'd always been a rubbish person, or if he'd sprouted privilege and brattiness in recent years, when he realized I'd stick around for the perks? My guess was he'd always been a twat, and I simply looked the other way. Well, it was safe to say my nose was now deeply shoved in BJ's bad behavior. And that no amount of wealth in the world was worth sticking to a terrible partner.

I was running the iron over the crinkle in the sleeve again when I felt something hard and hot pressing between my thighs from behind. Oh, no. Did I wee myself? I could swear I wasn't drunk anymore.

Wait, no. It was a palm. A *human* palm. Riggs's palm?

Ohmigod.

I clenched involuntarily around his hand, ribbons of warm tension uncurling beneath my navel. He cupped me from behind, and I wasn't sure if I was more confused or more hot and bothered by this surprising turn of events.

I wanted to ride his hand to a climax but stayed perfectly still, afraid it was some sort of a game or payback for my utterly selfish behavior.

"We'll be breaking the house rules." His voice was so deep and thick it sounded like it was coming from the bottom of the ocean.

I licked my lips, remembering the silly contract on our stupid fridge. "We don't even live in a house, do we? It's a flat, and really, rules are born so we could break them like an artist. Or so Picasso—"

"This doesn't mean we're a couple," he continued, his voice rough. His middle finger traveled up, skimming my slit through my underwear and trousers teasingly.

"I know," I said, my voice breaking.

His finger pressed into me, bunching the fabric of my knickers between my folds. I let out a growl, dumping the iron and straightening my back. He pressed his free hand to the base of my spine, keeping me bent.

"I like the view better from here," he whispered into the shell of my ear.

"Riggs! How dare you?" I huffed prudishly, trying to preserve the minuscule pieces of my pride.

"Easily. You're objectifying me and using me as a revenge fuck to dangle in front of your little boyfriend for when he comes back. I've seen that movie a hundred times, Poppins. I'll be your leverage. Your eye for an eye. And he'll have to swallow the fact I dicked you down, because he's been unfaithful too. But eventually, you'll forgive each other and live miserably ever after in a big house in the burbs, complete with an au pair who looks just old enough not to be a temptation for Cocksucker."

He used the rest of his fingers to pry my thighs open crudely. I widened my stance without protest, even though everything he just said sounded outrageous.

"Maybe I won't take him back," I said.

Riggs chuckled darkly. "Don't write checks you aren't willing to cash. You're too enamored with the idea of being Mrs. White Bread, with the silver-spooned spawns and country club membership."

I gulped, feeling both humiliated and aroused. I really wasn't going to take BJ back, but I also didn't want to discuss him at present.

"The thing about being bad . . ." Riggs leaned over, pressing his hot erection against me, his lips skating over the side of my neck. "Is that it's no fun unless you own up to it. So own up to it. You're about to fuck the husband you think is a broke-ass, no-good loser, and you're doing it just so you can throw it in Cocksucker's face."

I opened my mouth to protest, but nothing came out. When I didn't say anything, he snickered. "Good girl. Now we'll do it my way, because you want it not to suck, and I want to test my theory."

"What theory?" I finally found my voice. It sounded like there was gravel stuck in my throat.

Riggs pressed his open mouth to my jawline, sending goose bumps down my spine. He gathered my hair, letting it fall on my opposite shoulder.

"I want to see if corrupting the good girl really *is* more fun than taming a bad one."

Anxiety and heat gathered in the pit of my stomach. It was a delicious mix, expecting the unexpected, wanting to cross my own red lines, to sprint past them, to the unknown. To a man I'd never consider under normal circumstances.

"You thought about having sex with me?" I squeaked.

His hard abs trembled with a chuckle against my lower back.

"All." He pushed his index finger deeper into me.

"The fucking." He sank his teeth into the flesh of my neck.

"Time." His hand snaked to my trousers, unbuttoning them expertly.

He slid my slacks down, then my panties. I craved his kisses. The taste of him when he devoured me in the courthouse like I was his favorite dessert.

With my clothes still gathered around my ankles, I stayed bent, waiting for his next move. Riggs decided to neglect my southern region, using his finger to skim the shape of my areola through my shirt. A ripple of desire blasted through me, and I pressed my heavy breast into his palm, begging for more. I didn't recognize myself in my actions. In my need for something so primal and basic.

"You like it?" he whispered in my ear, his scent drugging me.

"Yeah."

He grabbed the edge of my shirt, jerking it down along with my bra. My breast sprang free from its confinements. He cupped it from the bottom and pushed it toward my face. "Lick."

I swirled my tongue around my breast, no questions asked. He groaned behind me and desire flooded me, making my blood sizzle inside my veins. The thought that I could make this near-perfect creature react this way made me gratified.

He clutched my waist, grinding his erection along my bum, his forehead dropping to the back of my head with a sigh.

"Your body's too delicious to be wasted on a prick like Cocksucker."

"Thank you," I managed. Barely.

"It's not a compliment, it's an observation." His hand—coarse like sandpaper—slid down from my hip bone to between my legs. "Never have I wanted to kiss a mouth and shut it up so equally."

"I—"

"Just ride my fingers and don't ruin this moment for me, Poppins."

He tugged me up by my hair, plastering my back against his chest. I let out a whimper. My head dropped against his shoulder. He was still grinding against me when his thumb found my clit, swirling teasingly around it, never quite touching it. I squirmed, chasing his touch, desperate for more.

"Please . . . ," I moaned.

"Please what?" His lips moved against my throat.

"Please touch me there."

He did. Oh, he did.

My eyelids drooped and I shuddered all over. I was close to climaxing, and I never had orgasms while having sex. It was why sex with BJ had become taxing. I considered it mandatory cardio. Like Pilates.

Riggs's tongue ran along the side of my neck, toward my shoulder. He picked up the pace between my legs, thumbing my sensitive bud in circles, applying the perfect amount of pressure and withdrawing just when I was teetering on the edge. Of course he was better than a vibrator. I should have known. What a curse of a husband Riggs Bates was. Wrong in all the places he needed to be right—no prospects, no money, no emotions, no loyalty—and good where sin and abandon were concerned.

After a few minutes, I felt my knees buckle and I released a loud sob. The pleasure was insufferable, and a wave of heat washed through me. I writhed and twisted, the sensation too much, too good, too loud.

"Ahhhhhhh," I moaned.

"No." Riggs moved his hand from my sex—which was still throbbing—pushing my lips open with his thumb and forcing me to taste myself. "Say my name."

"Riggs," I panted loudly. "Riggs. Riggs. Riggs."

Was I a screamer?

"Bugger," I muttered. "I can't believe I screa—"

Before I could finish the sentence, I was yanked backward and somehow found myself lying down on the floor.

"My turn." Riggs's face was close to mine, looming over me. My lips parted on their own accord, inviting him to kiss me. But he was already frowning at the space where our bodies would connect soon, freeing himself of his jeans.

I started kicking my underwear and trousers down my ankles, eager to speed up the process. He grabbed one of my thighs and pinned me down, holding me in place.

"Keep 'em on. More friction."

He wanted to do it with my legs practically closed?

"Would it fit, though?" I asked. I looked up from his cock, which he held in his hand.

He gave me the brightest, most heartbreakingly dimpled smile. To think that this smile belonged to no one, that it had no home, no person to love it, to look forward to it at the end of the day, made me want to weep.

"It'll squeeze through." He raised two fingers in the air. "Scout's honor."

I raised an eyebrow. "Were *you* in the Scouts?"

"Fuck no."

He reached down to the breast he had set free earlier, scraping his teeth over my puckered nipple. I trembled. I was going to come again, and he wasn't even inside me yet. This man was going to ruin me for all others, and he bloody well knew it.

Riggs reached between my legs, pushing two fingers, curling them to hit the spot BJ had never even attempted to find. His lips ran over my forehead, and he groaned, his breath fanning the hairs bracketing my face. "You're so wet, Duffy."

I blushed, ducking my head. He grabbed the tip of my chin and angled me to look him in the eye. Still, he wouldn't kiss me, and it drove me mad.

"Do you still want this?" he rasped. "It's never too late to change your mind."

"God, no."

His expression hardened.

"I mean *yes!*" I amended hysterically. "I still want it. No, I haven't changed my mind."

The relief on his face made my pulse accelerate. I watched as he produced a condom from his pocket and rolled it on. Secretly, I was thankful I was on the pill. Condoms were only 98 percent effective, and I definitely didn't want to become a part of the statistics.

Riggs reached between us, pushed my thighs open as much as he could with my trousers still at my ankles, and slid into me slowly, inch by inch. We both watched his penis disappear inside me with awe, our foreheads touching. It was the hottest thing I'd ever done with anyone in bed. Ironically, I wasn't even technically *in* a bed.

"Oh, God." I dropped my head back to the floor, closing my eyes. "It's like watching a magician pulling ribbons from his mouth, but in reverse. Your cock is never ending."

He tipped his head back, groaning and laughing at the same time. "You're doing good, Poppins."

I squeaked in response. I felt uncomfortably full. Like I'd been stuffed to the brim. It was odd but not unpleasant. After he was done pushing into me, he stayed still, giving me a chance to adapt.

"Told you." His gaze trekked up my torso and landed on my eyes, a private smile on his face. "It fits."

"Just barely." I pouted. "Well, at least it feels good."

Or so I thought. Because then he started moving.

And it wasn't good. It was *divine*.

He thrust once . . . twice, before I realized there was absolutely no connection between what BJ and I had been doing in the sheets and what was happening here. This was so good I wanted to cry. I felt like Riggs had lit a match and incinerated the entire room. The dancing flames around us licked at my skin.

My second climax arrived after five minutes, but I stayed on the ride for fifteen more before Riggs's nostrils tightened, his jawline ticked, and he finished inside me.

With his face angled up, blond curls framing his face like a halo, his strong Roman features sharp as a blade, it was hard not to see him as a brutal temptation.

This was the most deliriously satisfying sex I'd ever had, hands down.

And, sadly, it was also a one-off.

Riggs sagged on top of me after he finished, still inside me. My gaze etched to his face, fascinated. He was the first to speak.

"Well? Got it out of your system?" He sounded blasé, and I could already see him in my head in five minutes, lighting himself a joint and sitting at the window overlooking the street, shirtless.

"Eh . . . yes, thank you."

He dropped a kiss on my exposed shoulder. "Anytime, wifey."

I gulped at the word. It sounded so agonizingly perfect coming from his mouth, but I knew he'd never mean it.

Do you want him to mean it? You're polar opposites. You started out hating each other, and that was only a month ago.

But maybe I did want it. Why should it matter that Riggs wasn't making a load of money? I could be the breadwinner. We could be happy. Too bad he'd never consider it.

"Uh, Poppins?" He snapped his fingers in front of my eyes, and I realized he'd pulled out of me at some point during my brief visit at Fantasyland.

"Yes?" I cleared my throat.

"Why does it smell like your apartment's on fire?"

I stared at him drowsily before remembering I'd forgotten the iron on my bed while it was still working.

"Oh, shit!" I pushed him off, bolting up to my feet. I forgot my trousers were still on and almost fell onto the bed. A bed that was likely on fire.

Riggs tugged me back, pulling me to safety. He stood up. We both watched my mattress with astonishment.

The iron had burned through my entire blouse's sleeve. There was a black ashy hole that ate at most of the beautiful shirt. The heat had also passed through the board and created a dark stain on my duvet. Riggs picked up the iron, trekked over to the living room window, and flipped it over to cool down.

"Hope you're not banking on it working again."

Riggs grabbed a Sharpie from the pen box on the kitchenette counter, uncapped it with his teeth, and waltzed over to the fridge, narrowing his eyes at the list we'd laminated. He then crossed one item from it.

House Rules
 No pets
 No hookups
 ~~No fraternizing with your spouse~~

But rules *were* meant to be broken.
Too bad I couldn't say the same about my heart.

CHAPTER NINETEEN

DUFFY

I woke up to the scent of something carby and sinful.

Unbothered by the empty calories I'd consumed the day before in the form of vodka, my mouth began to water. I shifted in my bed. Since my duvet was half-burned from last night's indiscretion, I'd slept without a blanket. I couldn't believe I'd nearly burned down my flat to have sex.

Come to think of it, I couldn't believe I'd *had* sex. Enjoyable sex at that.

Last night's events flooded back into my memory, and with them a mixture of giddy excitement and crushing dread.

I'd shacked it up with my husband. My hotter-than-Hades husband.

After consummating our marriage, we ordered pizza (pizza! On a weekday!), had watermelon margaritas Riggs made with jalapeños (delicious), and went to sleep in our separate beds. Well, in Riggs's case, the couch. No doubt I could have offered him my bed for the night, but I didn't want to seem needy.

Plus, I didn't want him to see that as an invitation to stick his knob in me whenever he fancied. Even if I did want a rerun of last night's showing. I felt like my body had been possessed by a woman who was actually capable of having fun.

After I finished brushing my teeth and putting on a sensible dress, I padded to the living room, where I found a pile of fluffy and warm waffles stacked neatly on a plate on the coffee table.

"My God, talk about beauty and grace!" I cooed, rushing to the waffles.

I grabbed the plate and brought the waffles to my nose, sniffing. "You innocent little babies. Who put you here, in harm's way?"

Saliva gathered in my mouth. These waffles were the real deal. Where did Riggs get them?

The bathroom door opened, and Riggs walked outside, looking twice as wicked as the treat I was holding.

"Finally, you're up." He ambled over to the kitchenette, where he popped open butter and chocolate syrup.

I deduced he'd bought them, since there wasn't a weapon in the world you could threaten me with to make me willingly welcome chocolate into my home. "Hurry up, we gotta eat them before they get cold."

"Eat them?" I gasped at the blasphemy, putting the plate down before I did something stupid. "Riggs, I can't do back-to-back cheat days, and we already had pizza yesterday."

"You can and you should. I checked, and there are no laws against having fun in the state of New York." He squeezed the chocolate syrup all over the waffles. "Besides, I've seen you naked, so I have the authority to say you can definitely afford it."

I felt myself blushing from head to toe.

"I'm sorry. I appreciate the gesture, but I just can't . . . Where did you even buy them?"

"Buy what?" He sat down and, using a fork and a knife, cut a huge bite of waffles and chocolate for himself.

"The waffles," I heard myself say, my stomach grumbling loudly.

"Didn't buy them." He took the bite, chewing. "Made them."

"*Made* them?"

"Yup." He popped another bite into his mouth. The bloody man was going to eat all of them before I could have a taste. "Just bought an old-school waffle maker downstairs, and the ingredients. Easy-peasy. Wanna try?" He angled a forkful of goodness my way.

I shouldn't. I really shouldn't. But oh, I wanted to. I bit down on my lower lip.

"*Nr, buh thrrr fr degestte,*" I mumbled.

"Do you have that in English?" He raised his head from the HALF-EMPTY plate. I needed to work fast if I wanted a taste. "Couldn't hear you with your tongue swimming in saliva."

I opened my mouth begrudgingly. "No, but thank you for the gesture."

"No prob. I figured if you ate them, I'd win brownie points for best husband, and if you didn't, I could torture you by showing you what you were missing."

"Knobhead," I huffed and laughed simultaneously.

"Stuck up," he said cheerfully, taking another bite.

This was too much. The smell. The aesthetically pleasing, golden squares. The melting butter. The chocolate. The man who ate them.

"Oh, fine!" I plopped down next to him, prying the fork from his hand savagely. "I'll try your bloody waffles."

He watched me intently, a smile on his face. The bastard was gloating. I was about to stab him with the very fork I'd just pried from his fingers.

I took a bite with a perfect waffle-butter-chocolate ratio, then proceeded to close my eyes and moan. This was unreal. Sweet and salty in equal measures. Still hot, crispy on the outside, and soft on the inside.

No way the man was this gorgeous, this good in bed, *and* knew how to make the best waffles in America. He was a weapon of mass destruction.

"This is awful," I cried out, taking another bite.

He was full on grinning now. "Yeah, looks like you're suffering."

"By that, I mean that it's delicious. Where did you learn how to make them?"

"Belgium."

I almost forgot he traveled the world, picking up tricks and tidbits everywhere he went for his bag of talents.

"Do you always learn how to cook the local food everywhere you go?"

He slipped an arm around my shoulder. "All I can say is, you should try my pizza."

Ugh. This man was great for my sex life and horrible for my waistline.

"This"—I pointed with my fork—"is the best waffle I've ever tasted. Better than the one at that diner. What's your secret ingredient?" I demanded. "It's not yeasted batter. I know because I've tried."

He made a zipping motion with his mouth.

"You're seriously not going to tell me?" I thundered. So far we'd managed not to broach the subject of us having sex. Maybe he'd forgotten about it altogether? He did seem to smoke pot quite excessively.

"My waffles are my leverage. I'm not going to give it away without serious concession on your behalf." He stood up, trekked to the kitchenette, and seized a beer from the fridge. He felt at home. He *looked* at home too. And that was an even bigger problem.

He shut the fridge with his foot. "What's up with you? What are you doing today?"

I groaned, finishing off the rest of his waffles. "Looking for jobs, what else?"

"Didn't you say no one would consider you before you get your visa?"

I nodded solemnly, running the pad of my index finger over the chocolate residue on the plate, sucking it clean. *The visa.* We hadn't even discussed the blasted thing since we got married, because I'd been avoiding him. Since when was I so bloody scatterbrained? "I think they're worried it's going to take time. The timeline for being granted a visa can be unpredictable. Not to mention, the last place said they're interviewing to fill out the positions in the next few weeks. They can't wait four or five months."

He took a pull of his beer, and I pretended not to notice he was drinking at eight thirty in the morning. "So why don't you wait it out?"

I smiled calmly. "That's a very good question, Riggs. The answer is—because money doesn't grow on trees."

At this point, I was seriously considering doing the odd admin job and getting paid under the table just to resume the money flow. I was worried about paying my rent and all the bills without a steady income. There was only so much strain I could put on my savings.

"Take the day off," he suggested unhelpfully.

"I can't do that," I said.

"Tag along with me."

"I'm sorry, did you lose your hearing in the time between now and five minutes ago?" I frowned. "I can't afford to take a day off, Riggs. I'm literally on the verge of shoeshining to keep my head above water."

He looked bored with the conversation. How couldn't he understand? Clearly, he was no stranger to hardship.

"Tell you what." He spun the beer bottle's cap on his index finger, like it was a basketball. "We'll make a stop at that lawyer lady's office and fill out our visa application."

"All I can hear is more money for me to spend."

"Would you stop talking about money?" he asked through gritted teeth.

"Would you stop pretending it is not an issue for both of us?" I countered.

"I'll pay you to spend the day with me!" he snapped. "Happy?"

I jerked back and laughed so hard my stomach hurt. "Thanks for the laugh. I needed that." I stood up, carrying the plate to the sink.

"And for the waffles too. They were marvelous. Shall I grab ramen for dinner? My treat."

His gaze followed me. "I'm serious. I'll pay you to spend the day with me. I need an assistant for my *Discovery* project."

"Since when do you need an assistant?" I narrowed my eyes.

"Since today," he said grumpily.

"You've never needed one before."

"Don't question my process." He scowled.

Suppressing a smile, I asked, "All right. What does an assistant do for you?"

Please say "Suck me off," I thought, followed by the harrowing question—*Since when did I start talking like that? Even in my head?*

Riggs rubbed his chin, mulling over the question. "Carry my equipment, help me set up the lighting, serve as a placeholder when I try out different lenses . . ." He frowned. "Polish my shoes, wipe my ass, stroke my co—"

"As much as *this* assistant would like to sue you for sexual harassment, I can do without the rest of this sentence," I singsonged, rinsing the plate in the sink. "How much are you paying?"

Not that it mattered. I wasn't in a position to negotiate. Minimum wage would be fine.

Riggs slung his elbows over the counter, his body angled toward mine. "What's the rate for photography assistants these days?"

"I have no idea." I laughed. "I just became one fifteen seconds ago."

"Two grand? Flat rate for the entire date?" he suggested.

"Two *grand*?" I spluttered. "Riggs, how are you going to come up with that kind of money? You can't even pay for the subwa—" I zipped it, perhaps a moment too late, seeing as he was now looking at me with an unidentified expression that made me want to swallow all my words back.

"It's all about money for you, isn't it?" he asked quietly.

"I mean . . . isn't it to everyone?"

He shook his head, looking pensive.

"To answer your question, while I can't afford it, the company can. *Discovery* pays for my photography aide. It's a perk. So I'll pay you and send the bill to them."

That sounded so . . . *odd*. At the same time, for a reason I couldn't quite fathom, I knew Riggs was going to come up with that money. He'd never let me down before and had always made good on his promises. *Unlike BJ.*

Speaking of the knobhead, I could use a distraction. Working with Riggs for the day would not only be good for my wallet but also my psyche. Besides, how bad could it be, working for the man I'd married to deceive the authorities and had had wild sex with just yesterday? What could *possibly* go wrong?

"What if the solicitor doesn't have time for us today?" I asked, remembering we needed to send our application to the USCIS.

He laughed sardonically. "Do you know who I a—" Riggs stopped abruptly, clearing his throat. "She will. She's a good friend of Christian's."

Did he just pull the Do-you-know-who-I-am routine? How peculiar. He was literally . . . well, I was going to say no one, but that wasn't right. He was a *lot* for me.

"So where are we off to, partner?" I offered Riggs my pinkie.

"The most romantic place in the world." He laced his pinkie in mine, swinging our arms together while taking another sip of his beer. "An abandoned prison."

Felicity Zimmerman had a corner office in one of Manhattan's glitziest skyscrapers. She was a freakishly attractive woman in her forties and treated us as if we were royalty. She said she'd hold our hands through the entire process, first filing for a CR1 visa and then, two weeks after, a green card.

She went on to fill out the I-130A form with us and said she'd send it from her office and pull some strings with her friends in the immigration office. It all sounded very reassuring and terribly expensive.

Felicity explained that since Riggs was the petitioner, he wouldn't have to attend the interview himself, but that it would look lovely if he accompanied me when the time came.

"Optics are the name of the game." She looked between us, making eye contact to ensure we were on board. "And since everything you've filed in your I-130A is fairly recent, establishing a strong relationship and for Mr. Bates to show up with you would put the adjudicating officer at ease. Even if he won't be able to enter the actual interview."

"That's fine," Riggs said. "I'll make sure I'm there."

At the end of the hour, I asked Felicity how much she charged. Probably I should've begun with that question, but I didn't want to be anxious the entire meeting.

"Nine hundred per hour." She smiled.

"*Cents?*" I hoped.

Riggs laughed. I whimpered. When we left her office, he patted my back.

"Don't worry, Poppins. We'll sell your organs on the black market."

CHAPTER TWENTY

DUFFY

Riggs wasn't joking.

Abandoned prison wasn't a euphemism for something else.

It was *actually* where he'd taken me.

"Is that . . . ?" My breath hitched. I put a hand to my heart, only to find it trying to drill its way out of my chest and run away, like the rest of me should.

Riggs and I were upstate, at the Northeastern Penitentiary, where he'd so far taken hundreds of pictures of eerie kitchens, exposed walls, rat-riddled corridors, and dirt roads. Now we were in a particularly small room, and I was standing in front of a funny-looking seat, running my fingers over its headrest.

"An electric chair?" Riggs crouched on one knee, camera in hand, taking a picture of the chair. "Yup. That's Old Sparky, all right. Now get out of the frame, Poppins."

I gasped, jumping back. "Bollocks. I touched it."

"You do know it's not plugged in anymore, right?" He moved across the room to take a picture from a different angle.

"So what? I *touched* it, Riggs." I was hyperventilating. "People died on this thing. Their eyes popped out while they were sitting here."

"That's a myth, kid."

"Is it, though?"

"They used to cover their eyes so they wouldn't roll on the floor and weird everyone out." He snapped his gum, taking position on the other side of the room, his camera *click-click-clicking* away. "Besides, it's not like now that you touched it, the ghost of a gnarly-looking executed murderer is going to chase you."

"I think I'm gonna throw up." I clutched my stomach.

"I see a theme here." Riggs chuckled. "You should get checked for reflux."

Mumbling something unintelligible toward him, I created more space between the chair and me. The chair was rooted to the floor, its red vinyl pads still pristine, in contrast to the ruins around it.

Wait a minute. Red vinyl pads . . .

It was a barber chair.

I hurried to Riggs, smacking his shoulder. Said shoulder was already quivering with barely restrained laughter, making the camera shake in his hands.

"You bastard!"

"Come on! In the words of every asshole who deserves to be locked behind bars for rape—you were asking for it." He snickered, straightening.

"Just like them, *you* deserve to be castrated." I shoved at his chest.

He grabbed my wrist and kissed the inside of it, in the sensitive spot where you spritz your perfume. "That's very convenient of you, Daphne."

Daphne? "Convenient how?" I eyed him suspiciously.

"You using the goods, then throwing them away." He gave me his back. "Grab my backpack. Let's get more pictures of those rusty exposed pipelines. They were cool."

I grabbed his heavy backpack, trailing behind him. Riggs had put me to work in the five hours we'd spent together. If I thought he was going to hand me free cash because he felt bad for me, I was sorely mistaken. I set up umbrella reflectors, carried his equipment, cleared spaces he wanted to take pictures of, fetched him water, did all the driving from prison to prison, and kept a chart of all the places we'd been to, the names, the rooms, the history—everything.

As we were working, I was already writing down notes about each section of the penitentiary, which Riggs could later give to his editor. To be honest, I loved doing this more than any job I'd held in the news. It wasn't glamorous, but it was fascinating. It made me rethink my entire way of operating. What if money *wasn't* the most important thing after all? What if it was passion for life that gave you satisfaction? There was something about capturing a moment in time—a moment you were present in, that belonged uniquely to you—that called out to me. I thought about all the times I'd pulled out my album pictures from the attic to revisit my favorite memories, and realized I liked timeless things. Pictures were timeless. The news? Fluid and ever changing.

The prison we were in had operated from 1842 to 1966 and housed some of the most lethal criminals and murderers in New York's history. At least 215 men had been executed here. It felt surreal to be in such a place. I hadn't felt this challenged, this alive, this acute, in a long time.

We were walking through a long corridor with high ceilings and cobwebs and dirt everywhere. The place looked like it was caving in to itself.

"Didn't you say you have a few more prisons to take photos of tomorrow?" I pried, trying to keep up with my fake husband's pace.

He was still snapping his gum, flipping through the pictures on his camera without slowing down. "Yeah. Why? You in the mood to make more cash?"

I pressed my lips into a thin line. It wasn't just the money. I was genuinely having fun.

"Two more grand wouldn't hurt," I admitted demurely.

He laughed, slinging his camera over his shoulder. "I bet."

I was surprised by how professional Riggs was. Ever since we started working, he had been laser focused. He was a completely different creature and had a strong work ethic. He was serious, talented, innovative, and above all . . . he took really bloody good pictures. I would hang them on my wall if I could ever afford them.

Well, maybe not the ones we were taking now, of rusty pipes, but still.

"Let's see how your trial run goes." Riggs cut a corner suddenly, and I followed his lead.

"Rubbish!" I cried out. "You know I'm the best employee you've ever had. Possibly the *only* one, but also—"

I sent my foot forward and suddenly felt nothing but air beneath it. We were on the third floor of the building. I had a cartoon moment as I looked down beneath me and realized I was in the air.

Oh, shit. I'm going to die.

Riggs grabbed the back of my dress quickly and pulled me with a low growl. I staggered backward and fell on my arse.

Holy hell. He saved me from a sure death. One of the building's outer *walls* was missing.

"You okay?" He squatted, offering me his hand. I took it, still panting. Adrenaline laced through my veins like poison, and I felt sick with fear and relief.

"I . . . I think so. *Whoa.*"

"Yeah." He glanced around us, dark fury clouding his features. "I'm going to rip Emmett a new one for not telling me about this missing wall. You sure you aren't hurt? You took a tumble." His hands were all over my face and shoulders, and they were shaking. Why were they shaking? And why did I find it more pleasurable than any encounter I'd had with BJ?

We were standing in a tiny cell. The brick walls were completely covered in moss, and there were dozens of old, doorless laundry machines stacked in lines. But the most interesting thing was the missing wall. A part of the building had collapsed, which made for an amazing view. Endless green fields with high weeds swayed under the sun.

"I'm sure." I dusted myself off. "I'm a little shocked, but I'm fine."

"Good." He rolled his tongue over his inner cheek. "Because you on the floor with your panties exposed brought back good memories." He grinned.

What . . . ? *Ohhh.* The night at Gretchen's. Of course.

But also . . . *Gretchen.* That cow.

I hadn't thought of her for so long, too busy with the fake wedding, the visa, and BJ. Had Riggs been in contact with her? He hadn't talked about her since the day at her office, but I wasn't so stupid to think they didn't sleep together anymore. Which made me queasy. Sharing a knob with Gretchen Beatty was a bitter pill to swallow.

"What's wrong, Poppins?" Riggs peered into my face. I really had my heart on my sleeve, didn't I? "You sure you aren't hurt?"

"Yes, yes." I wiped my forehead. "Brilliant."

I didn't want to ask him, but I didn't want to not-ask him either. I needed to know.

It was already three o'clock, and we still hadn't had our lunch, so I decided this was a good opportunity to redirect the subject.

"I packed us some lunch!" I said, perking up. "You know, because I'm the best assistant in the whole world and you should absolutely hire me tomorrow. Shall we take a break?"

He frowned. "I say I need to see what you packed first. You're very good at making gross food—no offense."

I shot him a scowl. "Sandwiches."

"With carbs? And meat? And *flavor*?" He squinted suspiciously.

"A breadless lettuce sandwich for me and a normal wheat sandwich for you. With salami and cheddar and plenty of sodium and cholesterol."

Riggs nodded. "You speak my love language."

But when we sat down with our sandwiches, the great vibe we had going all day was gone.

"So, you planning on going back home for a visit soon? Take advantage of your vacation?" Riggs took a bite.

"Hmm, no."

"Why?"

I ducked my head and blushed.

"Right. Money." He said the word like it was dirty.

"Actually, not *just* money," I said. "I can't leave the US while my visa application is processing."

Which was a shame, because I missed my family dreadfully.

"Any other summer plans?" he probed.

"Not really." I nibbled on my iceberg lettuce, which had veggies, tofu, and quinoa inside it. "I should probably start working on my contacts in the city, though. Put myself out there."

"Find another rich groom to lock down?" he asked wryly.

I ignored his jab.

"Might get a facial next week. I have an unused voucher." I shrugged, staring at my food dispassionately.

He scratched his head. I looked everywhere but at him. After two full minutes of silence, he snapped.

"Okay, can you tell me what the fuck happened between my saving your ass and you acting like I pushed you to your death? Because I *know* you're not this boring."

"How do you know?" I challenged, annoyed that he'd called me out on my childish behavior.

"Because"—he let out an exasperated growl—"you're the only woman in the world I like to speak with. And before you call me a pig, I don't like talking to men either. So just tell me what I need to apologize for and we'll call it a fucking day. I don't wanna hear about your *facials*."

I stared at him, miserable. I wanted to ask about Gretchen, but I knew the wrong answer would leave me agonized. BJ cheating was bad enough, but Riggs . . . I mean, no need to pile on the bad news.

"Nothing." I pursed my lips.

"Spill it or you're fired," he said with a straight face.

"You can't fire me—the day's almost over."

"Fine. Then forget about tomorrow. I'll give the job to somebody else."

"You don't know anyone else who needs the money." Oddly, his friends were really rich.

"Charlie," he said.

Shoot. Charlie would love tagging along with Riggs. *Double shoot.* I hadn't checked on him, even though I'd been meaning to.

Might as well get it over with.

"Are you still . . ." I gulped, buying time.

He raised an eyebrow, losing patience. "Am I still what?"

"In touch with Gretchen?"

His eyebrows creased. "*This* is what got your panties in a twist?"

I hitched a shoulder up. "Let's admit it, my knickers have been twisty since last night, when you refused to get rid of them."

He smirked. "Jealous?"

I barked out a laugh. "Don't be ridiculous. My only feelings for you are fondness and friendship."

"I meant of *Gretchen*." He stared at me like I was insane as he took a slow bite of his sandwich.

"Right. Of course. I knew that." I smoothed my dress over my legs, thinking about it. Was I jealous of Gretchen? Or had I been? I wanted to be honest with him, with myself. And I also wanted to know the answer to that question, because I never dared to ask that of myself.

"I think I envy her," I admitted, finally.

He ripped another piece of bread with his teeth. "What's the difference between jealousy and envy?"

"Envy builds you and jealousy destroys you." I rolled a piece of lettuce between my fingers. "Envy is wanting something someone else has and being inspired by it. Jealousy is knowing you could never have it. And though they oftentimes wear similar masks, you can always tell them apart. Jealousy will be louder, unrestrained, and often public."

Riggs reached to ruffle my hair. I secretly loved when he did that.

"You're smart, Poppins."

I bloomed under his hooded gaze, feeling prettier and smarter than I ever had before, and wondered if this was how love felt. To feel like you completely belong and are worthy, even when showing your true self.

"So that means Gretchen was jealous of you, and you were envious of Gretchen," Riggs concluded. "Because what I've seen in her office was sure unrestrained and public."

"What could Gretchen be jealous of?" I let out a bark of a laugh. "She has everything, and I have nothing."

"You have youth," he pointed out. "And wits. You're funny, you're smart, you think on your feet, and—fine, I'll give it to you—you're a great employee, and she knows that."

"Maybe." I *hmmed*. "But that doesn't answer my question—are you still in touch with her?"

He gave me a smart-ass smirk. "No comment."

I wanted to strangle him for not giving me a straight answer, but I didn't sulk and forced myself to take part in our conversation as we finished our sandwiches.

"So . . . how long have you been a mountain climber?"

"*Mountaineer*," he corrected. "Since I was eighteen. But even before that, I liked climbing shit. Rooftops, trees, whatever."

"You really want to die, don't you?" I squeezed a pitted olive between my fingers, watching it spurting oil.

He laughed. "Actually, climbing a roof when intoxicated is much more dangerous than climbing Everest with the help of oxygen bottles, a Sherpa, and months of preparation."

"What's the appeal, though?" I asked, genuinely wanting to know.

Riggs made a shocked face. "You're asking me what the appeal is in reaching the highest point a human could set foot on?"

I nodded, shrugging. "I don't get it."

"Well, believe it or not, I don't get the appeal in laminating supermarket lists." He set his elbow on my knee casually, and my heart did something funny in my chest. "But seriously. I get off on the notion my body is capable of crazy shit. Mountain climbing speaks to that part of me that wants the validation that I'm Peter Pan."

"Peter Pan?"

"Forever young."

I didn't say anything, I was processing, when he did the impossible and actually *volunteered* some information on his own accord.

"I climbed them all. Mount Everest, K2, Kangchenjunga—"

"Not all of them," I noted, remembering his inner-arm tattoo.

He elevated an eyebrow. "Did I leave out anything? You know that Mountain Dew isn't real, right?"

"Not Denali. And since mountains are measured from base to summit, Denali is technically taller than Mount Everest." *Yup, this girl googles.* Watching him, I carefully added, "Don't tell me you're scared of climbing Denali."

Instead of taking the bait, Riggs smirked, looking proud. "You know why I didn't climb Denali."

"Because you never want to visit Alaska."

"Ten points to the woman with the pretty purple eyes." He grabbed the bottle of water I'd brought for him, chugging it down.

"Why is that?" I pressed. "You don't strike me as someone who's afraid of anyone or anything. What's in Alaska that makes you so terrified of visiting there?"

Tipping his chin up, Riggs watched me through hooded eyes. I could practically hear the wheels in his head turning. How much should he tell me? And why should he, anyway?

"We might need that for the marriage-based immigration interview." I licked my lips, swallowing. "I should know."

"Why would they care that I've never visited Alaska?" He frowned.

"Because!" I laughed nervously. "They'll see that you've climbed all the other mountains. Your name is on the internet. You've done interviews. They'd want to know if you confided in me. Your loving wife."

It sounded like such a fantastically daft excuse, even to my own ears. And still, Riggs looked like he was torn between talking about it and shutting me down.

I waited quietly, holding my breath. I didn't know why it was so important for me to hear his Alaska story. Maybe because I knew, deep down, that he'd never shared it with anyone else.

"Guess it all boils down to mommy issues." He sighed, kicking back on his elbows, stretching his long legs.

"I thought your mom was from San Francisco?" I asked tentatively.

"She was. She died in Alaska, though." There was a pause, in which I could see him physically struggling to push the words out of his mouth.

"Alaska was the last place she'd run to after my grandfather told her to get her shit together and take care of me. Her no-good boyfriend was there, so that's where she went. Apparently, once she got there, she found Nameless Boyfriend in a compromising position with a teenybopper who wasn't her and lost her shit. She stole his pickup truck and drove off. Wanted to stick it to him, I guess." A bitter smile marred his beautiful face.

A terrible feeling crept over me, and I couldn't help but flinch, my muscles stiff, as I braced myself for what he was about to tell me.

"She might've been drunk or something, though they never found anything in her system." Riggs clucked his tongue. "Or maybe she committed suicide. Who the hell knows? All I know is that she drove herself right off the road with complete disregard for who she left behind. The bottom line is, Alaska made me an orphan—not just a kid with troubled parents, a straight up orphan—and, irrational or not, I refuse to set foot in it."

"I don't think it's irrational," I said quietly, drawing circles with my fingers over the dust on the exposed concrete. "I think you're protecting yourself. That's smart."

He tipped his head back and closed his eyes. I stared at him, mesmerized.

"But maybe you're not an orphan after all," I heard myself say. "Did you ever try to find your father?"

His eyes snapped open. "Shouldn't he be the one to try to find *me*?"

"Ideally," I admitted. "But we don't live in an ideal world."

"*Ideally*, he's currently six feet under."

"It wasn't his fault that she died." My voice was so quiet I was surprised he heard me.

"Maybe." His elbow was still on my knee, and his fingers tapped my leg absentmindedly. "But it was his fault she ran away. He was a cheater. That's why I'm not big on relationships. I don't want to cheat and don't want to be cheated on."

His words singed a path into my heart. His reasons for never wanting to settle down were all serious, thought through, and meticulous. That was enough to warn me against developing any kind of feelings for him. He wasn't going to change his mind.

But the need to make him feel better took over every cell in my body. I couldn't bear the idea that he was unhappy. I rolled onto my side. My bare knees hit the gravel and dust on the floor. I pushed my palms against the ground and crawled into his lap.

"Riggs," I whispered. He didn't answer, his eyes closed. The heat of his body rolled off his skin. Hesitantly, I pressed my hand to his stubbled cheek. It felt like the roles were reversed. A girl warrior saving a sleeping beauty of a prince.

"Riggs." I let my fingers skim over his face, run over the sharp angles of his cheekbones, trace the shape of his lips. "I know you're awake."

"Stop touching me," he answered gruffly.

Instead of feeling hurt and disappointed, I smiled. "Why?"

"Because you're making me want to bump uglies again, and apparently yesterday was a one-off."

I was glad his eyes were still closed. It spared me the embarrassment of being seen as red as a beet.

"It doesn't have to be a one-off." I could barely hear my own voice.

He popped his eyes open. He had that sultry James Dean look, a moment before he crushed your heart into fine sand.

"I'm the same," I admitted quietly. "Well . . . not the same. I do have a family. I'm very lucky and grateful for that. But my issues stem from the same dark place yours do. My biological father left us when Kieran and I were three. Just buggered off to an unspecified place in the world with his new girlfriend. One day, he just wasn't there anymore. Cell phone changed, no trace. Mind you, he was still married to Mum, which made her getting a divorce quite a pricey and long process. I don't know what would have happened if she hadn't met Tim. We wouldn't have survived." I pursed my lips, realizing I hadn't admitted this to anyone before, not even to BJ. Not even *Kieran*. "In the years before Tim, we couldn't afford electricity. We could barely afford bread. Kieran and I would sleep huddled together long after it was appropriate just to keep each other warm during the winters. People at school would throw sandwiches at me because I didn't bring a lunch box. Sometimes I was desperate enough to go back and pick some of them up, and eat them in secret, in the loo. I always blamed him, though. My dad."

I inhaled deeply, trying to stop myself from shaking. "When Tim entered the picture, things began to change. We're doing a lot better now. But I think . . . I think the damage has been done. I have daddy issues. Maybe that's why I accept BJ. I think deep down I've come to the realization that if I cannot have the security of being loved unconditionally by a man, at least I should marry one who'd make sure I'd never be like my mum. Merely scraping by, counting the pennies every week before she went to the shops."

Riggs stared at me, looking both sexy and contemplative. After a long silence, he reached to tuck a flyaway behind my ear.

"Thank you for sharing this with me." His voice was rough with emotions.

I smiled. "I'm better now. Even though I'm a gold digger."

"I'm better too," he assured me. "Even though I'll never fall in love, have children, do the whole mundane-life shit."

"What are you thinking about?" I let my fingers travel down his chest.

"I'm thinking . . ." He bit his inner cheek, his eyes becoming smoldering in a nanosecond. "Why is the objective of golf playing the least amount of golf? Doesn't it defeat the purpose of golfing?"

"Wh-what?" My fingers stopped moving across his chest, and I blinked in confusion. To my expression, he threw his head back and laughed. I started laughing too.

"You're such an eejit," I murmured.

"To answer your question." He rearranged himself while I was still atop him. "I'm wondering what you taste like."

"You already know what I taste like, silly."

"No." His gaze traveled down between my thighs. "Not in the way I want to."

"Oh," I said.

"Two O's." He winked, then took my hand and put it on his hard-on through his pants. "Guaranteed."

He crashed his mouth against mine, thrusting his tongue between my lips. He knocked the oxygen out of me, and I had no choice but to surrender, my toes curling in my sandals as he deepened the kiss, conquering every part of my mouth while flipping our positions, with him towering over me again and me pinned on the ground beneath him.

There was something almost punishing about the intensity of that kiss, of his weight pressing against mine. Like I'd pried his secret out of him—and now I needed to pay.

Reaching down, he grabbed my arse cheeks and pressed my core against his erection, releasing a feral growl. This was divine torture.

"Riggs—" I was about to give him the okay to ravish me to a point of extinction when he dragged his hard-on against me, making my entire body clench in anticipation. My clit throbbed. I didn't understand it. We'd touched for an entirety of eighty seconds, and I was already so close to the edge.

"Ahhhh." I let my head drop to the floor, not caring about how filthy it was. "Please suck at oral. I cannot afford to be married to a sex legend."

His muffled chuckles reverberated inside my body as his mouth moved slowly from my neck south. "You're the best thing to happen to me this year, Poppins."

I wished he hadn't said that, because my systems were crashing all over to this statement. Moving from *Goodness, he really likes me* to *Just this year? How seasonal. How small. How insignificant.*

Before I could dwell on his last sentence, his mouth clamped onto one of my tits through my dress and bra, creating a warm, wet stain that engulfed it. I shivered, lust coursing through me. The pleasure was unbearable, and it built up even more when his hot mouth moved across my dress farther down, leaving damp, hot kisses I could feel through the fabric.

Then he did something terrible and decided to focus on kissing my hip bone, again and again and again. I wriggled and wailed, thrusting my groin up toward his face savagely. I'd never realized how sensitive that region of my body was. Each time his tongue swirled around my hip bone teasingly, I giggled, feeling a wetness pooling in my knickers.

"Please, just stop." My teeth sank into my lower lip.

He stopped immediately, raising his head to look at me.

"What do you think you're doing?" I barked.

"You told me to stop." He smirked.

"Ohmigod, *continue!*"

"Getting mixed signals over here."

I took his hand and brazenly shoved it between my legs. Even through my knickers, my body gave a clear message. "I'm ready for the final act!"

"You're really bossy for an employee, you know that?" Riggs finally—*finally!*—decided to put me out of my misery, flipping the hem of my dress up and reaching to stroke me through my underwear.

"I'm not wearing my employee hat," I informed him, pressing against his hand, begging for more friction. "I'm wearing my wife hat."

"Well, Mrs. Bates." He tugged my knickers to one side, the tip of his index finger tracing my opening deliciously slow. "You may leave your metaphorical hat, but all the other clothing items, I'm getting rid of."

He pushed my dress all the way up my neck and released my breasts from my bra without removing it, pushing it down. He dipped his head between my legs and, with my panties still drawn to one side, had his first taste of me.

I shuddered all over. "Had I known sex could be this way, I'd actually give it a real go."

Riggs bit and nibbled, licked and stroked, but completely ignored my clit. I took it to mean he wanted to spare both of us the embarrassment of my reaching an orgasm before the event even started.

But this was almost worse. The bringing me to the edge, only to pull me away, was horrible. It was surreal. Watching his blond head between my legs and the backdrop of a summer field overlooking the abandoned prison we were in. I realized that one day I was going to remember this moment—replay it in my head countless times—as one of my sweetest, most cherished and joyful moments. I couldn't, for the life of me, think of one moment with BJ that could compete with the total bliss I was feeling right now.

"I'm sorry," Riggs groaned between my legs, his hands hiking up to catch my waist and pin me down so I couldn't fidget.

"Sorry for what?" I mumbled, confused.

"I can no longer not pay attention to this beautiful clit of yours."

His lips closed down on my clit, and he sucked on it hard before using the tip of his tongue to stroke it.

I fell apart. It was like nothing I'd ever experienced before. The sheer pleasure was so foreign, so potent, I thought I might expire in his hands.

Death by an orgasm. Not the most elegant way to go, but a lovely one nonetheless.

After my climax had subsided, Riggs fell next to me like a heavy beast, our shoulders brushing. I turned to him, grinning. "My turn."

He shook his head. "I hate reciprocated oral sex. The second one to give the goods always does it out of obligation."

I frowned. "That's not true. I want to do that. I've been wanting to do that since . . ." I hesitated.

Riggs stared at me intently.

"Since I first saw you," I admitted. "Oh, blast it. I said it out loud, didn't I?"

"You did," he confirmed. "And I believe you. But now's not a good time."

"When then?"

"Surprise me. I'm not short of morning wood, and you're not short of waking up way too damn early."

Ten minutes later, we were already up on our feet and dressed. The space between my thighs was still throbbing and pulsating.

"Grab the gear. We're outta here," Riggs said, heading out through the laundry room like he hadn't just served me with the best oral sex of my life.

I followed him, watching his muscular back and his lithe movements. Guess we were back to being an employer and an employee.

"Poppins?" he asked, his back still to me.

"Yeah?"

"I'm not in touch with Gretchen. Haven't been since that day in her office. Stopped taking her calls."

"How come?" My heart beat so hard I could swear it was bruised and mangled in my chest.

Riggs didn't turn to look at me or break his stride. "Nobody says things like that to my wife and keeps their teeth to repeat them." He pulled the door open for me. "Since they cost a fortune at the dentist, I spared her teeth, but I'm done picking up her calls."

Undiluted pride filled my chest, spreading to other organs in my body. Or maybe it wasn't pride. Maybe it was something much more dangerous.

Something that I didn't want to think about.

Something I had never felt in my entire life.

By the time we got back into the city, it was already late in the evening. The sun hung low, grazing the skyscrapers.

Riggs and I lazed to our front door. I was exhausted. I couldn't remember the last time my limbs had felt so deliciously sore.

"Please tell me you're too pooped to make a salad smoothie or whatever and that we can just order in." He pushed the door open for me with his shoulder.

I sighed. "You're a bad influence."

"The good one is boring, so don't pretend like you aren't having fun."

We took the stairs up side by side, even though the stairway was narrow. He slowed down to my pace.

"Fine," I bit out. "As long as it's Thai."

"Fuck Thai." He took his equipment from me, probably realizing I was about to drop and break it. "We had that last week. Let's try the kebab shop down the street."

"I don't eat kebab," I informed him. "Or any other fatty meat."

"But you just said earlier you wanted to blow me."

I swatted his shoulder on autopilot. We had routines now. That was terrifying. Riggs laughed, but when we rounded the stairway to our floor, the laughter died in his throat. We both halted. Charlie was in the hallway, trying to pick a lock.

Our lock.

"Charlie?" I frowned. "You all right, mate?"

"Yeah . . . yeah . . ." Charlie—big, tall, handsome, movie-star-look-alike Charlie—spun slowly on his heel, looking left and right. More than anything, looking confused. "I'm just . . . I think I forgot my key?"

"*And* your door," Riggs muttered under his breath. Aloud, he said, "Let's track your last steps. Where'd you come from just now?"

"The diner, I think." Charlie grimaced. "Or was it yesterday?"

Riggs and I turned to each other. What was going on? Charlie didn't *look* drunk and didn't smell drunk. This seemed more like an episode of sorts.

"Charlie . . . ," I said softly, stepping forward. "I think you've got the wrong door."

He whipped his head toward my door and scratched his head. "Huh. Right. Mine says twenty-four, not twenty-two."

"We can call a locksmith," I suggested.

"I don't have anything on me," Charlie said, patting his front pockets. "No ID, no wallet . . ."

My gaze instinctively dropped down to said pockets, and I let out a gasp, slapping my mouth. There was a large, round stain around his groin area. He'd *soiled* himself. This vital, handsome grown man, who wasn't intoxicated or impaired in any way I could see, had peed himself.

Riggs must've seen the same thing, because he made his way toward us quickly, inserting himself as a buffer between Charlie and me, like the sweet man could ever hurt me.

"Why don't you head inside, Poppins? I'll join you in a second."

My eyes snapped from Charlie's pants to my husband. My mouth was still agape.

"I . . . I . . . he said he doesn't have any docs on him. No wallet. A locksmith won't open the door for him."

"I'm not calling a locksmith," Riggs said dryly.

Was he going to break into Charlie's flat? That was a terrible idea. Charlie was renting, like me.

"Riggs, you can't—" I started, then saw the resolute look on his face. My shoulders sagged. "I'll be inside."

"Thank you," they both said, in harmony.

Same tone. Same voice. Same low rumble.

I turned to look at them again, blinking. And suddenly, I saw something very horrible and potentially very destructive. And also improbable.

You've watched too many soap operas. Stars do not align this way in real life. Only this wouldn't be a case of stars aligning. More like a supernova full of explosions and multiple casualties.

"Well?" Riggs grumbled in frustration, no doubt eager to help Charlie without my watchful eye.

"Right. I'm leaving."

I closed the door to my flat behind me and plastered my back against it, panting.

Reeling from my new discovery.

CHAPTER TWENTY-ONE

RIGGS

Knocking down Charlie's door was the easy part. I didn't even need momentum for it. A front kick did the trick, *and* I got to feel like Kyo the Enforcer. Figuring out what had made him all confused and try to unlock *our* door and piss his pants was the impossible part.

"Hey, Charles, did you have a little drink today?" I asked, strolling into his minuscule apartment, assisting him by the elbow.

He shook his head. "No. Not in the last few days." Ah, fuck. It would have been great if he was just a sloppy drunk.

"Let me grab you some water and Advil. Be right back." I sat him on his couch.

His place was actually decent, in a Manhattan shithole standards kind of way. Lots of interesting geography and history books, cool art, shit he'd obviously collected from around the world. The sort of place I would have had, had I not been allergic to routine.

"Sure . . . ah, thanks." Charlie sat on his couch and stared at his hands, elbows propped on his knees.

I stalked to his bathroom, straight to the medicine cabinet. This wasn't about getting him a painkiller. It was about digging through his crap and figuring out what kind of pills he was taking. Maybe he'd skipped a few, and that's what had caused this episode.

In his bathroom, I went through his medicine cabinet. Xenazine, Zyprexa, Klonopin . . . I'd never heard of those before. I needed to get him that Advil before he started wondering if I was taking a shit, and then a shower right afterward.

I emerged back with two Advil and some water. Charlie gulped everything down. He stayed silent for a while. I thought about helping him to a shower but then concluded he'd just be embarrassed if I offered. Best to ignore the stain between us. A stain, by the way, that must have been itchy and was starting to smell now.

"Is there anyone I can call?" I sat on a recliner opposite him.

He shook his head. "Nope. I have no one. How pathetic is that?"

"Stop with the self-pity, Charlie." It was like looking at a mirror thirty years from now. I didn't like what I was seeing.

"I don't pity myself." He smiled. "I deserve to be alone."

Despite telling myself I didn't give a shit, I did stay with Charlie for a couple of hours. I fixed him a bowl of cereal and some coffee, wrote down my number and stuck it on his fridge, then cleaned the place a little so he wouldn't have to.

"Do you need anything else before I go?" I stood in the doorway. Truth was, I wanted to get back to Duffy as soon as I could and check on her. She liked the old man, and she'd seemed distraught to see him this way. It was grossly inconvenient that the wife I told myself was a shallow, money-grabbing stuck-up could feel so deeply for her old neighbor.

"No," Charlie said. "You've already done more than I'll deserve."

"Jesus, Charles. Dramatic much? You didn't kill my cat."

I closed the door behind me and shook my head.

Asshole was too sentimental for his own good.

◆ ◆ ◆

I checked in on Charlie in the days after the hallway incident. He seemed off, but not off enough that he was pissing his pants or forgetting where he lived. Still, he was irritable and pensive, which worried my ass. Was it time to step up and actually do something for someone else? The thought made me nauseous. At the same time, the temptation to offer him help had never been greater. Stupid fucking heart. It had been dormant for nearly forty years and all of a sudden decided to beat for all the strays in New York. Donating handsome amounts of money annually to charities and getting tax relief for it was so much more convenient. I wanted to get back to doing that.

Speaking of strays, I had another, hot issue on my hand—namely Duffy.

I ended up "hiring" my wife for three more days, a gesture of good-will I had never previously made before. If Duffy suspected the post wasn't real, she didn't say anything. I paid her in cash, since she couldn't technically work. And while it was laughable that *Discovery* would ever fund me a two-grand-a-day assistant, *she* didn't know two grand was the kind of money my eightieth butler could wipe his ass with, if I wished to have one.

She clearly needed the money, and I was clearly so pussywhipped that I saw fit to start paying her for simply existing.

Duffy was actually a good employee, even though I had to pull tasks out of my ass to keep her busy.

Ever since that first time in her room, where we'd almost burned down the building, all I could do and/or think about was putting my penis in any hole in her body that was willing to accept me. We'd been going at it like rabbits. In the apartment, in abandoned prisons, in the rental car to and from those prisons. A small part of me wanted to take her places—restaurants, the movies, picnics, vacations—just so we could screw there, but that was treading too closely to real-relationship territory, and apparently, falling in bed with her hadn't robbed me of all my gray matter.

Just 99 percent of it.

CHAPTER TWENTY-TWO

RIGGS

"How do I look?" Duffy marched out of her room, wrapped in one of her dresses. It killed me to see her hiding those curves in ruffled blouses and weird-ass frocks more fit for a runway. And I'm not talking a Victoria's Secret runway. I'm talking the designer shit I used to see when I accidentally landed on the Fashion Channel in the middle of the night as a teenager while I was high, hoping to catch a nip slip. The kind of weird, asymmetrical, sharp-edged dresses that made you wonder how much pot the designer had been smoking prior to sending out their sketches.

Couldn't she fill her closet with pencil skirts and edible thongs? What kind of gold digger was she?

A terrible one, obviously.

But she twirled in her tiny living room, looking hopeful, and I refused to kill her vibe.

"Yeah, the dress is very . . ." I cleared my throat. *"Dressy."*

I was slung on the couch, stroking my dick through my briefs. I was still crashing on the sofa, which worked well for both of us, because it made us remember there was a red line made out of fucking lava, and we were both unauthorized to cross it. "Where're you off to today?"

"The Social Circle." She bit her lip nervously, her purple eyes glittering. "It's an exclusive social club for the rich and famous. They're looking for an assistant manager. Great salary. Superb benefits. And, of course, this is the playground for the kind of men I want to bag, so Cocksucker could finally be out of the picture."

"They'll love you," I said, and meant it, still touching my cock, in case she noticed and wanted to go for a joystick ride before the job interview. "You're hardworking, highly motivated, not to mention fucking stunning. Most places just can't sponsor you at a moment's notice."

"I know." She sighed, then walked over to the shoe rack and pulled out a pair of heels. "It's so bloody frustrating."

The offer to have her work for me full time was on the tip of my tongue. Especially now, when she was shopping for her next meal ticket. I'd be able to pay her under the table, take her with me around the world, fuck her, *and* work. A quadruple win in my books, and a pretty sweet arrangement altogether. The only thing stopping me from doing so was the knowledge I was going to get bored with her in a few weeks, max. I always did.

Good thing Duffy didn't expect anything from me. When we weren't working together or screwing each other, we were just roommates who got along well. Nothing more. Nothing less.

"Well." She blew out air. "Wish me luck."

"Break a le . . . never mind." I shook my head. "It'd be a nightmare to nail you. Best of luck."

She rolled her eyes, grabbed her purse, and swatted my shoulder with it. "Check on Charlie, will you?"

251

Groaning, I peeled myself off the couch and wobbled to the fridge. "Sure. Why not. It's not like I have a job to do."

"Has Emmett said anything about the pictures?" She twisted her head to follow me while I opened the fridge.

"Yeah." I took out the milk and guzzled it straight from the carton.

"Well?" Her purple eyes lit up. I loved that she honestly cared.

"That they were perfect." I wiped my mouth with my arm before returning the milk to the fridge. "But now I need something else to keep me busy. I'm feeling claustrophobic."

"He'll give you another project soon." Her face was a vision of sympathy and hopefulness. "And soon, this will all be over and you can go back to traveling the world."

With Duffy out of the apartment, I had plenty of time to burn. I went downstairs and did some grocery shopping for that high-maintenance neighbor of ours and tried to ignore my traveling itch. The only way to scratch it was to board a plane and get the hell out of here. But I'd promised Duffy I'd be here to help her with the visa application. Responsibility sucked balls.

On my way back to the building, I stopped by a diner and grabbed Charlie some coffee and apple pie. Then I went up to check on the old man. I knocked on his door, feeling like a fucking sitcom character from the seventies. Neighborly visits didn't exactly scream the rock star life. He didn't answer.

It was possible he'd gone out somewhere.

. . . but it's also possible he's bit the dust.

Stifling a grunt, I rapped on his door again. "Charlie, it's Riggs. Answer."

Nothing. It wasn't like Charlie, who usually fell all over himself when I visited like I was the pope or something. I punched the doorbell, growing both uneasy and pissy with myself for giving two shits about this whole thing.

"Open up, Charles, or I'm kicking this door down. Gotta keep the tradition alive."

It seemed like half my time in this building was spent tearing doors down and then paying to put them back up. Was there an Olympic sport for that kind of thing?

When there was still no answer, I let go of the paper bags, took a step back, angled my shoulder, and smashed against it. The flimsy door flew open. I stepped over the brown bags I'd left on the floor earlier and waltzed inside. It had only been twelve hours since I'd last checked on him, and the place reeked.

Oh, fuck, if he died, I was going to be stuck here forever, answering police questions.

I looked around, relieved to see that the sulfur smell was coming from boiled eggs he'd left on the counter and not his decomposing body.

"Charlie?" I asked, moving around the apartment. It was bigger than Duffy's but still small enough to cover in less than two minutes. "You sick fuck, who boils eggs and keeps them on the counter?"

I walked into his bedroom. Empty. I dashed to the bathroom and opened the door. Something hard and heavy pressed against it from the other side, making it difficult to open all the way.

Shit.

Carefully, I squeezed through the gap in the door before stepping over a . . . what the hell was it? A leg. I glanced down. Charlie was lying on the floor, his eyes closed, his arms spread like he was making a snow angel. He looked young and old at the same time.

If he'd kicked the bucket, Duffy was going to be really sad. And to be honest, I would be too.

I crouched down and ran my fingers under his nose. His hot breath fanned over them, faint, but there. I let out a sigh of relief.

I fished out my cell phone and shook my head. "You're lucky I'm calling an ambulance and not the police. I would've killed you twice over if you'd messed up my day like that."

The next hour moved fast. Charlie was taken to the hospital in an ambulance. He was still unconscious, and the paramedics told me they weren't authorized to give me any information about his health, since I wasn't next of kin, but that I could visit him once he was in the books. They also said I "did the right thing." Like there was anything else to do when you find your neighbor unconscious on the floor.

I shot Duffy a message informing her about what happened, then proceeded to the Brewtherhood. The good thing about this bar was that it opened at noon, which made getting trashed not only easy but legitimized.

I was well into my third drink when my phone buzzed with an incoming call. I fished it out of my pocket and frowned. Gretchen's name flashed on the screen. I couldn't ignore her for eternity, because maturity or something. Plus, I had a thing or two to say to her.

"Hey, Riggs!" She sounded like a bundle of sunshine, like we hadn't parted ways with me being pushed to marry her assistant, who she then humiliated on their last day at the office. "How've you been, hon?"

"Did you have a personality implant last time you went for a lipo?" I leaned against the bar, squinting. "You sound—"

"Happy?" she chirped.

"*Nice*," I corrected.

"Isn't that a good thing?" It appeared like she was driving. Or, more likely, being driven.

"No." I picked up my beer and brought it to my lips. "I enjoyed your wrath in bed and never stayed long enough for the conversation."

She let out a shrill laugh. "I swear, the things that come out of your mouth."

"The things that get into yours," I retorted.

That made her laughter die. "Where are you?"

"My usual spot." She knew about the Brewtherhood because, before she moved to DC, every time I was in New York, we had an arrangement. We'd meet here and then go to her apartment.

"Great. I'm on my way." She hung up.

She was in New York? What happened to DC? Maybe POTUS had realized she had a radioactive personality and an attitude to match.

Ten minutes later, Gretchen was sitting next to me in the Brewtherhood, looking like the bombshell I'd enjoyed so much over the years. Interestingly enough, she did nothing for me now.

"I thought you were in DC," I said, wondering if my dick was broken. Gretchen never failed to make me hard. There was something about her unapologetic ruthlessness and six HIIT workouts a week that spoke directly to my cock, which was an avid listener.

"I am." She turned toward me, flashing some serious leg through her gray pencil skirt. She had that whole sexy-secretary look down to a T. "Aren't you going to ask how working for the White House is?"

"How's working for the White House?" My voice was so flat you could use it to cut a fucking salad.

"Great." She leaned into my arm. "Wonderful. POTUS is a real gem. Such a lovely man. So mild. And he sings my praises."

There was no nice way of telling her I didn't give a crap if POTUS was going to divorce his wife and marry her, so instead, I steered the conversation to where it mattered. "So what brings you to New York?"

"Meetings, back to back." She wiped invisible sweat from her brow. "One of my meetups got canceled, so I thought we'd catch up. We haven't spoken in weeks! Why is that, remind me?"

"Because you're a bitch?" I offered, remembering how she'd treated Poppins. "Also, because we only speak when one of us is in town and wants to screw the other."

She nodded, motioning toward her body with her hands. "And here I am."

I blinked at her before throwing my head back and laughing. It took me two full minutes to calm down. And in those minutes, she sat there and stared at me, wearing an expression of confusion and annoyance.

"You wanna fuck?" I asked, finally.

She pressed her lips together. "Don't act like we haven't been doing it for years, Bates."

"We had." I took a swig of my beer. "But aren't you forgetting a teeny, tiny detail?"

She tilted an eyebrow up. "Enlighten me?"

"I'm *married*."

"Married!" Now it was her turn to laugh. "Please, Riggs. We're both married by name only."

"But you do recall falling to your knees, begging me to marry your assistant, correct?"

I was starting to lose my patience. We hadn't discussed her little showdown with Duffy in all the weeks since it had happened, and now she wanted me to fall into bed with her?

Gretchen batted her long eyelashes, and all I could think about was how her eyes were boring blue and not exotically purple. "Yes. As an arrangement."

"Well, it's been arranged."

"Not to save my ass, that's for sure." She was starting to drop her sweet charade and show her true colors. "Something else made you say yes. You made it clear you didn't care about me or my career the night she caught us."

"The why isn't important. The fact that I did it is."

"Again." She sipped her wine through pinched lips. "How does it matter? The marriage isn't real!"

"It matters because I'm not going to cheat on my wife, who is waiting for a US visa, just to wet my dick," I bit out.

Now that I'd verbalized it, I realized I hadn't screwed anyone other than Duffy since that night she caught me with Gretchen. Not that I thought that the US government was the moral police. Half the politicians had affairs, drug scandals, sex tapes, and DUIs. But there was no need to pile more difficulties on Operation: Getting Duffy a Visa.

Meanwhile, Gretchen's face looked like it was about to melt into her wineglass. *Abhorred* didn't begin to cover it. She looked like I'd just informed her that I'd given her gonorrhea.

"Don't tell me . . ." She touched her neck delicately. "That you're having an *affair* with her?"

"Can you have an affair with someone you're married to?" I wondered aloud. "Kind of like being a fuck buddy with your girlfriend, no? It's all baked into the cake."

"So it's a yes!"

"It's a 'no fucking comment,'" I corrected. Then, realizing Daphne might expire if she thought her boss knew she was sampling her leftovers, I added, "I should be so lucky."

Gretchen flew up from her seat, shaking her head, her eyes wide. "No, no. Don't give me that. There's no way you're not having sex with her. Are you two living together?"

Feeling a little concerned Gretchen was going to out us, I stood up too. I grabbed my wallet and threw notes onto the bar, covering both our bills. "Don't forget this whole mess started because *you* were afraid Duffy was gonna run to the press and rat us out," I warned.

"You didn't answer my question." She blocked my way out with her body. As if that would help if I wanted to bulldoze past her.

"You didn't answer my unspoken one," I countered.

Her nostrils flared, and she took a step back. "Are you asking if I'll do something to hurt Daphne's chances of being granted a visa?"

"I'm making sure." I folded my arms over my chest.

"Well, no. I'm not that person. But now that I have a government job and rules to abide by, I can't chance a scandal. I reserve the right to—"

I raised my hand. "Stop it right there. You have no rights. None whatsoever. You lost your rights when you decided to fuck someone who wasn't your husband. You'll keep your mouth shut and stay out of our life."

Our life? Dafuq was I saying? We had no mutual life together.

"Or?" She tilted her chin up, her eyes tapering.

Seriously?

"Or I'll be the one singing to the press about our affair. I'll spare no detail, Gretchen. The props, the frequency, the faces you make when you come . . ." I let loose a spiteful, sly grin. "Trust me, I can be *very* chatty when prompted."

She took another step back, her eyes glittering with rage. "I can't believe the bitch got you."

I grabbed my phone, having had enough bullshit for the entire day. "There's only one bitch in this story, and I'm looking at her right now. Duffy may not be everyone's cup of tea—hell, who in this world is?—but what you did to her the last day of her job is unforgivable. And the worst part . . ." I shook my head, chuckling. "Is that you didn't even ask for forgiveness. Your narcissism looked really good up close when we were screwing, but from every other angle? It's really ugly. Have a good life, Gretchen. Or better yet—don't."

With those parting words, I shoved the door open and made my way to the subway. I knew Gretchen would never contact me again. Her ego was too big to sustain this kind of blow. Which worked out well, because her ego was also too fragile to survive the tell-all interview she knew I'd give the *Enquirer* if she messed with Duffy's visa somehow. I had nothing to lose.

Or so she thought.

Because now I was starting to wonder . . . *did* I have something to lose?

Was Duffy mine to lose?

I don't know, idiot, is she? Because last I checked, she is still talking about Cocksucker in the present tense and scheming how to work somewhere where she could bag a millionaire.

One thing was for sure. I had feelings toward my wife. They weren't always positive, but they were in existence.

And that was becoming a very big problem.

CHAPTER TWENTY-THREE

Riggs

Later that day, I went to the hospital to visit Charlie.

Duffy was helping her friend Laura by taking her cat to the vet, since she had a last-minute presentation. Laura, not the cat. She sounded really upset on the phone that she couldn't make it earlier and promised to visit him in the evening, once she was done.

I told her I'd keep her posted and spared her any mention of my meeting with Gretchen today. What was the point of ripping open that old wound? It wasn't like I had any news to tell. Gretchen was still an asshole.

Joining me for moral support, or more accurately so we could all get trashed afterward, were Christian and Arsène. Most people would shy away from meeting a complete stranger in a vulnerable condition. These two didn't flinch at the sight of misery, though.

"I want to see the person who makes Riggs go grocery shopping," Christian explained as he power walked through the hospital's corridors in his Tom Ford suit. "It's unfathomable that you'd give a damn about someone you don't plan on bedding."

It was a good thing I didn't tell them about my hookups with my wife. First of all, I wasn't eager to hear them say "I told you so." Second, I was strangely protective of Daphne and her privacy, especially after she'd gone viral since meeting me. *Twice.*

"I'm capable of feeling," I protested, my jaw locking in annoyance.

"Only without a condom," Arsène sneered. Christian snickered.

"What's wrong with the old man, anyway?" Arsène wondered.

"Dunno." I stopped in front of Charlie's room number and knocked on it. "Guess we'll find out now. He's supposed to be awake."

"Come in."

I heard Charlie's voice and pushed the door open.

Charlie was sitting upright in his bed, white as a Colorado Christmas but looking better than I'd seen him last week.

"Hey, R." His face broke into a tired smile. "Thanks for coming. And you brought some friends." His eyes scanned the two men behind me. "How . . . inappropriate."

Christian and Arsène chuckled behind me.

"The one in the obnoxiously expensive suit is Christian." I stuck a hand in his direction, yawning. "And the one who looks like a vampire and doesn't need a six-grand suit to feel like he's better than God is Arsène. They're my best friends."

They both reached to shake his hand.

"How's Duffy?" Charlie turned to me.

"'How's Duffy?'" I echoed, taking out my stoner kit and then rolling him a joint. Surely, he was in pain. I could wheel him out of here for a quick smoke. "I found you passed out in your bathroom. Tell me how *you* feel."

"First of all, that must be the stupidest thing anyone's done in a hospital." He pointed at the joint I was rolling. "And second, I'm good. Just had a little accident. Those happen."

"Don't bullshit a bullshitter. What's going on with you?"

Charlie looked away. "Nothing."

"Is it about these two?" I jerked my thumb behind my back. "'Cause I can kick them out. They're used to it."

Charlie munched on his inner cheek. "Drop it."

"That bad?" I asked gently.

"*Worse.*"

So it must be terminal. My heart slowed, heavy in my chest. If he didn't want to say, I didn't want to press.

"Got it. No more questions." I nodded.

"Appreciate it."

"Other than one," I amended, holding my joint up in the air between us. "Where's your wheelchair, asshole?"

It took charming two nurses and flirting with one doctor before I could get a wheelchair for Charlie. Then another fifteen minutes for us to find our way out to the communal garden. It was mostly empty. Better for us, since I'd brought over Blue Dream, my favorite weed. Chef's kiss. Michelin-starred marijuana.

I put the brakes on Charlie's chair and leaned against a fake plant, giving him the honor of lighting up. He took a long hit, waited until the smoke reached the bottom of his lungs, then released, coughing a little.

He kicked his head back and closed his eyes. "Haven't had one of those since I was twenty."

"A doobie?" I asked, surprised. "Don't like the effect?"

"On the contrary. I love it. Not so much the person it turns me into, though."

I decided not to pry, since he was already dealing with a terminal disease and the shit ton of problems it brought with it. I couldn't help but wonder what it felt like to die alone, since that was exactly what was about to happen to Charlie. And, one day, to *me*.

"Well, now that you have a mysterious disease, you can be whoever you want." I watched as he puffed on his spliff. "The perks of dying are never ending."

He laughed and coughed at the same time. "Everything has an ending. That's the point of living." There was a brief silence. "So. How *is* Duffy?"

"You're like a dog with a bone."

"Give me the meat then."

"She's fine." Then, when he kept looking at me and grinning, I groaned. "She's coming to visit you tonight."

"I'm more interested to know how *you* feel about living with her. You guys seemed close when I met you in the hallway the other day."

I liked that he didn't feel embarrassed about the state he'd been in that day.

"She's way too young." It was the only thing I could think of saying, since "She's too hell bent on marrying up" sounded lame and "I'm too scared of commitment" seemed too personal.

"If anything, you're too young for *her*." He wiggled his brows, taking another toke.

I laughed. "Are you gonna pass me that joint this century?"

"Nope."

"*Pfft.*" My eyes grazed the side of his face. "You're lucky you're dying, you know. I'm normally not that forgiving."

"So lucky." Charlie nodded weakly.

After he was done, I wheeled him back to his room and asked if I could grab him something from the cafeteria before I left. Charlie said he was good. That whole time, Christian and Arsène were waiting in the room's small balcony.

They slid the glass door and walked back inside when they noticed me helping Charlie back into his bed. There was something really

263

depressing about helping out this big, muscular man do something so trivial.

"Ready to go?" Christian clapped my shoulder.

"Yeah." I glanced at the time on my phone. "But I think I'm heading home."

"Home?" Arsène raised an eyebrow. "Nice choice of word."

"Don't read too much into it," I quipped. "Bye, Charles."

"Bye, kids." Charlie was already engrossed in a *Discovery* magazine he was flipping through.

The three of us made our way to the elevator. Christian and Arsène exchanged looks.

"Who should tell him?" Arsène asked, businesslike.

Tell who what? I was too preoccupied for his brand of bullshit.

"Not me." Christian held up his hands. "If he goes through a mental breakdown, Arya's gonna expect me to spend time with him. I lack the patience. *And* sympathy."

"Who's having a mental breakdown?" I asked, thinking they must've been continuing their conversation from the balcony.

"No one," Christian said, at the same time Arsène said, "You, idiot."

"Why would I have a mental breakdown?" We all stopped by the elevator.

Christian glanced behind his shoulder, to the room we'd just left Charlie in.

"When the old man dies."

I gave him a puzzled look. "He's a nice guy, but a meltdown is a stretch."

The elevator slid open.

"Maybe it's my destiny"—Arsène shook his head, looking upward—"to be surrounded by morons."

The day just kept going progressively shittier.

After bailing on drinks with my friends, I made my way back to Duffy's. When I got to her floor, I couldn't find the door. Not because it had disappeared, but because there were approximately eighty thousand fucking roses waiting for her, blocking the path to the entire hallway.

Who did something so stupid? Sent someone who lived in a tiny apartment in New York thousands of roses, cramming up the entire goddamn building? But the answer was clear—Cocksucker. Cocksucker, who never had to live anywhere smaller than four-thousand-square-foot houses, even in college, I bet.

There were roses everywhere. Red roses. White roses. Pink roses. Yellow roses.

Roses didn't make up for the fact that the man fucked someone else in Thailand. *Or* that he was in Thailand, not Nepal. *Or* that he'd left her. Man, if she took him back, she'd be the biggest idiot on Planet Earth.

No. That would be you. For buying into your sham fucking relationship.

Upon closer inspection, I realized that on each of the roses was a petal with the imprint *Please forgive me.* I bet he thought it was a nice touch.

Somehow, I managed to push through and get to the door. Normally, if any packages were outside, I brought them inside. Not this time. We didn't have space to store all of BJ's *I know I fucked up* flowers. Even if we did, I wasn't going to help his cause.

Inside was a Tupperware container waiting on the counter, along with a note.

I walked over to it and picked up the note.

> Riggs,
> Interview was cut short due to my visa situation (it's fine, I'm over it), so I had time to stop at the flat.
>
> I made you some stuffed zucchini. You can't live off junk. Eat it. It's an order.

Also, the neurologist's office called. They had to move your appointment. Please call them to reschedule.

BBL.

Poppins.

It was that gesture that really did it. I wasn't planning on getting rid of Cocksucker's flowers. But seeing how thoughtful and inherently fantastic this woman was, I couldn't chance her going back to this jerk. She was too good for him. It was time to intervene and do the world a favor.

I marched back outside and threw out all the roses. Stuffed all of them into a dumpster downstairs.

She was going to find out sooner or later that he'd sent her flowers and that I threw them out, but not today, and probably not tomorrow either. Besides, the momentary satisfaction of sticking it to that asshole was worth her future wrath.

I went back upstairs and wolfed down her zucchini dish. It still tasted too healthy for me to seriously enjoy it, but at least it wasn't a lettuce sandwich.

I hopped into the shower, got out, and walked over to the couch. Duffy had left her iPad there, probably when she was in a hurry to get out and help Laura with her cat. I picked it up to put it aside. It was an old-school iPad, without an automatic password authenticator.

As soon as I grabbed it, the screen flashed with an incoming message. It must've been connected to her phone.

The message was from BJ.

I'm coming home for you, Duffy.

CHAPTER TWENTY-FOUR

DUFFY

I'm coming home for you, Duffy.

Rolling my eyes so hard I was stunned they didn't end up all the way in Hoboken, I swiped my finger to delete the message. The alternative was to reply with something snarky to BJ, along the lines of "I know you're good at coming, but I wish you'd reciprocate sometimes." These days, I'd been riding the O train at least three times a day. It was always on time and reached its destination unfailingly. The only reason I didn't rub my relationship with Riggs in BJ's face was because I didn't want to reduce Riggs to a mere rebound. He was so much more than that.

Oh, and because the relationship wasn't, you know, *real*.

The latter was something I had to remind myself repeatedly as I found myself doing wifely things for him. Cook for him, cuddle with him, tell him about my darkest secrets and naughtiest desires while we were wrapped up in one another, limbs tangled, hearts beating to the same rhythm.

Slipping my phone back into my purse, I dashed down the corridor to Charlie's hospital room. I felt bad for not dropping everything and rushing to his aid when I found out he'd been admitted, but earlier today Laura called to tell me her kitten, Bubsy, had fallen from the top cabinet of her kitchen. She saw him on the nanny cam while at work but couldn't tend to him until later tonight. I wanted to repent for how shitty I'd been to her in recent years, so I rushed to her aid.

Now I was in front of Charlie's door, dreading to open it and see what waited inside. Not only did I like my old neighbor quite a bit, but if I really was right about who he was to Riggs (which seemed unlikely and yet so incredibly obvious at the same time), I had a moral dilemma on my hands.

I knocked on the door.

"Come in, Daphne."

I pushed the door open and padded inside sheepishly. Charlie was lying in the hospital bed, hooked up to all sorts of monitors. He looked pale and sickly and not himself.

I plastered a smile on my face and presented him with a slice of pineapple pizza—his favorite—and a can of Coke.

"Medicinal junk food," I announced.

"Just what the doctor ordered." His eyes lit up, but the rest of him remained dimmed, curled over the big bed like a book-pressed flower.

Plopping on the recliner, I speared him with a chiding look. "You've got a lot to answer for, mister. You should've told me."

He coughed into his fist before tucking into the pizza, not meeting my eyes. "You've been busy recently. Plus, I don't go advertising my sickness for all to see."

"That's not what I'm talking about." I followed him with my gaze. His movements were slow and labored. "You know bloody well I'm not talking about your illness. Though we'll get to that too."

He sighed, dropping the pizza onto the paper plate. *"Fuck."*

So it was true, then. My chest felt like someone was trying to wring it dry.

"Language," I said haughtily. "But yes, *fuck* sums it up nicely."

"I guess someone needs to know." Charlie looked around us, as if making sure we were indeed alone. "And I guess that someone must be you, since you're the one constant person in my life."

"Don't sound so depressed. You could've had worse company. Have you met my *roommate*?" I wiggled my brows.

I watched his reaction hawkishly. He let out a tired laugh but stopped quickly. It must've hurt his lungs. I had no idea what he was here for. I assumed it had something to do with his episode earlier that week.

"Can we talk about it in a second?" He gulped, his face wrinkling with anxiety. "Because what I have . . . it's bad, Duffy. Really bad."

"Alcohol-poisoning bad?" I asked. He'd been moved from the ER to the ICU, but I still had no idea what he was here for.

"No."

"Cancer bad?"

He shook his head. "Huntington's disease."

My spine went rigid. *Huntington's disease?* The name was familiar, but I knew nothing about it. Only that it was quite rare and deadly.

"You look so surprised you'd think I told you I was pregnant." He reached for his nightstand to pop open the can of Coke. "To make a long story short, it's a disease in which the nerve cells in your brain rot progressively, until you can barely move, think, or speak."

"You mean . . . like ALS?" I gulped.

Charlie unleashed a soft smile. "No. ALS at least leaves your mind unaffected. Your healthy mind is essentially trapped in a body that deteriorates. Huntington's disease is an overachiever. It robs you of your mind *and* your body."

I had so many questions. So many things I wanted to know. But the one big thing that stood in front of me was the realization that Charlie was dying. Dying and lonely. The only people who'd visited him were Riggs and me, and we lived next door.

"How long have you been suffering from this?" I tucked my hands between my thighs so he wouldn't see me shaking.

He blew out air, swinging his gaze up to the ceiling. "Probably close to six years, I'd say."

"I never saw you looking . . . uh . . ." I trailed off. I wasn't sure what the warning signs were.

"Yes," he said, and I noticed that his speech was slower than usual. "I've been good about taking my medication, keeping up with my appointments . . . did everything right. I've even stopped traveling because I needed to be close to my health care personnel." His eyes gleamed with unshed tears, and now he *did* look at me, but I almost wished he hadn't. His misery sucked away whatever sunshine I still harbored. "Just because you didn't see it, didn't mean it didn't happen. I suffered through all the phases. Big and small. The memory lapses, the clumsiness, the muscle spasms, the impaired speech."

"How did you hide it?"

"I got good at slinking away whenever it was necessary." He smiled grimly. "I disappeared on the few people I was in contact with. And I wasn't always in such pain. The time from the first symptom of Huntington's disease to death is between ten and thirty years. I've been dodging the real bad stuff for a while. Looks like it finally caught up with me."

I closed my eyes, drawing a deep breath. This was why he'd soiled himself the other day. He had little control of his muscles. It took everything in me not to cry.

"You've been coping with this alone for six years?" I pressed my lips together to stop myself from crying.

He tried to nod. "Though each year felt like a decade."

"Well, what are they planning to do to help you here?" I demanded, rising up. "There's a lot to be done. You've been practically fine before this week!"

He looked at me sympathetically, like I was in complete denial.

"I wasn't fine, and there's not much they can do. Huntington's disease is incurable. You can slow it down and sometimes manage it, but I've already done those things before. They don't work anymore. This is my final act, I'm afraid."

"How can you say that?" I began pacing the room, frantic. "You just got here!"

"It's not my first stint at the hospital," he admitted. "You know all those times I told you I was going out of town?"

My eyes flared. Charlie would text me randomly that he couldn't make it to our weekly drinks every now and then because he was away. I never questioned his excuses. He was a dashing, cosmopolitan man. I figured he took trips to see friends and family, not lie in a dark hospital room all by himself.

"Oh, Charlie." I cupped my mouth. Despite my best effort, tears leaked from my eyes. "Don't worry. We'll get you out of here—"

"*Duffy.*" His voice sharpened. "Listen to me. I'm not getting out of here alive this time. If I do, it's straight to a hospice. I've been pushing it for the last year. Things aren't getting better for me, angel."

"How could you give up so quickly?" I whined childishly, fire burning through my lungs.

"I'm tired." He looked down at his fingers, which were curled into themselves, prawn-like. "And in pain. All the damn time. I just want it to stop. I'm ready for it to stop. Even if I wasn't . . ." He took a labored breath. "Our lungs? They're a muscle too. I'm sure you know that. Mine are slowing down, making it difficult for me to breathe. I'm at a thirty-percent capacity right now. Which is . . . not great."

"What about a lung transplant?" I leaned forward, clutching his hand.

Charlie laughed, then coughed. "I ain't young and have a deadly disease. I'll never qualify." Silence blanketed the room for a moment. "Goodbyes are hard, angel, I know. But this is what makes great hellos so significant."

I buried my face in my hands and began sobbing uncontrollably. When I'd first walked in here, I couldn't imagine Charlie would tell me something like that.

I thought he'd confess to drinking a bit too much, or to a mini heart attack that would finally push him in the right direction, of living sober and eating meals that weren't frozen. I was entirely unprepared for what he'd just hit me with.

"You said this is the end." My weeping had subsided some. "How close are you to said end?"

"A few more weeks. A month, maybe? I've already contacted my landlady and told her the apartment's all hers to rent out."

I moaned into my palms, knowing I needed to be strong for him and somehow still shamefully allowing myself to break. My thoughts spun into a messy knot. He was too young. Too good to die. He was my only friend in New York. And if my suspicion was true . . . he had so much more to live for. An entire human to dedicate his life to.

As if reading my mind, Charlie cleared his throat and tried to scratch the back of his shoulder.

"Now about that other thing we were going to discuss . . ."

I forced myself to look up. I was now furious with myself for not paying attention to the small clues. To his limited range of motion. To the way he sometimes slurred. To the fact that he'd forget basic things I'd told him about my life.

"It's about Riggs." He winced.

I was nauseous with fear, having put together the picture in my head.

"Huntington's . . ." He swallowed hard. "It's an inherited disease."

I closed my eyes.

This was his admission.

His confirmation that my theory was correct.

It was mad *not* to notice it, even though on paper, Riggs and Charlie were from different states, places, coasts, and backgrounds; if you put them both in the same room, they looked like a mirror image of one another. They had the same height, the same build, the same golden, striking hair. The same eyes—blue with golden flecks swirling around the pupils, like tiny oil spills—and the same Roman nose. They spoke in the same low, sexy baritone. They both moved like panthers in the savanna, out to catch their next prey. They were passionate about the same things: nature, photography, extreme sports. They drank the same alcohol, had the same tics, and had the same addictive laugh. Based on their case, nature versus nurture had a clear answer: nature all the way. They'd lived their entire lives apart, and yet they were practically identical twins.

My muscles tightened. "When did you know?"

Charlie tipped his head back, looking anguished. "That he was mine?"

"Yes."

"That very first second. That time he slipped through the entrance door of our building. It was like staring into a mirror thirty years ago. It knocked the breath out of me. All the times afterward, I waited for him to say something about it. He never did."

"He could hardly know, though, could he?" Fresh anger slammed into me, and I momentarily forgot Charlie was sick. "Why would his mind even go there?"

"You're right," he said grimly. "It shouldn't. He shouldn't even be thinking about me at all."

An avalanche of questions swirled inside me—why did he leave? Why did he never look for Riggs? What happened the night of Riggs's mother's death? But ultimately, I didn't have the right to know anything before Riggs did. Even having this conversation felt like betraying him.

"When are you going to tell him?" My voice turned metallic and cold.

"*When?*" His eyes widened. "Never, angel. Why would I do that to him?"

"Because you're his father!" I roared. "He deserves to know."

"He'd never forgive me. Both for deserting him and for telling him." Charlie's chin wobbled. I couldn't deny that he was probably right. "And I wouldn't blame him. What's the point in telling him? More heartache? More disappointment? He's done well for himself. I always knew he'd be all right, with his granddad and everything, but Riggs surpassed my expectations and became an accomplished artist all by himself."

What did he mean about his grandfather? Why did he know Riggs would be okay? Before I had the chance to ask, he continued.

"And Riggs doesn't want to know. If he did, he'd have found me easily. Though Abby didn't put my name on his birth certificate, she gave her father my full name. All he had to do was ask. Funny, I always assumed that he would."

Abby. Riggs's mother. The woman I hated with every atom of my body.

I pressed my lips together, trying to keep calm. "Both his grandfathers died when he was a small boy."

Charlie's face became as pale as the walls behind him. He looked torn to pieces. A part of me wanted him to hurt for what he'd done to Riggs. The other wanted to cry because he was in pain. Emotions really were quite a messy ordeal.

"Where did he grow up?" Charlie's mouth remained open.

"Ask him." I stood up. "When you tell him you're his father. Which is going to be tomorrow, next time he comes to visit you."

"I already told you—"

"Enough!" I raised my voice, smashing my purse against the foot of his bed. "I don't care that the truth is uncomfortable. It is still the truth. Not to mention, it's not a family reunion that I'm after." My palms and the back of my neck began to sweat. "Riggs has been having . . . headaches."

Charlie frowned. "Okay . . . ?"

"Nagging headaches that won't go away and have no explanation." I raised my eyebrows, staring at him pointedly. It took a second before the penny dropped. Headaches were a telltale sign of something worse, and I imagined Huntington's disease was one of them.

Charlie was green in the face now. "He needs to know."

"He *must* get checked," I agreed.

What I left out was that I had already booked Riggs an appointment. He just needed to reschedule it. That was because I wasn't only worried for his health—he deserved to know the truth. What he chose to do with it afterward was his business alone.

"Tomorrow." I bent down to kiss his cold cheek. "Otherwise, I'll do it, and he'll kill you himself."

By the time I got home, I was proper knackered. I felt like I hadn't slept for a hundred years. My mind was reeling with the revelations that Charlie was dying and that he was Riggs's father. Amid all this, I also had to deal with the uncomfortable knowledge that I couldn't stop thinking about my husband every second of the bloody day. I was obsessed with the man, and the prospect of him finding out about Charlie and getting upset made me want to hurl myself under a bus. I didn't even want to unpack the idea of Riggs possibly having Huntington's disease, which alone was a breakdown-inducing prospect for me.

Riggs was on the settee, smoking a joint and drinking a beer when I walked in, the picture of clean living. I flung my purse onto the coffee table, resisting the urge to scold him to take better care of himself, because his no-show dad could have passed a deadly disease to him.

"Hello," I greeted. I tried to maintain "icy and proper" whenever we weren't in bed together. "Look at you, being a health guru. Would you like a few lines of cocaine to go with your beer and weed?"

"You mean a bump?" He chugged the rest of his drink carelessly, rising to his feet. "Sure, if you have it."

"I do not."

"I'm shocked and shaken," he replied acerbically, clutching his chest.

"How was your day?" I ignored his sarcasm.

"Terrible, yours?"

"Same." I paused, frowning. "Why was your day terrible?"

He didn't answer, but he *did* look like he could murder someone. And rather enjoy it too. I'd never seen Forlorn Riggs before. Cheeky Riggs? Yes. Annoyed Riggs? Most definitely. Even Angry Riggs made a cameo once or twice. But this was new and unwelcome.

We stood in front of each other, our gazes clashing like titans. I didn't know what had changed between earlier this morning and right now, but something had. There were secrets between us. Unspoken things that could ruin us.

"Why are you looking at me like that?" I huffed. I was tired, sad for Charlie, devastated for Riggs, and mostly—terrified. I couldn't fall in love with my husband. I simply couldn't. He had no interest in my heart. If I gave it to him, he'd chuck it in a bin on his way to his next, leggy conquest.

"Never mind about my shitty day. You seem off." Riggs squinted.

"Well, because Cha—" I started, then zipped my mouth shut. I wanted to tell him it was about Charlie dying, but Charlie never told Riggs what was wrong with him. It wasn't my place.

I shook my head. "I've had a long day."

"Full of calls and texts from Cocksucker, I'm sure." Riggs fastened his mouth into a taunting scowl.

My God, who cared about BJ right now?

"Have you rescheduled your appointment yet?" I grabbed his empty beer bottle and his ashtray, then carried them to the kitchenette.

"Soon." He crept behind me like a hungry predator.

"Pack a bag." His words hit my back, almost bringing me to my knees.

I disposed of the ashtray's contents into the bin and swiveled on my heel to face him. My spine pressed against the counter. Riggs was crowding me, in my face.

"Excuse me?" I arched an eyebrow.

"Pack. A. Bag," he enunciated slowly, like it was my hearing that was problematic.

"Are you kicking me out of my own flat?" I let out a sardonic laugh.

"No. We're going on vacation."

"*Vacation*? Where?"

"London."

"London?"

"Are you just going to keep repeating everything I say in a higher pitch?" he asked, looking irritated and put-off.

"Until you make sense, yes. Riggs, what do you . . . okay, first of all, personal space, please." I waved a hand between us, shooing him away. I couldn't concentrate when his body was so close to mine.

He took a step back, still staring me down with the rage of the entire Roman army.

"Second—what do you mean, we're going to London? When? For how long? And perhaps most importantly, with what mone—"

"Stop worrying about money," he hissed out, trapping me by slamming his hands on each side of me over the counter, leaning in close. "Just pack a bag and let's go."

My eyes widened and my jaw dropped. "You mean, you booked us tickets for *tonight*?"

"No better time than the fucking present, kid."

"I can't leave the country, remember?" I asked frantically. "My visa is pending."

"Your form I-131 just got approved." He raised his hand, in which my passport was tucked, a brand-new visa inside it. "The USCIS expedited it because you have an emergency at home."

"I have an emergency at home?" I shrieked.

"No," Riggs said. "Kieran and I manufactured one, though. I knew you missed your parents, and Zimmerman was more than happy to help out and receive the extra ca—" He stopped unexpectedly, but I was too dazed to follow this thread of the conversation.

My head spun. He needed to talk to Charlie tomorrow. This couldn't wait.

"But we've already filed our visa petition," I said, scrambling. "We don't need to pretend anymore."

"Contrary to what you may think, I don't live, breathe, and exist for your visa."

"Jesus, Riggs." I ducked my head under his muscular arm, making a beeline for the loo. "Now's not a good time. I . . . I . . . I have a job interview tomorrow."

You need to talk to Charlie. I don't know how much time he has left.

"You won't get it." He followed me. "You are unemployable until you get a work visa. There, I hit you with a truth bomb. Now stop trying."

I threw the door to the bathroom open, pushed my pants down, and squatted for a pee in the toilet. He balanced against the sink, knotting his arms over his chest.

"You're being unnecessarily overbearing," I pointed out.

"You're being unnecessarily stubborn." His gaze dropped between my thighs, and a small smirk graced his face. "But I like that we've reached this level of intimacy. I draw the line at number two, though."

"Eyes up here!" I snapped my fingers. "What about Charlie? We can't leave him."

"Fuck Charlie. He's not our kid." Riggs shrugged. "Besides, it's just for one weekend. He'll survive that long."

My stomach roiled. He had no idea it was his father he was talking about. I felt like Judas Iscariot. A deceiving Demas.

"Well, I don't want to go." I had a feeling there was something he wasn't telling me.

"Then I guess I'll just have to invite my next available hookup. Can't let your ticket go to waste, can we?"

I flushed, bulldozing toward the sink. Riggs didn't move. I purposely splashed water at him while washing my hands.

"You're being a bully," I seethed, scrubbing my fingers unnecessarily hard.

"You're being unreasonable," he clapped back. When I finished washing my hands, he clasped my wrist and tugged me to my room. "Now, get packing."

"What's the hurry?" I buried my heels in the floor, refusing to budge.

"Just wanting to get this sham marriage over with, and what better way than to finally meet the bride's family?"

"You didn't seem so eager to be done with me yesterday, when we shared a bed," I said conversationally.

Riggs sneered. "First of all, it was a shower, and second, don't confuse fucking with romance."

We stopped in my room. I turned around. We were both panting hard.

"Riggs." I used my shaking hands to pull my hair back. "You're scaring me. What's happening?"

"Look, I'm feeling very confined right now. I haven't been outside of this goddamn state in over a month. I'm growing antsy, and this was the one trip I could write off as legitimate in Emmett's eyes. A honeymoon. And since I can't take you anywhere else because of your visa application, I thought you'd enjoy seeing your family."

I felt selfish and completely self-absorbed. Of course he felt claustrophobic. Never before had he stayed in one place for so long. He was only here because we needed to pretend. And I hadn't seen my family in so long. So bloody long, and my heart squeezed at the thought of hugging them again. Charlie could wait for one weekend. It wasn't ideal, but Riggs's world was about to detonate, and he deserved one last happy weekend.

"I'll pack a bag right now."

CHAPTER
TWENTY-FIVE

Emmett: Getting claustrophobic yet?

Riggs: New York is a big place.

Emmett: Not big enough for your brand of issues.

Riggs: I didn't know you moonlight as a shrink. There is just no limit to the things you can do without talent, is there?

Emmett: Did you pay her to marry you?

Riggs: Are you listening to yourself?

Emmett: Well, did you?

Riggs: Goodbye, E.

I wasn't claustrophobic.

Of course staying in the same place sucked, but it had nothing to do with why I'd booked Duffy and me two tickets to the English capital, and had Zimmerman use all her pull at the USCIS to issue Duffy an emergency travel document.

No, this had everything to do with Cocksucker's forest of flowers and his text message that he was on his way to New York. If he was heading to the Big Apple, I was going to drag Duffy out of it. Simple fucking math. Two could play this game.

I felt zero guilt over getting rid of the flowers without telling her. He owed her an engagement, loyalty, and about ten thousand orgasms. I'd given her everything he hadn't in the weeks we were together. And still, to her, he was a better prospect than me.

The worst part, though, was that Duffy fought me tooth and nail. She probably wanted to stay in New York and wait for that cheating scumbag.

Now, as we made our way to JFK in an Uber (YES, Cocksucker, YOU CAN TAKE A FUCKING UBER TO THE AIRPORT), I tried not to think about how all I was doing was postponing the inevitable. Soon enough, my wife was going to reunite with the moron who'd left her. Soon, he was going to skim his lips over her delectable curves. Bite her neck where I had just bitten her last night. Grab her by the hip bones as he plowed into her from behind.

And you care because . . . ?

Things got worse when we got to JFK. The terminal was jam packed with holidaymakers trying to get home, carrying the worst type of travelers—*children*. The lines were long. The flight-departure boards flickered on and off due to electricity shortages because of the heat wave, and drunken tourists crashed into Duffy, accidentally spilling beer all over her dress.

By the time we passed TSA, we were both agitated, thirsty, and *really* fucking late. Blame it on Duffy taking two and a half years to pack for one weekend.

There was nothing remotely romantic about the entire trip so far. Not that I was shooting for it, but it'd be nice not to hold the worldwide record for shittiest honeymoon on earth.

It was bad enough that Kieran and I had had to fake his impending death to put her on that flight. A secret we agreed to keep between us.

"I forgot how hellish traveling is for the poor," Duffy moaned, pressing her forehead against my shoulder as we trekked through the moving walkway. "BJ and I used to travel business. It was one of the perks of being with the arsehole."

"Suck it up, buttercup." I quickened my pace, not wanting us to miss the flight. She struggled to keep up, because of course, she had to wear pumps to a red-eye.

As per Murphy's Law, our gate was on the edge of the fucking universe. About five miles by foot from the TSA point. We ran, shouldering past the thick crowd of travelers, rushing past duty-free shops, the time slipping between our fingers.

It took us twenty minutes to make it to the gate, and by the time we got there, the rows of seats were empty, and the person behind the check-in kiosk was snoozing.

That Guinness record for worst honeymoon ever was becoming an actual prospect.

"Oh, bugger." Duffy collapsed against a wall. "We missed our flight."

"Fuckers," I muttered. "Could've waited."

"We were forty minutes late," Duffy pointed out, perching her ass on her trolley with a sigh. "I knew I shouldn't have taken so long to pack."

"Why did you then?" I barked out. I wasn't really mad at her. More about the part where we were about to head home and wait for fucktard to knock on our door and sweep her off her feet.

She shot me an injured look. "I haven't seen my family in almost a year. There was a lot I bought for them but didn't send because shipping's too expensive."

I rubbed my mouth, looking away. *Fuck.* "Wait here."

I trudged to the check-in point, where a sleepy airline representative was playing *Best Fiends*.

I rapped her counter. "Two tickets to your next London flight."

She looked up, dropping her phone. "Heathrow or Gatwick?"

"Whatever's earlier."

"Let me check, handsome."

She began clicking away on her computer. I shot a glance at Duffy behind me. She was gnawing on her inner cheek, childlike. What an idiot I was to book us a flight we had three hours to prepare for. Now she might not see her family.

"Sir?"

I whipped my head back to the woman.

"I'm sorry, the next flight is leaving in forty-five minutes and is completely booked."

"Give me your list of passengers," I demanded. "And their phone numbers."

I could easily buy two tickets from well-meaning, well-paid travelers for double the price, and Duffy would be none the wiser.

She shook her head. "We don't give out our customers' information. Company policy."

"I'll pay you."

Since when was I so desperate? Since when was I paying people to do ridiculous stuff? That was more my friends' thing.

The woman glared at me, undeterred. "That won't fly, pardon the pun."

"There must be a solution," I insisted. "For us to go on that flight. We're just two people. One of us is, like, less than a hundred and ten pounds." I motioned to Duffy.

Her eyes dropped back to the screen, and she pounded the keys with a huff.

"Actually . . . there are two business class seats."

"How much?" I pretended to care.

"Four thousand eight hundred and seventy-five per ticket, sir."

I fished out my credit card, dumping it between us. "I'll buy them."

She clasped the card between her fake nails, eyeing me skeptically. I didn't look like money. I couldn't remember the last time I'd flown business. *Discovery* bought us economy seats, and I never fussed about it.

She swiped the card. We both held our breaths, like I didn't know what my checking account looked like. After a few seconds, she nodded.

"It's printing now. Thank you for choosing Unified Airlines."

"Thank you for pretending I had a fucking choice."

"I still can't believe they upgraded us to North Star seats just because *we* missed our flights," Duffy squeaked excitedly beside me an hour later, while we were both tucked in two bluish booths on the airplane. "My seat is a proper bed!"

See, *now* I was feeling guilty. But what was I supposed to tell Duffy? That I spontaneously decided to shell out nine thousand dollars I wasn't supposed to have on a last-minute trip?

"Lucky us," I muttered noncommittedly.

"Wait till I tell Kieran about this." She rolled onto her side, beaming up at me. "He's going to start missing all of his flights. He might even show up a couple days after."

"It's probably a one-off," I said, not wanting the Markham family to miss their family vacations. "Best not to try it at home."

Duffy laughed, patting my hand. "You're right. He can be so literal. Oh, I can't wait for you to meet him."

This won her a sidelong glance from me. "Yeah? Why?"

Did she want me to meet the family? Was she going to introduce me as her roommate? Her boyfriend? Her husband? Her partner in deceit?

While we were on the subject—Poppins looked so happy now. Would it really be the end of the world if I told her I was filthy rich and was taking her for a spin for a year or two until she got out of my system? I had the means and she had the will.

You're not buying your wife, you idiot. If she doesn't love you poor, she doesn't deserve you rich.

She accepted a Bloody Mary from an air hostess and bit the tip of the celery, chewing thoughtfully. "Because you're both teetering over the same mental age of thirteen."

I smiled tightly. "What was that? All I heard was the word *teat*."

"You're hilarious." She pointed at me with the celery stick. "You know, I could really get used to this sort of lifestyle. See why I want to marry someone rich?"

You already did, Poppins. But I'll die before letting you find out.

CHAPTER
TWENTY-SIX

RIGGS

The Markham family lived in a three-bedroom semidetached house just off Tooting Broadway's main street. It was a redbrick, old-looking thing that definitely didn't scream privilege. There was a beat-up Saab 900 parked out front, and a laundry-line pole with an array of old undergarments greeted us.

Poppins blushed and ducked her head as we made our way down the pathway leading to her front door.

"Sorry about that. Mum loves skipping the dryer. Saves her loads of money."

I shrugged it off. "Feasting my eyes on the Markham clan's underwear is a hobby at this point."

"The house is a bit old from the inside too . . ." She drifted off, munching on her lip. Her eyes looked faraway, and I bet she remembered being teased about her financial situation as a kid.

I clapped a hand over her shoulder, looking her straight in the eye. "I don't fucking care. You're valued by more than your net worth."

She nudged my shoulder with a sniff before pushing the doorbell. Our arrival was a surprise to her parents. Hopefully not one that was going to give them a heart attack. I was considerably older and a fucking stranger for all intents and purposes, and I'd just showed up on their doorstep with their only daughter.

We waited outside, the sun rising sluggishly behind a field of red and gray chimneys.

"Are they going to think I'm an old creeper?" I grunted, just when the sound of feet padding over carpeted floor came from the other side of the door.

Duffy turned to look at me, surprised. "Why would they think that?"

"Because there's over a ten-year gap between us," I drawled. "Kieran knows we're married."

"He won't breathe a word," she assured me, moving her palm over my back in a soothing motion. "And they're going to adore my new—"

The door swung open, and in front of us stood a man in his early sixties, wearing a wifebeater, fluffy slippers that clearly belonged to his wife, and old-school Adidas sweatpants. His sleepy expression vanished at the sight of Duffy, swapped with astonishment and delight.

"Daphne-doo!" he clucked, reaching for her and then tossing her in the air like she was a toddler. I watched with confusion as he put her back down and held her hand. She gave a princess spin, flinging her stained dress, as if verifying her own existence.

He gasped. "What are you . . . how did you . . ."

"Stop it, Tim, you'll wake Mum up." She giggled. *Giggled.* Who was this person?

He shook his head. "I'm just blown away. This is the best surprise."

"We took an overnight flight from New York and thought to spend the weekend here," Duffy explained, clutching him by the arms, sparkling with joy and warmth and love. "Is that all right?"

"*All right?*" he spluttered. "I'm the happiest man alive right now."

No, that would be me, watching your stepdaughter happy.

Tim's eyes darted to me. "And who is *we?*"

"Tim, meet Riggs. Riggs, this is Tim, my stepdad."

I reached out to shake his hand. He took it, squeezing hard to assert some kind of authority.

Too late. Already sampled her from every possible angle. And some not-so-possible angles. She almost sprained her ankle once.

"And what is Riggs to you, darlin'?"

Good fucking question. I was all ears myself.

"A royal pain in the arse," Duffy answered, avoiding a straight answer. I inwardly groaned. The jokes were getting old, and as she liked to point out every so often—so was fucking I. "He's also my roommate."

Roommate. That did not feel nice at all. I could tell you that much.

"Don't you live in a one-bedroom?"

"Riggs is crashing on my couch until he finds a place."

"Eh." Tim gave me a long once-over. I could read his mind. *Almost forty. Sleeps on someone's sofa. What a winner.* "And he decided to tag along? Sightsee, ay?"

The conversation was turning from painfully awkward to catastrophically bizarre.

"Actually, I just got two tickets to London, and since Duffy had a place to crash, we made it work," I said, interfering.

Tim's forehead creases smoothed, and he nodded.

"Makes sense. Well, don't just stand there! Come on in."

In, we came. The house wasn't too shabby, but Duffy was right: it didn't look like something you'd see on a Netflix reality show. Tim offered us a *cuppa*, and I prayed to shit it wasn't some code to fondling my junk. In a matter of minutes, the entire house was on its feet. Mrs. Markham came rushing down the narrow stairway in a fleece robe, howling when she saw her daughter. They exploded into a hug, crying into each other's hair, mumbling incoherently like war prisoners reunited. Next was Kieran, who trotted down in an adult Mike Wazowski onesie, holding a half-empty jar of peanut butter and a can of beer.

After everyone hugged and kissed and cried (I did not do the third one, which, at this point in my infatuated existence, was a relief), we sat for a full English breakfast Mrs. Markham somehow whipped up in twenty minutes.

I never understood English breakfasts. Potatoes, beans, sausages, and black pudding were all lunch and dinner ingredients, unless your idea of fun was to clog your arteries with enough fat to fill a bathtub. Mrs. Markham also couldn't be accused of being the best cook to grace this planet, as the sausage was both soggy and cold, the potatoes half-raw, and the black pudding . . . well, to be fair to her, I didn't think anyone could make it edible.

Still, as we all sat at the round table, chugging screwdrivers, I was beginning to see the perks of this whole family-concept thing.

"So BJ doesn't mind you rooming with a dashing young man like this?" Mrs. Markham motioned to me with her knife. Interesting table manners. I wondered if the Windsors approved.

Duffy rolled her eyes. "Riggs isn't that young."

"But he is *that* dashing." Tim pointed at me with a sausage-laden fork. "And Brendan . . . well, I've met more confident blokes, let's just say that."

"Yeah, Duff." Kieran sat back like a fat cat, grinning. "Doesn't BJ care? I mean, what kind of boyfriend is he?"

Kieran and I shared a knowing glance. *A nonexistent one.*

Duffy licked her lips, pinking. "He's fine with it."

"And is he still in . . . what's it called?" Her mom snapped her fingers.

"Denial about his receding hairline?" Kieran offered with a grin.

"Need to hurry up and pop the question?" It was Tim's turn to ask.

"—Tibet, was it?" Mrs. Markham completed.

"Kathmandu," Duffy corrected, turning bright red now. "He's still in Asia, yeah."

Kieran turned his attention to me.

"So Riggs, what do you do?" He chewed loudly, with his mouth open, just to piss people off, I suspected. He spoke like we hadn't been planning and executing the Conquest of Shelby in the last few weeks. She was thawing real nice. He'd even managed to get a date with her next week.

I sipped my screwdriver, sticking to eating the eggs and hash brown on my plate.

"A photographer." But he already knew that.

"That's an interesting job!" Mrs. Markham said perkily.

"Not much money in it, though, right, son?" Tim popped a fried cherry tomato into his mouth.

"Not much," I confirmed.

Tim nodded in approval. "Good. I like people who go after their heart's desire without giving a toss about the paycheck."

Now if only your stepdaughter was of the same mind.

"What do you do for a living?" I asked Tim.

"Fulfill my heart's deepest, most passionate wish." He opened his arms wide. "I make fish-and-chips."

Laughing, I leaned in to give him a fist bump. "A divine mission."

"I like to think of myself as a modern-day Jesus."

"Riggs, do try your black pudding," Mrs. Markham urged. "I know it looks a bit funny, but I swear it's good."

"*Mum,*" Duffy scolded, now bloodred with discomfiture. "Leave the man alone."

"Actually, I was saving the best for last." I smiled charmingly, picking up the round black thing between my fingers and bringing it to eye level. There was no way to sugarcoat it—it looked like crap. And I mean that literally. There were also yellow bits in it, which made it look like corn-infested shit. But for a reason beyond my understanding, it was important to me to win these people over.

Halting my breath, I shoved the whole thing into my mouth, chewed just enough to help it pass through my pipeline, and swallowed. I reached for the orange juice quickly, guzzling it.

"Delicious."

"Thank you!" Mrs. Markham radiated joy. "Tesco's finest."

"You want to vomit, don't you?" Duffy whispered through gritted teeth beside me.

"Very much." I dropped my voice.

"Well, Mum, let me show Riggs to his room!" Duffy stood up, covering for me.

A minute later, I was kneeling in their bathroom, throwing up into their toilet while Duffy patted my head.

"There, there. Now that you survived Mum's cooking, it is safe to say you are immortal."

The Markhams had a tradition. They went apple-picking the first day of the season. Since Duffy wasn't around for that this year, they decided to do it now that we were visiting.

"You don't have to come, obviously." Duffy was standing in the matchbox-size room they'd assigned for me, which used to be her room. She wore a yellow summer dress and looked like an orgasm waiting to be unleashed. "It's just a silly tradition. You probably want to explore London."

I drank her in from my spot on her childhood bed, arms propped behind my head. The room was so Duffy it was ridiculous. With stripy beige-and-lavender wallpaper, pleated curtains, and all her memorabilia organized in drawers labeled with the year they were from. There were also some Prince William posters I was sure she didn't want to talk about.

"I've been to London twelve times. Did all the tourist shit," I said, trying to downplay it. "Apple-picking sounds good."

We hadn't slept together since yesterday, when she'd received that text from Cocksucker, and I was becoming antsy. And worried. And fucking *mental*, as Poppins liked to call it.

"Okay, brilliant. We leave in thirty minutes. Does that work for you?"

"Let me look at my schedule." I picked up my phone and scrolled through the blank screen. "Yup. I have an open window between today and FIFTY-SIX FUCKING MONTHS FROM NOW WHEN YOU FINALLY GET YOUR PERMANENT GREEN CARD."

"They'll grant it to me beforehand. The lawyer lady said so herself. She has connections with the immigration office. That's why we're here," she rushed to promise me, no doubt thinking it would make me feel good. "Then you'll be off to your next exotic destination."

"As soon as you get your visa, I'm out of here," I said, forcing the words out of my mouth.

"Understood. And . . . thank you."

I shrugged, putting on a cockney accent. "I'd like to think I have the patience of a saint."

She winced. "Tim's a character."

"I like characters. Never apologize for your tribe. They're your people. Everyone else is just a visitor in your life."

Duffy loitered at the door, still not ready to leave.

I arched an eyebrow. "Can I offer you anything? A drink? Advice? *Anal?*"

She bit down on the edge of her fingernail, frowning at the floor.

"I just wanted to say thank you."

"You already have."

"No. Not for the visa. For bringing me here. I really appreciate it."

"Don't mention it. Now go get me a couple of painkillers. My headache's killing me."

◆ ◆ ◆

We crammed into Kieran's Saab.

The journey to the apple orchard felt like being a part of a clowns in a car circus act. There were no seat belts to be found in the damn thing, and one of the windows had collapsed into itself, now permanently open. Duffy had to sit on top of me, which was great for my morale and tragic for my cock. Kieran drove like he was blindfolded, veering between lanes and casually stealing red lights, while Mrs. Markham kept whacking his neck from the back seat with shrieks of horror. Meanwhile, Tim, in the passenger seat, belted out Slade songs to a CD in Kieran's stereo. It felt like I'd taken a molly that had transferred me back to the nineties, if I was adopted by an unbalanced yet endearing family.

"I still can't believe that radio show rated Slade behind Pink Floyd in that greatest British bands special," Tim complained loudly as Kieran zipped past a row of Scouts, almost running them over *GTA*-style. "Shoulda gone on air and given them a piece of my mind. Your mum stopped me."

"People like Pink Floyd," Duffy explained, wiggling her ass over my erection unintentionally while trying to pull her dress down. "They were experimental."

"McDonald's made bubble gum flavored broccoli once," Tim reminded her. "That was an experiment too. It was also *shite*."

"If it makes you feel any better, if the competition was about who had the better hair, Slade would . . . well, still lose," Kieran offered.

Duffy laughed, her ass bouncing on my crotch.

My penis was seriously going to snap in half if Poppins didn't get off me in the next ten minutes.

"What do you reckon, Riggs?" Tim stabbed me with a look through the rearview mirror.

I think your stepdaughter is about to inflict permanent damage on my reproductive organs.

"About what?"

"Pink Floyd. As a band."

"Not a fan," I said decisively. "As a band, as a racing horse, et cetera. Grossly overhyped."

"Good man, good man." He smiled to himself, then twisted in his seat to look at Duffy. "You should dump that posh boyfriend of yours, Brendan, and date this bloke instead. A bit old, yeah, but we like him better."

"Tim!" Duffy's eyes almost popped out of their sockets.

"Yeah, Tim." Kieran neglected the wheel in favor of thwacking his stepdad's shoulder. "Duffy doesn't want to hear what everyone is thinking."

"Even if BJ and I don't work out, Riggs and I are just friends," Duffy announced.

"Did you move in together because you're very poor, Duffy?" Mrs. Markham implored tactlessly, just as Kieran slowed down and peered through the windows, in search of a parking spot. *Thank fuck.* "Is Riggs paying your rent for you?"

"No, Mum. I still have some savings."

"Let us know if you need anything, is what your mum's saying," Tim clarified. "Because we can always pull some strings and find money to give you. There's no shame in getting a bit of help. Things are not so dreadful anymore."

"I even got my dental done last month—finally!" Mrs. Markham squeaked. "I can't stop smiling now. I no longer have to cover my mouth when I do."

Okay. I was starting to see what all the hype about family was about. Must be nice to have a support system to lean on. I guess I could lean on Christian and Arsène if I really needed someone, but it wasn't the same. These people were imprinted into each other's existence permanently.

Kieran pulled into a gravel parking spot right in front of a sprawling wrought iron fence. There were lines upon lines of apple trees behind it, as far as the eye could see. Ribboned straw baskets were stacked neatly by an entrance booth, with a price sheet written in cursive letters.

"It's the one bougie thing we Markhams do. And only once a year," Kieran explained, reading my mind.

We ambled to the gate and picked up our baskets. The Markham family seemed perky, elbowing each other excitedly.

"Not many people out here, eh?" Tim beamed. "Got the place all to ourselves. This is what Kate and Wills must feel like."

We started apple-picking, and I think I figured out why the Markhams were such huge fans of this get-together. They were all competitive as *fuck*. I'd seen less bad blood between the various *Game of Thrones* houses. Kieran climbed those trees like a fangirl on a nineties rock star, trying to get to the high branches with the most untapped apples. Meanwhile, Tim jumped and swatted branches down, shaking tree trunks in a bid to get as much fruit as possible. Mrs. Markham resorted to gathering fallen apples from the ground, some of them squashed and inedible. The only person who didn't try to outperform her family was Duffy. She looked pensive and thoughtful. I plucked apples from high-hanging branches, watching her alertly.

"Is your head okay?" Duffy asked about twenty minutes into the carnage her family was inflicting on the place.

"More or less."

"Is it more, or is it less? Because I gave you two paracetamol. It should've done the job."

"My head's fine." I gave her a WTF look. "Why so constipated, Poppins?"

"I'm allowed to be worried about my fake husband," she said hotly.

"Aw." I looped my arm around her shoulder, jerking her close to plant a kiss atop her head. "Is someone catching feelings?"

She huffed, "I need you alive to get a visa, remember?" It was ironic that Daphne had dreamed of a tiara growing up. She'd have nowhere to put it even if she had married a royal. The woman clearly had horns.

I chuckled bitterly, strolling into the thick of the apple orchard, wandering away from her family.

"When are you going to reschedule your appointment to the neurologist?" She followed me. She'd been going on about this like it was open-heart surgery.

"Soon. *Ish.*" I picked an apple from a branch midstride, took a juicy bite, and tossed it on the ground. "Why do you care?"

"I already said, I need—"

"Me for your visa. Right. Pretty sure I've got a few more months in me."

She pressed her lips together, catching up with my pace. I was getting fed up with the hot mess referred to sometimes as our relationship. Us fucking, then reassuring one another that we didn't give a shit. I ventured to the corner of the apple farm, looking to get away from the Markham clan. They were a good bunch, but not enough that I wanted them privy to our next conversation.

"Why are you like that?" Duffy was practically running after me.

"Like what?"

"You've been in a mood ever since I got back home from visiting Charlie yesterday."

That's because your boyfriend's coming home and you're not addressing the elephant in the room, even though the fucker took a huge dump and is stinking up the place.

"I'm not in a mood." I picked an apple and cleaned it against my shirt. "Bored, maybe."

"Do I bore you?" Her expression wilted, crestfallen.

Say no. Don't be a dick. Don't take your frustration out on her.

Running a hand over my face, I grunted, "It's the whole situation. Nothing personal."

"Fuck you, Riggs."

"Right now?" I tsked. "No, thanks. But I'm thinking of maybe sampling the local crop later tonight."

I didn't know what I was saying or why I was saying this. I just knew I wanted to hurt her as much as it hurt me to think of her crawling back into that asshole's arms once she realized he'd cut his trip short to get her back.

Duffy stopped behind me, and I knew immediately that I'd gone too far. I wished there was an unsend button on my mouth. I'd pay good money for one right now.

"Jolly good, then. Have fun with your local crop," she spat out. "See if I care. All you've done since we first met was highlight how little you think of me. Well, congratulations. I finally feel as disposable as a plastic fork."

"Hold on a minute!" I swiveled, trekking toward her. She was making a beeline to the other side of the farm, getting farther away from her family. "*You're* the one who keeps reminding me I'm a working dick with an American passport."

She spun on her heel, staring me down, her eyes dark and furious. A drop of sweat trickled down her face and neck, disappearing into the valley between her breasts. She was heaving. I was panting.

"You didn't want to marry me," she reminded me, shaken.

"But then I *did*," I bit out, my eyes scorching the strip of earth between us.

"Do you regret it?" Her chest rose and fell to the rhythm of her breaths.

"No." I closed my eyes. *It was the best decision I've ever made.* "You?"

"Yes," she admitted, bowing her head. "I miscalculated my pragmatism-to-soul ratio, Riggs. I think . . . I think I *did* catch feelings."

She was so incredibly sweet I didn't know what to do with myself.

Drawing a breath, I said, "Come here, Poppins."

She sauntered over wordlessly and stood in front of me. Apple trees arched above our heads, cocooning us from the world. I palmed her cheek, dropping my forehead to meet hers. Our hot breaths mixed together. Her heartbeats against my chest calmed me some.

"I wasn't expecting this either," I admitted, my mouth moving against hers.

"Expecting what?" she croaked.

"Wanting you so badly. All the goddamn time. Day. Night. The space in between."

The thought of her conquered every second of my day. My hand skimmed her curves, gripping her hip and jerking her closer. My erection pressed between her legs, and I let out a growl.

"I can't stop thinking about you."

"Right back at you," she whimpered, her lips latching to the side of my neck, her tongue peeking out to swirl against it. "What are we going to do about it?"

I lowered her to the ground, my hand reaching between her thighs to spread her open while I peppered wet kisses over her entire body through her clothes. She clawed at my hair, moaning with abandon, giving less than half a shit about her family being not too far from us.

"We can't." But as she said that, she also pushed me down between her legs.

"Says who?" I pulled her panties off, not even bothering to lift her dress up. It'd be hotter if she couldn't see me at all when I went down on her.

"Society . . . ?" She groaned. "And this can't be hygienic. People eat here."

"I second that statement." I licked her center, top to bottom, making her whole body tremble as I ate her out. "Besides, all I'm doing is giving you mouth to mouth."

"That is *not* my mouth."

"I'm an old man, remember? My eyesight isn't what it used to be."

She laughed throatily, bucking her hips, thrusting herself into my mouth. I slipped two fingers into her.

After she came against my mouth, I flipped her over, propped her up by the waist, and pounded into her. She cried out in ecstasy when she came, so I did what any gentleman would do and shoved her face in the dirt to stifle her moans so her family wouldn't think she was being mauled by a coyote. Then I kept thrusting into her from behind, waiting and expecting the rush of a normal climax to run through me. This was what I did. I had meaningless sex and enjoyed it. But every time I was within reach of an orgasm . . . every time I thought I was going to come . . . I kept picturing faceless Cocksucker knocking on our door.

And I couldn't.

I couldn't fucking come.

So I did something I'd never done before. I let loose a low grunt and pretended to find my release. I stayed inside her for a few more seconds before withdrawing and knotting the condom quickly so she couldn't see it was empty. She stood up, pushing her dress down, looking flushed and happy.

Her hair was a mess, full of leaves and tiny twigs, and she had a mud patch on her left tit. "I'm losing the apple-picking battle."

"Don't worry, I'm at least one foot taller than Tim and Kieran." I patted her head. "I'll give you those apples if I have to touch the sky to get them."

CHAPTER TWENTY-SEVEN

DUFFY

I ended up winning the apple-picking battle. It wasn't even much of a competition. Riggs did a wonderful job filling my basket to the brim. And yes, there *was* a euphemism there. #SorryNotSorry.

The rest of the weekend was a blur of drinks with my childhood mates (Riggs made all of them swoon, and one even tried to take him home, thinking he was just my flatmate, which gave me a small heart attack), a visit to Tim and Kieran's chippy (Riggs approved, wolfing down three servings; I found pride in that, since BJ absolutely detested anything fried), and a day in Camden, going through old record shops and secondhand finds.

It was both lovely and soul crushing, knowing the interview letter from the immigration office would come in the mail any day now. After that, there'd be no need for us to physically stick together, and we'd go our separate ways.

But the haze of vacationing with my fake husband didn't evaporate until we were tucked in the cab on our way back to our Manhattan flat. Something about the tall, imposing buildings and unbearably fast pace of the city anchored me back to reality. With it came the reminder that I had pressing issues to tend to. None of them related to BJ, my visa, and finding a job.

"You know what today is perfect for?" I toyed with the soft tuft of blond curls behind his ear.

"Sex on the beach?" Riggs was scrolling through his phone, looking largely unbothered by the fact our so-called honeymoon had come to an end. "The act, not the cocktail. I still have my balls intact, thank you."

My cheeks were so hot you could make well-done burgers on them. "That too. But you need to schedule your appointment with the neurologist."

If looks could kill, I'd be stuck in an underground fridge right now.

"I can book it for you if you're busy," I suggested, not particularly enjoying playing his mum.

"I'm a big boy. I'll do it, eventually."

"But your headaches—"

"You're contributing to those with your constant nagging, Poppins." His voice was soft, but his expression hardened.

I opened my mouth, then clamped it shut. He needed to know about the potential risks he was up against.

"You should also go see Charlie in the hospital."

"Yeah, I'll drop by tomorrow on my way to Christian's."

"No, not tomorrow. Today."

His head finally snapped up. "Why're you pushing this?"

"Pushing what?" I played dumb.

He circled the air with his finger. "All of this. My headaches. Charlie. Why do you give a fuck? I'm not your business. We've already gone through this. Fuck buddies with benefits, right? Nothing more."

You'd think the frequency with which he said it would make the pain dull, but it never ceased to hurt me.

"Just because the marriage isn't real doesn't mean the friendship isn't," I mumbled.

"You think BJ's gonna like you being friends with the guy you're married to, the guy who fucked you in every single position in the Kama Sutra?" He snorted.

Actually, I was quite sure we were about eight positions short.

I licked my lips. "I'm not sure I'm getting back with BJ."

Why couldn't I simply spit the truth out? That BJ hadn't even been in my thoughts for weeks? That Riggs haunted them, day and night, and at some point through it all, I'd realized love was more important than money?

Because that would be admitting to yourself that you're in love with your bloody husband.

Riggs let out a rusty laugh. "Is that why you didn't tell your parents you've broken up?"

The reason why I hadn't told my parents about BJ and me was because I was embarrassed. I wasn't ready for Riggs to witness the cringe when I had to explain to Mum and Tim that BJ had run off to a Thai island to sample exotic beauties while I twiddled my thumbs and pined for an engagement ring.

"Now who's the one overstepping?" I answered.

A muscle jumped in his jaw. "My bad. I have no right giving a shit about you and BJ. It's not like I'm your husband."

When the cab dropped us off at our building, I went straight to the mailbox. I unlocked it and flipped it open, my heart stuttering in my chest. The usual junk mail spilled out of it, landing at my feet. Riggs shut the door behind me, dragging my trolley along.

Among the leaflets and commercials was one white letter. I bent down to pick it up. Riggs used the opportunity to slap my ass, forever the gentleman.

I ripped the letter open with unsteady fingers, holding my breath. My eyes ran over the text, drinking it in.

"Planet Earth to Poppins, copy," Riggs grumbled behind me. "We going up, or what?"

I turned to him, holding the unfolded letter from the US Citizenship and Immigration Services. Riggs's eyes skimmed the short text. His jaw was squared and locked.

It was going to be over. Him and me. The little kingdom of take-outs and midnight giggles we'd built in my shoebox flat.

"October twenty-second, huh?" Riggs sucked his teeth in, nodding. "Not too long." October 22 was three weeks from now.

"Yeah." I licked my lips, feeling quite light headed.

"That's good." The words sounded like he'd forced them out.

"Exactly what we wanted," I agreed, choking on every single vowel.

Riggs glanced around, running his rough palm through his angel hair. "Ah, fuck," he groaned.

"Didn't you say you wanted to wait until we were home?" I joked weakly.

"I need to tell you something, Poppins." He dropped his backpack onto the floor. My suitcase went down in a thud too.

"Yes?" I angled my entire being toward him. I wanted so badly for him to say something I could hold on to. That maybe he could stay here for a while after the interview. Or perhaps I could accompany him on one of his trips and work for him. I'd even do it for free. Or . . . I don't know, even that we could try to see each other casually whenever he was in New York and see where it led.

"I—" he started. The entrance door to the building swung open with a whoosh.

A male nurse in a blue uniform breezed inside, peering down at his phone. He scratched his forehead, looking up at us. "I'm looking for apartment number twenty-four?"

Charlie's apartment.

"Th-third floor . . . ," I stuttered.

"Thanks." He started climbing the stairs.

"Wait!" I called. Guilt made its way quickly and efficiently up my body, its hold tightening around my neck. Poor Charlie had been all alone in his hospital room over the weekend while Riggs and I got drunk and had filthy apple sex. "How's he doing? Charlie?"

The man hesitated, holding on to the banister with a wince. "I . . . uhm, I'm not supposed to tell."

"You can tell us. We're family." I jerked my head slightly in Riggs's direction, without him noticing.

The man took one look at Charlie's clone, and his shoulders eased. "Oh. Okay. Yeah, he's . . . struggling."

"Elaborate," Riggs quipped.

The man looked straight into my husband's eyes. The same dazzling shade of blue as Charlie's. "You should probably pay him a visit."

He vanished upstairs. I turned back to Riggs, looking for any sort of understanding or recognition.

Riggs shook his head. "As I was saying—"

"You need to go talk to him," I interrupted, resolute. I wanted to hear Riggs's confession more than I wanted my next breath, because I had a small, pathetic hope that maybe he was going to say what I wanted to hear. That maybe in all of this fakeness, something real had grown.

Riggs clamped his mouth shut, giving me the stink eye.

I put my hand on his chest. "You know you're Charlie's favorite person."

"If that's true, then A, he needs to meet more people, and B, that's creepy."

I gave him my disappointed-parent look.

He grunted. "Fine. I'll go. You're lucky you give good head."

"I give good hugs too. Would you like one of those?"

He hitched a shoulder up, downplaying it. "I guess."

I squeezed him tight, trying to transfer to him every bit of my inner strength. He was going to need it. He was going to see Charlie today, and both their lives were going to change forever.

"Tell me how it goes when you see him."

He glowered. "What do you mean, tell you? Your ass is coming with me. You're the one who's been preaching about visiting him."

I can't come with you because he is about to tell you he is your father, and there's a good chance you'll want to murder someone, and that someone could very well be me.

I'd considered that Riggs would be mad at me for keeping the information about Charlie from him. However, I'd tried to reason with myself, I'd only really known the truth about them for one weekend. And I'd been doing everything I could to rub his nose in the truth.

"I've got things to do . . . ," I stuttered out. "Laura needs help with her kitty again."

He nodded seriously. "Pussy first. Trust me, I get that more than anyone." Then, before I had the chance to let loose another weak lie, he picked up his backpack and my suitcase like they weighed no more than a coffee mug and headed upstairs. "Fine. But we're finishing that conversation when I get back."

The next couple of hours seemed to stretch over a month and a half. Time dripped like honey, slow and thick. I kept glancing at the clock, annoyed with every leisured tick it made.

I tried to keep myself occupied. I cleaned the place—twice—did all our laundry, applied to a couple of jobs, answered all my starred emails, and even had the audacity to look for discounted, sexy lingerie on the internet for Riggs, even though I had no business spending money on anything, now that I was neck deep into unemployment, paying an expensive immigration lawyer (shouldn't I have gotten my first invoice from her by now?), and fully committed to helping Riggs on his possible health journey.

An hour dragged by, and then another. Riggs hadn't come back. Paranoia began creeping into me—what if he'd had a big blowup with Charlie and decided to up and leave? Riggs's entire worldly possessions were in his backpack. It wouldn't be terribly far fetched that he'd left it behind. But no. His camera equipment was still here, and that was expensive. Maybe he got hit by a train? A bus? A *plane*? Or maybe he got attacked. Crime was rampant in New York.

"If you're that worried, you know what you need to do," Laura said on the phone when I decided my Riggs problem was now *our* Riggs problem.

"I can't call him." I plastered my forehead to the wall, grunting.

"*Call*? Of course not. What are we, in the Middle Ages? But you could text. Ask where he is."

I could. But I didn't want to seem too needy and hysterical. Riggs already thought I was neurotic, and I could no longer pretend I didn't want him to like me.

"No. I'll wait." I scrubbed the counter in my kitchenette for the twentieth time. "He should be here any minute, shouldn't he?"

"Well . . ." I could hear Laura munching on a crispy apple on the other line. "I'm not his secretary, so I can't tell for sure, but you said it's been two and a half hours, right?"

I flicked my wrist, glancing at my watch. The same watch I'd told myself over and over again I should remove because it was a present from BJ, but never quite got to doing so. No wonder Riggs thought I still had feelings for that wanker.

"Three hours now," I corrected.

There was a thump on the door, followed by the sound of the key swirling in its hole.

"Oh. He's here. Wish me luck."

"You don't need luck, you just need to remember you're worthy," she chirped. "Loving, caring, smart, ambitious. He'd be lucky to have *you*." She paused. "And if that doesn't work, then at least remember you're super fit, and he cannot help himself around you."

I tossed my phone onto the couch and tucked stray flyaways behind my ear as I rushed to the door. I opened it. "Riggs, I—"

But I didn't get to finish this sentence.

Because it wasn't my husband standing in front of me.

It was BJ.

◆ ◆ ◆

"Babe."

BJ's voice broke, and apparently so did he. He sank down to his knees melodramatically at my doorstep, his face marred with anguish. He had a deep tan, overgrown hair, and a new beer belly. That pet name—*babe*—I'd never thought of it before, but now that I did, I loathed it. How lazy. How impersonal. I loved *Poppins* so much more.

He was kneeling in front of me, and strangely—*infuriatingly*—the only thing I felt was disappointment and annoyance it wasn't Riggs at the door.

All I needed was one look at this man to know that I could never marry him, never forgive him, and never imagine my future with him, no matter how many zeros were in his bank account. I'd outgrown him completely, perhaps because I'd also outgrown the version of myself that had found his swanky flat, designer clothes, and filthy rich parents attractive. Without these props, he was sadly lacking in all the places that mattered.

And, while I was being completely honest with myself, he *was* a mouth breather. And that trilby? Pure ridiculousness.

"What are you doing here?" I reared my head back, looking at him like he was a piss stain I had to rub off the carpet. I wanted *Riggs*. Wanted to talk to him. Wanted to stroke his pretty head and tell him everything was going to be all right. To help him sort through the complicated emotions of finding his biological father and, yes, of losing him soon too.

"I cut the trip short." BJ choked on his words, still on his knees, which frankly made me feel like I was talking to a toddler bargaining for a treat. "God, Duffy, I just couldn't concentrate on anything after how we left things off."

"That's an interesting narrative to what happened between us." I looked around, distracted and disinterested. "Oh, BJ, do stand up. This is so melodramatic and improper."

As he stood up and shuffled inside, it occurred to me that nothing was ever improper or indecent when Riggs did it. In fact, when Riggs strolled around completely naked in this place, even bending down to pick up a piece of cereal he'd dropped, I found it sexy, funny, enchanting, and bold.

BJ approached me with puckered lips, expecting a kiss. I turned around and gave him my cheek, revulsion bubbling inside my stomach.

"I've missed you." His lips skimmed my ear.

I stepped back. "Please, take a seat."

He plopped on the settee, and I took the recliner, happy to put distance between us. Honestly, I'd have loved to skip this entire conversation altogether, but I suppose we both needed closure. Plus, even though I despised BJ these days, we'd still shared quite a few years together.

"I got you a ton of gifts—had a layover in Singapore, and they had awesome designer stores at the airport—but they're in my suitcase downstairs." His face scrunched. "I came straight here from the airport. Didn't even make a pit stop to my apartment for a shower, and trust me, the business class in Jet Giant Airlines stinks."

If this was supposed to make me swoon, he'd failed spectacularly.

"Not impressed?" He gave me a fake, humble smile. "Yeah, okay, fair enough. I guess I have a lot of explaining to do."

Still, I said nothing. BJ's face was becoming red under his new tan. He looked genuinely stressed, and I couldn't help but marvel at the irony. A month ago, I'd have killed to get this reaction from him.

"Tough audience." He gulped, rubbing his palms over his ridiculous Bermuda pants. "So, here's the thing. Six months ago, a friend of mine from prep school, Kane, saw me at a bar downtown. He told me he got engaged to his girlfriend and that he was going on a six-month, last-hurrah-type vacay in Thailand. You know, just rent a place on the beach on an island, eat well, drink well, do water sports . . ."

"Shag around?" I finished the sentence for him, folding my arms over my chest.

BJ's chest caved in on a sigh. "He didn't present it that way, and I didn't go there thinking I was going to cheat on you or something."

Like a spontaneous infidelity was less immoral than a planned one.

"Do go on." I smiled sweetly, cupping my knee.

"Kane asked if I wanted to tag along. He knew that I was getting ready to propose to you and pointed out that I'd never really done the whole bachelor thing. You and I met when we were so young, Duff."

"Yeah, I know, I was there." I rolled my eyes. "Believe it or not, BJ, I had urges too. Needs that weren't fulfilled. Low points. Second thoughts. It's a part of being human in a serious relationship."

"You're right." He stood up and paced around. "But at the time, I was really stressed. I knew you were the one, that I wanted to spend the rest of my life with you, but Kane's idea was so tempting."

"So you decided to lie to me instead of telling me how you felt," I concluded, feeling nothing. No rage, no anger, no disappointment, no heartache.

BJ shook his head. "No, no. I mean, yes—I did. I fucked up. I lied. I knew how selfish it sounded, that I needed some time to fulfill the carnal, self-indulgent needs of mine before I could commit. The whole Kathmandu story just sounded better in my head. And then when I got there . . . well, I didn't wanna talk to you too much because I was scared you'd be onto me. That you'd expose the lie."

"How unlucky that you were daft enough to do the job for me," I muttered.

"I was so ashamed I couldn't even call you to say I'd made it safely," he said, ignoring my snark.

"My heart bleeds for you."

"Please, Duffy, please." He rushed toward me but stopped short when I gave him a look that made it clear that if he touched me, he would lose a finger. "You're the love of my life. My soulmate. I fucked up, and I own up to that—"

"No." It was my turn to stand up. Every time he spoke my logic shriveled deeper into itself, feeling personally attacked. "You don't own up to that, and you're not holding yourself accountable. You're just sorry you got caught."

His face paled. "That's not true—"

"Anyway." I spoke over him. "It doesn't really matter. As I said before, you boarded a flight to Thailand and left me here, visa-less and jobless. I had to take care of business. So I got married."

The last word exploded between us, and the room was blanketed with silence for a few seconds. He looked shell shocked, like he'd just watched his dog get run over. If he ever had a heart to adopt one. BJ didn't like pets, and thought that dogs were dumb and high maintenance. What did I ever find in the bloke?

"What do you mean you got married?" he asked, finally.

"What part wasn't understandable?" I replied tersely. "Don't you know what marriage means? Or is it the *got* part that you're struggling with? I have a dictionary in my room, if you need one."

Dazed, he looked around, registering the proof that I was indeed with someone else. Riggs's photography equipment. Clothes. *Scent.* "I mean . . . when? How? *Who?*"

"A bit after you left." I looked down at my nails, bored. "His name is Riggs. You don't know him. Cheers for the idea, by the way. Of me marrying someone else. Worked well."

Too well, as it turned out. The line between real and fake had never been so blurred.

"But it's . . . it's . . . just for the visa, right?" He looked perplexed. Like he genuinely thought I was a dumb cow who'd wait for him forever.

"Of course." I smiled politely before delivering the final blow. "Though we *did* consummate our marriage. Including yesterday. Just to be on the safe side."

He hung his head between his shoulders. Holy eye roll moment. The man cockblocked me out of an engagement, ran away to the other side of the world, and picked up randoms. At least I'd stumbled into bed with Riggs *after* knowing of BJ's indiscretions.

"You *slept* with him?" He looked up, his eyes wide and haunted, as though he was witnessing a crime against humanity.

I waved a hand between us. "Only once or . . ." I did a quick mental count. "Eighty-six times." I frowned, remembering that time on the washing machine. "Make that eighty-seven, actually." Pause. "And a half, I guess."

I wasn't even including oral in that.

I could tell there were so many things he wanted to say but couldn't. It'd be hypocritical of him to chide me for something he'd done himself.

BJ shook his head, probably trying to rid himself of the mental image of his reserved, English-rose ex-girlfriend getting defiled several times by a faceless man.

"You say you want to see accountability? Well, there you have it. I'm *happy* you slept with the guy. I deserve it too. But I'm a changed man, Duffy. And I still want you. I want us to start over. To do it again, the right way this time. Please, would you give me a chance?"

Old Duffy wanted to say yes. New Duffy, however, had both a spine and healthy self-worth.

"I can't divorce him now," I said coldly. "We're in the process of getting me a visa."

It was easier than telling him the truth—that I felt nothing at all toward him anymore, and even if I had still loved him, his actions were unredeemable. My mum had a saying—jam could never become fruit again. That was how I felt about BJ and me. We were jam. We could never return to our initial form.

Plus, there was something else that was bothering me about my relationship with BJ. Something completely independent from the way he'd wronged me. And I could only point that out now.

I had always felt like I'd faded away in my story with Brendan Abbott Jr. If we were a picture, I'd be the landscape. That thing in the background that exists solely for the purpose of emphasizing the subject of the story. I was tired of being his plus-one.

BJ pressed his lips together, looking down. "I'll wait."

"It'll take years."

He nodded, not looking at me. "I'll give you decades if need be."

There was a beat of silence while I tried to think of ways to turn him down politely. It annoyed me that after everything that had happened, all the heartache and wrongdoing, all I was left with was dull disappointment and a bit of sadness for BJ, who was daft and arrogant enough to think he could get away with having his cake and eating it too.

"BJ . . . ," I started on a sigh.

"No. Don't say a word. Not before I do this." BJ held up a hand. He turned around and hurried to his bag, retrieving something square, black, and velvety from it. He returned to me. When he was about a foot away, he lowered himself to one knee and stared up at me like I was a sky full of stars. Like I held the answers to all his prayers.

"Daphne Markham. I will wait until my last breath if need be. Begging for a chance to prove myself every day. We could move in together, or we could stay apart. I'll be a good husband to you. Loyal and faithful. I'll give you everything you ever wanted. Money, class, prospects, opportunity. You won't have to work a day in your life ever again. All I ask is one thing—say yes. Marry me."

He flicked the box open. The diamond inside was square and big, surrounded by small shiny diamonds. It looked gorgeous and sinfully expensive. Upper-six-figures expensive. The kind of engagement ring you flaunted once, then shoved in a safe, since it was unsafe to carry around.

It was perfect, but not for me.

I loved Riggs's ring. The unusual, quirky, classy heirloom. It was rich in things that weren't money. With history and memories and nostalgia I wished I knew more about. It was something I could pass one day to my own child.

A crazy thought invaded my mind. Did Riggs know me better than BJ did? Even during the week he gave me that ring? When we were still complete strangers?

Oh, God. He did, didn't he? He knew me then and had got to know me even better every day since.

And me, I loved him. *I love him.*

So much it hurt to breathe when he wasn't around. That the thought of him boarding a plane and going somewhere for months made me want to wither into something tiny that he could put in his pocket just so I wouldn't have to say goodbye.

That tangled web I'd woven around me, made of rusty barbed wire to fend off genuine feelings to a man, had somehow been cut, ripped, and destroyed by a man who had zero aspirations to fight for my heart.

I was in love with my husband.

I had to tell him. Not tomorrow. Not in a few hours. *Now.*

Tears prickled my eyes, and I cupped my mouth in astonishment.

I was so shaken with the revelation that I didn't even notice the door dragging open and Riggs walking inside. He looked ashen. But when he stopped in front of us and saw the scene of BJ on one knee, and me standing there with tears in my eyes, his face turned from ashen to destroyed.

And that was the moment when I knew what love truly was—the need to know you're someone's entire world, and still not want to ever witness what your power over them could cause.

"Riggs . . ." I gravitated toward him like a moth to a flame, almost tumbling over BJ in the process, forgetting he was there. The latter finally came to his senses and seemed to comprehend that a heartfelt reunion wasn't in the cards for us and stood up. "Wait . . ."

Riggs chuckled bitterly, shaking his head. "You surprise me sometimes, Poppins. Breaking your own rules over and over again. Thought we said no hookups inside the apartment. By the way." He turned to BJ with swagger, a cocky smile on his face. "I'm the guy your girlfriend has been fucking the entire time you thought you were winning at life."

BJ gasped, raising a fist to wave at my husband. "Don't you dare talk about Daphne like that."

Riggs narrowed his eyes, stepping into BJ's sphere. The latter stumbled back, whitening under his (fake?) tan. For a moment, I thought I was going to witness murder and was ready to jump between them. Their noses nearly touched when Riggs spoke again.

"Don't tell me what to do. Not when you fucked off and left me someone who doesn't trust men, doesn't trust her own emotions, doesn't believe in love. You ruined her, Cocksucker, with your selfish ways. And lookie now." He stepped back, his eyes ping-ponging between us. "Seems like you both figured it all out. Enjoy your reunion. Just don't do it on the couch," he spat out before storming off. "After all, it's my bed."

CHAPTER
TWENTY-EIGHT
RIGGS

Three hours earlier

"I gotta stop smoking." Charlie pressed his head against the hospital wall in the garden area, closing his eyes.

I side-eyed him, prying the joint from between his fingers and taking a drag. "It's just a little weed, Charles."

"Weed doesn't agree with me."

Charlie was a bummer today. I had a feeling he was bracing himself to tell me what was wrong with him. Whatever it was, it was serious.

"What makes you say that?" I passed him the joint anyway, and he took it.

He gnawed on the side of his cheek, staring down at his feet. He'd lost a bunch of weight since I last saw him, and his hands were shaking now.

"You ready for story time, Riggs?"

L.J. Shen

I jerked my chin to confirm I was.

Even though the old man was surprisingly bearable for a human, I mainly gave him my time and attention because of Duffy. As selfish as it may sound, if it was up to me, I'd be with her right now, telling her we needed to cut the bullshit and decide what we were doing next. What would having a girlfriend entail? I didn't know, and I still wasn't sure I wanted to give up my nomadic lifestyle.

But I was also just as sure I didn't want to give her up.

"When I was young, really young, I used to smoke all the time. Until something happened to make me stop completely. I hadn't touched a joint in thirty-seven years before you came to visit me in the hospital." Charlie scratched his stubble, focusing on an ivy-laced wall in front of us.

"Okay . . ." I frowned. I hoped he wasn't about to launch into a drugs-are-bad, straight-edge routine. Smoking weed recreationally and responsibly was fine. And yes, it was my hill to die on. Happy and stoned, *thankyouverymuch.*

"I tended to do a lot of bad things when I was high. Maybe I blamed it on the weed . . . I don't know. But I always found myself up to no good. Driving recklessly, missing work, cheating on my girlfriend . . ."

"That was almost forty years ago," I reminded him. "Fucking around and driving under the influence were shit moves, but you were a kid."

When I was twenty, all I did was drugs, booze, and sex with as many people as I could find.

"One time . . ." Charlie ignored me, forcing himself to unglue his gaze from the wall and look me in the eye. "I really messed up. We were at a river. I worked the zip line at a park, so I had a lot of time to burn until opening hours. I'd rented out a dirt-cheap cabin nearby and goofed around most days."

318

He licked his lips and swallowed. I had no idea where all this was going, but I was starting to feel uneasy. He seemed really stressed, considering this was four fucking decades ago.

"I had put up a tent on the river and forgot to zip it. I smoked a few and went down on some tourist. My girlfriend caught me."

I puffed my cheeks, shifting uneasily. "That sucks, man. Is that the one who got away?"

"It is."

"Well, sorry—"

"I'm not done," he said sharply.

Dafuq did they put in your IV drip?

"She ran away. It took me a full five minutes to realize she'd walked in on me. That was how high I was. When I found out, I took the car and chased after her. Needless to say, that was a gigantic mistake."

He shook all over in his wheelchair. I took the joint from his fingers and put it out, alert now. If he'd killed the woman, I was 100 percent telling the authorities.

"You chased her by car while you were high?" I repeated. "Were you competing for the Dumb-Fuck Award?"

He nodded grimly. "She sped up to escape me. I didn't want to give up. I thought if I could just explain myself, she'd forgive me. We were going to go away, you see. She'd finally convinced me to move to California and assume my responsibilities. Start a family. I mean, we already *had* a family, I guess. A son. His granddad took care of him while we were working at this adventure park."

I was beginning to feel very, very sick.

Either this was a tasteless joke made by Duffy and Charlie that they were going to pay for, or today just became the shittiest day of my entire existence.

Staring at him, I said nothing.

Charlie looked me straight in the eye. I held his gaze. I saw the guilt there. And it killed me just like it killed *her*. The woman I didn't remember and would never meet again.

"She veered off the road trying to take a turn. Her car totaled right then and there in front of my eyes. I pulled off onto the shoulder of the road and ran to her. She was still alive when the paramedics were called. She told me to take care of our son. She really wanted to get her act together and become a mom to him."

I didn't move. Didn't even blink. We did look alike. Fuck, we looked so alike it was comical. But when you meet a complete stranger who looks like you in a huge-ass country, in a city of multi-digit-million people, your mind doesn't immediately go to *Maybe he's my dad. Yippee-yay, can we go to Disneyland together?*

"Riggs?"

"What?" I couldn't fucking breathe.

"This happened in Denali National Park. In Alaska."

I stood up. If I didn't leave now, I would punch him in the face. I was halfway to the sliding doors when I turned around and stormed back toward him. He stayed in the same spot in his wheelchair, looking like a miniature LEGO version of the man I'd met only a month ago.

"She wanted to come back to me?" That was my first question. Maybe that was what had been bothering me the most about my origin story. How a mother could turn her back on her son for a steady dick.

He managed to nod, just barely. Whatever was wrong with him, it put a huge strain on his muscles.

"Yes. She talked about you nonstop. Went to visit you every few weeks. She wanted us to be a family. Me, I was the asshole. I'd only seen you once. Your grandfather dragged me by the ear to meet you. He thought it'd make a difference, make me change my ways. You were tiny and angry and fragile. Colicky and very red. I took one look at you and figured it was too big a responsibility, too hard a job."

A revolted smirk found my lips. "And I guess you extended that notion to after she died too. You never came back for me."

Charlie's skin budded with goose bumps. "Not for lack of wanting to. You don't have to believe me—hell, I don't expect you to—but that's not why I didn't come for you."

"Why then?" I was yelling now. I needed to tone it down before I got kicked out of a hospital for abusing a patient. A *dying* patient.

"Shame. Embarrassment. Seeing your grandfather doing my job so much better than I ever could. Knowing deep down that you were better off without me." He stared at the ground. "I took your mother away from you. And I treated her goddamn poorly. I only knew what you looked like from pictures. It seemed insane to go to California and rip you apart from the only constancy and stability you'd ever known. Your grandfather loved you. You were his pride and joy. I thought I was doing both of you a favor."

How did a conversation about a fucking joint escalate to *this*? Charlie *Black Mirror*ed my ass to oblivion. And yes, I used *Black Mirror* as a verb.

"Yeah? Well, thanks a bunch." I bowed mockingly. "Your sainthood awaits at the counter in heaven. Make sure to collect it—you get great discounts for your halo and wings."

He winced. "You have every right to be angry."

"I'm not angry." I laughed. "I'm *delighted*. You're right. I wouldn't have loved spending my life under your wing. After all, I could've ended up like you. A washed-out, lonely, soon-to-be-former hunk with no family, barely any friends, no ties. Oh, *wait a minute*." I pressed my finger to my lips, frowning. "That's *exactly* what I am right now. Well, well. At least you didn't have to watch it happen. Don't worry, Granddad was kind enough to drop dead only *after* I was old enough to go to a private prep school, so I skipped the whole foster-family routine. Of course, I had to stay on school grounds every Christmas and Thanksgiving because I had no one to claim me."

He swallowed again. His eyes were misty. I hoped he had a disease where you would drop dead if you cried. He deserved it.

"Where did you spend summer vacations?" he croaked.

"I'd usually convince one of my friend's parents to sign me out to spend the summer with them and pick me up from school. But I didn't want to impose, so they usually dropped me off halfway to their house, and I'd just hitchhike. At least I had money for nice hotels. You know I'm loaded, right?"

He bit down on his lip, reclining his head. A silent yes.

I tilted my head sideways. "Please don't tell me this entire confession happened so I could pay for your lengthy hospital stay. I'd rather burn the money. Literally. On fire."

He snarled, turning in his wheelchair sideways so as not to face me. "I'd never do that."

"No, of course not," I said easily, feeling like worms were eating at me from the inside. "You hold yourself to such high moral standards. I almost forgot."

"What I did was inexcusable. I'm not looking for forgiveness." He sounded stern and serious. Almost—and that was really ironic—like a *father figure.*

"What are you looking for then?" I crossed my arms, leaning against the wall. "Why did you even tell me? No, wait." I held up a finger. "Before you answer that—when did you find out? And how?"

Charlie blinked at me, like the answer was clear. "The first time we met. It was damn obvious you were mine. You looked like me, talked like me, smelled like me." He paused, lifting his hand with great effort to pull the collar of his hospital gown down at his neck. "We both have a birthmark the shape of South America on our neck. Kind of like a pointy tooth."

My hand went instinctively to my neck.

"Now answer my other question," I prompted. "Why now?"

Charlie closed his eyes. "Because I have a rare genetic disease that is killing me. And you might have it too."

◆　◆　◆

My hatred and shock were put on pause. He told me about Huntington's disease while I sat on the bench next to him and read about it on my phone. When I saw that headaches were a part of the symptoms, I speared him with an icy glare.

"You told me you had a daughter. That she died when she was eight months old. Was that true?" I asked, remembering the time we went working together in Harlem.

Charlie tried to shake his head, moaning in pain halfway through. "No. But I couldn't tell you the truth. Leaving you behind felt like mourning a child. So that's how I articulated it."

"Liar on top of a shit dad. Your talents know no bounds." I paused. "Duffy knows you're my father, doesn't she?"

"She found out, yeah."

"When?"

"On Friday."

So, she kept it from me an entire weekend. No wonder she acted weird.

Charlie added, "She told me to tell you, or she would. She was never going to keep you in the dark about it."

Not that it mattered. Being mad at her was redirecting my rage where it didn't belong. If anything, I now knew why she'd spent the weekend nagging me about getting checked.

"So, I might have Huntington's disease," I said to sum it up. "And could die."

"No," Charlie said dryly. "You *will* die. That is a guarantee for all of us. But if you have the disease, it'll happen sooner rather than later, so you better get your ass in gear and get checked."

The more I looked at his face, the more I debated beating it to a pulp. "You don't seem very sorry for passing it on."

He laughed and coughed at the same time. "I'm only sorry for things I can control. I didn't even know I was a carrier until I was in my fifties. I had no way to protect you. And I don't think your headaches have anything to do with the disease. Now, neglecting you, I take full responsibility for that. But I want you to know that there hasn't been a day—an hour—that I didn't think about you. That I didn't wonder who you were now, what you were up to, what you were doing. Every day, when I fell onto the mattress at night, I praised myself for not yielding to temptation and seeking you out." He sucked in a breath. "And when I finally met you, man, you exceeded all expectations. You were all I ever wished for, and much more. My biggest punishment is knowing who you are and not having the privilege to spend time with you."

I digested all of this, feeling . . . hell, how *was* I feeling? Sad, angry, disappointed, startled, annoyed, frustrated. All of the above, multiplied by a fucking hundred. More than anything, I was confused. Because even though he had ruined my life, arguably killed my mother, then neglected me (and on top of that maybe passed on a dangerous disease to me), I still couldn't hate him all the way.

I rubbed at my jaw. "Now I get why you were all buddy-buddy with my ass. Wanting to meet up, go on vacation together. I thought you were hitting on me."

He made a face. "Not everyone who wants your company wants to screw you."

"You'd be surprised."

I thought about Christian and Arsène. The looks they exchanged when they saw Charlie and me together. They knew. Or, at the very least, heavily suspected.

"So." Charlie cleared his throat, looking very childlike all of a sudden, staring up at me with azure eyes. "What now?"

I thought about his question, then stood from the bench.

"Now's the time I tell you to go fuck yourself, remind you that you're a selfish bastard, and thank you for the heads-up about the disease you might've given me that will ensure I die a slow, painful death."

"It's not gonna be so slow," he said, coughing out a joke.

I laughed, too tired to be mad at him. Yeah, he'd screwed up my life, but he was right in saying his situation sucked even more.

"Believe it or not, I hope the rest of your life isn't terrible." I tipped an imaginary hat down in his direction. "However short it may be."

"That is very charitable of you." He sat back in his wheelchair, eyeing me. "So does that mean I shouldn't expect you back?"

"Correct."

His throat bobbed. "Just making sure you're aware—I don't have much time. The nurse you met, Malcolm, he grabbed my stuff from the apartment because I'm not coming back."

"Yeah . . ." I reached to rest a hand on his shoulder. "I understand why you didn't come for me when I was young. Now it's time you understand why I won't come for you when you're old."

He put his hand on mine on his shoulder, trying to squeeze, and it seemed wild that I was holding hands with my *father*. The faceless figure I had spent so many nights secretly imagining in my head.

"I do understand." He looked down, and I knew by the quake of his shoulders that he was crying. "Have a nice life, Riggs."

I turned around and didn't look back.

When I walked out of the hospital, I made two phone calls.

The first was to my health insurance provider, to get my blood work done and get myself checked for Huntington's disease. I paid a hefty fee to get it done that same afternoon, at a private lab, for a quick answer.

The second was a conference call to Christian and Arsène. They both picked up instantly, probably because I was notorious for never calling anyone about anything.

"Did you knock Duffy up?" Arsène greeted me. "If so, no, I won't be the godfather."

"No offense, but I wouldn't put you in charge of a Pet Rock." I forced myself to smirk, like I didn't just find out I had a father *just* so I could say goodbye to him for the last time.

"Do you need us to bail you out?" Christian continued along the same theme. "Because if so, you'll need to give me the details now. Arya has a charity event, and we need to be there in two hours."

"I hate both of you," I informed them calmly. "And I called to ask a question."

"The answer is right on top, between the labia. A small bud." Arsène yawned. "Bean-like."

"Why didn't you tell me?"

Arsène sighed. "With the amount of porn you watched, we figured you knew—"

"Cut the bullshit. You know what I'm asking."

"Why didn't we tell you what?" Christian asked.

"That he was my father."

There was silence for a few seconds before they spoke.

"We weren't one hundred percent sure," Christian admitted. "That's the main reason."

"The secondary one being that if he really did neglect you, he didn't deserve closure," Arsène continued. "You're insufferable but still worthy of more than this bastard gave you."

"He gave me nothing." I held up my arm once I got to the street, hailing a cab. The lab where I was going to give my blood was quick about withdrawing it. They said I should get the results back as early as twenty-four hours, sometimes sooner, if I came in today.

"Exactly," Christian said. "Are you mad?"

"No." I slipped into a cab. "Just weirded out. I'll get over it."

I couldn't wait to get back home and talk to Duffy. She had the tendency to make sense of things.

And so, when I climbed up the stairs, I naturally started feeling a little better. Yeah, life was shit, my father was dying (and also in fucking existence), and, yes, I was on edge about the blood work, but there was Duffy.

Then I opened the door, and there wasn't *only* Duffy.

There was also Cocksucker, bent on one knee.

A knee I wanted to snap with a baseball bat.

CHAPTER
TWENTY-NINE

DUFFY

"Riggs, wait!"

I stalked down the stairway, stumbling over my own feet, gripping the banister for dear life. Riggs was faster and determined to get out of there. He slapped the entrance door open and let it swing back, almost hitting me in the face. I pushed through and ran down the street after him. It was evening, and the sky was painted in purples and blues. The sidewalk was overflowing with people. Pedestrians, bikers, people walking their dogs. I slammed into two men in suits and a teenager in Lululemon pants on my quest to reach him.

"Please!" I cried, trying to catch the back of his shirt. "I can explain."

BJ was still in my flat, presumably, and I very much hoped he realized by now we weren't getting engaged or married, or even getting friendship bracelets together.

Riggs picked up his pace. At this point I was desperate and decided to throw myself over him. Maybe I'd have practiced more self-restraint if it was just about BJ. But the man just found out that his father was alive and dying a slow, painful death. Now was not the time to worry about my precious pride.

I grabbed the back of his shirt, falling atop him. He swiveled, demonstrating excellent instincts, and caught me in his arms before I pancaked on the sidewalk. He righted me and took a step back.

"What do you want?" He was panting so hard I could see his muscles contract under his shirt.

You, I thought miserably. *Nothing less, nothing more. Just you. Flaws and insecurities included. No returns. No money. No prospects. I'll sign on the dotted line right now.*

But this wasn't about me. It was about him. I knotted my fingers together, my hands in my lap.

"How was it?" I winced.

A dirty smirk tarnished his face. "You mean, finding out Charlie was my sperm donor?"

I flinched at the words, even though they were more than fair.

He snorted. "It was fine. I told him he was a fucker, an idiot, and a rotten soul. Informed him that I was done with him, then went my merry way, straight to get a blood test. No need to see your neurologist now. Your nanny position has been officially terminated."

He was being mean, but I tried to tell myself he had a lot to digest. An incurable disease, potentially.

"Are you really not going to see him again?" I bit down on my lip.

Riggs laughed sarcastically. "Are *you* really going to marry someone who needed six full months to cheat on you to 'get it out of his system'?"

"I'm not marrying anyone!" I exclaimed.

He turned around and resumed his journey. I followed him.

"Course you're not. You're already married. Wouldn't wanna pass up a sure thing, huh?"

"Can we not talk about the visa for a moment?" I reached for his shoulder. He shook my touch off.

"The visa is why we're here. Don't pretend otherwise."

"You're being ridiculous!" I cried out in frustration. It was unlike Riggs to be unreasonable. He was always levelheaded. "I turned down his marriage proposal. I told him I don't want him anymore. What more do you want from me?"

He stopped again, turning to me sharply.

"You'll change your mind, Poppins. Women like you always do. Even if you're infatuated with my dick now. BJ will continue courting you—why not? You're the entire package, certainly the best he could ever hope for—and one day down the line, in a couple months, maybe, you'll cave in. Because he is rich, and comfortable, and familiar, and that's what you gravitate toward. Money. Money you won't be getting with me."

Dumbfounded, I blinked, praying this was nothing but a hallucination.

"Is that truly what you think of me?" I asked in a strangled voice, when I finally found my words again. "That I would choose money over . . ." *Don't say* love. *Even if you feel it.* Especially *if you feel it. He'll crush you like a bug.* "You?"

His nostrils flared, and his jaw pulsated.

"Yeah," he said smoothly. Coldheartedly. "I honestly think you'd choose money over me. Let's not forget, we started out with extortion, graduated to a fake relationship, engaged in some meaningless rebound sex, and for dessert, you kept the fact Charlie was my father from me an entire weekend. You're not trustworthy, and neither am I. Now go back to your boyfriend."

Riggs swiveled and stalked off.

Even if I wanted to follow him, I couldn't. My legs wouldn't move. His words cut me bone deep. I had thought he and I had a connection. A special bond. That we'd changed one another. Subtly. In the same way a blank mug decorated by your child becomes your favorite because of the meaning attached to it. I was still the same Duffy. Just . . . a bit better.

It took everything in me to drag my feet back toward the flat. I didn't know where Riggs was going, when he'd come back, or *if* he'd come back.

When I reentered my living room, I was surprised to find BJ at the stove, burning eggs in my frying pan with an apologetic smile on his face.

"Thought I'd make you dinner. Hope it's okay."

That was when I truly and genuinely lost it.

"Get the *fuck* out!" I threw my mobile in the air, letting it fall to the floor and crack. "Christ. It wasn't enough that you slow burned our relationship for years until it was completely charred, screwed me out of an engagement and a visa, lied to me about your whereabouts, sprang a half-year stunt on me last minute, and cheated on me—now you've made the *only* man I truly ever loved leave me. You are one talented man, Cocksucker. Unfortunately, your talent is to mess up my life!"

There was a five-second pause before he spoke again.

"Cocksucker?"

"OUT!" I pointed at the door.

He scurried away like a rat, leaving me to collapse on the floor.

CHAPTER THIRTY

RIGGS

Emmett: I saw that you put in a request to cover the Sri Lankan economic crisis. That's two months in South Asia.

Riggs: Really? I thought I could do it remote from my local Starbucks.

Emmett: Thought you were all loved up with Desiree McFake.

Riggs: We ran into a crisis.

Emmett: Ran is the right word. That was quick.

Riggs: You're a little too smug about this for my liking. Wanna bet I can ruin your marriage in less than an hour if I put my mind to it?

Emmett: Not funny.

Riggs: Not kidding. Give me the Sri Lanka assignment. I want to get out of here.

◆ ◆ ◆

It was time to cut the cord.

If there was one thing I was sure of, it was that if I got attached to someone, they'd end up leaving.

Hell, people I *hadn't* had the chance to get attached to had left me. Giving Daphne Markham a chance was going to completely annihilate me.

And I'd seen her face. All flushed and rosy when I walked in on her with Cocksucker.

Yeah, I wasn't going to get my heart broken by my wife.

No matter the price.

CHAPTER THIRTY-ONE

DUFFY

House Rules
No pets
~~No hookups~~
~~No fraternizing with your spouse~~

Someone had crossed the no-hookups rule. And that someone wasn't me.

Riggs didn't believe me when I said BJ and I were over.

He didn't return home that night, or the night after that. I tried to burn time by visiting Charlie, who seemed reluctant to provide any details regarding his showdown with Riggs, and with Laura. But for the most part I was alone, as I had been for years, ever since I'd moved to New York for BJ.

Thing was, I'd never *felt* the loneliness. It simply existed alongside me, like an ugly painting you get used to. Not this time. This time, the feeling was big, and vast, and took over the entire flat. It suffocated me when I was awake, pressed against my chest when I was asleep.

I wanted to call him. To reach out. It wasn't my pride that stopped me. It was the notion that I didn't stand a chance. Riggs still saw me as the superficial gold digger he'd met at Gretchen's flat all those weeks ago. He wasn't going to change his mind. We were done.

And still. The thought he was somewhere else, likely in another woman's bed, made my stomach roll. He owed me nothing, and me? I wanted everything.

Most of all, I wanted to know the results of his blood test. I needed to know that he was okay. So on the second day, I broke down and texted him.

Duffy: Did you get your blood test results yet?

Riggs: Yes.

Duffy: Are you going to share them with me?

Riggs: No.

Arsehole. I closed my eyes and took a deep breath, sitting on the edge of the settee, where I'd slept the last couple of nights, breathing in traces of his scent.

Duffy: Shall I be expecting you at some point this century?

Riggs: If you're asking if I'll make it to our interview on Oct 22nd, the answer is yes.

Duffy: It is not what I'm asking at all.

Duffy: Have you moved out?

Riggs: I still have my equipment there, don't I?

Then where the bloody hell was he? I decided I was fed up with his attitude.

Duffy: Dunno. Do you? I just might toss it out to make some space for my own stuff.

Riggs: You will do no such thing.

Duffy: . . .

Riggs: Don't do anything stupid, Poppins.

Four hours later, Riggs walked through the door. He actually looked quite cheerful, which made me perk up at first. Then I realized it wasn't his reunion with me that was making him happy. He was holding something between his palms. Hopefully not acid to throw in my face. Gingerly, I got up from the settee and strolled over to him. His photography equipment was still tucked in the corner of the living room, in one piece. *For now.*

"What're you holding?" I asked, suspicious. His grin was far too big for it to be something I'd be happy to see.

"It starts with a *C* and ends with a *T*."

I made a face. "Don't tell me you brought a cunt over. I thought we'd agreed indiscretions would be left out this door."

He actually chuckled a bit before frowning, remembering that I was his new public enemy. He opened his palms. Inside sat the most ridiculously tiny and adorable kitten. It was all black with bright-blue eyes. It was caked in mud, with crusty eyes and very little meat on it.

A stray. Of course he took in a stray. That's how he viewed himself. I swallowed hard. "My landlord doesn't allow pets."

"That's not true. When we made the house rules, you said you'd never asked." Riggs proceeded into the living room, a cardboard box tucked under his arm. He lowered the cardboard box by the coffee table, and I saw that there was cat food, two bowls, and a little kitty bed there. "I'll go back down to get the tray and litter in a sec, Micko."

"You gave it a *name*?"

He put the kitty in its bed, and it yawned happily, stretching its legs.

"Why wouldn't I? It's mine."

"We can't keep it." Again, I found myself following him as he headed over to the kitchenette.

"We can, and we are." Riggs grabbed the Sharpie by the fridge, stood in front of our laminated list, and crossed out another one of our house rules nonchalantly.

House Rules
~~No pets~~
~~No hookups~~
~~No fraternizing with your spouse~~

He turned around, smiling big at me. "There you go. I'm stretching your horizons."

"More like tearing them apart." I stood next to him, furious. I was happier when he stretched other parts of me. "You can't just adopt a pet without consulting with me first. Especially as I'll be the one to take care of it."

Riggs stepped forward, getting in my face. His eyes were dark and thunderous. "I don't think you understand the meaning of this word *can't*. Because that's exactly what I'm doing."

He turned around and went back downstairs to bring the rest of Micko's things, refusing to speak another word to me. And when darkness peered down at us from the window, he slid into the settee like he'd never left, turning his back to me.

Riggs was different. Changed. And he wanted to destroy my house rules, my anchor, my sense of control.

If he didn't have control, he didn't want me to have it either.

The message was loud and clear.

We were over. For good.

CHAPTER
THIRTY-TWO

D U F F Y

The next couple of weeks were hell on earth.

Foolishly—and with complete disregard to logic—I decided to break the news to my family via FaceTime that BJ and I were done. A dreadful idea, really. Mum and Tim were technologically challenged and kept frowning at the screen and leaning into it, as if I was trapped inside Kieran's mobile.

"My goodness, darling! Broken up? Completely, you mean?" Mum clutched her fake pearls. The same ones that usually made my skin crawl but these days seemed like a funny anecdote about the woman I loved so dearly.

"Yes, Mum, he cheated on me in Thailand. Kier, I thought you told her?"

"I did." Kieran threw his hands in the air in the background. "She asked how many times, so clearly we didn't get the reaction we were shooting for."

"Mum!" I chided, appalled. "Once is more than enough! It's like murder. You don't have to be prolific to get into the halls of villaindom."

"Was he pissed when he did that?" Tim asked seriously. "You know the bloke can't handle his liquor."

"Stop making excuses for him!" I fumed.

"We just don't want you to think you've wasted so many years on nothing, darlin'," Tim explained sheepishly. "You seem to like that twat, for a reason beyond our grasp."

"Mum, Tim, a time with the wrong person isn't wasted. It's like going to school. You're paying your dues and getting educated about what you want in a partner . . . and what you certainly don't."

"Does she look heartbroken to you?" Kieran barked out a laugh. "Look at her. She has that bedding-someone-a-decade-older-than-me-who-is-also-my-roommate-oops-the-secret-is-out glow."

Kieran was lucky we were an ocean apart, because I'd have loved to throw one of my heeled shoes at him right now.

"Is that so?" Mum lit up like a Christmas tree. *On fire.* Oh God, so awkward. Also—so *raw*. I wasn't prepared to tell them Riggs and I were already finished.

"No, Mum, it's not." I shot Kieran a scowl. "Riggs and I are only roommates."

"Who have sex together," Kieran finished. Did Riggs tell him, or was it one of those twin psychic things?

"You snitch," I accused.

"You prude!" Kieran laughed.

"Mum, Kieran wanted to moon our neighbor to ask her out," I snitched back. Two could play this game. His mouth went slack.

"Mum, Duffy got married to Riggs to stay in America."

Everyone went completely still. Nobody said a word. By the look on Kieran's face, I saw that he hadn't intended to let the cat out of the bag. It just rolled off his tongue, like all the other nonsense he spewed on a regular basis.

I lowered my gaze to my feet. Mum shoved her entire face into the camera, showing me an impressive close-up of her nostrils.

"Is this true, Daphne?"

"Yes, Mum."

She frowned, mulling this over. "Do you love him?" Okay. *That* reaction, I did not expect.

"It's just for show," I reminded her, depressed. "Riggs is helping me out."

She tilted her head. Now I had a close-up of her chin. "But do you love him?"

Ah, bugger. I couldn't hide my emotions at all, could I?

"Yeah," I admitted miserably. "Very much. But he doesn't love me back."

"Rubbish." Tim laughed, delighted. "The man stared at you the entire weekend with worry and anxiety, like you held his balls in your pocket. He's definitely smitten."

But if Riggs was truly smitten, he wouldn't be coming home every night reeking of alcohol and other women's perfume, much to my chagrin. He wouldn't ignore me so thoroughly. He wouldn't move around with a disgruntled frown that made me feel like he was waiting for October 22 like it was the second coming of the Messiah Himself.

"I appreciate it, Tim, but Riggs is not like that."

"Like what?" he boomed. *"Human?"*

"He doesn't do feelings."

"Eh, famous last words."

But those were some of the very *first* words Riggs had said to me, when we made the deal. And now? I knew better than to doubt them.

Then there was Micko, who seemed to be growing by the nanosecond and spending every waking moment clawing through every single item in my flat. The settee was already tarnished. Micko had decided to use it as her nail filer. The rest of the furniture, she just used as her bed and made sure to leave loads of hair on. In fact, Micko, being a typical cat, had decided to make every single surface in the place her bed, other than—of course—her *actual* bed.

I spent the vast majority of my time trying to shoo her off furniture, and the remaining time I cuddled with her, because I felt bad about limiting her sleep spots. What I *didn't* do was apply for jobs. Somehow, I'd lost all motivation after Riggs shut me down. I told myself it was fine. That after October 22, I'd get my visa and become more attractive to employers. But deep down, worry began gnawing at my gut. I had never been so apathetic. Everything in New York reminded me of him. Without him, the city was a shell. Hollow and empty.

Riggs and I probably could have gone on like this for the remainder of the three weeks together. Him, giving me the silent treatment, and me, trying to hold my head up high and not fall apart.

We could have, but then something terrible happened.

That evening, I waited for Riggs to come home, sitting on the settee as I ogled the door. Not one to disappoint, he stumbled inside at half past six, looking disheveled, eyes glazed over. After dropping his backpack at the door, he kicked his Blundstones against the wall and headed straight to the fridge.

I stood up. I was over being punished by him for something I didn't do. I'd made it clear BJ and I were done. If Riggs didn't want me anymore, which he was entitled to, he should end it respectfully.

"Had a good day?" I asked politely, hands clasped behind my back.

Shrugging, he took out a can of beer from the fridge, then chugged it.

"Where's Micko?" Riggs glanced around.

"In her litter tray, doing a poo," I said through gritted teeth. I really didn't care for his attitude. "We need to talk."

"I can see." He gave me a once-over, looking none too happy. "This'll have to wait until I come back from Morocco, though. I got a last-minute paid-content assignment. I'm leaving tonight."

"It's not going to be dreadfully long." Panic laced my voice, and I hated that I became the same small woman I was in my relationship with BJ. I promised myself to never be that person again. He'd told me about his upcoming work trip, but I must've penciled in the wrong date.

"Sorry, don't have time." He lumbered toward a pile of his clothes in my living room before plucking some clean items and shoving them into his backpack.

"You can't go to Morocco." I hadn't a clue what inspired me to say this. He clearly could.

Riggs chuckled, not looking back from his backpack. He slung it over his shoulder, patting his pockets down to ensure he had his wallet and passport. For him, traveling around the world was akin to taking the subway to Williamsburg. "See you on October twenty-second."

He headed to the door. Rage simmered up my throat, and my fists balled painfully, my nails digging into my skin.

"Charlie is gonna die tonight."

He stopped in his tracks but didn't turn around to look at me. The only sign that he'd heard me was the tiny nod of his head.

"What do you want me to do with that information?" Riggs asked frostily.

"Say goodbye."

"I didn't even want to say *hello*," he reminded me, slowly turning on his heel to meet my gaze.

"I know." I didn't waver. Didn't look away. "But the hello happened, so a proper goodbye shall follow too."

Riggs blew out air. "I appreciate the heads-up, but I don't think it's a good idea."

Stepping forward, I couldn't help myself and grabbed his hands. A shot of electricity ran through me. He was warm and rough and familiar and no longer mine, and my heart broke all over again. I hated myself for not telling him how I felt when I still had a chance. When there was a minuscule chance of us being together.

I inhaled. "Trust me, you'll regret it if you don't see him before he passes away."

"How do you know?" His eyes tapered.

"Because even though I hate my father, and haven't seen him in over twenty years, I'd still want to see him if he was dying. It's not about his welfare. It's about *yours.*"

I was fully bracing myself for the sting of rejection. After all, Riggs had made it clear I no longer had any sort of hold on him. But he surprised me by sighing and glancing at his watch.

"Fuck. Fine. On one condition."

I blinked up at him, waiting.

"You're coming with me."

Willing myself not to jump to conclusions—it was hard, with my heart soaring madly in my chest—I gave him a curt nod. "I was going to pay him a visit, anyway."

"Meet you there in an hour?" His voice was flat and disinterested.

"Yes." I paused. "Where are you going?"

"I have some loose ends to tie up."

With that, he was gone.

CHAPTER THIRTY-THREE

RIGGS

Charlie wasn't in his usual room when I came to see him. They'd moved him to another unit, which made finding him a real bitch. There seemed to be an unwritten rule that hospitals were impossible to maneuver. Once I found him, I wished I hadn't. He was sound asleep in his bed and looked like he'd aged three decades overnight. He was hooked to an IV, and I guessed they'd pumped a ton of painkillers into him. He didn't look alive. Not by his color or his weight. It looked like his soul—or whatever it was that made people *look* alive—had already exited the building.

I sucked in a breath, hating him and myself and Duffy for being in this situation. I forced myself to walk inside.

Since I didn't want to disturb his sleep, I waited. I had no doubt Daphne was going to show up, but I still couldn't understand what made me want her here. Even if she wasn't back with BJ yet, the fact that I'd spent the last few weeks drinking myself into oblivion and avoiding the apartment like it was radioactive must've shown her I wasn't boyfriend material. Still, I couldn't escape her. She wasn't just in my head; she was in my veins too. A permanent part of my DNA. A fixture I could never get rid of. She consumed me like a snake eating its prey, swallowing me whole.

Twenty minutes after I walked in, Charlie began to stir back to life. More like groaned his way back into it. The man made it sound like it was impossible to breathe, and even though I wanted to take pleasure in seeing him in pain, I couldn't muster the pettiness.

He opened his eyes, and when he saw me, his whole face lit up. For a second, he looked like my friendly neighbor again.

"Riggs," he grumbled. His hand twitched. Did he want me to touch it? Well, I wasn't ready for that. "You came."

"Duffy told me—" I started, then stopped. There was no polite way of saying "You're about to drop dead."

Charlie exhaled. "I'm hoping they'll pump enough drugs into me that I won't feel it."

"You should've said something. I'd have scored you some."

He arched an eyebrow. "Ain't too late for that."

I forced myself to laugh, not sure if he was kidding or not.

Awkward silence swathed the room. Neither of us acknowledged the giant elephant inside it, which was my being here after making it clear I would never give him the time of day again.

Finally, Charlie spoke. "So . . . what's in the bags?" He jerked his chin toward a few paper bags at my feet.

"Ah, yeah." I reached down, pulling out an Aussie meat pie, a craft lager from Scotland, and Maharaja Bengali sweets from India.

"We haven't had the chance to get to know each other," I said ruefully, leaning on his bed with an iPad with a playlist of my favorite songs, movies, and galleries from around the world. "I figured I'll give you the bulletin points of all my favorites. So when you're stuck in the elevator between hell and heaven, you can bullshit your way and say you had a son, and that you actually knew him."

Charlie pressed his head against the flat pillow on his bed and closed his eyes. His throat moved as he tried to swallow in a sob. His chin quivered. I stopped unloading my bags and watched him intently. I'd never seen a grown man cry like that, but I was beginning to see that life had a way of breaking you, no matter who you were.

"You're my biggest regret." He shrank in front of my eyes into something small and fragile. "I want you to know that. If I could turn back time and do one thing different, it would be being a real father to you. I know it means jack shit right now. Way too little, way too late. But for what it's worth—it's the truth."

Did I forgive him? No, I didn't think so. If I did, it was only because he was dying, which was not a solid reason at all.

Instead of ridding him of his guilt trip, I cleared my throat. "How do you know it's time?"

"Cachexia."

"And in English?"

"I'm wasting away, Riggs. My systems are shutting down. My muscles are no longer functioning. In fact, speaking to you right now hurts. Hell, *blinking* hurts."

Oh, fuck. I couldn't take it anymore. The emotional overload Charlie and Duffy had put me through in the last couple of months. I was about to tell him that in my book, he was forgiven, when Duffy rushed through the door.

"Bloody hell, you'd think an established hospital would know how to find a patient in their system if he got switched to another unit . . ." She froze midstride when she realized she'd walked into a tense moment. Her frown melted.

"Shall I come back later?" She jerked a finger behind her shoulder.

"No," I said, at the same time Charlie said, "Yes."

Charlie took one look at me, probably realizing I needed her in that moment.

"Just kidding." He forced out a smile. "Come in, angel."

Cautiously, she made her way in and took his hands in hers, squeezing them tight. My eyes landed on where their skin touched, and I wondered what it said about me that I was jealous of a dying man because Daphne was touching him.

It says that you're a fucking coward who doesn't want to give this thing a chance because you're afraid of getting hurt, as if you're not already in shambles.

Unable to deal with my own bullshit and with the tragedy unfolding in the room, I stood up and excused myself. I went outside and postponed my flight to Marrakech. I wasn't going to board a plane tonight, that was for damn sure.

The next eight hours were passed watching my movies, going through galleries of my photos, eating my favorite food, and drinking my favorite drinks (probably should have thought that one through, since Charlie wasn't in a condition to swallow anything other than his own saliva). I showed him pictures from my mountain-climbing adventures, and he alternated between crying and laughing. Duffy was crying too. Quietly, sitting in the corner of the room and looking at us in awe. I couldn't understand how this self-proclaimed gold digger ended up having a heart of gold, but somehow, she did.

Nurses and doctors breezed in and out of the room, checking in on Charlie. They didn't offer us much information, just sympathetic looks, which was how I knew we were close to the end.

Eight hours after I arrived, Charlie's pain became unbearable. He stopped talking altogether and only smiled or nodded in response to everything around him.

"All righty, darling. I think it is time to up your morphine levels. Nod to confirm I can jack it up." Duffy walked over to his IV and picked up a red button that was hooked to it. Charlie gave a faint nod. I watched, fascinated. I'd never seen anyone die. Least of all one of my parents.

She pressed the button, then sat on the edge of his bed, taking his hands in hers. She rubbed a spot with her thumb, smiling calmly. "You're okay, Charlie."

He nodded weakly again. My throat tightened, and my eyes burned. Even if he wasn't okay, he could no longer open his mouth and ask for help.

A lone tear rolled down his cheek. Duffy was kind enough not to acknowledge it.

"Shall I prop you up a bit more?" she cooed sweetly. "Might help with your lungs."

This time his nod was barely visible. She pushed a button on the side of his bed and helped him into a full sitting position. His head lolled sideways.

No functioning muscles. Duffy grabbed one of the many flat pillows lying around and secured it around his neck to keep him steady.

And that was it. I knew Charlie would die in the next hour. That there were a lot of things to say, and that none of them would be said. He was taking the answers to all my questions to his grave. If I'd been more forgiving, more open, I could've known more. As it was, my origin would always be largely a mystery to me.

Sensing the same thing I did—that Charlie was in the process of passing away—Duffy stood up. She leaned down to kiss his cheek.

"Goodbye, sweet friend. Thank you for being my family away from home. Thank you for giving me the most precious thing one could give—time. And thank you for the man you became. I know you have your regrets, but I can assure you, Charlie—you're up there with Tim. A man worthy of restoring a little girl's faith."

She rubbed at his cheek, smiled, kissed his head, and withdrew. A moment later, her hand found my shoulder.

"I'm going to get some coffee for us. Would you like anything to eat?"

I shook my head absently, still amazed that Charlie's looming death was hitting me this hard, along with the realization that Daphne was the loveliest person one could perish in front of. Caring, loving, sweet, and warm. She was everything I'd wished my mother was.

She was everything my mother could have been, had she been alive.

And just like that, with the reluctant forgiveness I granted my no-show dad, I also came to the realization my life was one poor decision by my mother away from being completely different.

My abandonment issues, my fear of loss, my anger—all gone. And maybe, if everything was so fluid, so fragile, it was better to spend time being grateful for the people you did have in your life than resenting those who were absent from it.

Duffy closed the door behind her gently. If there was a **Do Not Disturb** sign for hospital rooms, I bet she'd have put one on our door. She was clearly desperate for Charlie and me to have some kind of a resolution.

Charlie blinked my way, the simple movement slow and labored.

"Hey," I said.

His gaze dropped to my hands. I had my elbows on my knees, and I was crouching forward, toward him. My stare followed his. My jaw ticked.

He wanted me to hold his hand.

I didn't want to. Didn't want to forgive him, to touch him, to love him, to hurt because he was hurting. But somehow, without permission, he'd managed to make me feel all those things.

Reaching out, I placed my hand over his, clasping it firmly. Maybe it was the adrenaline, or the morphine—hell, maybe it was the dying—but I swear I felt him shaking underneath me.

I choked on my saliva, willing the words to leave my mouth, knowing that I meant every single one of them.

"I forgive you," I heard myself say, and underneath my hand, he began shaking harder. His whole body trembled, his eyes clinging to me so hard he didn't dare blink. "I'm not making excuses for you, but you were young and extra-fucking stupid—the apple didn't fall too far from the tree, by the way. I was a goddamn demon in my twenties." I squeezed his hand in mine. "Besides, I still can't commit to a girlfriend at thirty-seven, so I'm not one to criticize anyone in that department."

Though Duffy hadn't asked to be my girlfriend. She hadn't asked me to be my anything.

Charlie stopped trembling. His eyelids slid shut, even though I could see he was fighting to stay awake.

"Don't fight it, Charles. It's okay. We all have our day. And you had a good run." I licked my lips, watching his expression as it became horrifyingly neutral. "I bet if she were alive, she'd forgive you too."

His hand became cold as circulation stopped flowing. Everything turned slack and lifeless. The pale became paler—other than his lips, which took on a blue hue.

I was there in the most intimate moment of his life. And I wouldn't change it for the world.

I stayed still when he flatlined, holding his hand when he slipped from the living to the dead. It was hard to make sense of what I was feeling. In a way, I was grateful for the journey with him. In another, I despised him for putting both of us through it.

A nurse rushed into the room a few moments after his EKG had signaled his loss of life. I slipped my hand away and sat straight.

"I'm sorry about your father," she said quietly, buzzing in someone with another one of the endless buttons by Charlie's bed.

"What makes you think he was my father?" I eyed her.

She looked between us, confused. "Oh, sorry, I thought . . ."

"He was," I interjected, and I realized that weirdly enough, today, he *did* feel like my dad. "You're right. He was."

Duffy opened the door, looking ashen. Her eyes were red, and her shoulders were slumped. She'd never looked more beautiful than she was right here, in front of me.

"Oh, Riggs." Her eyes filled with fresh tears, and she cupped her mouth. "I'm so sorry."

◆ ◆ ◆

That night, Duffy and I went home together, stumbled into her bed together, and had sex together. We both needed that, and the excuse was there—we were broken, we were hurt; if there ever was a chance to make one last mistake, it was tonight. Besides, sex was the antithesis of death. It symbolized life. Lust. Passion. Warmth.

We touched slow, we kissed slow, we loved slow.

When the sun rose and I woke up—now truly orphaned, no second chances, no returns, no surprises—Duffy wasn't in bed.

I strolled out of her bedroom shirtless, scrubbing the sleep from my eyes. She stood in the kitchen, making us both oatmeal and fruit.

She swiveled to the sound of my approaching feet. She wore an oversize shirt of mine and threw a small smile my way. "Hey, you. How'd you sleep? Hope you're hungry."

I could tell by the look in her eyes that she thought last night was a reconciliation. I should've made it clear that it wasn't. The hope swimming in her irises was about to be doused with gasoline.

"Let's talk." I tilted my head toward the couch.

She followed me to the sofa, sitting primly with her hands crossed in her lap. I was going to miss her stance. The little, disapproving purse of her lips. Her sarcasm, and goodwill, and quirky fascination with waffles. But it had to be done. I couldn't go around getting hurt by people. Sticking around, making sacrifices, only to be disappointed. Plus, Duffy was a high-risk investment. Women who were after money were after power, and there would always be someone with more power in their vicinity. I didn't want to spend my life trying to keep her.

"I'm boarding a plane to Morocco today."

Her facial expression didn't change, other than one minor flinch. "Of course. You said you have work there. Maybe when you get back home—"

"I have no home," I said, cutting into her words. "This is your apartment, not mine. In fact, I've outstayed my welcome. We've already filed our application, complete with all the necessary proof that we live together. No point in prolonging the inevitable."

"You're moving out?" Her mouth slacked. Micko used the opportunity to jump on the couch and settle in the small gap between us, shifting her glare left and right to see who'd be the first to pet her.

I rubbed behind her ear absentmindedly. "Don't worry about Micko. Winnie wants her. Arsène is going to kill me, but I know she'll take good care of her."

Besides, Arsène had always wanted to kill me. Nothing new under the sun.

"Wh-where will you stay in New York?" She blinked.

"Christian's. Arsène's. The usual." I stood up, knowing that every moment I stayed brought me closer to changing my mind and begging her for a chance. "Don't worry about the interview, though. I'll be there, and we'll ace it. All right?"

I could tell she was in shock. I could also tell that I was fucking in love with this woman. Seeing her hurt destroyed me so thoroughly I was surprised I was still able to stand on my two feet. I felt like my soul had been pulled from my body by a rusty rake and tossed into the depths of hell.

But that was exactly why I had to leave.

I was in love with a woman who wanted an arrangement.

And me? I wanted the whole fucking deal.

"So it's over?" She rose up slowly. "You and me?"

Say no. It's not. Grab her. Kiss her. Throw your heart on the line. Be a fucking man, Riggs. You've climbed mountains. You've braved rain forests. Do it, goddammit.

"This has no future." I motioned between us, my tone dead. "You knew that."

Her eyes roamed my face wildly. Whatever she was searching for—doubt, second thoughts, regret—she didn't find it.

"Yeah." She licked her lips, averting her gaze. "I guess you're right."

Kill me now.

I went over to my pile of clothes and started thrusting them one by one into my backpack. Grabbed a white henley and put it on, then shoved my feet into my boots.

I couldn't look at her. Hell, I couldn't even stand her looking at *me*.

"Can I just ask you one thing?" I felt her eyes following my movements.

"Yeah," I said. "Sure."

"Did you get the blood work results? And if so, what were they?"

I stopped, a balled pair of pants still in my fist. I looked up and smiled at her sadly. "I'm not a carrier of the disease. I actually spoke to a specialist. He said the migraines were likely due to elevation issues from being a mountain climber."

Her frame drooped with relief. "That's good to hear. Thank you for telling me."

"Thanks for caring."

"Course I care, Riggs." She looked away so I wouldn't see the tears in her eyes. "I'll always care. I want you to know that. You'll always have a home in me. No matter where you'll be."

This was torture. Plain torture.

"And . . ." She inhaled shakily. "If you need any money . . . well, I still have some savings."

I stared at her, flabbergasted. "Huh?"

"Yeah." She pretzeled her fingers, looking embarrassed to offer. "I mean, it's not much, but whatever I have is yours. I know those medical bills can pile up."

"And how will you afford rent?" I asked, fascinated. The woman who was obsessed with money had just offered to give me whatever was left of her measly fortune.

"I won't." She bit on her lip, moving around the small apartment, helping me look for belongings of mine. "I'll crash at Laura's. Don't worry, she owes me plenty of favors."

"You're a terrible gold digger." I sighed, thinking it'd be so much easier if she was actually good at being a heartless bitch.

"I know." She smiled delicately. "It's ridiculous. I wish they gave classes."

This charade had gone on long enough. I couldn't fucking do it anymore. I was about to do something that'd earn me a place in the Dumbasses Hall of Fame, a Guinness record, and possibly an *I'm a moron* hat.

"Oh, shit." I pressed my forehead to the cool wall, shaking my head on a chuckle. "You're really going to make me do it."

"Make you do what?" She blinked, confused.

I looked up, ripping the words out of my mouth before I could change my mind. "I'm Victor Bates's grandson. The grandfather I told you about. That's him. The so-called American Armani. I'm rich. Filthy rich. One-point-three-billion-dollars rich, to be exact."

She stared at me. The air stood still.

"You're joking, right?" she choked out once she'd found her voice again.

I threw my arms out in a What-can-you-do? motion.

"I'm rich, which makes *you* rich. In fact, after this is all over"—I signaled between us—"you'll be entitled to half of what's mine. And I'm not going to fight you on it. You'll be welcome to every penny. Please, *please* take that into consideration if you ever think of going back to Cocksucker. You deserve better. So much fucking better. And now you don't need his money. You have mine. Just . . ." I drew in air. "Next time you fall in love, do it with someone who deserves you."

She stared at me with so many conflicting emotions I couldn't tell them apart. Shock. Hurt. Anger. Sympathy.

"But why—"

"Because back then you were just a woman who wanted to marry her way up," I explained. "You meant nothing to me. Now you mean something." *Everything.* "Something that's much more than the number in my bank account. I'll leave you my accountant's number. He'll fix you up with a generous allowance so you'll be comfortable while you wait for the visa and find a job. Enough for a swanky apartment, for a closetful of designer clothes, and no need to work ever again."

I'd just given up half my fortune, and instead of feeling like an idiot, all I felt was dull anger and a lot of fucking pain for leaving this woman. She was going to suck every penny out of the arrangement, and I'd have no one but myself to blame.

The worst part was—I wanted her to have it. Wanted her to have nice things, to live the luxurious life she'd always dreamed of. I wanted her to shove it in her ex-classmates' faces.

"Riggs." She started toward me, no doubt wanting to thank me for making her minted *and* soon to be the proud owner of a green card. Poppins had impeccable manners. But I didn't want to hear it. I seized my backpack and photography equipment.

"I'll see you on October twenty-second."

"Wait!"

I pressed my lips to her forehead and rushed out before she could utter the words.

I didn't want her thank-yous.

I wanted all of her, every single piece. Especially the one she'd put up for sale—her heart.

CHAPTER
THIRTY-FOUR

DUFFY

My husband was a billionaire.

Riggs Bates, who could fit his entire worldly possessions into his backpack, who walked around with holed socks and avoided subway fees, was rich beyond my wildest dreams.

He'd hidden it from me. And who could blame him, with the way I'd been behaving? I was so wrapped up in this idea of marrying up that he didn't want me to . . . what? Try to make this thing real? Bamboozle him and run with the money? And why didn't he make me sign a prenup? It wasn't unheard of that I'd somehow find out about his financial situation.

The big irony was that I didn't even care about the bloody money. I cared about him upping and leaving. I cared that he was healthy—I almost dropped to my knees and sobbed with relief when he told me that.

Last night, I really thought we'd patched things up. When Charlie passed away, it seemed like the universe was rearranging itself around us, making us realize what was important in life. Now I saw that for Riggs, stumbling into bed with me was nothing but a mishap.

After Riggs left, I called Laura for an urgent BFF conference. Or rather, an ex-BFF-turned-former-BFF-turned-back-to-BFF conference. She arrived with a huge Häagen-Dazs tub (bourbon praline pecan) and some wine. Before she even walked through my door, I pounced on her, crying hysterically. My reaction took me aback, because I'd been a lot more reserved and removed when BJ had announced he was buggering off for half a year.

"My goodness, Duffy, you're showing actual human emotions." Laura mock-checked my temperature, ushering me to my settee. "Do you have a fever? Shall we get you to the hospital?"

This, of course, only made me cry harder. I cried for two hours straight before I could find the words for what I was feeling.

"What if I can't live without him?" I blew my nose into something that was once a tissue, I was certain of it. "He thinks I'm going to take his money. Call his accountant and . . . I don't know, ask for an allowance or something." I frowned at my bowl of ice cream. "Honestly, I wouldn't even mind if we lived here, in this crappy flat, until the day we die. I just want him. Nothing else. No designer clothes, fancy handbags, and snail facials." I sniffled. "Okay, maybe *one* snail facial, just to see what all the fuss is about. They say it's life changing, you know."

Laura patted my back, her face scrunched in pity. "Oh dear, you're more hopeless than I thought." She tucked her feet under her bum on the settee, and for a moment, I was filled with illogical rage that she was putting her scent and her cells and her *everything* over my precious Riggs couch. "Why don't you call him and tell him how you feel? He was obviously hurt over the whole thing with BJ, which means he cares."

"He cares," I agreed, "and that's exactly the problem."

I replayed yesterday in my head. Remembered Riggs's face as his father drew his last breath. When he realized he couldn't help it—that he cared deeply for Charlie. I was there when Riggs gave Charlie the best day of his life—even if it was his last one too—so I knew exactly where my husband was coming from.

He wanted nothing and no one to hold him back. He didn't want to be chained, didn't want responsibilities, a family, a wife; I'd agreed to it in our terms and conditions. It wasn't fair for him if I ripped our verbal contract apart.

"I don't think anything I could say would change his mind." My chin quivered as I shoved another spoonful of ice cream into my mouth.

"Then," Laura said, reaching to rub at my arm, "I'm afraid you need to do what he did to you and let it go."

CHAPTER
THIRTY-FIVE

"Did you get a photo of the pool from this angle? With the carriages and the fruit baskets?" Elin, the marketing and commercial executive at *Discovery* magazine, trotted on the edge of the Marrakesh pool. She wore a white beach kimono and a tiny bikini while giving me meaningful looks that could only be translated into *I want you to fuck me again.*

Last time I did was two years ago, after a company Christmas party, along with two attractive interns who'd wanted a taste of an orgy. Ho, ho, ho, indeed.

I lumbered over to the angle she was talking about, clicking my camera.

I hated doing commercial work, and probably would've found a way to avoid it if it wasn't for Duffy, who was too much of a temptation as long as we were cohabiting a continent.

Unfortunately, an entire ocean still wasn't enough to keep her off my mind. I'd been miserable ever since I landed in Morocco, feeling homesick, lovestruck, and, worst of all—like a coward.

Problem was, you're never homesick for the walls or the furniture. You're homesick for the people who share it with you. My wife had grown on me in the weeks we'd spent together, and now being away from her felt like an unscratchable itch. I could turn my skin inside out and still go wild with misery.

After taking a gazillion pictures of the pool, which was bracketed by acres of green grass, luxurious orange recliners, and dining tables, I walked over to the outdoor spa, with its velvet burgundy seats and golden walls.

Elin followed me, her heels clapping the marble beneath us. "It's beautiful out here, isn't it?"

"Hmm."

I was only able to provide monosyllabic answers these days. Even that was a stretch.

"Do you have any plans after we wrap this up?" Elin purred. "We're almost finished."

"I think I'll call it an early night." I hoisted my camera over my shoulder.

Elin bit down on her lip in my periphery. "You know I broke up with Neil, right?"

I didn't even know who Neil *was*. Only that four months after our Christmas sexcapade, when I'd called her to see if she was interested in a sequel, she'd said she had a boyfriend.

"Sorry to hear."

"You shouldn't be. He was an asshole."

We got to the spa. I started taking pictures, wishing she'd take a hike. But Elin, while good at writing marketing pieces about luxury hotels, was bad at reading signals, so she decided to hammer the suggestion home while grinding her tits against my arm.

"We could have dinner together."

"Not hungry."

"Then we can go straight to dessert." She giggled.

I turned around to her, a frown on my face. "Didn't you hear I got married?"

The news must've made the rounds. Emmett had a mouth the size of Montana. Gossip was his favorite sport.

This made Elin pale. "Emmett might've mentioned something."

"And you still thought I'd be game?"

Her mouth hung open. Good-natured, always-up-for-fun Riggs was obviously MIA.

"You've never been in a relationship the entire time I've known you. I just figured—"

"Figured what?" I knew I was directing my anger at the wrong person but still couldn't help myself. I was on edge, waiting to see how much money Daphne was going to ask from my accountant and what kind of legal documents would be waiting for me back home to secure my wife's personal wealth.

"Figured it wasn't serious. Your marriage, I mean." She pursed her lips, then said, "I mean . . . is it? Is it real?"

Maybe it was Emmett who'd sent her to ask. Hell, maybe he'd sent her to tempt me, just for funsies.

"It's very real," I heard myself say. "It's the realest thing I've ever achieved, so do yourself a favor and never ask again."

The weeks leading up to Duffy's visa interview were spent taking every bullshit assignment Emmett could give me to get me out of New York and crashing at my friends' places, watching as they did lovey-dovey shit with their wives. I finally got it. Why they were content losing their freedom for someone else. I'd never felt so trapped in my life, living without the woman I was in love with.

The day before October 22, I sent Duffy a message. I convinced myself that I needed to see if there was still a point in showing up for the interview. Maybe she'd called the entire thing off. Hell, maybe she was working on her wedding to BJ right this moment. Maybe she was dead, and that's why she hadn't touched my money yet. My mind went weird places every day we were both engaged in radio silence.

Riggs: We still on for tomorrow?

Her reply came three hours later, which made me wonder what the fuck was more important than her precious green card. Or—her billionaire husband, for that matter.

Duffy: Absolutely. Again, thanks for doing that.

Riggs: Noticed you haven't contacted my accountant yet.

Duffy: No.

Riggs: No post-nup letters from your lawyer either.

Duffy: 'My lawyer'? I cannot afford a pedicurist anymore, Riggs. You should see my nails. I look like a sloth.

This made me laugh. Fuck, I missed this woman.

Duffy: I'm not going to touch a penny of your money. I already owe you so much.

Riggs: It's fine. Have at it. I've never been enamored with wealth.

Duffy: Good. I'm beginning to see being money-hungry has a terrible price.

I stared at her message. What did she mean? I wasn't dumb enough to ask via text.

Duffy: Anyway, see you tomorrow.

Riggs: Yeah. Tomorrow.

CHAPTER THIRTY-SIX

DUFFY

THE INTERVIEW

The Holy Grail had arrived. The final stop in the process of getting a visa, and, afterward, a green card—*the interview*.

Riggs and I met outside the USCIS building. It was the first time I'd seen him in weeks. He wore dark jeans and a button-down denim shirt, the first three buttons undone, sleeves pulled up to his elbows, exposing his muscular forearms. His hair had grown in the time I hadn't seen him, and he looked especially delicious and grown up. So much so I wanted to cry.

"You look good." He grinned down at me, and I mustered all my strength not to melt into a pool of emotions at his feet.

"You too. How was Morocco?"

"Humid. How was New York?"

"Same, only crowded."

We both stared at each other, smiling like loons. Riggs was the first to break the spell. He tilted his head toward the building.

"Ready to knock 'em dead?"

"I don't know if I am." I ducked my head nervously. "Is . . . not knocking them dead an option? Perhaps slapping them until they're dizzy?"

Laughing, he reached for my hand, bringing it to his mouth, and my heart stopped when he brushed his lips against my knuckles.

"You're the girl who does dioramas out of traffic cones and laminates supermarket lists. You're ready for anything, always. Knock 'em dead, Poppins."

The adjudicating officer was a nice man named Asher. He had a large pile of documents in front of him, next to an array of family pictures propped on his desk.

He began by apologizing for the stuffy side office we were occupying.

"Oh, don't worry. It's still larger than my flat." I giggled. Asher raised his eyebrows, flipping through the pages on his desk.

"That small, huh? I'm surprised, with your husband's net worth."

He referred to Riggs's tax return, which I hadn't seen at the time we filled out the petition form. Guess we were diving straight into it. All righty, then.

"My husband is not a materialistic person," I said with confidence, knowing each word spoken was the God-honest truth. "In fact, if you get to know him, you'll see that he is the least money-oriented person you'd ever meet. The first few times we hung out, I bought him socks because his were holey and I was worried about him come winter."

Asher listened intently, a small smile on his face. I felt myself blushing.

"Sorry, should I . . . stop talking? Wait for you to take the lead?"

He shook his head. "No. This was perfect. Okay." He clapped. "Ready?"

"Yes."

"Please state your spouse's full name, date of birth, and place of birth."

"Riggs Carson Bates, born February eighth, in San Francisco."

That was an easy one.

"How did you meet?"

"Mutual friend." *Who screwed him while I was watching.*

"What are his hobbies?"

"He loves mountain climbing, passionate about nature, food, friends. He is actually quite the cook. Makes great waffles . . . oh, and watermelon margaritas! And he is naturally fit, so even though he'd tell you he doesn't do sports, he is rather athletic."

I could go on about him forever. I blushed again, feeling like I'd given too much away. Surely he thought I was overdoing it to prove the authenticity of my marriage.

Asher jotted something on a document in front of him with a frown and continued.

"Tell me a little about his social life outside your marriage."

Omitting Riggs's endless list of sexual conquests, I told him about Christian and Arsène, about Riggs's upbringing at Andrew Dexter Academy, and about his family background. The more I spoke, the more confidence I gained. It occurred to me that I knew everything there was to know about my husband. Sadly, that only made room for me to doubt the fakeness of my marriage. If I felt so deeply connected to the man—how could our marriage be a sham?

The interview lasted twenty minutes, even though Felicity had told us to expect something more substantial. This meant it had gone either terribly bad or exceptionally well. I tended to lean toward the latter.

"Well, thank you very much, Mrs. Bates. I'm confident that you will hear from us very soon." Asher stood up and winked.

Oh, bloody hell. We did it. We actually did it. A wink is the international "You passed the test" sign. Everyone knows that.

"Cheers. I mean . . . thank you!"

"Best of luck with your future."

Yeah, I'll need it.

When I got out, Riggs was there, on the stairway leading up to the building, smoking a spliff. He was pacing, looking genuinely concerned. He *cared*.

I stopped and watched him for a bit, taking him in. A pang of pain pierced through my chest. This was quite possibly the last time I was going to see him. All the other things we needed to do—namely get a divorce—could be done via emails. We would liaise by text messages and the occasional phone call, like strangers. I would no longer be able to kiss him silly. He would no longer chase me around our small flat. No one was going to walk around naked anymore to make the other feel comfortable. There would be no waffle sampling, no sex on the floor, no apple-picking laced with kisses . . .

I felt myself hyperventilating.

I couldn't do it. I couldn't say goodbye. But I had to.

He's fulfilled his part of the bargain. Now you do yours and let him go.

Somehow, I dragged my feet toward him. He only noticed me when I was about a foot away from him. He looked preoccupied and a little confused.

"How'd it go?" He flicked his joint off to the street.

"Well, I think."

"Good. Good."

Pause. Blink. Gulp. Repeat.

"When are you gonna hear back from them?" Riggs ran a hand through his hair.

"Ten to fifteen working days," I chirped.

"Nice."

"Yeah."

Another silence. It was my turn to keep the conversation going.

"I found a job."

"You did?" He looked jaded and distracted.

I nodded. "Junior producer for a local news channel."

I couldn't muster any excitement for the new role, which I would be starting after Christmas, by which time my visa would arrive. The truth was that I made the news because it was familiar territory, not because I loved it. I quite loved helping Riggs with his photography, but now that I knew about his financial situation, I was aware there was no such role as a photographer's assistant, and even if there was, you don't get paid two K a day for it.

"That's amazing." He grabbed me by the waist and lifted me up, spinning me in the air, laughing. "I'm so proud of you, Poppins."

"I couldn't have done it without you. Like, *literally*."

I contemplated begging him not to leave, but I wanted to spare myself the humiliation and him the trouble. He didn't want me anymore. And me? I had to figure out what I wanted to do with my life.

Before he left, a tear escaped his right eye, rolling down his sculpted cheek. He made no move to wipe it away, which was even worse somehow than if he'd tried to conceal it. This was classic Riggs. He didn't hide how he felt. He just strongly preferred not to.

After the next awkward silence, I finally mustered the courage to make a move. It wasn't like I had any choice.

"So . . . it should take me around two years before I actually get my permanent green card, but I know you said you didn't want—"

"I'll wait," he said, cutting me off. "There's no rush on my end. I'm not planning to marry anyone else."

"You don't know that."

"Trust me, I do. You're the real deal. The end game. If we didn't stick, no one else would."

I wanted to die. For the earth to crack and swallow me whole.

"Maybe in another life?" I sniffled.

He smiled. "I'll hold you to it, Poppins."

CHAPTER THIRTY-SEVEN

DUFFY

Three months later

"Great job, Daphne." Rita, the executive producer of the evening news show I worked for, patted me lightly on the back as she breezed out of the studio. "Follow me to my office."

I snailed behind her, passing my new colleagues in the hallway. Rita entered her office, grabbed her handbag from a hook at the back of her door, and tossed her phone into it.

"We're all going to get some drinks down at the Dead Rabbit. You in?"

"I wish I could," I said on autopilot, smiling politely. "I have plans."

"Yeah?" Rita dug in her bag for a cigarette, already making her way out of the place. She ran everywhere, making me do the same. Gretchen used to do it too. Storm places. "What're you up to?"

"Huh?" I asked.

"You said you have plans. What are they?" We both stopped by the revolving door in the main entrance. I blinked, caught off guard. The truth was, I had no plans whatsoever. It was just the thought of having to pretend to have fun—even among genuinely nice people—that I didn't care for. I rather enjoyed spending my time in my flat, scrolling through professional photography pages on Instagram. I couldn't stop thinking about the prisons tour. About the magic of capturing something and giving it your own spin, rather than simply reporting about it.

"I . . . am . . . knitting . . . ," I said slowly, avoiding any questions about my new hobby.

Rita arched an eyebrow. "Sounds . . . thrilling. You a big knitter?"

"Yeah," I heard myself say. "Huge knitter. My entire flat is basically yarn."

Her expression was doubtful, but she nodded. "Okay. But you should join us next week. It's Monique's birthday. The weatherwoman?"

I'd met Monique. She was gorgeous and nice and abnormally passionate about the subject of precipitation.

"Of course," I mumbled.

"Although even before that, we're going to pull two all-nighters together." Rita laughed, taking out her phone and ordering an Uber. "We have all those Valentine's Day pieces to work on, remember? Which reminds me, can you make it here at seven in the morning tomorrow, not nine?"

I glanced at my watch. It was 11:45 at night. I appreciated a good work ethic, but I'd almost forgotten how demanding working the news—even the local news—was.

"Sure," I said absently. "I'll be here."

"Okay. See you tomorrow then! Or, technically." She jutted her lower lip out, thinking. "Today, in fifteen minutes."

I poured myself out to the street. The weather was bitter cold, the sky pitch black. Christmas had come and gone, and I spent it alone in my flat, too skint to buy a ticket to England. Touching Riggs's money wasn't an option. He'd given me something priceless, and demanding anything more would be greedy. He'd taught me how to love.

As I made my way down to the subway, tucked inside my black peacoat, I marveled at how absolutely dreadful life had been in recent months. I lived on autopilot, working, meeting up with friends, and going to the gym. The highlight of my week was usually FaceTiming Kieran. He was now in a steady relationship with Shelby. I'd even met her once on a video call, and she'd confirmed my suspicion that she wouldn't have been taken with him had he mooned her. 1–0 to team logic.

I thought about Riggs every single minute of the day. I had no idea where he was or what he did these days. Time seemed to run like water. I'd received my visa, started working, and got steady paychecks, and BJ was still calling me every now and then to test the water. Spoiler alert: I still wanted him to drown.

I'd received everything I wanted—BJ's undivided attention, a job as a news producer, and my precious visa . . . and I couldn't be more miserable.

I trudged the streets of Manhattan, passing by bundled-up couples and loved-up tourists. Everybody seemed to be paired off. Bowing my head to avoid the influx of young lovers, I stared at my shoes and picked up the pace. I was almost at the subway when I collided with another body. Another *hard* body.

My first thought was *Riggs*. He was here.

"*Whoa*. You okay?" a raspy male voice chuckled. I looked up. It wasn't Riggs. Just a fairly attractive young man with dimples and wearing running gear.

No, I am not okay. I'm in love, and miserable, and want cake. Loads of cake.

"What are you doing jogging in the middle of the night?" I grumbled. "I could've gotten hurt!"

"I have to run at night. I work shifts at the hospital and have a weird schedule." He was running in place and seemed friendly, despite my almost biting his head off for simply existing. "Why didn't *you* look where you were going?"

"Because," I gritted out, "I'm sick and tired of watching everyone in this city so in love and intimate and . . . and . . . and gross!" I flung my hands in the air. "Seriously, you Americans have no decency. Get a room, all of you."

"Hey, I'm not being intimate and in love with anyone." He put his hands up.

"Right," I said sourly. "Sorry. I'm a bit prickly. Well, have a nice jog."

I bulldozed past him, but he blocked my way, entering my line of vision.

I narrowed my eyes. "Please don't bother harassing me. I have a Taser, pepper spray, and at least fifty hours of Krav Maga training under my belt. You're not going to win this."

The Krav Maga bit was bollocks, but he couldn't know that.

The man rolled his eyes. "I wasn't going to harass you. I was going to ask if you wanna grab a drink. I'm Chad."

Of course he was. He had a Chad face.

I didn't take his offered hand. "I'm Daphne, and I can't have a drink with you."

"Now or never?" He withdrew his hand, not looking one bit offended.

"Both," I said assuredly. "I'm horribly in love with someone else, and having sex with you won't be satisfying because you're not him and because most men are quite useless in the sack, especially the first few times."

He stared at me, clearly staggered. "Ma'am, do you have *any* filters?"

"No!" I flung my arms up. "He's taken all of them, the bastard. You should've met me before him. The picture of proper and reserved."

I could tell Chad didn't find me adorable-eccentric, but in-need-of-being-heavily-medicated eccentric. Which was why he took a step back, keeping his good-natured smile intact.

"At least you know what you want in life, huh?" He was already jogging lightly away from me. "I'm still looking for that one thing to make me happy. Have a nice one, Daphne!"

With that, he turned around and *literally* ran away.

I stared at his back as an epiphany struck me with the force of a lorry.

My work. My career. My need to be perfect. They were all distractions. Avoidance to ensure I wouldn't take a good look at my life. At my relationship with BJ.

This whole entire time, I'd got it all wrong. I'd been worried Kieran and Mum and Tim were living small, uninspired lives. I'd wanted more for them than working the chippy, wanted them to care about designer clothes and lavish hotels and mansions in impeccable school catchment areas. But they were *happy*. Happy with who they were, with what they did, with how much they had. There was no pretense with them. They owned up to who they were and weren't ashamed of it.

And Riggs, he was the same. Unapologetically himself.

I'd confused greed with aspiration.

Money with motivation.

Comfort with love.

Riggs made me see the errors of my ways, but he was gone now, doing what he did best. Traveling to faraway locations, grabbing life by the bollocks.

I'd outgrown New York once I realized living the glitzy life here wasn't going to make me happy. And staying in the flat that held every lovely memory I'd created with Riggs Bates was going to taunt me to an early grave if I didn't do anything about it.

I needed to cut my losses. Go back home and reassess. Buy a camera. Make something of myself. Document. Appreciate. Find beauty in the small things.

On their own accord, my legs turned me around and made me stomp my way to the Dead Rabbit. It only took me ten minutes to get there. I pushed the door open. I spotted Rita and a few other colleagues lounging on dark-green stools in the corner of the crowded room. They were enjoying cocktails and bar snacks. The place was loud and rowdy, but I didn't have time to do this in the morning.

I marched Rita's way and tapped her shoulder. She turned around, a look of surprise on her face.

"Hey, Daphne! So glad you decided to join us."

"I quit," I announced, proud of myself for the assertiveness.

"Yes!" Rita clapped her hands together. "You were quick. We're still debating whether to eat here or grab something from a food cart."

I shook my head. "No, no, I said I quit."

"This place *is* lit."

I was going to strangle someone.

Throwing my hands in the air, I proclaimed on a scream, "I'm quitting my job! Handing over my resignation! I'm done! Finito! No longer working for you!"

At this point, I'd happily communicate it to her via mail pigeons, smoke signals, and rock piles. Rita's face sobered, and her smile vanished. Everyone around her went quiet. Normally, this was the point I'd be mortified for making a scene. Tonight, I couldn't care less.

"Are you serious?" She wrinkled her nose.

"Unfortunately." I sighed. "I have to go home. To England."

"What's wrong?" she asked, and I could tell by her tone she was already losing interest. After all, I'd only been employed at the channel for a few weeks. She wasn't that invested in me. "Do you miss your family?"

I smiled dejectedly. "Yes, I miss my family. But I miss myself more. I can't wait to find myself again."

CHAPTER
THIRTY-EIGHT

RIGGS

The Sri Lankan job came and went. I'd spent most of it wondering why the fuck it felt like I was missing an entire limb from my body while taking pictures of mass protests, temples, and ancient ruins. I was preoccupied pretty much the entire time and managed to produce work only by chance. Surprisingly enough, Emmett wasn't on my ass. Maybe he'd finally found interest in his own miserable existence.

I thought about Charlie often, but rarely with sadness. I preferred to remember him playing in Harlem with kids like he didn't have a care in the world, even if he knew back then that his days were numbered.

I spent the flight from Bandaranaike Airport to JFK mentally counting all the reasons not to reach out to my wife:

1. She hasn't reached out to me
2. She is busy with her new job (yes, I found her employee page online)

3. I'm not looking for a serious relationship
4. She hasn't reached out to me
5. Just because she hasn't touched my money doesn't mean that she won't once we get a divorce
6. She might be back with Cocksucker. In fact, he might be fucking my wife this very minute
7. SHE HASN'T REACHED OUT TO ME, WHY THE FUCK NOT?

All great, valid reasons. And still, halfway through my journey, I decided to text her.

Riggs: Gonna be in your neck of the woods soon. Drink?

It sounded noncommittal enough. Plus, it was my obligation to check in on her and make sure she was well. I stared at my phone for three minutes straight and, when she didn't answer, flipped it so I couldn't see the screen. I browsed the movie channels, looking for a distraction. There was a limit to how pussywhipped I could be. Sitting here pining for her when she could be sitting *on* Cocksucker's face was bad form.

An hour after I'd sent the message, I glanced at my phone. No answer. Two hours. Three hours. *Four* hours. By the time I landed at JFK, I wasn't worried—I was *pissed*. I'd set her up with a whole-ass green card, committed federal fraud for her, and pretty much handed her half my fortune, and she couldn't even reply with *No thanks, I'm busy*?

Fuck. That.

The cabbie waiting for me at the airport must've picked up on my mood, because he grabbed my small suitcase without a word and only spoke when we were out of the elaborate hell that was John F. Kennedy International Airport.

"Where to?" he asked curtly.

I gave him Christian's address. No way was I in a mood to tolerate Arsène's smart ass in my current condition. When the driver rounded the curve to Christian's street, I had a change of heart.

"You know what? I need you to drive me somewhere else."

I gave him Duffy's address. The little English rose was going to learn some manners from this American hooligan. I didn't even consider that she hadn't seen the text. Duffy was fused to her phone. She'd never taken more than fifty seconds to answer a text, even in the middle of the night.

Still, when I was about five minutes away from her apartment, I began to sweat. What if she was with somebody? What if she was with *Cocksucker*? I didn't like the prospect of going to jail, but there was no chance on earth I'd be able to hold myself off from at least breaking his jaw.

"This is you," the driver announced moments later.

I grabbed my shit, tipped him, and trudged up the stairway to her apartment, refusing to flinch when I passed by Charlie's door. When I got to her place, I rang twice. When she didn't answer, I banged on the door. Since it was the weekend, I knew she wasn't at work. And since it was Duffy, I knew she wasn't up to much, which made me wonder for the first time—had something happened to her?

The whole Charlie thing had made me a little raw when it came to people passing out in their own homes. Without thinking much of it, I pulled out the key she had given me months ago and had never asked for again.

I shoved it into the keyhole.

It didn't fit.

Gritting my teeth, I pressed my forehead against the door and took a ragged breath. She didn't answer my text *and* locked me out of her apartment? Good luck with her getting a divorce, because I was going to drag her to the depths of the legal inferno just to spite her so she could never marry her precious boyfriend.

Actually, that wasn't true, and I knew it. I was going to give her whatever she wanted, because watching her happy trumped whatever trivial notion I had. But fuck, that hurt.

I pulled my phone out and called Christian.

"Hey," he said, sounding sleepy. "What's up?"

"How much time will I get for breaking and entering?" I snapped, skipping the *hello* part.

"Time?" He let out a chuckle. "They're sending rapists to house arrest. Prisons in this state are overcrowded as it is. Ain't nothing going to land you in jail unless you plan on going on a prolific killing spree."

"A whole spree?" A mental vision of Cocksucker assaulted my brain. "Nah. Just one person. A crime of passion."

"Passion, you say?" He sounded thoughtful. "Might get early parole for that. People love a good romance."

I started for the stairway, having had enough of standing by Duffy's door like an idiot.

"So, are you gonna tell me why we're having this weird conversation?" Christian probed.

"Duffy isn't answering her door or taking my calls." I didn't feel humiliated saying that. Not after this motherfucker jumped through hoops to win his wife after what he'd done to her back when they were dating.

"Oh, yeah, about that. You should probably come here."

"Come where?" I took the stairs down.

"To my place."

"Why?" I slapped the door open, already looking for a cab to hail. "You know something about that?"

"She left you a letter."

"A letter?" My mind was reeling. She left me a fucking *letter*, and Christian didn't see fit to fill me in on that?

"Yeah. Said she didn't want to bother you while you were on an assignment."

"Forget her, why didn't *you* bother me?" I raged. "You sure as shit don't mind bothering me about anything else that's going on in your life. You called to tell me Louie started counting *backward*, for fuck's sake."

"Hmm. I'm picking up some high-stressed vibes here," Christian said flatly. "To answer your question, according to you, there was never anything between you and Duffy, nor have you ever felt something more than friendship for her. I thought it could wait."

Of course he knew Duffy and I were messing around and didn't tell me about the letter just to win an unspoken argument about the importance of settling down and blah-blah-conservative-fucking blah. Classic goddamn Christian.

"I'm going to kill you." I was now screaming in the middle of the street—definitely not a good look. In an unbelievably cunty move, I bypassed a Nordic-looking tourist who tried to hail a cab, entering before him and giving the driver Christian's address.

"Wow. You really go ham for your platonic friends," Christian said in a deadpan. "So when should we be expecting you?"

"Five to eight minutes."

"I'll cock the gun for you," Christian said. "You know, for when you murder me."

"Thank you."

◆ ◆ ◆

It wasn't a letter.

It was a giant-ass pile of documents crammed into a manila envelope. The envelope was sealed securely, so at least I knew Christian and Arya hadn't peeked. This wasn't a given, since they were ogling me eagerly, little Louie sitting in Arya's lap.

"Do I look like Netflix?" I carefully removed the handwritten letter from the envelope.

"Not at all." Arya shook her head, mesmerized. "If you were, I could skip the intro. Unfortunately, I'll have to sit here and watch in slo-mo until it finally hits you that you've just lost the love of your life because you're a chicken."

Know all the inspiring sayings about good friends? They did not apply to the assholes I surrounded myself with.

I'd have gone to another room for privacy purposes, but there was poetic justice in being served humble pie by my friends after all I'd done.

> Dear Riggs,
> If you're reading this, that means you're back from Sri Lanka. I hope you had a splendid time there, and that you were able to do what you love more than anything—explore and find new adventures.

Actually, as it turned out, there was something I loved more than that. Namely—Duffy.

> Let me preface this by saying I don't wish to appear ungrateful. On the contrary. In our short time together, I have managed to grow more than I have in my entire lifetime. I cannot thank you enough for the sacrifice, devotion, and commitment you've shown for me. I am truly grateful and beyond indebted to you.

Blah, blah, fucking blah. It reminded me of all the nice things people said to their partners before they dumped them for someone else. This reeked of "It's not you, it's me."

> As you know, I've recently come to find employment.

Only Duffy would sound like an eighteenth-century noblewoman when telling someone she got a job.

As it turns out, the position wasn't what I'd been hoping for. I am not quite sure what I'm looking for, to be honest, which was why I thought it best to go back to London and stay with my family as I explore my passions and talents, and how to contribute to this world.

She moved? To London? I didn't know how I felt about it. On one hand, I was greatly relieved she wasn't with Cocksucker anymore. On the other, I felt weirdly naked, now that I knew she wasn't in the same city as me. The one comfort I had in Sri Lanka was knowing where Duffy was. It gave me a false sense of control over the situation.

Since I don't think I'll be coming back to New York City, and the last thing I want is to hold you back, I am granting you this divorce with no further ado. There is no need for us to wait for a green card, since I do not intend to seek employment in the States. I now realize that deceiving the authorities, atop committing a crime, all while dragging you into this, was wrong. I would also like to take this opportunity to apologize for trying to blackmail you.

No. No, no, no, no, no. Just no multiplied by a hundred thousand. This wasn't happening.

Finally, as a token of my regret for all the inconvenience I've caused you, I have purchased you a ticket to Alaska. Not because you cannot afford it, but because you need the push to go there.

I know it's none of my business, Riggs, and I do respect that, but in all the short but intense time I have known you, you've never shied away from a challenge. You can do this. You can conquer Denali.

Besides, that's what Charlie would have wanted.

With love and affection,

Poppins.

Along with the letter were a ticket to Alaska and reservations for a hotel, as well as divorce papers. The tickets alone had probably drained her bank account.

She blew all her savings so I could go to Alaska and fight my demons. Somehow, I wasn't even slightly surprised.

Daphne Markham was never a gold digger. She aspired to be one, sure. But she also had those pesky things called *morals*. She was caring, good, and so far out of my league we weren't even playing the same fucking game.

And still, I wanted her. Every inch and cell in her body. Every snarky remark and innocent smile.

"Well?" Arya prompted. "Fill us in, lover boy."

I looked up from the letter, my jaw clenching so hard my teeth nearly crushed to dust. "Short story? She moved back to England, granted me a divorce, not gonna take a penny from me even though she knows I'm a billionaire, and bought me a ticket to Alaska."

"But you hate Alaska." Christian frowned.

"Exactly."

"She's making you do something you don't want to do just to prove a point?" Christian stroked his chin. "You sure the marriage isn't legit?"

"She's trying to help him overcome something." Arya clutched Louie close to her chest in a snuggle. "Ugh, I really like this one, Riggs. Please, can we keep her?"

"Apparently fucking not." I waved the letter in my hand.

"*Language*," Christian drawled.

"English," I confirmed. "But not a very good one, according to our former lit teacher, Ms. Maren."

"Uncle Riggs said a potty word!" Louie clapped, twisting in his mother's arms and watching her expectantly. "Mommy, put him in the naughty spot."

"That's all right, kiddo." Christian ruffled his son's dark hair, lounging back. "Uncle Riggs is in a worse place than the naughty spot."

"He is?" Louie's eyes widened.

"He's in the doghouse, after spending the last twenty years living like a gap-year student."

I folded my arms over my chest, curving an eyebrow that said, *Really?*

"He's not wrong." Arya dropped an imaginary mic.

"Thanks for the judgment. Exactly what I needed right now. So, what do I do?" I barked out, like it was their fault Duffy had decided to bail. "My wife just dumped me via letter."

"She didn't dump you," Christian said, disagreeing. "She gave you an out. Nice girl. Kind of hot too."

Arya nodded. "*Totally* hot."

"Talk about my wife like that again, and I'll smash your teeth in." I pointed at Christian, then turned to his wife. "You can still say these things, just as long as you remember I'm notoriously bad at sharing."

Louie blinked, fascinated. "*Now* does he get a time-out?"

"No, but Mommy is about to *throw* him out if he doesn't watch his mouth around you, sweetie," Arya fussed.

Louie was the only kid I was in contact with. I forgot how coddled they were.

"I can't let her go." I gathered the divorce papers and ripped them to shreds, letting them rain down on Christian's marble floor. "Especially after she fu—" I started, then saw Christian's and Arya's bulging eyes. "*Forgot*," I amended, "her ex-boyfriend and dropped him like a hot potato. She's single now. Fair game."

Arya looked at me like I was a complete moron. "She's not single, Einstein. She's married. To *you*."

"It's not a real marriage." These words had never felt so much like a lie on my tongue.

Arya bowed an eyebrow. "This is news to me, since you have all the components of a real one—you love each other, there's enough angst between you to last for an entire season of *Grey's Anatomy*, and the physical connection is there."

"What're you gonna do?" Christian asked, amusement twinkling in his eyes.

"Go to London, fu—fabulously, obviously." I produced my phone from my pocket, already going through flights. "I'm not ready to give her up."

"Good thing your suitcase is already packed." Christian jerked his chin to the suitcase by his door.

I whipped my head up, scowling. "My clothes smell like shit."

"Shit!" Louie exclaimed, giggling. "Shit, shit, shit!"

"That's it, out of my house!" Arya stood up and pointed at the door. "By the time you're done with my precious baby, he'll have the vocabulary of a drunk sailor."

"At least let him do his laundry first." Christian chuckled. "He can't try to win her heart smelling like cra—*crab*."

"He's a billionaire." Arya was already halfway into the vast hallway, about to put Louie down for his nap. "He can afford a nice please-marry-me-for-real suit."

CHAPTER
THIRTY-NINE

DUFFY

The night Kieran finally convinced me to watch *The Damned United* was the rainiest day of the year.

I wore my fluffiest, most ridiculous pair of jammies for the occasion. The ones I'd stuffed into the back of my closet in my adolescence when I decided I wanted to be an ice queen, but I couldn't quite bring myself to throw away. They were my first Christmas gift from Tim and held a special place in my heart, since they were one of the first "real" gifts I'd received since my biological father had left us. Up until then, it was all rewrapped items we already had at home or things I knew were hand-me-downs from the neighbors.

There were dozens of printouts of me laughing on the PJ bottoms. Custom-made sleep attire that was supposed to please me but really mortified me as a teenager. The PJs were magnificently ugly, but I'd been wearing them a lot since I returned to England a few weeks ago. They reminded me of the old me. The one who'd blossomed the first time Tim took her for a Nando's and wasn't ashamed of how completely enthralled she was by the small gesture. I missed that person. A lot. But I was beginning to reconnect with her. My accent had morphed back to its South London self. I was beginning to take more interest in arts and creativity, less in brands and stilettos. I stopped going to SoulCycle—I never much liked it, anyway. The spinning machine's seat did horrendous things to my lady bits—and I got my workout walking places and watching old-school fitness DVDs with Mum like the last couple of decades had never happened.

"I can't believe it took me almost a month to convince you to watch this masterpiece." Kieran shoved a raspberry Jammie Dodger into his piehole.

"I can't believe you convinced me, period." I rolled my eyes, slurping fountain Diet Coke, a leftover from our nutritious McDonald's dinner. "It's about footie, has virtually no fit men in it, *and* it's about footie."

"You already said that." Kieran shifted on our living room couch.

"Not enough." I shook my head solemnly. "Never enough."

A few minutes into the movie, I was properly annoyed.

"It's not even set in our era!" I waved a hand at our TV. "Literally, there was nothing good about the seventies other than ponchos. I miss ponchos."

"The seventies are still your era, you dimwit." Kieran laughed.

I kicked him across the couch, and he kicked me right back. Amused, I took another drag of my Coke. Being back home felt weird, but somehow right. I'd slipped right back into my family's life, like a piece of a puzzle they'd been waiting for so they could complete the picture.

In the mornings, I worked at the chippy with Tim and Kieran, which was lovely. The fresh air by the Thames felt good in my lungs; talking to tourists, *seeing* people happy put me in a good mood. I was no longer holed up in a stress-filled studio or stuffy offices. Then I usually clocked off and went around the city taking pictures. Of buildings. Of people. Of trees. The Thames. I wanted to show them all to my husband, but even if they were all just for myself—I took pride in them.

In the evenings, I had dinner with the family. Real dinner, with carbs and a glass of wine. Sometimes I went down to the pub with Kieran. Watched cable shows with Mum. Played cards with Tim. The more time I spent with my family, the more I struggled to remember what it was that I'd found so atrocious about my pre-Manhattan existence. These days, the only thing I missed about the place was Riggs.

Riggs, who still hadn't contacted me. With every passing day without a word from him, I anticipated that my wretched hope he'd seek me out would've evaporated. It never did, though. Each morning, I woke up with a fresh sense of grief.

I still felt as I had the day I'd boarded the plane to London. Like he'd torn my heart out of my chest and ravaged it like a pomegranate, blood trickling down his muscular forearm. It was ironic, how I'd always wanted to trade love for comfort, but once love struck, comfort became the last thing on my mind.

"Duffy? *Duffy!*" Kieran kicked my ribs across the settee. Guess I'd been zoning out. Who could blame me? I'd be better off watching paint dry.

"Bloody *what*?" I whipped my head toward my brother.

"First of all, good to hear your *real* accent is back." He wiggled his brows. "Second of all, there's someone at the door. Go answer it."

"*You* go answer it," I raged. "It's pissing outside, and I'm a delicate flower."

"I got us dinner." Kieran stubbed his chest with his finger. "And you're a pesty weed at best. It's your turn to unplaster your arse from the couch."

"It could be a murderer," I pointed out smartly, crossing my arms over my chest. "You'll have better luck shooing him away, with your size and strength."

"*Him?*" Kieran's eyebrows jumped to his hairline. "So now we're under the assumption all murderers are males? I reject that framing."

"Eighty-five percent of serial killers *are* male, and eighty-two of them are white," I countered, squinting at him. "Which means I might be looking at one right now. Should I be worried?"

Kieran gave me a look, throwing a Jammie Dodger at my arm. "Go get the door, smart-ass."

"Ugh, fine."

I kicked the throw off my waist and trudged to the door. Mum and Tim were upstairs, watching *The Age of Innocence* for their book club (the book, according to Tim, simply had "too many pages to even count"). Besides, they clearly had keys to their own house, so I was taken aback that someone was paying us a visit this late at night and in this weather.

Maybe it *was* a serial killer. If so, hopefully my jammies alone would scare them away.

I swung the door open with a sigh, expecting to see a volunteer asking for donations for something. "Hi. Let me get my purs—"

The rest of the word died in my throat.

In front of me stood Riggs. Tall, gorgeous, rugged Riggs. His floppy blond hair wet from the rain, bracketing his face. There were so many emotions in his stare I couldn't even begin to untangle them.

And . . . he wore a *suit*. A proper one too. With a jacket and bow tie and everything. For the first time in his life, my husband looked like a groom.

I'd never seen him looking so formal. So . . . *drenched.* My heart skipped three beats before trying to bulldoze its way out of my rib cage and jump into his arms.

Riggs is here. Riggs came to London to see me. Riggs, my husband. And . . . I'm wearing the most atrocious thing to ever be created, bless Tim.

The first thing I did was not trust my own eyesight. This was clearly a hallucination. Another step in my cognitive decline since I'd started eating junk food and drinking soda. I reached to pinch my arm, then immediately regretted it when I gave myself a bruise.

"Aw, Duffy, you daft cow."

"Hey, don't talk about my wife like that." He frowned.

Oh. My. God.

Seriously, what was happening?

Too shocked to produce words, I simply stared at him, clutching the doorknob for dear life.

It seemed like a lifetime passed before he said anything. For the first few moments, he just drank me in, as I did him. Taking inventory of the person who used to share a roof with me and was now across a threshold.

"I brought waffles." He raised a Tupperware container between us, then handed it to me. The condensation of hot, fluffy pastry adorned the plastic dish from within. I grabbed it and held it tightly, knowing my shaky hands weren't to be trusted.

"Ch-ch-cheers . . . ?"

I needed to say something. *He* needed to say something. Somebody definitely ought to start this conversation. Was it an official breakup conversation? A let's-get-back-together conversation? Were we even really together in the first place? My head was spinning.

"How did you make the waffles?" I blurted out. "You don't . . . live here."

Really? That's your main focus right now?

"I rented an Airbnb." He looked very intense, as though the task of making these waffles was the most important thing in the world to him. "They're still hot, by the way."

They were. They made my chest feel fuzzy from the heat.

"This is why it took me a couple days to get here after coming back from Sri Lanka," he explained, still looking a little startled to find himself on my doorstep. "Hmm . . . are these PJs full of little pictures of your face?"

"I'm afraid so." I glanced down on a sigh. "Actually, I'm quite terrified so, seeing as I wasn't expecting any guests."

Especially ones I consider the love of my life.

"Duff?" Kieran boomed from the living room. "Is it a serial killer? Did he finish the job? More food for us, I guess."

"It's fine!" My voice was high pitched. Riggs was still standing in the rain. In my shock I forgot to invite him in. "I'm wrestling him down to the floor and rolling him in the carpet before calling the police."

"Brilliant. Let me know if you need help." I heard Kieran munching on something crunchy. My eyes shifted back to Riggs.

"Is this a bad time?" he asked.

"What?" I gasped. "No, no, no. We're just watching a stupid football movie where everyone is fully clothed. In horrible seventies clothes, no less."

Riggs let out his familiar You're-cute-when-you're-neurotic chuckle.

"So, uhm, what's up?" I asked after a pause. "I mean, I appreciate the waffles, but . . . why are you here?"

Was he here to hand me the signed divorce papers? I hadn't asked for anything. Maybe he appreciated it and wanted to thank me in person for not turning out to be the money leech I appeared to be. Or maybe he wanted something else. I didn't dare hope. Hope was the worst thing one could have when disappointment waited just around the corner, with its rust-tipped talons, ready to squeeze your soul out of you.

"Why am I here?" He let out a short breath, as if the question had just occurred to him. Raindrops clung to the tips of his lashes, and he looked like a beautiful vision. Something completely unreal. "I'm here because I thought about you every single day, every single hour, every single minute, every single second while I was in Sri Lanka."

My insides felt like dominos, falling atop each other at an escalating speed.

"I'm here because everything you've ever offered Cocksucker, I want from you. Every kiss, every argument, every baby, every*thing*. I've been wanting those things for a while from you, I think. But telling you this was admitting defeat. I promised myself very early in life I wouldn't care. Would never be chained to a person, to a place. Which made watching you agonizing over him so fucking frustrating." He took a ragged breath. "I'm here because if it weren't for you, I'd have never met Charlie, and looking back at the whole thing . . . I'm glad I did, even if I only got to know him for a little while."

My eyes felt hot, and I knew I was about to cry.

"I'm here because you made me feel, and no one else ever had, so I'd be a world-class fool not to explore that. I'm here because I loathed that you didn't touch my money, because it proved that all the things you tried to be—untrustworthy, materialistic, superficial, ruthless— weren't true at all. You are, and always will be, the girl who blew her entire savings on a poor stranger who couldn't afford a subway ticket just because she cared."

My entire body rocked back and forth with sobs now. Okay. That *did* escalate quickly.

"I'm here because I don't want to get a divorce. I want to give this a fair shot. I think we can do it. But most of all . . ." His eyes met mine, and they seemed eager, anxious, full of determination. "I'm here because I'm fucking in love with you, Daphne Bates. And if I have to buy your love, then I'm not above that either. Mansions, yachts, country clubs, designer bags. Anything you want, I'll give you. Just be with me."

Daphne Bates.

I dropped the waffles at my feet, and we crashed into one another, like a perfect storm. Rain pounded on my head, my back, and my arms as I wrapped myself around him, my legs lacing over his waist. Riggs searched my lips instantly, and I tilted my head up and kissed him hard, rough, feeling his fingers twisting inside my hair, keeping me in place as his tongue invaded my mouth.

I moaned when his mouth descended from my lips to my neck. His face was cold, but his kisses burned hotter than the blazing sun. His fingers sank into the soft skin of my bum, and he ground me against his cock, making sure I knew he fancied me despite my silly jammies.

"Duff! Have you managed to roll our serial killer into the carpet yet?" Kieran's voice pierced our little bubble. Riggs groaned into my shoulder. I could still feel his erection pressing against my center and cursed my twin brother inwardly when my husband disconnected from me, putting me down gently.

By the tone of Kieran's voice, I knew he was aware it was Riggs at the door and was now simply taking the piss.

"Yes," I groaned, rolling my eyes and tugging Riggs inside, where it was warm and dry. "The police are on their way."

"Goodie. Let me know when they're here so I can put the kettle on."

Riggs and I looked at each other again. He was dripping water all over the carpet, and I was quite sure Mum was going to kill us both when she found out.

"Can we take this to the kitchen?" I asked.

"Is that where you're going to tell me you've moved on and aren't interested in giving us a try?" A guarded look clouded his face.

"As if." I swatted his chest. "I'll go get the waffles. You go upstairs and dry off before you catch pneumonia. I have loads of plans for you, and you need to be healthy for all of them."

Fifteen minutes later, Riggs, Kieran, and I were all in the kitchen, wolfing down waffles with Nutella, nursing steaming-hot teas. Kieran was leaning against the kitchen counter, finishing off the Nutella by dragging his finger inside the tub.

"So, does this mean you two are back together now? Shelby would love a double date."

I turned to look at Riggs for confirmation from my vantage point of sitting in his lap. He didn't even spare me a look.

"Book that double date. While you're at it, tell all of Duffy's admirers to stop knocking on the door unless they want their fingers broken."

Kieran's eyebrows lifted. "I'll try to get the message to the press. And since Duffy told me you're a gazillionaire, does this mean you're going to invest in our chippy?"

"Kieran!" I chided, appalled.

"Do you want me to invest in your chippy?" Riggs's arms tightened around my waist, and I felt a thrill, knowing I belonged to him and he belonged to me.

"I want a Covent Garden branch," Kieran said, ignoring me completely. "Tourists love Covent Garden. We can make bank."

"Because there isn't any fish-and-chips in any of the hundred pubs in Covent Garden?" I huffed.

"Not like ours, no," Kieran said with conviction.

"I'll invest in you," Riggs said airily. "On one condition."

"The answer is yes." Kieran dumped the empty Nutella jar in the bin. "Unless the condition is I snog the fox that lives in our backyard, in which case the answer is still yes, but let's all pretend I tried to negotiate it."

Riggs laughed. "I'll never do that to the fox. But I do need you to give us some space. Duffy and I aren't done talking."

"'Talking.'" Kieran used air quotes. "All right, then. I'll be in the living room if you need me, trying to mentally block what's about to happen here, next to my beloved food."

"We won't be needing you," I assured him.

Kieran crept out of the kitchen. I turned to look at Riggs, who grinned down at me wolfishly, slipping his big palm into the front of my jammies.

I'd missed this. No matter where we were or what we were doing, the man was always in the mood.

"So?" he asked. "What do you say? Are we giving this thing a chance?"

"We better." I rubbed my nose against his affectionately, hugging him. "Since I'm in love with you, too, and have absolutely no interest in mansions, yachts, and country clubs."

I left the *designer bags* part out. I wouldn't say no to a new Chanel or two. You know, down the line.

"That's good to hear." His palm patted me down there, his tone turning smoky.

"What made you come here?" I asked. "I mean, what made you change your mind?"

"My mind was never changed. I've always wanted you." Riggs started drawing lazy circles between my thighs. It was incredibly hot. "But I was always sure you'd turn your back on me and get back with BJ. And I didn't want to disclose my financial situation because I didn't want you to be with me for the wrong reasons. Actually . . ." He pushed one finger in, through my jammies. Ahhhh. "That's a lie. I did. I did want you to be with me and fuck the reason why. But the prospect of losing to Cocksucker even if I had a fatter bank account was paralyzing. So I convinced myself I didn't do monogamy. But then I saw your letter when I got back from Sri Lanka and realized not only that you weren't with Cocksucker, but that you actually wanted to grant me a divorce. And divorce isn't something I'm ever going to consider, just so you know."

I moaned, partly because what he said was swoonworthy, and partly because he was now circling my clit with his thumb.

"Now, do you have any questions for me?" He looked at me seriously.

How could he expect me to think straight when I was so close to an orgasm? He dipped his index and middle fingers into me, still encircling my tight bud with his thumb, gaining speed and using the perfect pressure.

"Did you . . . uhm, *you know*, when we were apart . . . ?" I choked out halfway through the question.

Sleep with other women?

He shook his head. "Not when I was mad at you and we lived together. Not after I was gone. Not during my travels. Not ever. I've been faithful to you from the day I moved in with you."

"But I smelled other women's perfume on you."

"Arya's." His chest quaked with a chuckle. "I crashed at Christian's when we were on bad terms. Their entire apartment smells like lilies."

"What about Gretchen?" I started panting. I was very close to climaxing.

"Gretchen?" He sounded surprised. "I told her to go screw herself months ago. She was in town from DC while you and I were married."

"Why didn't you tell me?" My question was more of a sigh. The pressure building between my legs was unbearable, and I knew I was about to come apart any moment now. Riggs increased the pressure, and I tried not to think about how we were doing this in my parents' kitchen and any one of my family members could walk right in at any moment and catch us.

"There wasn't a point." He trailed his tongue along my jaw. "You were stressed about finding a job, and it wasn't like Gretchen stood half a chance. From the moment I saw you, Poppins, I was all yours."

I came riding his hand. Riggs watched me the entire time. When the brain fog of the orgasm began to evaporate, I got up on shaky legs and hurried to get some water. Riggs leisurely stood up and washed his hands.

"So . . . what's next?" I heard myself ask tightly. I still couldn't believe my luck. "You'll be traveling the world and coming to visit me here?"

I couldn't help but remember what had stopped me from fantasizing about something more with Riggs. His inability to stay in one place for a long period of time was always there, and I doubted he wanted to change.

Riggs smiled. "I was thinking our marriage could be more traditional. As my wife might say—I'm no spring chicken anymore. Besides, settling down is not all that bad when there's someone next to you you're obsessed with."

We met halfway in my parents' kitchen.

"London or New York?" I asked.

"Let's flip a coin."

He produced one from his wallet.

"Heads New York, tails London," I said.

He tossed it in the air, then flipped it on the back of his palm, covering it.

"You ready?" He looked up at me. I nodded.

Riggs revealed our future location.

We both laughed.

"Perfect." He kissed my forehead. "Absolutely perfect."

EPILOGUE

RIGGS

Emmett: Free for freelance work?

Riggs: Where?

Emmett: Croatia. Some of the shots require special skill, mountain climbing, etc.

Riggs: I'll ask my wife and get back to you.

Emmett: Thanks.

Emmett: And Riggs? You're missed.

Riggs: Don't make me barf my lunch, Emmett.

A month after my reunion with Duffy in London, we both traveled to Alaska to fight my demons. We declared it our real honeymoon, the one that never was. We took the opportunity to spread Charlie's ashes in Auke Lake, which—he told me on his deathbed—was his favorite place growing up.

We went to all the places my mother spent time in, and it also felt like coming full circle. It humanized her further in my eyes. To see where she partied, where she worked, where she fell in love.

Speaking of coming, we did a lot of that too. Which was good, because Duffy finally decided what she wanted to do with her life—become a mother and a newborn photographer. "They're the best clients," she explained. "Cute, sleepy, and never self-conscious about their bad angles." I loved that she loved photography. And I loved that I was the one to introduce it to her. Of course, not everyone was dazzled by my wife's mere existence.

"That's your aspiration?" Arya bellowed while we were FaceTiming them from our Juneau hotel. "To become a *mother*?"

"Aren't you one?" my wife asked briskly, shrugging Arya's abhorrence off. "And aren't you pregnant with another child right now?" Duffy added. She'd become pretty close with Arya and Winnie this past month, once they were both positive it was okay to get to know her without running the risk of my giving her the boot.

"Well, yes, but you need something for yourself that isn't the newborn photography stuff." Arya frowned. "You know I hear there are poop accidents on a daily basis? And some of those things they tuck the babies into are just ridiculous."

"This *is* what I want to do for myself," Duffy said with conviction. "I want to raise really great humans. And I think it's a purpose just as high and good as becoming an engineer or a marketing manager or an architect."

Attagirl.

Arya sighed. "I guess you could have your first client in me when that baby pops out."

Winnie, who was also on the line with Arsène, giggled. "And I'll be booking you right after. Three weeks apart, if my OB-GYN is correct."

Duffy turned to Winnie. "By the way, Win, I wanted to say congrats on *your* pregnancy too."

Winnie blushed deeply, ducking her head with a shy smile. "Thank you. I got your flowers and card too. I really appreciate it."

Winnie and Arsène had been trying for a while. I knew because the bastard was extra butthurt about everything to do with his wife while they were trying to conceive. If I breathed the wrong way under their roof, he'd throw a fit, thinking it made her uncomfortable and gave her unnecessary stress.

"When are you coming back, anyway?" Arsène asked, sounding more put off by the idea than interested.

"*Where* are you going back to is the better question?" Christian added.

Duffy and I exchanged looks. I decided to do the talking, since Duffy still felt a little intimidated by Arsène.

"We purchased a condo in Chelsea," I announced.

"New York or London?" Arya asked.

"Both," I replied, slinging an arm over my wife's shoulder.

When the coin showed tails, I think both Duffy and I knew that we weren't ready to give up either of our favorite cities. Besides, now that I was getting into business with my brother- and father-in-law, I needed to take a closer look at the space we were renting for the restaurant in Covent Garden.

"So exciting!" Arya and Winnie cooed.

"Not too shabby for a gold digger." Duffy pretended to dust off invisible lint from her cardigan.

"Gold digger, my ass." I kissed her temple and rumpled her hair.

"Oh, that's a good location." Her eyes lit up, and I laughed. "Better than both Chelseas."

In the end, Duffy got exactly what she wanted—a life of luxury—without even having to pretend to be someone she wasn't, only to find out what really mattered was the person you shared the wealth with.

As for what she taught me, that would be that family came first.

And that for the right person? You would change your whole entire world.

DUFFY

Six months later

"I'm doing it."

"Don't you fucking dare, Poppins. I'm watching you."

I leaned over the round table at the Manhattan café where we'd stopped for a quick lunch and slowly pulled a piece of pastrami from his sandwich. Riggs shooed my hand away with a napkin like a stern governess, then picked up the sandwich and shoved the whole thing into his mouth.

"What are you doing!" I groaned. That was half a sandwich. He could choke.

"Saving my baby. He can thank me later."

Screw listeria. My love for cold meats knew no bounds, and it pained me to have to part ways with my favorite food while I was expecting. Especially now, when I'd passed the first trimester and was officially back in eating-everything-in-sight mode.

"You don't know that it's a he yet." I munched on my grilled cheese reluctantly.

"Of course I do. Little Charlie." He smirked.

"Charlie? Really?" My heart stopped beating for a moment. What a gorgeous homage.

"Fuck no." Riggs snorted. "I just wanted to see your reaction. But I just think that, since Arsène and Winnie are having a girl, and Arya and Christian are having a girl, it'd be too much of a coincidence if we have one too."

"I don't want any gender disappointment." I wiggled my finger in his face, taking yet another bite of my food.

"There's never any disappointment where you're concerned, Poppins." He gave me a lopsided grin.

I was opening my mouth to tell him the feeling was mutual when someone stopped in front of us on the sidewalk eating area, blocking the sun from our faces.

"*Riggs?*"

My husband and I both turned to look at the person. A beady-eyed, slender man with freakishly long fingers. He was standing there with a pretty lady, staring at me like I was a ghost.

"Can we help you?" I asked in a crisp tone.

"She *is* English," the man said, his jaw slacked with shock. "And she's real. She really exists. *Whoa.*"

"Told you," Riggs said smugly, leaning over to press a kiss on my mouth. I accepted the gesture greedily. I didn't care who this man was—kisses from my husband were always welcome. "And I also said she was the most beautiful woman on Planet Earth. Did I not? Brutally honest."

Riggs pivoted to look at the man, tipping an imaginary hat at the woman. "I assume you're Mrs. Stauce."

"You assume correctly." She blushed under his sultry gaze.

Riggs nodded. "My condolences. Duffy, this is my former boss, Emmett."

"You never did answer me about Croatia." Emmett turned to look at Riggs, accusation carrying in his voice. "Why's that?"

Riggs gestured toward me. "We're working on our legacy and will be popping out babies for the next five years or so. Feel free to ask me afterward."

After Riggs had come to London to confess his love for me, he quit *Discovery* magazine. Emmett had been trying to convince him to freelance for them ever since, with little luck.

"Five years is a long time," Emmett said, looking extra surly.

Riggs shot me an adoring smile. "Not when it's with the right person."

ACKNOWLEDGMENTS

It is always bittersweet to finish a series you've been working on for a few years, and it is especially sad for me to say goodbye to these three men, who have burrowed their way into my heart. But every end of a series is (hopefully) the beginning of a new one, and I'm so excited to see what's in store for me. As always, this book couldn't have happened without my support group, in which I include beta reader (and PA extraordinaire!) Tijuana Turner, as well as Vanessa Villegas, Ratula Roy, Marta Bor, Pang Thao, and Jan Corona. Special thanks for all the love to Lena and Steph.

This book also couldn't be here in your hands (or ears) if not for my agent, Kimberly Brower, and the amazing Montlake team who held my hand through it.

Special thanks to the word wizards who made this book possible (and coherent!), editors Anh Schluep, Lindsey Faber, and Bill Siever, as well as proofreader Elyse Lyon. A big hug to the designer who worked on all three books in the series, Caroline Teagle Johnson.

And to you—the readers, Instagrammers, TikTokers, bloggers, and avid book lovers—I am so grateful to have you in my life and so humbled that you keep choosing to read my books.

If you've made it all the way here, please consider leaving a brief review to let me know what you thought about Riggs's and Daphne's journey.

All my love.
—L.J. Shen

Before you leave, here is an excerpt from another book of mine, *The Kiss Thief.*

PROLOGUE

What sucked the most was that I, Francesca Rossi, had my entire future locked inside an unremarkable old wooden box.

Since the day I'd been made aware of it—at six years old—I knew that whatever waited for me inside was going to either kill or save me. So it was no wonder that yesterday at dawn, when the sun kissed the sky, I decided to rush fate and open it.

I wasn't supposed to know where my mother kept the key.

I wasn't supposed to know where my father kept the box.

But the thing about sitting at home all day and grooming yourself to death so you could meet your parents' next-to-impossible standards? You have time—in spades.

"Hold still, Francesca, or I'll prick you with the needle," Veronica whined underneath me.

My eyes ran across the yellow note for the hundredth time as my mother's stylist helped me get into my dress as if I was an invalid. I inked the words to memory, locking them in a drawer in my brain no one else had access to.

Excitement blasted through my veins like a jazzy tune, my eyes zinging with determination in the mirror in front of me. I folded the piece of paper with shaky fingers and shoved it into the cleavage under my unlaced corset.

I started pacing in the room again, too animated to stand still, making Mama's hairdresser and stylist bark at me as they chased me around the dressing room comically.

I am Groucho Marx in Duck Soup. *Catch me if you can.*

Veronica tugged at the end of my corset, pulling me back to the mirror as if I were on a leash.

"Hey, ouch." I winced.

"Stand still, I said!"

It was not uncommon for my parents' employees to treat me like a glorified, well-bred poodle. Not that it mattered. I was going to kiss Angelo Bandini tonight. More specifically—I was going to let *him* kiss *me*.

I'd be lying if I said I hadn't thought about kissing Angelo every night since I returned a year ago from the Swiss boarding school my parents threw me in. At nineteen, Arthur and Sofia Rossi had officially decided to introduce me to the Chicagoan society and let me have my pick of a future husband from the hundreds of eligible Italian-American men who were affiliated with The Outfit. Tonight was going to kick-start a chain of events and social calls, but I already knew whom I wanted to marry.

Papa and Mama had informed me that college wasn't in the cards for me. I needed to attend to the task of finding the perfect husband, seeing as I was an only child and the sole heir to the Rossi businesses. Being the first woman in my family to ever earn a degree had been a dream of mine, but I was nowhere near dumb enough to defy them. Our maid, Clara, often said, "You don't need to meet a husband, Frankie. You need to meet your parents' expectations."

She wasn't wrong. I was born into a gilded cage. It was spacious, but locked, nonetheless. Trying to escape it was risking death. I didn't like being a prisoner, but I imagined I'd like it much less than being six feet under. And so I'd never even dared to peek through the bars of my prison and see what was on the other side.

My father, Arthur Rossi, was the head of The Outfit.

The title sounded painfully merciless for a man who'd braided my hair, taught me how to play the piano, and even shed a fierce tear at my London recital when I played the piano in front of an audience of thousands.

Angelo—you guessed it—was the perfect husband in the eyes of my parents. Attractive, well-heeled, and thoroughly moneyed. His family owned every second building on University Village, and most of the properties were used by my father for his many illicit projects.

I'd known Angelo since birth. We watched each other grow the way flowers blossom. Slowly, yet fast at the same time. During luxurious summer vacations and under the strict supervision of our relatives, Made Men—men who had been formally induced as full members of the mafia—and bodyguards.

Angelo had four siblings, two dogs, and a smile that would melt the Italian ice cream in your palm. His father ran the accounting firm that worked with my family, and we both took the same annual Sicilian vacations in Syracuse.

Over the years, I'd watched as Angelo's soft blond curls darkened and were tamed with a trim. How his glittering, ocean-blue eyes became less playful and broodier, hardened by the things his father no doubt had shown and taught him. How his voice had deepened, his Italian accent sharpened, and he began to fill his slender boy-frame with muscles and height and confidence. He became more mysterious and less impulsive, spoke less often, but when he did, his words liquefied my insides.

Falling in love was so tragic. No wonder it made people so sad.

And while I looked at Angelo as if he could melt ice cream, I was the only girl who melted from his constant frown whenever he looked at me.

It made me sick to think that when I went back to my all-girls Catholic school, he'd gone back to Chicago to hang out and talk and *kiss* other girls. But he'd always made me feel like I was The Girl. He sneaked flowers into my hair, let me sip some of his wine when no one was looking, and laughed with his eyes whenever I spoke. When his younger brothers taunted me, he flicked their ears and warned them off. And every summer, he found a way to steal a moment with me and kiss the tip of my nose.

"Francesca Rossi, you're even prettier than you were last summer."

"You always say that."

"And I always mean it. I'm not in the habit of wasting words."

"Tell me something important, then."

"You, my goddess, will one day be my wife."

I tended to every memory from each summer like it was a sacred garden, guarded it with fenced affection, and watered it until it grew to a fairy-tale-like recollection.

More than anything, I remembered how, each summer, I'd hold my breath until he snuck into my room, or the shop I'd visit, or the tree I'd read a book under. How he began to prolong our "moments" as the years ticked by and we entered adolescence, watching me with open amusement as I tried—and failed—to act like one of the boys when I was so painfully and brutally a girl.

I tucked the note deeper into my bra just as Veronica dug her meaty fingers into my ivory flesh, gathering the corset behind me from both ends and tightening it around my waist.

"To be nineteen and gorgeous again," she bellowed rather dramatically. The silky cream strings strained against one another, and I gasped. Only the royal crust of the Italian Outfit still used stylists and maids to get ready for an event. But as far as my parents were concerned—we were the Windsors. "Remember the days, Alma?"

The hairdresser snorted, pinning my bangs sideways as she completed my wavy chignon updo. "Honey, get off your high horse. You were pretty like a Hallmark card when you were nineteen. Francesca, here, is *The Creation of Adam*. Not the same league. Not even the same ball game."

I felt my skin flare with embarrassment. I had a sense that people enjoyed what they saw when they looked at me, but I was mortified by the idea of beauty. It was powerful yet slippery. A beautifully wrapped gift I was bound to lose one day. I didn't want to open it or ravish in its perks. It would only make parting ways with it more difficult.

The only person I wanted to notice my appearance tonight at the Art Institute of Chicago masquerade was Angelo. The theme of the gala was Gods and Goddesses through the Greek and Roman mythologies. I knew most women would show up as Aphrodite or Venus. Maybe Hera or Rhea, if originality struck them. Not me. I was Nemesis, the goddess of retribution. Angelo had always called me a deity, and tonight, I was going to justify my pet name by showing up as the most powerful goddess of them all.

It may have been silly in the 21st century to want to get married at nineteen in an arranged marriage, but in The Outfit, we all bowed to tradition. Ours happened to belong firmly in the 1800s.

"What was in the note?" Veronica clipped a set of velvety black wings to my back after sliding my dress over my body. It was a strapless gown the color of the clear summer sky with magnificent organza blue scallops. The tulle trailed two feet behind me, pooling like an ocean at my maids' feet. "You know, the one you stuck in your corset for safekeeping." She snickered, sliding golden feather-wing earrings into my ears.

"That"—I smiled dramatically, meeting her gaze in the mirror in front of us, my hand fluttering over my chest where the note rested—"is the beginning of the rest of my life."

ABOUT THE AUTHOR

L.J. Shen is a *USA Today*, *Washington Post*, and number one Amazon bestselling author of contemporary, new adult, and YA romance titles. Her specialties are unapologetic alpha males and the women who bring them to their knees.

Her books have been sold to twenty different countries and have appeared on some of their bestseller lists. She lives in Southeast Florida with her husband, three sons, pets, and eccentric fashion choices and enjoys good wine, bad reality TV, and catching sunrays with her lazy cat.

Connect with Shen at www.authorljshen.com and sign up for her newsletter at https://bit.ly/3LhsIrb.